GROVER WILCOX GOES TO THE CIRCUS

CANNIBAL
PRESS

Also by Martin Lastrapes

NOVELS

Inside the Outside
The Vampire, the Hunter, and the Girl
The Vampire, the Hunter, and the Witch
The Vampire, the Hunter, and Frank

SHORT STORIES

Dolph the Unicorn Killer & Other Stories

PRAISE FOR . . .

Inside the Outside

"There are some books which stick in your mind, even years later. *Inside the Outside* by Martin Lastrapes is one of those books."
Joanna Penn, *New York Times* bestselling author

The Vampire and the Hunter Trilogy

"Is there anything new to say about vampires? Martin Lastrapes proves there is and it is creepy and sexy and definitely full of fresh blood."
Diana Wagman, author of *The Care and Feeding of Exotic Pets*

Dolph the Unicorn Killer & Other Stories

"If Hunter S. Thompson and Neil Gaiman got together for a surreal spin through Vegas, this is the kind of madness that might have come from their minds."
Self-Publishing Review

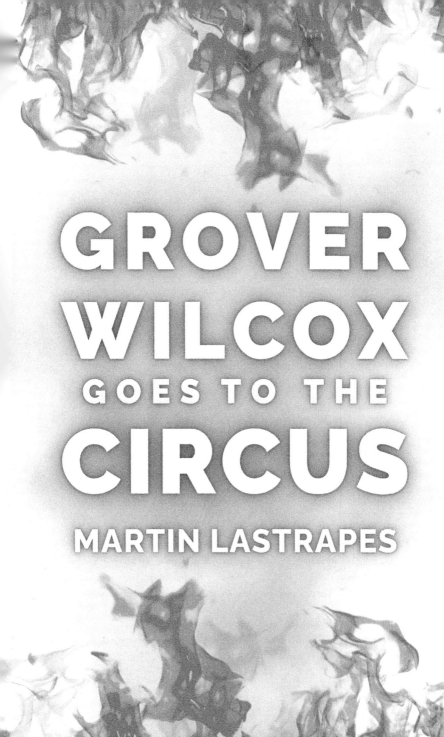

GROVER WILCOX

GOES TO THE

CIRCUS

MARTIN LASTRAPES

For Chanel

Money is in some respects life's fire: it is a very excellent servant, but a terrible master.

P. T. Barnum

The price of anything is the amount of life you exchange for it.

Henry David Thoreau

The road to hell is paved with good intentions.

Proverb

PROLOGUE

"**F**OLLOW ME."

I do as he says.

"Take your place."

I step onto the platform, standing with my back against the wooden pole as he wraps the heavy rope around my arms, chest, and belly, cinching it into a knot so uncomfortably tight that I know, even without having to try, I can't break free. It's a strange feeling to cooperate so freely in my own execution. For what it's worth, I don't want you to think I've lost my will to live. Like somebody stranded in the middle of the ocean, staring into the wide-open jaws of a great white shark, I want to live. Like somebody heaved over the highest ledge of the Empire State Building, gazing at the clouds as they move further and further away, I want to live. But, regardless of my desperate want to live, I know that boxing a row of razor-sharp teeth is every bit as futile as screaming at the sky to reason with gravity.

The inevitable is undefeated.

PART ONE

Chapter One

IGNITION SOURCE

F IRE.

Right this very moment, I'm alone and covered head to toe in fire. As certainly as I know you can hear these words, I know this is how I'm going to die—thrashing about my kitchen floor, systematically swallowed up by flames, my final breath filled with hot, black smoke—and it's all my fault because I didn't make myself a peanut butter and jelly sandwich. I can only hope that whoever finds me will assume this was all the result of spontaneous human combustion, because the truth is much more embarrassing. For what it's worth, even before my unfortunate fiery mishap, my life prospects weren't looking very good.

To begin with, I live in a tiny studio apartment (for the time being, anyway, since that bit of truth will be past tense once I'm burned to a crisp), and, logistically speaking, the minuscule square footage of my humble abode helps tell the tale of my flaming epic fail. Picture this: one corner of my apartment is designated as both the kitchen *and* the dining room; in the middle of the kitchen/dining room, just a few feet away from my stove, is a table with a heavy wooden top that is big enough for two grown adults to enjoy a meal together (but, since I have no roommates, close friends, or romantic prospects to speak of, I've never had the opportunity to put its capacity to the test). Now, imagine this heavy wooden table standing directly behind me as I, in turn, stand over the stove, reheating yesterday's Chinese food.

Because I'm an adjunct English professor with a thirty-minute window between classes, I was short on time and definitely should've thought twice about preparing any sort of meal that involved fire and haste. But just so you don't think I'm a total dunce, I'd like to point out that, while racing home for my ill-fated lunch, the thought *did* occur to me—however fleeting—to make a peanut butter and jelly sandwich. Unfortunately, the peanut butter and jelly sandwich idea had barely taken shape in my frenzied brain when my appetite convinced me to squeeze in a much more satisfying lunch involving grilled shrimp marinated in a mysterious brown sauce.

I mean, what could go wrong?

Given that my plan was to eat leftover seafood, I assumed the biggest potential catastrophe might be an upset stomach or, at worst, a bout of emergency diarrhea during my lecture on inductive and deductive reasoning. But the fear of food poisoning didn't scare me away from my plan, nor did it curb my hubris when, after realizing leftover shrimp wasn't going to be enough, I decided I would also grill some peppers and onions with my meal. Even now, writhing around the kitchen floor in a fiery cocoon, I can't stop thinking about how, if I'd just skipped the peppers and onions and nuked the shrimp in the microwave, none of this would be happening.

After hastily parking in the filthy, unkempt lot of my complex, I dashed from my car to my tiny studio apartment. Bursting through the front door, I checked the time on my phone—which was firmly grasped in my clammy fist—and saw that I had roughly seventeen minutes to prepare my lunch and scarf it down before racing back to Chandler College for my next class. If traffic were to be in my favor and the God of Greenlights smiled down upon me, I figured I could make it back in approximately seven minutes, leaving me with ten minutes to do both the cooking and the eating.

While checking the time, I happened to notice my phone charge was dangerously low, so I plugged it into the charger beside the couch before rushing into the kitchen, where I clicked the stove burner onto the highest possible flame. Now, while I'm not a master chef, I *do* recognize that cooking on a high flame is poor culinary technique—not to mention it's very unsafe—but I was desperate, hungry, and short on time, so danger was the least of my concerns. At worst, I figured I might cause a grease fire, which I delusionally assumed I could handle because my dad's a firefighter and he taught me all about them when I was a kid.

Dad's lesson took place at our favorite diner as we sat at the counter waiting for lunch. I was watching the burgers cook in the open kitchen when a large flame blossomed on the grill, causing me to jump from my stool.

"It's okay, bud," Dad said, resting his hand on my shoulder. "It's just a grease fire."

"How'd that happen?"

"Well," he said, "the hamburger grease reached its flashpoint."

Now, Dad knew full well that I didn't know what a flashpoint was, but, as was his way—in lieu of giving me an outright dissertation—he preferred planting little seeds of curiosity.

"What's a flashpoint?"

"It's a term in chemistry that describes the lowest temperature at which a volatile material, like hamburger grease, can release enough vapors to ignite into a flame," he said. "Make sense?"

"Kind of," I shrugged. "What's a volatile material?"

"Good question," he said. "A volatile material is anything that can catch fire when exposed to heat or a spark." He pointed to the grill. "Take those hamburgers, for example. As they cook, they release grease, which is volatile. This means it can catch fire, but only when it gets hot enough."

"And the minimum temperature is the flashpoint?"

"Exactly."

"So, if the hamburger grease gets hot enough, it turns into fire?"

"You got it."

"Okay, but what ignites it?" I asked. "Doesn't the hamburger grease have to touch fire or something before it blows up?"

"Yes and no," he said. "What you're referring to is called an ignition source."

"What's that?"

"An ignition source is anything that provides enough heat or energy to create a combustion."

"What's a combustion?"

"Combustion is the process by which something catches fire," he said. "It happens when an ignition source meets a volatile material and then reacts with the oxygen in the air to create fire." He grabbed a napkin from the metal box on the counter, letting it hang between us. "For example, imagine lighting a match and then touching it to this napkin. What would happen?"

"The napkin would catch fire."

"Exactly," he said. "So, which is the ignition source? The match or the napkin?"

"The match?"

"You got it, bud," he said. "And that means the napkin is the volatile material."

"Okay, I think I get it," I said, turning my eyes back to the grill. "So, does that mean the hamburger grease is like the napkin?"

"Precisely."

"I guess that makes sense," I said, "but there's no fire on the grill."

"Good observation," he said. "That's what's called a flattop grill. It uses a gas burner below, which is why you don't see any fire."

"If there's no fire," I said, "then what was the ignition source that made the hamburger grease combust?"

This made Dad smile.

"Sometimes," he said, "under the right circumstances, combustion can happen *without* an ignition source."

"It can?"

"Yes," he said, "we call that autoignition."

"Autoignition?"

"Yup," Dad nodded. "It means the grease got so hot on its own that it burst into flames without needing a match or a spark."

"Wait a minute," I said, my mind fully blown, "you mean fire can just happen out of nowhere?"

"Under the right circumstances, yes."

"Like magic?"

"Yes," he said, ruffling my hair, "very much like magic."

A few minutes before engulfing myself in flames, I'd poured a few splashes of vegetable oil into the skillet, and, in my haste, I spilled some on my linoleum floor. Because I was in a rush, I decided not to clean the oil up right away, choosing instead to step over and around it while preparing my lunch. As the peppers and onions sizzled and smoked alongside yesterday's shrimp, I searched around the kitchen for a spatula. Stepping away from the hot skillet—careful to avoid the vegetable oil on the floor—I rifled through my kitchen drawers to no avail, before eventually finding the spatula in the kitchen sink hiding beneath several dirty plates and utensils.

Turning on the faucet, I let the water run for a minute so it could get hot, as I loathe washing dishes with cold water. Once the water was hot enough, I soaped up a sponge and began giving the spatula a thorough scrubbing. I was mid-scrub when the piercing squeal of the smoke alarm sounded overhead. Luckily, there was no fire yet to speak of—just an aggressive column of smoke barreling into the ceiling. Dropping the spatula back into the sink, I grabbed a dish towel and hurried into the corner of my tiny apartment designated as the living room, where the smoke alarm is located. Because I was operating in panic mode, I neglected to turn the stove off, which was still burning on the highest possible flame as it aggressively grilled my ill-fated lunch.

Standing beneath the smoke alarm—which actually looks more like a tiny UFO stuck to the ceiling—my arms burned with fatigue as I wildly waved the dish towel in an effort to clear the smoke away and stop the high-pitched squeal from its assault on my ears. When that didn't immediately work, I stepped up onto my coffee table to wave the dish towel in closer proximity to the tiny UFO. I'd barely settled my feet atop the coffee table when the familiar whoosh of combustion sounded behind me. Turning my head, I saw a raging grease fire erupting in the skillet.

Jumping from the coffee table, I ran back into the kitchen and, using the dish towel to protect my hand, lifted the dangerously hot skillet from the stove. I'd hoped to drop the flaming skillet into the sink, but the vegetable oil on the floor conspired against me. I managed to take only one step when the heel of my shoe landed flush on the oil, causing my foot to slide with such force that it swung up and over my head like a pendulum. As I fell ass-backward towards the linoleum, I was already anticipating the pain of my inevitable rough landing, but what I wasn't counting on was cracking the back of my head on the heavy wooden table on the way down.

At some point during my flailing descent, I lost my grip on the flaming skillet, allowing it to land squarely between my legs on the linoleum floor. Generally speaking, under most any other circumstance, I would've been acutely aware of a flaming skillet between my legs, but on account of the concussive blow to my head, I didn't immediately notice it. On the bright side, the flaming skillet wasn't actually touching me—but, on the not-so-bright side, it *was* touching the dish towel, creating a perfect conduit for the fire to travel from the skillet to my very flammable business slacks. By the time I made this critical observation, not only were my slacks engulfed in flames, but so was my equally flammable shirt.

And this brings us back to the moment of now: me all alone, covered head to toe in fire.

I begin rolling on the floor, harkening back to my grade school lessons of stop, drop, and roll—minus the stopping and the dropping—but my fiery cocoon is much too stubborn to give up without a fight, so I tear my shirt open like Clark Kent transforming into Superman, popping buttons all over the kitchen floor, before frantically working to unzip my pants. The primary struggle with my pants is trying to locate the zipper beneath the aggressive flames; this takes me several terrifying seconds, but once I successfully manage to unzip, I push my pants down to my ankles, where—son of a bitch!—they get stuck atop my shoes. I dig my toes into the back of one shoe and then the other, quickly prying them off before fully evacuating my flaming business slacks. Scooping up my charred slacks and shirt, I heave them into the sink under the running faucet before tossing the skillet in after them.

The piercing screech of the tiny UFO continues to assault my ears, so, in hopes of expediting its silence, I open the front door to let the smoke out. I also take this opportunity to step outside for some fresh air, standing on the porch with my quivering hands planted against my hips. As I take in several deep breaths, my mind racing around the reality of just how bad this all could've been, a couple of schoolgirls in plaid skirts giggle at me as they walk past. Looking down, I realize that—with the exception of my underwear and socks—I'm completely naked, so I hurry back into my apartment, where the tiny UFO has mercifully gone silent.

Plopping down on my couch, I lay my head back and close my eyes. It's not until this exact moment that it occurs to me to check for injuries. Even before I look, I know there's no way I got out of this fiasco without at least a few third-degree burns. I assume the reason I'm not currently in excruciating pain is that my body's in shock, which is just as well since I'm not in any hurry to experience whatever torture is coming my way.

I examine my arms first.

Nothing.

I look down at my chest and belly.

Nothing.

Legs and feet?

Nothing.

Not a single burn or blemish to be found.

Before I can properly process this inexplicable development, my phone rings.

It's my mother.

She's crying, barely able to talk.

"Mom," I say, "what's going on?"

"Oh, Grover," she says, "I don't know what's happening."

"Is everything okay?"

"It's your father," she says. "There's something wrong with your father."

Chapter Two

SCHRÖDINGER'S CAT

"**I**S GOD REAL?"

I was twelve years old when I first presented this question to my parents. We were driving to Disneyland for our annual Easter visit—Mom and Dad in front, me in the back with a Batman comic book.

"That's a big question, bud," Dad said. "What made you think of that?"

"I don't know," I said with a shrug. "I guess because I've never seen him before?"

We weren't a religious family, so I didn't spend a whole lot of time thinking about God or the Devil, Heaven or Hell. I was aware of the *concept* of God, and I suppose he existed in the same part of my brain as Santa Claus and the Easter Bunny. However, when I was old enough to learn that Dad ate the cookies and Mom hid the eggs, I naturally started to wonder what else wasn't true.

This particular Disneyland trip was delayed by a few hours as Dad wanted to attend Easter Mass at the local Catholic church. We weren't normally a church family, but my grandpa—Dad's dad—had passed away a few months prior, and Easter was the first holiday on the calendar since his passing. Unlike me, Dad *did* grow up religious—Catholic, to be specific—as my grandpa was a devoutly religious man. I think going to church that particular Easter was Dad's way of feeling connected to him. The only thing I remember about that Easter Mass was sitting on a wooden pew for three hours, bored out of my mind, wishing desperately for the man in the fancy robe to wrap things up so I could ride Space Mountain.

"For people who believe in God," Dad said, "part of their faith is based on not being able to see him."

"So, God exists, but we just can't see him?"

I watched Dad's eyes in the rearview mirror; they didn't have the all-knowing confidence I was accustomed to seeing.

"I'll be honest with you, bud," Dad said. "I don't know if God is real."

"Do you know, Mom?"

Mom closed the book she was reading, leaving her thumb inside as a placeholder.

"Well," she said, pausing for a few brief moments, "I know that *nature* is real. The moon, the sun, the stars. The air we breathe, the grass in our yard, the ocean, the ozone layer, dinosaur fossils. And I also know these are all big mysteries because nobody knows for sure where they all came from. Maybe there's a God who created it all, or maybe there's some other explanation that we're simply not aware of."

"Does that mean God *is* real?"

She smiled at Dad before looking back at me.

"I don't know either, sweetheart."

"You know, when I was in college," Dad said, "I learned about Schrödinger's cat."

"*Who's* cat?"

Dad laughed.

"Schrödinger's," he said, "but the cat wasn't real. It's what you would call a thought experiment."

"What's that?"

"A thought experiment is basically a made-up scenario," he said, "something that challenges your brain when you think about it. Make sense?"

"I think so."

"To begin the Schrödinger's cat thought experiment, you first need to imagine putting a cat into a box," he said. "Tell me when you see it."

I closed my eyes, picturing a black cat in a cardboard box.

"I see it."

"Now, imagine putting a piece of poisoned cat food in the box with it."

I opened my eyes, looking at Dad in the rearview mirror.

"That doesn't sound very nice."

"No, it's not nice at all," Dad said, "but it's part of the thought experiment. So, go ahead and put a piece of poisoned cat food in the box. Tell me when you see it."

I closed my eyes and gently laid down a piece of poisoned cat food inside the cardboard box.

"I see it."

"Now," Dad said, "close the box so the cat is sealed inside with the poisoned cat food. Tell me when you see it."

I took a deep breath before closing the box.

"I see it."

"Now, here's where the thought experiment begins," Dad said. "Is the cat dead or alive?"

"He's alive."

"Are you sure?" Dad said, smiling. "Can you see it?"

"No," I said, "but he was alive the last time I looked."

Dad laughed.

"That's true," he said, "but you also put a piece of poisoned cat food in the box with it."

"Yeah, but only because you told me to."

"That's also true," Dad said. "Nonetheless, the poisoned cat food is in the box with the cat. If the cat eats the poison, it'll die, right?"

"Yes."

"So, is it dead or alive?"

"I don't know," I said. "Can I open the box to check?"

"Nope," he said, smiling. "Part of the thought experiment is that you can't open the box."

"If I can't look inside the box, how do I know if the cat is dead or alive?"

"Ah-ha," he said, "you've just discovered the point of this thought experiment."

"I did?"

"You sure did, bud," he said. "Since you can't look inside the box, both possibilities are true simultaneously."

"What does that mean?"

"It means that Schrödinger's cat is both alive *and* dead at the same time."

"That's impossible, isn't it?"

"You're right," Dad said. "The cat can only be dead *or* alive, but not both. But the idea is that until you open the box and see for yourself, both possibilities are true."

"Okay, I think I get it."

"Good," Dad said. "For me, I sort of think of God as Schrödinger's cat. Because we can't see God, he both *does* and does *not* exist at the same time. Make sense?"

"Kind of."

In the rearview mirror, I saw Dad's mind searching for something more.

"Your grandfather was a very religious man," he said. "Right up until the day he died, he believed all of it was real. Heaven, Hell, the Devil, and *especially* God. It didn't matter that he couldn't see him. For my dad, God was every bit as real as you and me. So, while I don't know if *God* is real, I do know that my *dad* was real. And he was a good man who worked hard, took care of his family, and helped his neighbors. All my life, I could *see* my dad. I could *touch* him. I could observe his good deeds with my very own eyes. I know for certain that, because my dad believed in God, the world is a better place. Make sense?"

"Yeah, I think so."

"So, whether it's God or Schrödinger's cat," Dad said, "*you* get to decide what you want to believe."

"But what if what I decide to believe isn't true?"

"It doesn't matter if it's true," Dad said. "It only matters that you believe it."

Right now, as I race down Interstate 10 to Loma Linda University Medical Center, Dad is Schrödinger's cat. Mom said he had come home from the fire station for lunch, which was a nice surprise. She gave him a kiss in front of the TV, then went to the kitchen to make him a sandwich. Mom was barely gone a minute when she heard the crash. Hurrying back to the living room, she found Dad face down on the floor. She dropped to her knees, screaming for him to wake up, but his eyes wouldn't open. That's when she called 911. Then she called me. We were still on the phone when the paramedics arrived, so, before hanging up, she told me to meet her at the hospital.

I park my car in the first open spot I see, then run through the parking lot as fast as I can. With every labored stride, I resent how unathletic I am, childishly wishing I could run with super speed like the Flash. The next several minutes unfold in a blur, from raising my voice at the kind receptionist to finding Dad's room in the ICU.

He's alive.

Thank God.

"Oh, Grover," Mom says, sobbing against my shoulder, "I'm so glad you're here."

"He's going to be okay," I say, looking over her shoulder at Dad. There are several wires and tubes attached to him, each leading to machines and gizmos that I've never seen in real life. "What's wrong with him?"

"I don't know."

"What did the doctors say?"

"They don't know anything yet," she says. "They're going to do tests."

"What kind of tests?"

"I don't know, sweetheart."

I've seen Mom cry before, but this feels different, like she knows something she's not telling me.

"I just can't imagine a world without your father in it."

Me neither.

Dad is like the love child of Paul Bunyan and Wonder Woman. He's been a firefighter for the Rancho Cucamonga Fire Protection District since before I was born, moving steadily through the ranks from Engineer to Captain to Deputy Chief and eventually Fire Chief. He's something of a manly man, brawny and tough, always with a crewcut and freshly shaved face. Every time he hugs me, he kisses my cheek. When he speaks, he looks you in the eye, and he's never exchanged a cross word with anyone who didn't deserve it. He always says please and thank you, and you can never beat him to a handshake.

When I was a kid, nobody ever confused me with being cool or popular in school—I've always been pretty shy and introverted—but being the son of Chief Wilcox came with enough cachet that the kids who might otherwise have picked on me left me alone, while other kids who might not have given me a second thought embraced me as an acquaintance. All of my teachers loved me even before they got a chance to know me because they already knew my dad.

He routinely made appearances throughout the school district, so it was always a special treat when he visited my school, pulling up in his big red fire truck. A couple of his firefighters, whichever ones were lucky enough to tag along, would pull up behind him in the fire engine. Dad would stand beside his truck, helmet atop his head, looking out over an audience of at least a hundred kids. Everybody in the school—students and teachers alike—wanted an opportunity to listen to Chief Wilcox speak, so they'd have to bring the students out in groups. He spoke to each group without a microphone, his booming voice carrying effortlessly over the entire audience.

"What's this behind me?" he'd ask. "A fire *truck* or a fire *engine*?"

He'd smile as the kids shouted out their conflicting answers over one another.

"How about that one?" he'd say, pointing to the second vehicle. "Fire truck or a fire engine?"

More conflicting shouts and guesses.

"The vehicle behind me is a fire *truck*," Dad would say, "and that one there is a fire *engine*. Fire *trucks* are equipped with very tall ladders that extend up and up so we can reach tall buildings or save kittens from trees." That always made the kids laugh. "Fire *engines* have hoses, so we can spray water. Each vehicle is different, but they work perfectly together. When there's an emergency, each one does what the other cannot."

I'd heard him give the same talk many, many times, and I never tired of it. I loved being lost in the crowd of kids, admiring Chief Wilcox right along with them, overflowing with pride that he was my dad. Mrs. Levon, a second-grade teacher, always stood near me when Dad came to visit. I was never in her class, but she treated me like her favorite student. If I happened to be passing by her classroom at lunchtime, she'd offer me chips and a juice box, and if her class was having a movie day, she'd always leave some licorice and popcorn aside for me. Mrs. Levon did these things because, before I was born, Dad saved her son's life.

Mrs. Levon was divorced and had primary custody of her son, Clive. Before he was old enough to attend school, Mrs. Levon put Clive in daycare with a kind old woman who took care of kids in her home. One day, there was a short circuit in the front room that started a fire. Clive and the kind old woman were the only people inside the house. The fire moved fast, blocking the front entrance; by the time the kind old woman realized what was happening, the flames had already spread to the back door as well. She stood in the middle of the entryway, screaming for help, with Clive in her arms. Dad wasn't even working when he happened to see the house on fire. Charging inside without hesitation, Dad saved both Clive and the kind old woman.

I've heard stories like this about Dad my whole life—sometimes from neighbors and friends, sometimes from complete strangers.

So, is this how it ends for great men?

Unconscious in an oxygen mask?

Hooked up to strange machines?

Barefoot in a hospital gown?

It's not fair.

I want him to see me.

I want him to open his eyes.

I want to tell him how much I love him.

I want to tell him I'm scared and confused.

I want him to comfort me and make it better.

I want to ask him what happened to me in my apartment.

I want him to explain how I walked away without a single burn.

Without my dad's expertise, I can only come up with one explanation.

I'm fireproof.

But that's impossible.

Right?

Chapter Three

HERO'S JOURNEY

L EAVING THE HOSPITAL AND driving back to my tiny studio apartment, I pass through Rancho Cucamonga—the city
where I grew up and where my parents still live—and in an empty
dirt lot behind a high-end shopping center, I see a classic big top
circus tent with red and white stripes and several vines of swooping
string lights. A series of small tents and midway booths lead up to
the big top, but interestingly enough, there is no Ferris wheel, which
seems like a missed opportunity (but who am I to say?). Hanging
above the entrance is a banner that reads, "The Grambling Brothers
Traveling Circus Show."

I honestly had no idea traveling circuses like this even existed anymore. I'd assumed Ringling Bros. and Barnum & Bailey had swallowed the industry whole, but clearly, as evidenced by the dormant
promise of joy to my left, I was wrong. The sight of it puts a smile
on my face for the first time today. As a kid, I was enamored with
the circus from my first introduction to it in movies like *Dumbo* and
Big Top Pee-wee. A couple of decades ago, my parents took me to my
very first circus, and I was over the moon with excitement. I couldn't
believe I was actually going to see the whole amazing spectacle live

and in person; they may as well have been taking me to Gotham City or the planet Krypton, fantastical worlds of make-believe that only existed on the pages of my favorite comic books.

The occasion was a private charity event at the Los Angeles Sports Arena featuring the Ringling Bros. and Barnum & Bailey Circus. Dad had gotten us tickets, which was one of the perks of being Chief Wilcox. There was a red carpet at the arena entrance, with several news outlets covering the event. I saw that one kid from *Who's the Boss* talking to *Entertainment Tonight*, as well as several players from the Los Angeles Clippers posing for pictures and signing autographs. Mom held my hand as we entered the arena, and at every turn, we saw celebrities like the old lady from the "Where's the beef?" commercials and the fat guy from *Saturday Night Live*. I wish I could remember everything about the circus performance that night, but I can only manage a few fleeting details, such as the ringmaster's booming voice, the trapeze artists' gravity-defying flips, and the clowns' hilarious interludes.

For several months following that charity event, I became obsessed with building myself into a future circus performer, but because I had no applicable skills, there was a lot of building to do. First, I practiced my tightrope skills by walking along the grout lines of our tiled kitchen floor. With my arms out for balance, I'd step one foot in front of the other, heel to toe, moving methodically forward until I reached the pantry. Once I mastered the kitchen floor, I went outside and practiced on the curb in our front yard, walking from the mailbox to the fire hydrant. The curb was only six inches or so off the asphalt, so losing my balance had very low stakes. After mastering the curb, I progressed to the cinderblock fence that separated our backyard from the neighbor's. I lasted all of three steps before falling to the grass and breaking my arm.

My mom's sister, Aunt Ruthie, happened to be staying with us for a few days when I broke my arm. Aunt Ruthie's visits always felt like a party, even when I had to go to the emergency room to get my arm in a cast. Mom always called Aunt Ruthie a dreamer because she had such a big imagination. Aunt Ruthie believed in my circus dream the moment I told her about it, so with my arm in a cast, she took me to the library, where we checked out a book on juggling. We read about the drop, the toss, the exchange, the jug, the overhand grab, outside juggling, and on and on. Aunt Ruthie practiced the techniques for me, but we quickly learned she couldn't juggle any better than I could walk a tightrope. With tennis balls rolling around the floor, Aunt Ruthie and I laughed until we could hardly breathe. Mom came around to see what all the fuss was about, only to get swept up in our hurricane of laughter.

"Make me a promise," Aunt Ruthie said. "Don't ever stop dreaming."

After Aunt Ruthie's visit was over, I continued going to the library in pursuit of my circus dream. With each book I checked out, it became more and more clear that being a terrible athlete with no discernible hand-eye coordination was not going to get me to the Promised Land. But I wasn't ready to give up on my dream just yet, so I thought perhaps being a clown was the way to go. I went into Mom's makeup and decorated my face with white powder and red lipstick before standing in front of the bathroom mirror and attempting to be silly—but it turns out I was no better at being a clown than I was at walking a tightrope.

In a last-ditch effort to bring my circus dreams to life, I spent several fruitless hours trying to become a contortionist. When, after much effort, I couldn't even manage to touch my fingers to my toes, I decided it was time to give up on the dream. My obsession with the circus waned over time until it became a dusty memory sealed away in the attic of my mind with other childish fantasies such as growing up to become Batman or climbing walls like Spider-Man. In fact, I'd all but forgotten about my circus dream until I saw the big top of the Grambling Brothers Traveling Circus Show, and all those wonderful childhood memories bubbled right up to the surface.

I wake up bright and early, and for the first several minutes of my morning, it's as if yesterday never happened. I roll out of bed, and within a few short steps, I'm in the kitchen, where I see my charred clothes in the sink, and—in a flash—it all comes back to me.

Grease fire.

Hospital.

Dad.

Speaking of yesterday...

Am I fireproof?

I suppose since I'm in the kitchen beside the stove, there's an easy way to find out. So, I click the stove burner on to the highest flame, staring at the circle of fire as I contemplate the consequences of touching it with my hand. There's a big part of me that's afraid of burning myself—but then, there's an even *bigger* part of me that's afraid of *not* burning myself. If, by some wacky miracle, it turns out I *am* fireproof (which I can all but assure you I'm not), what would that even mean? It's not like I'm going to go off and become a superhero...unless that's *exactly* what it means!

What if the crazy events of yesterday were the ignition source of my hero's journey? For a guy who's spent his whole life with his nose buried in comic books, I know an origin story when I see one. There was the wild accident in the kitchen, the discovery of my superpower, and the tragic events surrounding my dad. That last bit is crucial because all the best superheroes suffered a personal tragedy on their way to fulfilling their destinies.

Bruce Wayne became Batman after watching his parents murdered.

Clark Kent became Superman after his father died of a heart attack.

Peter Parker became Spider-Man after his uncle was killed by a mugger.

Now, before you start worrying about my mental stability, I fully recognize that fixating on an adolescent fantasy is my way of coping with the terrifying reality that my dad may very well be on his deathbed. I know I'll never be ready to lose my dad, but I'm *especially* not ready now. It's too early in our story for this sort of ending. I always assumed that when the time came to say goodbye, it would be at the end of a long, satisfying life, each of us old men with white hair, me at his bedside, telling him how grateful I am that the universe chose Rex Wilcox to be my dad. Then, I'd let him drift peacefully off to whatever comes next after this life.

I turn off the burner without ever touching the fire. I don't need to burn my hand to find out what I already know to be true: I'm not fireproof. Plus, even if I were, I don't see a whole lot of agency in being a fireproof superhero, since the only way I'd be able to use my superpower is by letting things happen *to* me. Not to mention the whole problem with my aggressively unimpressive physique, which, on my best days, is soft and pasty—what you might call skinny fat. Let's just say there's nothing about my physical form that needs to be accentuated by superhero tights. Speaking of which, I'd have to find a fireproof costume; otherwise, my clothes would burn off every time I used my superpower.

Can't you just see it?

Me carrying a damsel in distress from a burning building, only I'm completely naked. That's a Human Resources nightmare the Avengers would want nothing to do with.

Frankly, I'm relieved not to be fireproof.

I grab breakfast from McDonald's for Mom and me on my way back to the hospital. Under normal circumstances, a fast-food breakfast wouldn't be Mom's first choice, as creating culinary miracles from scratch is sort of her thing. As much as she enjoys cooking, she also enjoys sharing her knowledge, so when I took an interest in learning how to cook as a kid, she was more than happy to indulge me.

One particular Saturday morning, I decided to make scrambled eggs all by myself while my parents were asleep. I was about seven years old at the time, so cooking was still very new to me, but I was confident I could handle scrambling eggs. The only problem was my favorite Saturday morning cartoon, *Super Friends*, was about to start, and I never missed a minute of it. So, in an effort to cook my eggs as fast as possible, I turned the stove burner up to its highest flame. With *Super Friends* just moments from starting, I left my eggs unattended and went to the living room to turn on the TV, making it just in time to watch the opening credits, which was my favorite part.

Once the credits were over, I figured I could watch the opening scene before checking on my eggs during the first commercial break, but before I knew it, a dark haze drifted into the living room, and the smoke alarm began squealing overhead. I raced back into the kitchen with the hot sting of panic zipping across my chest as I found my eggs curdling into something dark and unrecognizable. I stood frozen amongst the black smoke, tears streaming down my cheeks, until Dad burst into the kitchen. After first turning the burner off, he used a dish towel to wave the smoke away from the tiny UFO in the ceiling until the squealing alarm went silent.

"Let me guess," he said, wrapping me up in a hug. "You tried cooking your eggs on a high flame?"

"I'm sorry," I said, crying into his belly.

"It's alright, bud."

He slipped on an oven mitt, lifting the skillet from the stove.

"Now, I'm not the cook that your mother is," he said, setting the skillet in the sink, "but I happen to know that cooking over a high flame doesn't actually cook your food faster."

Turning on the faucet, he ran cold water over the sizzling skillet.

"But I'm guessing you probably figured that out, huh?"

I nodded, yes.

The memory of that morning winds through my mind like a grainy VHS tape as I make my way back to the ICU, where I find Mom standing at Dad's bedside, holding his hand. Her eyes are heavy, and she looks more exhausted than I can ever remember seeing her before.

"Morning, Mom."

She smiles when she sees me.

"Hi, sweetie."

"Hungry?"

"Not really."

"Too bad," I say, handing her an egg and cheese biscuit sandwich. "You need to eat, young lady."

This gets a chuckle out of her.

"I forgot to get coffee."

"They have coffee in the cafeteria."

"Perfect," I say, "let's eat in the cafeteria."

She's reluctant to leave, but eventually relents. We go down to the cafeteria, where Mom grabs us a table, and I buy a couple of black coffees from the nice lady at the register.

"Do the doctors know anything yet?" I ask, setting our coffees down.

"Nothing more than they knew yesterday," she says. "He has brain activity, so that's good, but otherwise the doctors have no idea what happened to him or why he won't wake up."

"There's no sign of a heart attack or a stroke?"

"No," she says. "Every test they've done so far says your father is a perfectly healthy man."

"How's that possible?"

"That's what they're trying to figure out, sweetheart."

We eat in silence for a few minutes.

"I drove by a circus last night," I say. "It made me think of Aunt Ruthie."

This puts a smile on Mom's face.

"When's the last time you saw her?" I ask.

"Last week," she says. "I should really visit more than I do, but it's hard."

Aunt Ruthie lives in an assisted living home these days, following a stretch of time in a mental institution. Mom had her committed some years ago, which tore her up inside. I know Aunt Ruthie's mental illness has something to do with hallucinations or delusions or something of the sort, but I can never quite remember the details—or maybe I simply don't want to. All things considered, I decide that now probably isn't the best time to ask Mom to refresh my memory.

We finish our breakfast and go back to Dad's room, where we mostly sit in silence (save for a few bits of small talk in between whatever TV shows we're only half-watching). Nurses come and go, exchanging pleasantries with Mom and me as they check on Dad. Finally, after a few hours, Mom tells me to go home.

"It's okay," I say. "I'm not tired."

"Too bad," she says. "Go home."

"But I want to stay."

"Grover," she says, "this isn't how I want you to spend your life."

"Honestly, I *want* to be here."

"Oh, sweetie," she says, touching her fingers to my cheek, "none of us *want* to be here."

She stands up from her chair and pulls me out to the hallway.

"Drive safe."

"Mom."

"I'm serious," she says, kissing my cheek.

"I don't even know what to do with myself."

"Do something fun," she says. "Maybe go to that circus you saw. I'm sure there's a nice girl you can take with you."

"I'm sure there is," I say, "but I haven't met her yet."

"Want me to set you up with one of the nurses?"

"Would you look at that?" I say, looking at my watchless wrist. "I've got to go!"

This makes Mom laugh.

"Call me if you need anything."

"I will," she says, hugging me. "I'll see you tomorrow."

Chapter Four

MILESTONES

I'D LIKE TO THINK I might one day have the sort of romance that my parents have enjoyed for the last several decades, but I've never had much luck with girls. Aside from being painfully shy and socially awkward, I just don't know how to talk to them. Remember that joke I made about having to leave when Mom offered to set me up with one of the nurses? Well, it wasn't really a joke. Just the thought of it filled me with anxiety. As much as I'd love to find myself entwined in an epic romance, my pathetic dating history is not a promising precursor of things to come. If you were to comb through my past, you'd find three milestone experiences with the opposite sex that, for better or worse, have come to define my life as a bachelor.

MILESTONE #1

I was fourteen years old.

A carnival popped up overnight in the parking lot of the local Catholic church—the sort of carnival that features rusty equipment and dubious employees. On the first night of the carnival, which was a Friday, I went with some friends to check it out, and, in surprisingly short order, a group of girls started talking to us. While my friends took to flirting with ease, I was too nervous to engage with the girls, so I stood by silently and watched. One of the girls had the idea that we should all go on the Ferris wheel, heavily implying that there was romance to be found in those wobbly carriages. So, everyone paired off, and before I knew it, I was sitting in a Ferris wheel carriage beside a pretty girl who I'd known for less than ten minutes.

We sat quietly as the Ferris wheel took us high up into the sky, the sound of its rusty gears filling the air as the precarious carriage rocked us back and forth. I occupied myself by marveling at the infinite landscape of city lights when, without warning, the pretty girl's lips were attached to mine.

This was my first kiss.

She and I spent the next couple of hours holding hands and stealing kisses, while our friends playfully teased us. I pretended to be embarrassed, but I enjoyed the attention. After that night, we talked on the phone a few times, but because we lived several cities apart, it was all but impossible to see each other again; this was a time before smartphones and social media, so keeping in touch with anybody was significantly more challenging than it is today. With each passing week, the phone calls became fewer and fewer, until, soon enough, it was as if we'd never met at all.

And I never saw her again.

MILESTONE #2

I was seventeen years old.

During my senior year of high school, one of my buddies asked me to be his wingman for a hot date he had with his dream girl. I wasn't so sure being his wingman was a good idea and told him as much because I had no idea what being a wingman entailed.

"It's easy," he said, "you just have to keep her cousin busy while I try to get laid."

"Busy how?"

"Just talk to her," he said. "Who knows, you might get lucky, too."

We ate dinner at Denny's and then went to the movies. We stayed in the theater for about an hour before my buddy got antsy to leave, which I suspect had something to do with his date losing her hand down his pants. We drove out to Beryl Park, which was dark and empty. My buddy parked in front of the playground before disappearing with his date somewhere under the jungle gym, leaving the cousin and me alone together for the first time that night.

"Do you have a girlfriend?"

"No," I said. "Do you?"

"Do I have a *girl*friend?"

My cheeks grew hot.

"I mean, do you have a *boy*friend?"

She giggled, pushing her seat back flat.

"Nope."

She put her bare feet on the dashboard, letting her dress slide down toward her hips. Stretching her arms over her head, she arched her back, moaning softly under her breath. Now, as I unfold this story for you, it's probably becoming progressively obvious that the cousin wanted to steam up the windows with some amorous activity, but, because I was so inexperienced with girls, I simply assumed she wanted to take a nap. So, being the gentleman that I am, I got out of the car and left her alone to sleep.

Given my aforementioned inexperience, it won't surprise you to learn that sex was a pretty infrequent occurrence in my high school years—and by "infrequent," I mean it never happened—so, despite *not* getting laid that night, my evening with the cousin stands as the closest I ever came to having sex in high school.

And I never saw her again.

MILESTONE #3

I was twenty years old.

During my second year of college, I finally lost my virginity. It happened in a seedy motel parking lot after once again being recruited to play wingman, this time for a guy I barely knew. He was charismatic, funny, and talked to everybody—especially girls—with an ease that I could only dream of. We met in one of my English classes, and I remember he had a girl's name (Tracy? Ashley?). He was several years older than me and, for reasons I never understood, wanted to be my friend. We'd often hang out after class, grabbing food in the cafeteria or studying in the library—by studying, I mean I would do our homework and he would tell me how much he appreciated it.

One day after class, Tracy (Ashley? Bailey?) invited me to hang out with a couple of girls he met at the mall earlier in the week.

"These girls are down to party," he said. "You in?"

"Sure."

Tracy (Ashely? Bailey? *Sloane*?) bought some beers and drove us in his windowless van to a motel in one of the less appealing corners of the Inland Empire. We spent a few hours drinking and laughing until Tracy/Ashley/Bailey/Sloane started making out with his chosen girl on the only bed in our motel room. I stood against the wall with a half-empty bottle of beer I'd been nursing all night; the second girl stood beside me as we watched like a couple of giggly voyeurs right up until their clothes started coming off.

Without a word, she took my hand and walked me outside.

"Those two are crazy," she said, laughing.

"I know, right?"

"I think they would've fucked right in front of us if we hadn't left."

"You think?"

She led me to Tracy/Ashley/Bailey/Sloane's van and got inside. The van had only two seats—driver and passenger—so she and I sat in the back on the floor.

"Wanna fuck?" she asked.

It was a very startling question, and not just because she presented her query as casually as one might offer their grandmother a cup of coffee, but primarily because we'd barely just met and we hadn't even kissed yet. Despite the immediate anxiety that wet my palms, I recognized that opportunities like this came along very rarely—or, in my experience, just this one time—so I didn't want to blow it.

"Sure," I said.

She leaned in and started kissing me, which was great because I sort of knew how to do that, but, when it came to sex, I'd never seen or touched a naked girl, so I had no real idea of what I was supposed to do. I mean, I'd seen plenty of porn, so I knew more or less where all the parts went, but I didn't know if there was a particular order of when things were supposed to happen or if there were rules about where my hands *were* or *weren't* supposed to go. While I was busy worrying about all the things I *didn't* know about sex, she slid her hand down my pants and started stroking my...um...

Sorry.

I don't mean to be coy, but I'm not sure there's a polite way to describe what happened next. Or maybe you're not worried about me being polite.

I don't know.

I suppose it's easier to just tell you what happened.

I kept my hands to myself for fear of accidentally doing anything I wasn't allowed to, until she grabbed my right hand and slipped it under her dress, placing my fingers perfectly between her legs. She was very wet, which was news to me because I had no idea that's how girl parts operated. I slipped my middle finger inside, causing her to moan, and at that moment I knew precisely how Neil Armstrong felt when he landed on the Moon. In very quick and impressive fashion, she took my erection out of my pants; dipping her head into my lap, she proceeded to give me the first—and quite possibly best—blowjob of my life. It's a minor miracle that I didn't finish in a matter of seconds, but in retrospect, I think the whole situation was so overwhelming that my body didn't know how to react. Following my inaugural blowjob, she hiked up her dress and straddled my lap, sliding me inside of her. I've never in my life—not before nor since—orgasmed with such speed or voracity.

"Oh," she said, "did you finish?"

I nodded, yes.

"That was fast."

"Sorry."

She climbed off of me and exited the van while I pulled my pants up. I stayed back for a minute, mostly out of embarrassment, before eventually going back to the motel room, where I found her getting fucked doggy style by Tracy/Ashley/Bailey/Sloane while the first girl masturbated with an empty beer bottle. I didn't get the impression I was invited to this portion of the party, so I slipped out of the room and took a seat on the pavement, resting my back against the brick wall.

Even though things ended poorly for me with the second girl, I thought we might have a future together. But, as it turned out, she was holding a flame for her ex-boyfriend and was only looking to make him jealous by fucking somebody else.

And I never saw her again.

I'm thirty-five years old now.

I wish I could tell you that my love life has improved since those three milestones, but, if anything, it's regressed quite considerably. Thanks to dating apps and Craigslist, I've managed a few unremarkable dates here and there, but most days my life is an endless cycle of teaching classes, reading comic books, and surfing internet porn. If I can squeeze in a hot meal and a decent TV show, then that's what passes for a good day anymore. I don't want to believe that this is what the rest of my life will be, but I have no idea how to change course.

Chapter Five

XYLA PEPPERMINT

I'M SITTING WITH MOM in the hospital room as *Judge Judy* plays on the TV. Three days in, despite their best efforts, the doctors aren't any closer to figuring out what's wrong with Dad. One of the doctors—a young guy with a wispy blonde mustache—comes in to see us.

"Hello, Lucy."

"Hello, Dr. Boudreaux," she says. "Have you met my son?"

"I don't believe I have," he says, giving me his attention.

"Grover," I say, shaking his hand.

"Were you there when your father collapsed?"

"No."

He nods knowingly, as if I'd given him something useful to consider.

"Remind me, Lucy," he says, giving his attention back to Mom, "how was your husband feeling in the days before the coma?"

"Fine," she says. "There was nothing out of the ordinary."

"No vomiting or headaches?"

"No."

"Do you recall what he was doing before losing consciousness?"

"He was on the couch watching TV."

"And he collapsed on the floor, not the couch?"

"Yes."

"Do you think perhaps he was making his way to see you when he collapsed?"

"Maybe," she says. "Why do you ask?"

"Well, as you know, your husband's condition is a very challenging mystery," he says, "so every little bit of information helps. In this case, I'm thinking that if he stood up from the couch and took two or three steps before collapsing, maybe he was coming to see you because he didn't feel well, as opposed to collapsing on the couch without any warning that something was wrong. Again, these are small details, but any information we collect has the potential to help us figure out what's going on. Do you recall anything subtle? A slurred word, maybe? Trouble remembering something?"

"No," she says, "he's as sharp as he ever was."

"Thank you," he says. "I'm going to do a little checkup on your husband, if you don't mind."

Dr. Boudreaux pokes Dad with something sharp, examining his movement and reflexes. He explains to us that he's looking for responses to physical stimuli, which Dad isn't giving him. Dr. Boudreaux next leans over the bed and speaks directly into Dad's ear, watching for any sign of a response.

Nothing.

"We should be getting the results back from the second round of blood tests soon."

I raise my hand like an elementary school student.

"What are we hoping to see in the tests?"

"We're looking at a few things," Dr. Boudreaux says. "Blood count, electrolytes, and glucose. We're also looking at his thyroid, kidney, and liver function. We want to determine if there was any carbon monoxide poisoning or any sort of drug or alcohol overdose."

"Rex doesn't drink or use drugs," Mom says.

"I'm sure that's true," Dr. Boudreaux says, smiling. "As I said before, every possibility we can eliminate gets us closer to figuring out what's wrong."

He finishes the checkup before offering a quick goodbye, leaving us alone with Judge Judy.

I kiss Mom goodbye and head out for the first of my two classes, arriving on campus about thirty minutes early. As recently as last year, I taught *four* classes: two at Chandler College and two at Saint Andrew College (aka the SAC). This was how I managed to scrape by in my tiny studio apartment in a city that becomes very unsavory when the sun goes down. But, thanks to California's economy dropping a hot, steaming pile of recession atop our collective heads, Governor What's-His-Name (not the boy band singer, but the other guy) decided the first line of defense was to pillage the education budget, leaving me with only half of the shit wage I'd grown accustomed to earning.

The only reason I haven't been left *completely* without a job is that I teach English composition, which, along with math, is a staple of higher education. While the powers that be can't fully eliminate

English classes any more than they can burn down the classrooms, what they *can* do is strip California's English departments right down to their piss-stained undies. The SAC, for example, took a blow torch to their English department, eviscerating any job security I was gullible enough to believe I had—in other words, they have no classes for me to teach for the foreseeable future. Chandler's blow torch, on the other hand, was a bit more merciful, leaving me and my anemic bank account with two classes for the current semester.

The embarrassing reality I live with is that most of my students are in college to pursue the American Dream in order to avoid earning the sort of money I make as their professor. Because I don't have an office to hang out in—as those are reserved for full-time professors—I usually go to the library when I have time to kill. But I know that if I go to the library, I'll just end up doing something awful like grading papers, and I don't have it in me to endure such torture today, so I decide instead to wander about campus, taking in the scenery and fresh air. Because I don't have an office to hang out in—as those are reserved for full-time professors—I usually go to the library when I have time to kill. But I know that if I go to the library, I'll just end up doing something awful like grading papers, and I don't have it in me to endure such torture today, so I decide instead to wander about campus, taking in the scenery and fresh air.

Passing through the quad—a large stretch of concrete flanked by the bookstore and cafeteria—I see a small crowd of students standing around an exotic woman handing out fliers. Her hair is long and brown. Colorful bracelets hang from her wrists. The hem of her flowy skirt sweeps atop her toes, framing the silhouette of her legs against the sunlight. Curious, I make my way to the crowd as the exotic woman gives her attention to one of the young men, pressing her fingertips against his temples. I see her lips moving, but I don't get to the huddle in time to hear what she says to him. I am, however, just in time to hear the young man's response.

"No way!" he says, almost yelling. "How'd you do that?"

A collective hum of astonishment floats amongst the crowd as the woman goes back to handing out fliers. She spots me in the back, and we lock eyes. Smiling, she offers me a flier, but, panicked by her attention, I scurry away to my classroom.

The class before mine is still in session, so I set my bag down and rest my back against the brick wall. Women have always made me nervous, especially beautiful ones like her. I don't know what I expect will happen if I talk to a beautiful woman, but I always assume the outcome will leave me humiliated in some form or fashion.

The classroom door opens, and students file out. I wait for them all to leave before entering, saying hello to their professor as we cross paths. I unpack my bag and set up a PowerPoint presentation as my students start filing in. My class isn't nearly as full as it used to be, but that's to be expected halfway through the semester. This is the time of year when the less motivated students stop showing up.

While it's now time to begin class, you never want to start teaching anything the moment the students sit down. It's important to give their brains time to acclimate to learning, so I like to engage them in a bit of mindless chitchat before jumping in.

"Afternoon," I say, smiling. "Any of you pass through the quad on your way to class today?"

No response.

"There seemed to be some sort of commotion," I say. "I was just curious if any of you knew what was happening."

One student raises her hand.

"Did you finish grading our papers?" she asks.

I dig through my bag, pretending to search for their ungraded papers.

"Sorry," I say. "It looks like I left them at home. But, rest assured, they *are* graded."

"No problem," she says. "Can you tell me the grade I got?"

I open a manila folder, engaging in more pretend searching.

"Sorry," I say, closing the folder. "I haven't recorded the grades yet. Next week, for sure."

She seems satisfied with this response but disappointed nonetheless. She has every right to feel disappointed, too, because I have no idea when I'll have their papers graded. It's not that I don't care, so I hope that's not the impression I'm giving you. It's just that the only thing I like about teaching anymore is talking about stuff that interests me, while everything else about the job—such as grading papers—mostly sucks. Even when the papers are good, which is rare, grading is still the bane of my existence.

Since the mindless chitchat isn't really going anywhere, I start the day's lesson.

"There are three points of view in writing," I say. "Anybody know what they are?"

No response.

"I'll give you a hint," I say. "*One* of them is first-person. Anyone want to guess what the *second* is?"

No response.

"It's second-person," I say. "How about a guess for the *third* point of view?"

No response.

"That would be third-person," I say. "Does anybody know what each point of view does?"

No response.

It's not unusual to have a quiet class like this. In my early days of teaching, I took it personally, like they were passive-aggressively ignoring me. But, over time, I came to realize that this is the standard DNA of a college classroom. It's not that they *aren't* listening, because mostly they are, but in general, college students are loath to engage. I think it has something to do with being afraid of saying the wrong thing or sounding stupid in front of their peers. I totally understand that feeling, too, which is why I don't press too hard for them to talk. When I know I'm going to be lecturing, I like to throw questions at them so as to give the impression of a two-way discourse.

"The easiest way to think about points of view is in the context of narrative storytelling," I say. "First-person point of view uses 'I' and 'we,' because the narrator is part of the story, and they're communicating what they experience from their own personal perspective. When a story is told in first-person, the reader is limited to what the narrator sees and hears. So, on the one hand, you can get a very in-depth examination of the narrator's mind and how they see and experience the world, but, on the other hand, you'll get limited insights into the characters around them because the narrator isn't in *their* heads. With that in mind, what might be some advantages and disadvantages of writing in first-person?"

No response.

"Do you think a reader will feel *more* connected to a first-person narrator or *less* connected?"

One student raises his hand.

"More connected?"

"Good," I say, "I agree with you. Now, why do you think a reader might feel more connected to a first-person narrator?"

"I guess because it feels personal," he says, "like the writer is talking directly to you."

"Excellent," I say. "How about disadvantages? Can anybody think of a disadvantage to writing in first-person?"

No response.

"Let me ask you this," I say. "Are people perfect?"

A chorus of noes fills the room.

"Do people have perfect memories?"

More noes.

"Have you ever had a friend tell you a story, only to find out they got some of the details wrong?"

A chorus of yeses fills the room.

"Now, does getting the details wrong make your friend a liar?"

A mixture of yeses and noes.

A girl in the front row raises her hand.

"I don't think they were lying."

"Why not?"

"Maybe they *thought* they were telling the truth," she says, "but just didn't remember the details correctly."

"That's a perfect explanation," I say. "Does anyone else want to add to that?"

No response.

"Moving on," I say. "Third-person point of view is where the writer uses 'he,' 'she,' and 'they.' In this way, the narrator is outside of the story, observing from a distance, kind of like watching a *National Geographic* documentary. In third-person, there are two versions: limited and omniscient. Does anybody know the difference?"

The brightest student in the class raises her hand, which is a relief, as I'm always happy when she has something to offer.

"I think third-person, limited, is where the author is writing specifically from the experiences of one character," she says. "Is that right?"

"That's perfect," I say. "How about third-person, omniscient?"

She hesitates.

"C'mon," I say, smiling, "you know the answer. What is it?"

"Is it where the author knows everything in the story," she says, "like God?"

"That's exactly right," I say. "Now, one advantage of a God-like narrator is that you can trust that everything they tell you is true. Can you guys think of any disadvantages?"

No response.

"How about in comparison to first-person?"

One student raises his hand.

"Maybe it's less personal?"

"Excellent," I say. "Essentially, an omniscient narrator has all the answers, but they're more distant. Any other thoughts?"

No response.

"Well, that brings us to second-person," I say, "which is arguably the most interesting of the points of view. If first-person uses 'I' and 'we,' and third-person uses 'him,' 'her,' and 'they,' what does second-person use?"

No response.

"You."

A boy in the front row points at himself.

"Me?"

"No," I say, "not *you* specifically. Second-person point of view uses the word 'you' in the narration. Now, this begs a very interesting question. If you're reading a story and the author references 'you,' who exactly are they talking to?"

A girl in the back raises her hand.

"Is the narrator talking to *me*?"

"Yes and no," I say. "In second-person, the narrator is technically addressing the reader. But they may also be addressing someone else. Imagine, for example, that the narrator is looking in the mirror. In that case, 'you' is actually them. Or maybe the narrator is staring up at the clouds, and 'you' is their interpretation of God. See, this is why I find second-person so fascinating."

No response.

"Okay," I say. "You guys want to watch a video?"

A chorus of yeses.

You might be thinking that I put on a video because I didn't feel like talking to my students anymore—and you'd be correct. Once class is over, I send the students on their way before packing up and following them out, locking the door behind me. Outside, I find myself face-to-face with the beautiful woman from the quad.

"Hello," she says. "I saw you earlier, right?"

"Um...maybe?"

"Yeah," she says. "I was handing out fliers."

She hands me a flier.

"I'm with the Grambling Brothers Traveling Circus Show."

"No kidding?" I say, looking at the flier. "I drove by your circus the other night."

"And you didn't come to see us?"

"Oh...well...I mean, I thought about it."

She smiles.

"Just teasing you," she says. "I'm Xyla Peppermint."

"Grover Wilcox."

"Do you like the circus, Grover?"

"I haven't been since I was a kid," I say, "but I used to love it."

"Well, that's all the more reason to come to our show."

My cheeks grow warm.

"I'm a fortuneteller, by the way."

"Really?"

"Have you ever sat with a fortuneteller?"

"No, never," I say. "I assumed they were fake."

"Well, I'm standing right here," she says. "Do I look fake to you?"

"Sorry, I just meant...I don't know what I meant."

I drop my eyes.

"You're not wrong," she says. "Most fortunetellers are charlatans."

I bring my eyes back up.

"But not me," she says. "I'd love to prove it to you, if you'll let me. Come to the show tonight."

"I don't think I can make it."

"How about I leave you a ticket at the box office?" she says. "Just in case."

"You don't have to do that."

"Too late," she says. "Stop by my tent before the show starts, and I'll tell you your fortune."

No response.

"See you tonight, Grover."

Chapter Six

THIS PARTICULAR DARK ROAD

I DRIVE BACK TO the hospital, thinking only of Xyla Peppermint. She's exactly the type of woman I normally never talk to, as I would never have the nerve to approach her, let alone engage in conversation. Dad never suffered from this kind of insecurity. Once, when I was in junior high, I told him about a girl I had a crush on; she was a real knockout, the kind of beauty who belonged on *Beverly Hills 90210*.

"Have you asked her out?" Dad asked.

"No," I said, "I've never even talked to her."

"There's nothing to be afraid of," he said. "What's the worst she can say—no?"

"I guess so."

"Sticks and stones," he said. "So, are you gonna ask her out or what?"

"Yeah, okay."

"Attaboy!"

I never did ask her out. Instead, I spent the rest of junior high and all of high school admiring her from afar. I assumed talking to girls would somehow become easier as I got older, but it's quite the opposite; somehow, women have gotten even more intimidating, which is why my brief conversation with Xyla represents something of an anomaly. As much as I'd like to see her again, I can't quite shake the suspicion that she had an ulterior motive; maybe if she hadn't seen me as a potential customer, she wouldn't have talked to me at all. I mean, I know she said she would leave me a ticket, so it's not like I have to spend any money, but I'm sure there's a catch.

There's always a catch.

I'm sitting alone by Dad's bedside while Mom stretches her legs in the hallway. I lean in, telling him about the pretty girl I met at school and how she invited me to go with her to the circus.

"Hello, again," Dr. Boudreaux says, startling me. "Sorry, I didn't mean to sneak up on you."

"It's okay."

"You know, it's good that you're talking to him like that," he says. "There are studies that suggest coma patients can benefit from familiar voices, especially from loved ones. They say it may help stimulate the unconscious brain, helping with recovery."

"Really?"

"There's no concrete proof one way or the other," he says, "but there's certainly no harm in it."

"I appreciate that."

"My pleasure," he says. "Is your mother around?"

Mom turns up right on cue.

"Hello, Dr. Boudreaux."

"Lucy," he says, smiling, "I just wanted to let you know that I've scheduled the spinal tap for tomorrow."

"Thank you for the update."

I raise my hand.

"What's a spinal tap?"

"It's a lumbar puncture," Dr. Boudreaux says. "We'll insert a needle into the spinal canal and collect a small amount of CFT for analysis."

"CFT?"

"Cerebrospinal fluid."

"That sounds serious."

"It's a routine procedure, I assure you," he says. "The CFT will allow us to check for any signs of infection in the nervous system, particularly in the brain."

"Will he be in pain?"

"No, not at all."

After a quick goodbye, Dr. Boudreaux leaves Mom and me alone with Dad.

"How was class?"

"It was fine," I say. "I met a fortuneteller."

"A fortuneteller?" she says, grinning. "How'd that come about?"

"She's with the circus that's in town."

"Well, that's fun," she says. "Did she give you a reading?"

"No," I say, "but she offered to."

"Why didn't you do it?"

"Well, she offered to do it tonight."

"Oh, yeah?"

"Yeah, she said she'd leave a ticket for me at the box office."

"Sounds like she likes you."

"I doubt it."

"You never know," she says. "Are you going?"

"I don't think so."

"Why not?"

"I should be here with you and Dad."

"Nonsense," she says. "You're going to the circus."

"I wouldn't feel right having fun while you're here alone."

"I'm not alone," she says, looking at Dad. "You know, your father and I have had many, many good years together, and we've enjoyed more than our fair share of fun. You may find it hard to believe, but much of that fun took place before you were born. Quite frankly, you were born as a *result* of some of that fun."

"I don't need to know about that."

She laughs.

"My point is this," she says. "Before we found ourselves on this particular dark road, your father and I traveled down a whole lot of bright roads together. But, unfortunately, the world isn't always bright. I guess it needs to balance itself out once in a while. I know seeing your father like this isn't easy for you. It's not easy for me, either, but I've had a whole lifetime of love with your father to prepare me for it. You, on the other hand, have many bright roads ahead, and getting a free ticket to the circus is just one of them. So, go and have a good time."

"Are you sure?"

"Positive," she says. "When you come back tomorrow, I want to hear all about it."

Chapter Seven

GROVER WILCOX GOES TO THE CIRCUS

T HE THING ABOUT BEING a bachelor is that you sort of have to get used to doing most everything in your life alone—like eating at sit-down restaurants or going to the circus. As soon as I graduated from high school and the handful of friends I had disappeared into the rest of their lives, I adapted to a life of social solitude. These days, I hardly give a second thought to going to a concert by myself or walking solo through the mall, but for some reason, I'm feeling overwhelmed with anxiety as I arrive at the Grambling Brothers Traveling Circus Show all alone.

It's pretty obvious to me—just as I'm sure it is to you—that the glaring variable here is Xyla Peppermint. If she hadn't personally invited me to the circus, then none of this would feel strange. It's not as though Xyla made any romantic advances or even implied that her invitation was anything more than a polite gesture, so, really, there's nothing at stake—and yet, as I walk through the sparsely populated parking lot, my heart is pounding so hard I fear it may topple me to the ground.

A small family stands ahead of me in line at the box office—a mom, a dad, and their infant son. I watch them purchase their tickets before heading to the makeshift entrance, where they're greeted by a heavyset clown. Beyond the entrance, the big top is in plain view.

"Sir?"

I look up and see the man in the box office waiting for me. I step up to the not-so-clean window, through which I see his arm is in a sling, and he's sporting a black eye. I expect him to initiate our transaction, but he just stares at me. Before the situation gets any more awkward than it already is, I get things started.

"I think there's a ticket here for me."

"You want to buy a ticket?"

He has a foreign accent that I can't quite place.

"No," I say, "I think somebody *left* a ticket for me."

"Name?"

"Grover Wilcox."

With his good arm, the injured man opens a drawer and retrieves an envelope. He eyes it with what appears to be skepticism before looking back at me.

"Xyla Peppermint left this for you?"

"Yeah."

"On purpose?"

"Uh-huh."

He looks at the envelope again, then back at me, before sliding it through a small opening at the bottom of the window. I see Xyla's name on it, and until this moment, I had no idea it was spelled with an X. I assumed it was spelled the way it sounds: Z-Y-L-A.

"Your ticket is in there," he says. "Take it to Charlie, and he'll let you in."

"Charlie?"

"Charlie Chuckles."

"Who?"

"The clown."

The injured man mumbles something in a foreign language under his breath as I make my way to the entrance, where Charlie Chuckles greets me.

"Hello there, young man," he says, clapping his hands like he's playing invisible cymbals. "Welcome to the Grambling Brothers Traveling Circus Show! Are you ready to have a fun time?"

"Sure."

"Wonderful!" he says. "Go ahead and give ol' Charlie Chuckles your ticket, and we'll get you into our land of silly-willy fun!"

I hand him the envelope, and, as he eyes it, Charlie Chuckles' silly smile morphs into a confused O shape.

"Xyla left this for you?"

"Yeah."

"On purpose?"

"Uh-huh."

Charlie Chuckles continues looking at the envelope, shaking his head in wonderment.

"Can I go in?"

"Sure, kid," he says without looking up. "Go ahead."

I step through the entrance, a wooden arch painted to look like the big top. Looking back over my shoulder, I see Charlie Chuckles at the box office having an animated conversation with the injured man behind the not-so-clean window. I pass through the wooden arch and see a weaving path of sideshow tents, midway games, and snack booths as I enter the circus grounds. There's something antiquated about this place. It's small but charming, like I've gone back in time to a circus during the Great Depression. As I walk further in, my olfactory senses are flooded with a menagerie of delicious aromas, from cotton candy and corndogs to snow cones and charred meat.

I walk past an old-fashioned popcorn wagon that, despite its red paint and yellow typography, looks like it would be right at home in a grainy, black-and-white photograph. Manning the popcorn wagon is a short man with thin hair. He watches over the kernels as they pop inside the glass case, taking a moment to smile at me as I pass.

All of the classic midway games appear to be represented, including the one where you try to knock down a pyramid of weighted milk bottles with a baseball. The woman manning the milk bottle game smiles and waves, inviting me over to play. I smile back but continue walking.

Without warning, a booming voice bursts through the air.

"You there," the voice says, "come be amazed!"

It's a barker standing in front of a sideshow tent.

"Step right up to see the most curious creature this side of Tutu Island."

There are two banners in front of his tent. The first advertises "Pedro the Orphan Wolf Boy" with an illustration of an adolescent werewolf. The second advertises "Geno the World's Shortest Giant" with an illustration of a hulking man in an undersized Hawaiian shirt.

"I'm just looking around."

"That's wonderful, my good man, because I have exactly what you've been looking for," he says, slapping the tent. "Come experience a world you never knew existed. A world where wolf boys howl and giants shrink. A world where your brain won't believe a word of what your eyes say is true."

The barker pauses, touching his finger to his ear.

"Do you hear that?"

I hear nothing.

"I repeat," the barker says, speaking directly to the tent, "do you *hear* that?"

A delayed growl sounds from inside the tent, followed by a hairy little arm pushing through.

The barker snaps his head towards me—eyes big, mouth agape.

"Do you see that?!"

The hairy fingers blindly claw at the air.

"Back!" the barker yells. "Back, I say!"

The hairy arm disappears back into the tent.

"It seems Pedro is absolutely *famished* for company," the barker says. "Come inside if you dare, and let your imagination feast."

"Maybe later."

"Now is far better than later, my good man."

"Sorry," I say, "I'm looking for Xyla Peppermint."

"In the market for fortunetelling?"

"Not really," I say. "She left me a ticket at the box office."

"Really?"

"Yeah."

"On purpose?"

"Uh-huh."

The barker eyes me like my face is a puzzle he can't quite solve.

"Do you know where I can find her?" I ask.

"Last tent before the big top," he says, scratching his head in confusion as he disappears into his tent.

As I continue walking the circus grounds, I come across another sideshow tent. This one is fronted by a woman who looks like she came directly out of a pinup magazine. She's wearing a red dress with white polka dots; the hem of her dress hangs just above her knees, showing off her very attractive legs. The top of her dress barely contains her claustrophobic cleavage, as if she's one deep breath away from popping out for all to see. Resting atop her exquisite breasts is a full and burly beard, cascading down from her jaw in long, fluffy waves. A manicured mustache frames her supple red lips.

"Hello, sweetie," she says, her voice soft and demure. "What's your name?"

"Grover."

"Nice to meet you, Grover," she says, squeezing my arm. "I'm Bettie."

The feeling of her fingers on my bicep sends a shock of excitement through my pants.

"You're just in time," Bettie says. "My husband and I are about to start our show. Would you like to come inside?"

"Oh, I don't know," I say. "I'm looking for Xyla."

"The fortuneteller?"

"Yes," I say. "She invited me tonight."

"Really?"

"Yeah."

"On purpose?"

"Uh-huh."

Bettie looks me up and down, a curious grin on her face.

"Well, I'm sure she's not going anywhere," Bettie says, fingering a lock of hair behind her ear. "Come inside with me, Grover. You can see Xyla after we're done."

She backs up into the tent, slowly, pulling me along with her eyes. I follow her inside, taking a seat in one of several empty folding chairs. There are three other people in the tent waiting for the show to begin. Bettie walks to the front, taking her place beside a menagerie of props, including a large trunk and a bed of nails. Sitting atop the trunk, hunched over with his elbows planted on his knees, is a very skinny man covered in tattoos from his gaunt face to his naked toes. His earlobes are stretched with black plates the size of my fists, and his fingernails are filed to fine points. Two thick silver hoops hang from his pierced nipples. A pair of baggy khaki shorts and raggedy flip-flops are all that keep him from being totally naked.

"Hello, you beautiful people, I am Bettie the Bearded Bombshell," she says, lifting the hem of her dress for a curtsy, "and this handsome fella is my husband, Lenny the Lanky Lizard Man."

Lenny stands up, his body unfolding to reveal a long frame. If he's not seven feet tall, he's pretty goddamn close. His height is exaggerated all the more by Bettie standing beside him; she's much shorter, five-foot-three or thereabouts. Lenny presses his hands together and bows to the audience before unleashing his surprisingly long forked tongue.

"Lenny," Bettie says, running her nails down his skinny bicep, "be a dear and open the trunk."

He unlatches the padlock in front of the trunk, gingerly lifting the lid.

"I believe I left some long needles in there," she says. "Won't you find them for me?"

Lenny reaches inside, pulling out a handful of needles.

"Each of these needles is eight inches long," Bettie says, "and they're every bit as sharp as they look. Now, the length you can see with your own eyes, but how can you trust they're as sharp as I say?"

Lenny takes one of the needles, running it against his bony forearm.

"Mmm," Bettie moans, "I think my hubby has an idea."

Lenny pinches a wad of flesh from his forearm, slowly stabbing the needle through until it pokes out the other side, eliciting gasps and groans from the small audience. With the first one done, he stabs two more needles through his forearm before walking through the audience to give us a closer look. Small trickles of blood streak across his predominantly green skin.

"Lenny, it looks like you're running out of room on your arm," Bettie says. "I think you need to find someplace else for the rest of those needles."

Lenny runs the next needle against his forehead before pinching the flesh of his eyebrow and piercing it through. After doing the same with his other eyebrow, he again weaves his way through the audience. Leaning over, he invites a girl to pull one of the needles from his brow; she does so reluctantly, squirming and giggling as his skin tugs back on the needle. Once it's removed, the girl hands the needle to Lenny; he nods a thank you before sliding it across his tongue.

For his next feat, Lenny removes his flip-flops and walks across a stretch of broken beer bottles. Next, he hammers a twelve-inch nail into his nostril. He follows that by lifting a kettlebell from the ground with his nipple rings, stretching his skin into a pair of tattooed stalactites. For the feat after that, Lenny lies down on a bed of nails while Bettie sets three cinderblocks on his torso. She flairs her dress as she sits down atop the cinderblocks; her high-heeled shoe dangles from her toes as she crosses her legs. Standing from the cinderblocks, Bettie pulls a sledgehammer from the trunk and, with impressive precision, crushes the bricks with Lenny still lying beneath them.

For the grand finale, Lenny pulls a large sword from the trunk. He holds it horizontally with both hands, letting the flat of the blade rest atop his open palms. Walking to me with the sword he holds it in front of my face.

"Open your hands, sweetie," Bettie says. "Palms up."

I do as she asks, and Lenny lays the sword across my palms.

"Heavy, right?" she asks.

"Yes."

"From handle to tip, this sword is four feet long," she says, "which is more than half the length of my handsome husband."

Lenny lifts the sword from my hands, nodding his appreciation, before standing it up on the ground and measuring it against his body. Sure enough, with the point of the sword at his bare feet, the handle comes up past his bony hips.

"A sword that long couldn't possibly fit inside Lenny's body," Bettie says, running her fingers down his tattooed chest. "Or could it?"

Lenny places the tip of the blade in his mouth, tilting his head back as he balances the sword straight up in the air, like it's an extension of his spine. Inch by inch, he methodically guides it down his throat, his sternum pushing out against the pressure of the blade. When only the handle remains in sight, Lenny opens his arms and drops to one knee, posing while the four of us in the audience give him a well-deserved ovation. As methodically as he guided it down, Lenny pulls the sword back out.

"On behalf of the Grambling Brothers Traveling Circus Show, we want to thank you for coming out and supporting us," Bettie says. "Good night!"

I join the sparse audience in exiting the tent, smiling at Bettie on my way out.

Walking the circus grounds, I consider playing the midway game where you try to pop balloons with darts when my attention is quickly seized by a sideshow tent whose banner advertises "Fernando the Fearless Fire Tamer." Unlike the previous sideshow tents, this one has nobody standing out front. I'm tempted to go inside, but, before I can, I hear somebody call my name. I turn my head in time to see Xyla Peppermint turn up beside me.

"Were you planning to hide from me all night?"

"No," I say, "I was actually looking for you."

"You thought I'd be in Fernando's tent?"

"I just got distracted for a moment."

She smiles.

"Follow me."

Xyla leads me to her tent, which has a banner hanging from it that reads "Xyla Peppermint: The World's Prettiest Fortuneteller." Inside, the tent is faintly illuminated by candles and string lights. Incense burns somewhere out of sight, flavoring the air with a sweet and spicy aroma. There's a small table covered with a colorful silk blanket and a crystal ball at its center. Xyla sits down at the table, inviting me to do the same.

"So," she says, raising her eyes, "are you ready for your fortune?"

"Sure."

Xyla waves her hands over the crystal ball, staring deeply into it. Her eyes grow big as she leans in for a closer examination.

"Wow," she says, "this is amazing."

"What is it?"

"I'm not sure I should tell you."

"Why not?"

"I get the feeling you don't believe this is real."

"Is it?"

"I simply tell you what I see," she says. "Whether or not you believe it is up to you."

I smile.

"Would you like me to tell you what I see?"

"Please."

She waves her hands over the crystal ball again.

"In just a few moments, you'll exit my tent," she says, "and you'll buy yourself some cotton candy before entering the big top."

"Are you sure it's cotton candy?"

"What do you prefer?"

"Popcorn."

She waves her hands over the crystal ball.

"Look at that," she says. "It turns out you buy popcorn instead of cotton candy."

"So, I didn't buy the cotton candy?"

"Let me check again," she says, squinting at the crystal ball. "I see here that you actually buy both."

"But I don't even like cotton candy."

"That is most unfortunate," she says. "The crystal ball also tells me that all sales are final. But, because you're a kind and gentle man, you give your cotton candy to a child."

"That sounds inappropriate."

"Yes, it does," she says, "which is why the child's father threatens to punch you."

"My fortune got dark in a hurry."

"Luckily, the child's mother intervenes as she recognizes you're just being kind."

"How do I know you're not making this all up as you go along?"

"I'm just the messenger," she says. "Now, stop interrupting me."

"Sorry."

She squints again into the crystal ball.

"You take your popcorn with you inside the big top."

"What about the cotton candy?"

"Do you want it?"

"No."

She waves her hands over the crystal ball.

"I see you throwing the cotton candy into the trash," she says, "and *then* you take your popcorn into the big top."

"What happens if I get thirsty during the show?"

"The crystal ball is unsure about this," she says. "Wait, strike that. I see here that you buy a Pepsi."

"I don't like Pepsi."

"Coke?"

"Better."

"I see you buying a Coke," she says. "With popcorn and Coke in hand, you enter the big top and take your seat. As you watch the show, you find that you're pleasantly surprised."

"Really?"

"Yes," she says. "It's not that you expected *not* to enjoy the show, you just didn't expect to enjoy it as much as you do. When it's over, you exit the big top and come back here to my tent. You sit exactly where you are now, at which point I'll give you a proper fortunetelling."

"So, this wasn't a proper fortunetelling?"

"No," she says, "I was making it all up as I went along."

"I knew it."

"You'd best head out," she says. "The show's going to begin soon."

"But I just got here."

"Don't worry," she says. "I'll be waiting for you when it's done."

Chapter Eight

THE BIG TOP

T HAT WAS UNBELIEVABLE!

I mean, not the fortunetelling part—that was nonsense. But the back and forth, the banter, the flirting. I felt like George Clooney in *Ocean's Eleven* in every scene with Julia Roberts. I wish I knew what I did right back there so I could commit it to memory and repeat it every day for the rest of my life. I'm still buzzing as I buy popcorn, cotton candy, and a Coke on my way to the big top. Xyla is still very much in the front of my mind as I enter the tall, striped tent and see one large ring in the dirt, surrounded by bleachers.

I've heard of one-ring circuses, but I've never seen one before. The circus my parents took me to as a kid was a three-ring circus, which is sort of the standard you expect to see when you enter a big top. As best as I can recall from one of the books I read with my Aunt Ruthie, the three-ring circus was the brainchild of P.T. Barnum (and a couple of other fellows whose names unfortunately aren't as well branded as their legendary peer). The idea was to create more excitement with three circus acts performing simultaneously, one in each ring. The number of rings also made it necessary to have bigger tents, which meant bigger audiences and bigger money. But in order to fill those extra seats, there must be a willing audience ready to show up and hand their money over. So, by the looks of the sparse crowd in this big top, the Grambling Brothers Traveling Circus Show won't be doing a three-ring circus anytime soon.

As I make my way up some creaky steps, I clock the tightrope overhead as well as the two opposing platforms, where I presume the trapeze artists will soon be perched. I find a good spot on one of the middle benches, so I take a seat. Looking around at the other bleachers, there can't be more than fifteen or twenty people inside the big top, including the family of three I saw at the box office—mom, dad, and their little boy.

I'm pretty bad at guessing kids' ages, but I'll say the boy is probably three or four years old. He's standing on dad's lap, eyeing my cotton candy as he reaches for it with his pudgy little fingers.

"Okay," dad says, "leave the nice man alone."

"It's alright," I say, offering up my cotton candy. "He can have it."

"That's not necessary," dad says. "But, thank you."

The boy doesn't take the hint and keeps grasping for the cotton candy, digging his toes into his dad's thigh for extra leverage.

Mom turns around next—smiling but clearly not in the mood.

"Thank you," she says, accepting the cotton candy. "That's very kind of you."

"My pleasure."

The boy's focus transfers to mom, as she's now the keeper of the cotton candy, but instead of giving it to him, she sticks it under her seat. I don't blame her, of course. That's just good parenting. I feel silly for even offering it, now that I think about it. I'm not sure what even put that idea in my head. The boy, on the other hand, doesn't appreciate mom's prudence and immediately bursts into tears. Mom, clearly short on patience, tells dad to go buy some cotton candy, so he hurries out of the bleachers, offering me a half-smile before he leaves.

Dad is still gone when the lights dim, signaling the start of the show. A spotlight hits the dirt in the center of the ring, and classic circus music fills the big top. A brawny man wearing a top hat and a long, red coat steps into the spotlight. Bringing a megaphone to his lips, he begins the show.

"Ladies and gentlemen, boys and girls, children of all ages," he says, "I am the Ringmaster, Claudius Xavier, and it is my esteemed pleasure to welcome you to the Grambling Brothers Traveling Circus Show! For the duration of your stay within this magical big top, you will be presented with the most spine-tingling, heart-pounding, death-defying collection of spectacles your eyes have ever seen."

He pauses as the sparse audience offers a smattering of applause.

"Now, if laughter is indeed the best medicine, then your first performers of the evening might soon find themselves trading in the pharmaceutical arts. Ladies and gentlemen, I present to you the silly stylings of Charlie Chuckles and the Clown Alley Hooligans!"

The spotlight shifts to the back of the tent, illuminating the hollow shell of a Volkswagen bug as it races toward the ring. Inside are three clowns, their giant red shoes scrambling beneath the steel husk like Fred Flintstone hurrying to work. They run a full lap around the ring before navigating to the center, stopping all at once like they've slammed the brakes. Charlie Chuckles, who's on the driver's side, hurls himself through the empty windshield, tumbling into a deceptively athletic somersault. The other two clowns—a man and a woman—set the Volkswagen down on the dirt before opening the doors and leisurely stepping out.

Charlie Chuckles does a double-take when he sees his clown compatriots unaffected by the whiplash stop. The nameless male clown offers his arm to the nameless female clown, and they skip around the ring while Charlie Chuckles watches from his seat on the dirt. He holds his chin between his thumb and forefinger like he's thinking really hard—then, in a big, theatrical motion, he pulls a crude drawing of a lightbulb from his big red overalls and holds it over his head. This gets a big laugh from the audience as he runs to the Volkswagen, retrieving three red balls. As the male and female clowns make their way back toward the Volkswagen, Charlie Chuckles jumps in front of them.

Cradling the red balls against his chest, Charlie Chuckles gives his attention to the female clown, grandly pantomiming the beating of his heart. The male clown tries to get the female's attention, but his efforts are thwarted when Charlie Chuckles begins juggling. The female clown is clearly taken with him, which prompts the male clown to retrieve his own set of red balls—he has four to Charlie's three. The male clown begins juggling his four red balls, which earns him the attention of the female clown. Charlie Chuckles retrieves two more balls and is now juggling five total. The female clown shifts her attention from one clown to the other, like she's watching the world's most absurd tennis match. The male clown retrieves one more red ball, only this one is the size of a basketball. The female clown appears very impressed with its size, causing Charlie Chuckles to stop juggling. He holds his emasculated balls in front of his crotch, dejectedly looking on as the female clown gazes at the male clown's substantially bigger ball. This gets a huge laugh from the audience as the big top goes dark.

When the spotlight returns, Charlie Chuckles and the Clown Alley Hooligans are gone, and the Ringmaster has returned in their place.

"I have a feeling we haven't seen the last of those three," he says. "Now, if Charlie Chuckles needs advice on how to win the affection of a lovely lady, he might learn a thing or two from your next performer. Ladies and gentlemen, please welcome to the big top, Handsome Harry the World's Prettiest Strongman!"

The spotlight finds Handsome Harry entering from the back of the big top and follows him as he struts toward the center of the ring. From the neck up, he looks like a dashing star from the silent film era, with his jet-black hair parted down the middle and thick handlebar mustache cozied atop his lip. From the neck down, he looks like a character straight out of *Conan the Barbarian*, with his furry underwear and equally furry boots. His golden muscles glisten under the spotlight as he flexes his arms in a double bicep pose, causing the mom in front of me to writhe in her seat. Her reaction is a microcosm of most every other woman—and a few of the men—inside the big top.

The wave of high-pitched squeals winds down in anticipation as Handsome Harry begins his first feat of strength. Bending at the knees with one hand planted on his hip, he lifts an enormous barbell up and over his head; the weights are as big as car tires, drooping the barbell into an arch. Handsome Harry walks around the ring this way without so much as a quiver of resistance. When he drops the barbell to the dirt, a loud thud fills the big top, followed by a round of applause. Handsome Harry performs several other impressive feats of strength, such as bending a steel pipe into the shape of a pretzel and snapping a chain in half with his teeth.

For his finale, Handsome Harry recruits six women from the audience to join him in the center of the ring, including the mom in front of me, who is in a noticeably better mood. With relative ease, Handsome Harry lifts all six women off the ground at the same time, three perched in each of his perfectly tanned arms. After setting them down, he taps his cheek with his fingertip, prompting each volunteer to give him a kiss. After the women are safely back in their seats, the big top goes dark. When the spotlight returns, Handsome Harry is gone, and Charlie Chuckles and the Clown Alley Hooligans have returned in his place.

The nameless male and female clowns are sitting together on a bench, while Charlie Chuckles stands nearby, gazing at the object of his affection. He looks at the audience and taps his temple, indicating to us that he has another big idea. Reaching into his red overalls, Charlie Chuckles pulls out a handful of deflated pink balloons. He shows them to the female clown before blowing each one up into large sausage shapes, then manipulating them together into a small poodle. The female clown swoons as she accepts the poodle balloon from Charlie Chuckles, prompting the male clown to leap up from the bench and retrieve a handful of his own deflated pink balloons. He blows them up and manipulates them into an even bigger poodle, before snatching Charlie Chuckle's poodle away from the female clown and replacing it with his own. The male and female clowns skip off together, arm in arm, as Charlie Chuckles watches with his hands over his heart and a pronounced frown on his face. The audience lets out a collective sigh as the big top goes dark.

When the spotlight returns, the Ringmaster is back in the center of the ring.

"Poor ol' Charlie Chuckles can't seem to catch a break," he says, "but something tells me he may have at least one more trick up his sleeve. Now, if daredevils are your fancy, then you're in for a treat, because your next performer is known around the world as the Beethoven of Balance. Ladies and gentlemen, I present to you Swift Sammy Tawker the High-Wire Walker!"

The spotlight captures Swift Sammy Tawker, a wiry young man, bursting through the back of the big top and jogging his way towards the rope ladder that leads up to the platform where the tightrope awaits. As he reaches the top of the platform, Swift Sammy waves to the crowd before picking up a balancing pole. Holding the balancing pole against his thighs, he expands his ribs with a deep breath before carefully taking his first step onto the tightrope, his foot folding over the taut cord like a taco shell. He milks this first step for drama, as well as the second step. On the third step, Swift Sammy wobbles, losing his balance, which causes the audience to gasp in anticipation of what will surely be a horrifying fall—but he manages to steady himself, inspiring an eruption of cheers and applause from the audience as he continues his journey across the tightrope.

As he reaches the center of the tightrope, Swift Sammy begins a series of leaps, bouncing like he's on a trampoline. Next, he lowers himself down until he's sitting on the tightrope, swinging his legs back and forth. As the audience applauds his death-defying feat, Swift Sammy ups the ante by laying all the way back on the tightrope with the balancing pole resting across his chest. After a few moments of this, he carefully brings himself back up to his feet before gracefully galloping the rest of the way across the tightrope to the opposing platform.

As the audience cheers, Swift Sammy picks up a trio of bowling pins and begins juggling them as he effortlessly steps his way back across the tightrope. On the other platform, he picks up a jump rope and takes it with him as he walks to the center of the tightrope. He begins jumping rope, alternating from one foot to the other, swinging the rope faster and faster until it looks like he's floating in a large, translucent egg. After several exhilarating moments, Swift Sammy stops jumping and takes a bow before crossing the tightrope one last time. From the platform, he waves his appreciation to the audience as the big top goes dark.

When the spotlight returns, Charlie Chuckles and the Clown Alley Hooligans are in the center of the ring once again. As they get started with their next routine, the nameless male and female clowns are skipping around together while Charlie Chuckles futilely chases behind them. Just as Charlie Chuckles gets within arm's reach of the other clowns—his gloved fingers ever so close—he falls face-first into the dirt, splaying out like a starfish. As the audience laughs at Charlie Chuckles' pratfall, the female clown skips over to him and kneels at his side; this prompts the male clown to begrudgingly do the same while also feigning concern for Charlie Chuckles' wellbeing. When the female clown isn't looking, the male clown wrinkles his brow and shakes his fist, which inspires boos from the audience.

Charlie Chuckles stands to his feet and dusts himself off before poking the male clown in the chest; he appears to be challenging him to some sort of contest, but the male clown shakes his head no. Not willing to give up, Charlie Chuckles turns his attention to the audience and begins clapping his hands in a steady rhythm, encouraging us to clap along with him—and we do. Succumbing to the pressure of our collective will, the male clown accepts the challenge. To begin the challenge—whatever it'll be—Charlie Chuckles raises his hands to the air to silence the audience, then, after waiting a beat, he falls face-first towards the dirt, but, just before he faceplants, he curls his body into an elegant somersault.

As the audience cheers, he invites his nemesis to go next. The male clown points and laughs before easily performing an equally impressive somersault. Charlie Chuckles next performs two consecutive somersaults, and the male clown matches him expertly. Charlie Chuckles next performs three somersaults, and the male clown does the same—only this time he wobbles when he's done, appearing to be dizzy. On his next tumble, Charlie Chuckles performs so many summersaults that I lose count; he tumbles around the ring like a stray tire rolling downhill, rousing the audience to its feet as we chant his name, cheering him on. After finally finishing his seemingly endless series of summersaults, Charlie Chuckles jumps to his feet, holding his arms out victoriously. The male clown elbows Charlie Chuckles out of the way and begins his own series of somersaults, but, after seven or eight, he falls face down in the dirt.

Charlie Chuckles steps on the male clown's back as he makes his way to the female clown. Pulling three red balls from his overalls, he briefly juggles for her but is interrupted when the balls fumble from his hands onto the dirt. Charlie Chuckles drops to his knees, as if to pick up the balls, but instead retrieves a comically large diamond ring from his overalls. The female clown clutches her heart, looking to the audience for guidance. We cheer her on until she holds out her hand, letting Charlie Chuckles place the ring on her finger.

The female clown holds her hand in the air, displaying the ring to us, which inspires the loudest cheer of the night. She and Charlie Chuckles walk arm in arm together back to the hollow Volkswagen and navigate it out of the big top, while the male clown chases after them as the light goes dark.

The spotlight returns with the Ringmaster in the center of the ring.

"How about that, ladies and gentlemen? In the end, the boy got the girl. Now that your hearts have been filled with the promise of love, let's get them racing with death-defying aerial amazement. Your final performers of the night come to you all the way from São Paulo, Brazil. It is my tremendous honor to present to you the world's finest flying family, the Soaring Silvas!"

The spotlight finds the Soaring Silvas entering from the back of the big top—three men and one woman—and follows them as they jog in lockstep toward the platforms. The first male Silva has a tight, muscular physique. The second is thin and wiry. The third is barrel-chested, with thick arms and hairy shoulders. The female Silva is petite but muscular, her raven black hair tied back in a tight bun. The Soaring Silvas climb the rope ladders up to the platforms, three Silvas on one side and the fourth Silva on the other; multiple spotlights capture the Silvas in all their glory while conspicuously refraining from lighting the large net beneath them.

The barrel-chested Silva grasps a trapeze in his hands and leaps from the platform, swinging back and forth like a pendulum. Mid-swing, he pulls his legs up and over the bar, hanging solely by the backs of his knees while his arms dangle toward the ground. On the opposite side, the female Silva takes the second trapeze and leaps, swinging toward him. They gradually approach each other until the barrel-chested Silva reaches out his hands, and the female Silva meets him, releasing her trapeze. Gripping each other by the wrists, they swing together in tandem as the empty trapeze swings back toward the platform. The muscular male Silva catches it, then leaps from the platform, swinging toward the tandem of the female Silva and the barrel-chested Silva. Once they're within a few inches of each other, the female Silva and the muscular Silva release their grips, hanging in the air just long enough to trade places, with the female Silva grabbing the abandoned trapeze and the muscular Silva latching on to the barrel-chested Silva.

After a pendulum of momentum, the muscular Silva lets go of the barrel-chested Silva, flipping several times in midair before catching the empty trapeze that the female Silva abandoned on the opposite platform. The muscular Silva swings back to the platform, handing the trapeze to the wiry Silva, who immediately dismounts. He pulls his legs up and over the bar, releasing his hands so he hangs only by the backs of his knees, mirroring the barrel-chested Silva. As he swings back towards the platform, the female Silva catches his hands and dismounts. At the apex of their pendulum, she releases her grip on the wiry Silva and tucks into a double flip, opening up just in time for the barrel-chested Silva to catch her by the wrists.

The next several minutes are a symphony of strength and grace as the Soaring Silvas swing through the air in various combinations, flipping and catching each other in breathtaking fashion. At the end of the performance, they all stand together on one platform, waving at the cheering audience as the big top goes dark.

When the lights return, the Ringmaster stands in the center of the ring. One by one, he calls out each of the performers, and they jog out to join him, taking each other's hands and bowing in unison. I stand up from my seat to join the small—but enthusiastic—audience in a standing ovation. After a final wave from the performers, they all disperse towards the back of the big top. The lights flood back on, and the audience inside begins filing toward the exit.

Chapter Nine

THE SPREAD

WALKING BENEATH THE MOONLIGHT, I'm overwhelmed with joy, reflecting on the show I just experienced inside the big top. It's not that I expected *not* to enjoy the show, I just didn't expect to enjoy it as much as I did. The midway games and sideshow tents all appear closed for the night as the small audience files through the circus grounds on their way to the exit. I stop at Xyla's tent just like she asked me to, but it also appears empty. I can't exactly knock, and I don't want to stick my head in, so I figure I'll just call it a night and head for the exit.

"Were you planning on standing me up?"

I turn around and see Xyla standing outside of her tent.

"No, I just thought—"

"Kidding," she says, smiling. "C'mon in."

I follow Xyla inside, taking a seat at the table with the crystal ball. She sits across from me, setting a deck of cards on the table.

"We'll start with a tarot reading."

"Is that like astrology?"

"Goodness, no," she says. "Astrology deals with horoscopes, which you can read in the newspaper."

"Does that mean it's not real?"

"Maybe it is, maybe it isn't," she says, shuffling the cards. "I'm a Taurus, for example. My symbol is the bull, my gemstone is emerald, and my element is earth. According to my astrological sign, I'm loyal, stubborn, and greedy."

"Is it accurate?"

"You'll have to find out for yourself," she says. "But for the sake of this conversation, let's say it's all true. Now, is it true because astrology preordained it? Or is it true because I'm a unique human being capable of choosing exactly who and what I am?"

"I don't know."

"What's *your* sign?"

"Sagittarius."

"Your symbol is the archer, your gemstone is turquoise, and your element is fire."

"Fire?"

"Yes," she says, spreading the tarot cards into a cascading arc before deftly sweeping them back into a uniform stack. "As a Sagittarius, you have an exuberance for life, which can be wild like a forest fire. You're adventurous but get bored easily, especially with routine. As a mutable sign, you're adaptable to change and are comfortable going with the flow, letting life unfold before you one moment at a time."

"So, it's not about literal fire?"

"It can be, depending on the context," she says. "According to astrology, you're good in a crisis, so if there was a literal fire, you'd be good to have around. There's also the matter of Jupiter, your ruling planet. As a mutable fire sign ruled by Jupiter, you're attracted to intellect and higher learning."

She smiles.

"Remind me what you do for a living?"

"I'm a college professor."

"And how long have you been a college professor?"

"Ten years."

"That's quite a long time," she says. "If astrology is to be believed, you would be happier breaking out of that routine and experiencing something new and exciting."

"That's surprisingly accurate."

"Well, then," she says, "is it accurate because astrology is real? Or are you a unique human being capable of choosing exactly who and what you are?"

"I don't know."

"Have you ever had a tarot reading?"

"No."

"Oh, goodie," she says, sliding the deck in front of me. "Shuffle, please."

"Me?"

"Yes."

"Didn't you already shuffle them?"

"Their destined order must pass through your hands."

"What if I mess up?"

"Impossible," she says. "Whatever is supposed to happen, will happen."

I do my best impersonation of a Vegas dealer, but before I get even halfway through shuffling the deck, the cards burst out of my hands. A ball of panic sprouts in my chest as I quickly pick up the cards that fell on the floor.

"Sorry," I say, putting them back on the table.

"Nothing to be sorry about."

"Let me try again."

"No need," she says. "That was perfect."

"Really?"

"The order the cards were in, the direction they flew, where they landed, and how they landed were all perfect," she says. "You created a unique moment that can never be replicated, not by anybody, including you. If you tried a million more times, the cards would never fall in exactly that same order ever again."

I smile.

"In just a moment, you'll draw three cards," she says, sweeping the cards back into a uniform stack, "but before you do, you need to ask a question of the cards."

"What sort of question?"

"Something regarding your fortune," she says. "Whatever it is you'd like to know."

I consider this for a moment.

"Will my dad be okay?"

"I genuinely hope your dad *will* be okay," she says, "but that's *his* fortune, not yours. You need to ask a question about yourself."

"I'm not sure what I want to know."

"I don't believe you."

I consider another question.

"Will I ever be truly happy?"

"That's more of a yes-or-no question."

"Is that not allowed?"

"Well, there are no real rules," she says, "but yes-or-no questions don't leave a lot of room for fortunetelling."

"What would you suggest?"

"I can't suggest anything," she says. "I must minimize my influence on your experience as much as possible. Just try to rethink your question, making it more open-ended."

I consider my question further.

"Don't think about it too hard," she says. "Just say it."

"What do I have to do to be happy?"

"Perfect," she says, tapping the deck. "Draw three cards."

"From the top of the deck?"

"From wherever you like."

I pull the first card, leaving it facedown.

"Flip it so you can see what it is."

"That's not cheating?"

"No," she says, "it's not cheating."

I turn the card over, revealing a knight in a black suit of armor with a skull where his face should be. He's sitting atop a horse and holding a flag with a flower emblem on it. A priest stands before the knight, and a woman with a small child kneels beside the priest. An old man lay dead beneath the horse's hooves.

"Death."

"Death?"

"That's the card you drew."

"That doesn't sound good."

"Death isn't a bad thing."

"Depends on who's doing the dying."

Xyla laughs.

"What does it mean?"

"We'll get to that," she says. "Draw your next card."

I select another card from the deck, laying it beside Death. It's a man strolling with his chin up and eyes closed—not a care in the world. Over his right shoulder, he carries a long stick with a bag attached, like a cartoon hobo. He holds a flower in his left hand. Beside him, a small dog stands on its hind legs. The man is unaware that he's one step away from falling off a tall cliff.

"That's the Fool," Xyla says. "Draw one more."

I draw my third and final card, laying it beside the Fool. It's a woman with long blonde hair. She's scantily wrapped in a long scarf that covers her between her legs while leaving her breasts fully exposed. She floats in midair, framed by a large green wreath and holding golden batons in each hand. In each corner of the card, floating in the clouds, are disembodied heads—a man, an eagle, a bull, and a lion.

"The World," she says. "So, there you have it. Death, the Fool, and the World."

She taps each card with her fingertip as she says their respective names.

"That's your spread," she says. "For clarity, a spread is the number of cards you draw and the manner in which they're arranged. The significance of each card in the spread is determined by the position you lay them in."

"Was I supposed to lay them out in a particular order?"

"Not at all," she says. "You laid them out exactly as they were meant to be."

"How's that possible?"

"To understand that, you must first understand that each position in the spread has a determined meaning, and the significance of each card changes based on which position they land in," she says. "In your case, is it fair to say that you laid the cards out in the order of your choosing, free from outside influence?"

"Yes," I say, "that's fair."

"And is it fair to say that I didn't even ask you to lay the cards down?"

I reflect on this for a moment.

"Yes," I say, smiling, "that's also fair."

"The only direction I gave you was to draw three cards," she says. "You could've done anything with them, but you intuitively set them down in a three-card spread."

"Is that a good thing?"

"Let's find out," she says. "The first card represents the past, the second card represents the present, and the third card represents the future."

She waves her hand over the spread.

"Death."

Tap.

"The Fool."

Tap.

"The World."

Tap.

"Repeat your question for me."

"What do I have to do to be happy?"

"First, let's look to the past," she says. "You drew Death. For the uninitiated, Death can be alarming, especially if it's the first card drawn. But Death in this context isn't meant to be taken literally. The implication of the Death card is that you've reached the end of a particular cycle in your life. It's a metaphor for transition, for moving out of one phase of your life and into another. What it means for you, Grover, given that it represents your past, is you're at a place in your life where you're ready to end one thing and begin another. So, if you're not as happy as you want to be today, it's because there is something in your recent past that is making you unhappy. Something that, perhaps, you need to end, allowing you to move forward into a new cycle of your life, one that will bring you more happiness."

Silence.

"Any of this ringing true?"

"Sure."

"Tell me," she says, "what rings true?"

"Well, I think I hate my job."

"Hate is a very strong word."

"It's not so much the teaching that I hate," I say. "When I'm in the classroom, standing in front of a group of engaged students who want to learn, I feel very satisfied. But the overall job itself is what I hate."

"The parts of the job that aren't teaching?"

"Exactly."

"Like what?"

"Grading is the worst," I say. "I don't mean the giving of letter grades. I'm talking about the process of poring over a student's paper—reading each paragraph, each sentence, each word—giving it all my careful attention to catch any errors they made while also noting examples of exemplary work they've achieved. It's tedious and time-consuming, and the students don't care."

"If your students don't care," she says, "why do you go through such painstaking effort?"

"I don't know," I say. "Just in case, I guess."

"Just in case, what?"

"Just in case one of them *does* care."

"And because it's not always clear which students do care and which students don't, you can't afford not to give each paper your close personal attention."

"Exactly."

"That sounds like a frustrating paradox."

"There's also the bureaucratic part that I'm not a fan of," I say. "Rosters, peer evaluations, parking permits, tuberculosis tests, and so on."

"Is it fair to say you can never be truly happy as a college professor?"

I shrug.

"Let's move on to your second card," she says. "For the present, you drew the Fool. This is an astonishingly apt card to follow Death because it represents new beginnings. Brimming with careless optimism and childlike enthusiasm, the Fool is willing to take chances and disregard risk, even if the outcome has the potential for devastating consequences. Of course, it's his disregard for consequences that makes him a fool. If he were more careful in his choices, the Fool would never enjoy the prosperity on the other side of chance. This card is telling you that now, in the present, you're going to have to take a risk in order to give yourself the opportunity for true happiness."

"What kind of risk?" I ask. "Like quitting my job?"

"Quitting your job would address your past," she says. "Your present is more about stepping into something new, something scary and exciting."

"Like what?"

Xyla smiles.

"Let's look at your final card," she says. "For your future, you drew the World. This is a very positive card that signifies completeness and accomplishment. The World represents you growing and evolving into a better place. Given that this card represents your future, it means you are on your way to something good. But it's not going to happen on its own."

Xyla waves her hands over the cards.

"Now, let's review," she says. "The past, the present, and the future. Death, the Fool, and the World. There is something in your recent past that is making you unhappy, something you need to bring to an end in order to move forward. In moving forward, you'll need to embrace an adventurous spirit, perhaps making a decision that you might otherwise think is foolish. If you do these things, you'll find yourself on the precipice of happiness, overlooking a horizon flush with new adventures and opportunities."

Silence.

"It feels like you're not satisfied," she says.

"No, it's not that," I say. "I think I was just expecting something more specific."

"The tarot doesn't provide specific answers," she says. "You'll have to determine that on your own."

She reaches her hands across the table.

"Place your hands in mine," she says. "I'll look inside of you and tell you what I see."

She closes her eyes as I give her my hands. We stay like this for a few quiet moments, until she opens her eyes.

"Did you see anything?"

Xyla nods yes.

"What did you see?"

"Fire."

"Fire?"

"More specifically, I saw two flames burning side by side, surrounded by darkness," Xyla says. "Each flame was like the head of a match, only one was slightly bigger than the other."

"You saw all of that by touching my hand?"

"Yes."

"That's amazing."

"Is it?"

"Yes," I say. "You have no idea how wildly on the nose that is."

She smiles.

"My God," I say, leaning in closer. "You're really psychic, aren't you?"

"Sort of," she says. "I can't read your thoughts or anything like that, but I *can* see inside of you."

"What does that mean?"

"When I look inside of somebody, I see what's significant to them," she says. "It can be a place, a memory, an unfulfilled wish—or, in your case, it can be fire."

"Can I control what you see?"

"No," she says. "I see whatever your unconscious wants to show me. Generally, the visions are unique to each individual, but what I saw inside of you is strikingly similar to another vision I once saw."

"You saw fire inside somebody else?"

"Not fire, but close to it," she says. "Did you see the bearded lady and her husband?"

"Bettie and Lenny?"

"Yes," she says. "One time, I looked inside of Lenny and saw two bolts of lightning, side by side, surrounded by darkness. They were frozen in place but animated at the same time, crackling with life. I've never seen anything like it before or since, not until tonight."

"What did it mean?"

"I don't know," she says. "I rarely know what any of these visions mean unless the person explains it to me."

"Lenny didn't explain it?"

"No," she says. "But maybe you can explain the fire to me."

"I'm not sure I can."

"You're not sure because you don't know what it means?" she asks. "Or because you *do* know what it means and you don't want to tell me?"

I hesitate.

"I think you know exactly what the fire means," Xyla says.

"Maybe," I say, "but I'm afraid to say it out loud."

"Why?"

"You'll think I'm crazy."

"You can tell me, Grover," she says. "I promise I won't think you're crazy."

"You can't possibly know that."

"Try me."

I take a deep breath.

"Okay," I say. "I think I'm fireproof."

Xyla sits back in her chair, crossing her legs.

"That's a new one," she says. "Why do you think you're fireproof?"

"A few days ago, I set myself on fire."

"On purpose?"

"No, of course not," I say. "I was cooking in my kitchen, and there was a grease fire. One thing led to another, and, before I knew it, I was engulfed in flames."

Silence.

"Do you believe me?"

"I'm not sure," she says, "but I want to."

Xyla slides one of her candles in front of me, the flame dancing as it reckons with the air.

"Prove it."

"Well, I mean, I don't know if I'm *actually* fireproof," I say. "I haven't touched fire since the accident."

"I think now is as good a time as any to find out," she says. "Don't you?"

I decide that maybe she's right, so I raise my hand over the candle. With my fingers splayed and quivering, I lower my hand until my palm touches the flickering flame.

Nothing.

I lower it closer.

Nothing

Xyla leans her head in for a closer look, examining the flame as it presses up against my flesh.

"You can't feel that?"

"No," I say. "Not at all."

Xyla sets her fingertips atop my knuckles, guiding my hand down further.

"Nothing?"

"Nothing."

She lifts my hand from the flame, turning it over so she can examine my palm.

No burns, no redness.

"How about that?" she says, smiling. "Looks to me like you're fireproof."

Xyla presses her fingertips against my palm.

"It's not even hot," she says. "That's amazing."

"I can hardly believe it myself."

"What are you doing tomorrow?"

"Nothing."

"Perfect," she says. "Come back tomorrow, I want you to meet somebody."

"Who?"

"You'll see," she says. "I'll leave you another ticket at the box office."

Chapter Ten

THE LEGEND OF JANET HORNE

I KNOW IT'S NOT possible to be in love with Xyla Pepper-mint—at least not yet—but I'm pretty sure I'm in love with Xyla Peppermint. I'll admit that this isn't exactly new for me. One of the byproducts of being shy and afraid of the opposite sex is that when a woman is nice to me, I can't help but develop instantaneously strong feelings for her. Nobody as beautiful or exotic or alluring as Xyla has ever given me the time of day, let alone made me feel as special as she did last night. The hazard, of course, is that I don't know if she feels the same way about me. For Xyla, being nice may just be how she treats everyone. I'd be open to talking myself down from this overwhelming crush I'm developing, but for one simple fact—she asked me to come back.

It's all I can think about as I shower for work.

And as I drive to class.

And as I give a lecture on present tense versus past tense.

"When you read a narrative that's in the past tense," I say to the handful of students who showed up to class today, "there is the implicit understanding that the story has already occurred. This means there are no surprises for the narrator. But when you read a story in the *present* tense, there is an immediacy to it because the narrator doesn't know what's going to happen from one moment to the next. And if it's a first-person narrator talking in the present tense, then it adds even greater urgency to the narrative because the events are unfolding in real time."

After class, I drive back to the hospital to see my dad and spend time with Mom, all the while obsessing over my rapidly developing feelings for Xyla—and, for reasons I'm not remotely smart enough to psychoanalyze, my obsessive thoughts about Xyla are interrupted by the memory of my last significant conversation with Aunt Ruthie, which occurred the day before she was committed to a mental institution. At the time, I didn't know she was going to be committed, and I assume she didn't either.

But who knows?

Well, actually, Mom probably knows since she's the one who had to put her baby sister in a mental institution. It's never been something she likes talking about, so out of love and respect—and a desperate need to avoid uncomfortable conversations—I've never asked her about it. That said, I've always suspected that the conversation Aunt Ruthie had with me was directly connected to why she was committed.

"I'm a witch, you know," she told me. "A real deal, bona fide witch."

I was still a kid, maybe twelve or so, when she confided in me. The way she said it, it wasn't so much a revelation or a humble brag, but the unburdening of a weight she no longer wanted to carry alone—the same, I imagine, as Clark Kent telling Lois Lane that he was secretly Superman.

"Adults don't like hearing stuff like this," Aunt Ruthie said. "It makes them think you're crazy, even if you're telling them the truth."

"I don't think you're crazy."

Aunt Ruthie smiled, kissing the crown of my head.

"Thank you, Grover."

"Do you do spells and stuff?"

"Sort of," she says. "It's not exactly how you see in the movies with cauldrons and broomsticks, but I do have a special connection to the earth and the elements that allow me to manipulate the world around me in supernatural ways. It also allows me to see the world and the people in it more clearly than others do. It's the reason I know you're a very special boy, more special than you even realize, and you're destined to do amazing things in this life."

"Really?"

"Oh, yes," she said. "It's also the reason I feel safe sharing my truth with you."

"Are there other witches in the world?"

"Absolutely," she said. "But unfortunately, for as long as there have been witches, there have also been small-minded people hunting them down. Persecuting them, killing them."

"Killing them? Why?"

"People are often scared of things they don't understand," she said. "Anything or anybody that's different or unique or in any way counter to the status quo threatens their cold lizard brains. In many parts of the world, for as long as my kind has been around, witches have been burned at the stake."

"What does that mean?"

"It's a form of execution," she said, "like the electric chair or lethal injection, but much more barbaric. Do you know what a stake is?"

"Like the food?"

"No," she said. "A stake is a piece of wood with a sharp point. You've probably seen them in movies or television being used to kill vampires."

"Are vampires real, too?"

"Everything is real if you allow yourself to see it," she said. "That's why fortunetellers are so special. Unfortunately, many of them were burned at the stake as well. The world can be a dangerous place for special people." She shakes her head, smiling. "Sorry, I'm getting off track. We were talking about stakes. Now, the stakes that witches were burned on were large pieces of wood that were stuck into the ground like light posts. Witches were tied to these stakes, then lit on fire. Burned alive. They could do nothing about it except suffer in the flames until death separated them from their pain. Sometimes women who weren't even witches were burned at the stake, too."

"Why?"

"Because somebody *thought* they were a witch," she said. "They were just normal women trying to live their lives."

"Who would accuse them?"

"Anybody," she said. "Friends, family, strangers. It hardly mattered. Once a woman was accused of being a witch, it was hard to avoid being burned to death."

"But why did people want to burn witches?"

"In certain parts of the world, fire was seen as the only way to properly separate a witch from her magic," she said. "Burning witches at the stake happened mostly in European countries, while in America, witches were hanged by their necks."

"In America? Really?"

"Yeah," she said. "It mostly happened in Salem, Massachusetts, during the Salem Witch Trials."

"Why?"

"It's hard to say," she said. "Maybe in America, people thought hanging was more humane than fire."

"Are witches still burned in Europe?"

"Sometimes," she said, "but it's not legal anymore. The last known woman to be legally burned at the stake for witchcraft was in Scotland. Her name was Janet Horne."

"When was she burned at the stake?"

"A long time ago," Aunt Ruthie said, "sometime in the 1700s. You probably won't learn about her in your history classes, which is a shame. She had a daughter whose hands and feet were deformed, so her neighbors thought Janet had used witchcraft to make her look this way. It was their belief that Janet used her daughter as a pony to ride to the Devil and stand by his side. So, after a hasty trial, Janet Horne was judged guilty and burned at the stake."

"Was she really a witch?"

"Probably not," Aunt Ruthie said. "I think she was simply misunderstood."

I never told Mom about that conversation—not that Aunt Ruthie asked me to keep it from her. I just felt like keeping it confidential was the right thing to do. Of course, it's possible Aunt Ruthie had the same conversation with my mom, and that's what led to her being committed. Then again, there's no rule that says being a witch and being mentally unstable are mutually exclusive. I guess what I'm getting at is that in a reality where I'm fireproof and Xyla Peppermint is a genuine psychic, anything—truly *anything*—is possible. As I reflect on that conversation with Aunt Ruthie, I'm grateful that Xyla exists in the here and now, as opposed to a time and place where being misunderstood would've gotten her burned at the stake.

As soon as I enter Dad's hospital room, Mom greets me with a hug. She tells me his condition is stable, but the doctors still don't know what's wrong with him. Then she asks me about my night at the circus, so I start telling her about Xyla and having my fortune read—but I barely get into the details when Mom bursts into tears.

"I'm sorry," she says, wiping her cheeks. "Keep telling me about your night."

"What's the matter?"

"It's nothing I want to concern you with, sweetheart," she says. "What did the fortuneteller say?"

"Mom, please," I say. "You're scaring me."

She shakes her head, hiding her face in her hands.

"It's money," she says. "I was on the phone with the insurance company all morning. Apparently, they can only cover hospital costs for a limited amount of time before the coverage runs out. It's not a hundred percent coverage, either, so there's going to be a great, big medical bill on the other side of all of this."

"How much?"

"More than we can afford," she says. "Just the last few days alone with all the tests and whatnot are going to add up to something astronomical."

"What can we do about it?"

"I don't know," she says, followed by more tears, "but I'm keeping your father here for as long as it takes, so there's no way around that."

"We'll figure something out," I say, wrapping her in a hug.

"I want to believe that," she says, "but I don't know. I just don't know."

Chapter Eleven

PUTTIN' ON THE RITZ

I SPEND THE DAY at the hospital with Mom before heading back to Grambling Brothers in the evening. The parking lot is just as empty as it was yesterday, and nobody is waiting in line at the box office. The same guy with the black eye and injured arm is still behind the not-so-clean window. He's reading a book when I arrive and seems annoyed when he has to put it aside to help me.

"You're back?"

"Yeah," I say. "I think there's a ticket for me."

He digs around and finds an envelope.

"Xyla left you *another* ticket?" he asks, making no effort to disguise his bewilderment.

"Uh-huh."

"Does Harry know?"

"Who's Harry?"

He slides the envelope to me.

"Not my problem," he says. "Enjoy the show."

He goes back to his book, leaving me with more questions than answers. I take my ticket to the entrance, where Charlie Chuckles is waiting.

"Well, what do we have here?" he says. "Did Xyla invite you again?"

"Uh-huh."

"Does Harry know?"

"That's what the guy at the box office just asked."

"That checks out."

"Who's Harry?"

"Xyla didn't tell you?"

"No."

"Not my problem," he says. "Enjoy the show!"

Charlie Chuckles leaves me to go talk to the guy at the box office as I step through the entrance. Just as it was yesterday, I'm greeted with the same sights, smells, and sounds that awoke my childlike joy—only now my joy is tempered by this newfound concern about someone named Harry.

The barker from yesterday sees me and waves me over.

"You're back?"

"Yeah."

"Did Xyla invite you again?"

"Uh-huh."

"Does Harry know?"

"You're the third person to ask me that since I got here," I say, "but nobody will tell me who Harry is."

"Handsome Harry," he says. "The World's Prettiest Strongman."

"Oh, the big guy from the show?"

"That's the one," he says. "Does he know Xyla invited you?"

"I don't know," I say. "Should he?"

"If you enjoy having all your limbs intact, it's better Harry doesn't know."

"Wait, what?!"

"C'mon inside," he says, putting his arm around my shoulder. "We shouldn't talk about it out here."

The barker guides me into his dim tent, where string lights and a couple of shadeless lamps cast ominous shadows against the canvas walls. Amongst the otherwise empty foldout chairs is a young couple giggling and holding hands. A big piece of plywood rests flat on the dirt in front of the chairs; beside it is a small blanket-covered cage. The barker sits me down in one of the chairs, so I assume he's going to give me more details about Handsome Harry.

"Welcome, brave souls," he says, resting his hand atop the cage. "My name is Bastian the Boisterous Barker, and I'm impressed you've found the courage to join us for this tasty tour of terrifying treats."

A growl comes from the cage, followed by a set of furry fingers pushing through the blanket.

"Back!" Bastian yells, rattling the cage with a hard slap. "Back, I say!"

He flashes us a knowing grin.

"It seems our ferocious friend is growing impatient," Bastian says. "Shall I let him out?"

Gripping the blanket, he counts down—three, two, one—then yanks it off the cage to reveal a chubby dwarf crouched inside. His head is shaved, and he's wearing furry gloves.

"Geno!" Bastian says. "What are you doing in there?"

Geno looks at Bastian, then at the three of us in the audience. He claws at the air with his gloved hand, prompting Bastian to open the cage and shoo him out. Geno stands barefoot in a pair of much-too-tight pants that reach barely past his knees and a Hawaiian shirt whose buttons are losing an epic battle against his rotund belly.

"Where's you-know-who?" Bastian asks.

Geno shrugs.

"You don't know?"

Geno shakes his head, no.

"Well, the audience is waiting," Bastian says, "so I suppose we have no choice but to start without him." Bastian gives his attention back to us. "What do you say, folks? Ready to get started?"

We all stay quiet, but Bastian moves ahead with the show as though we gave him an enthusiastic yes.

"Ladies and gentlemen, coming directly to you from parts un-known, standing at a staggering stature of four feet and eleven inch-es—"

Geno tugs at Bastian's sleeve, interrupting him. He then stands on his tippy toes as Bastian leans over to let him whisper in his ear.

"Correction," Bastian says. "Standing before you at a staggering stature of four feet, eleven and *one-half* inches, it is my esteemed pleasure to introduce to you the eighth verified Wonder of the World, Geno the World's Shortest Giant!"

Geno takes a big step forward, opening his arms in anticipation of our applause. The three of us go along with it, clapping as he flashes a smile with a few missing teeth. Bastian taps Geno on the shoulder, but Geno ignores him, beckoning for more applause.

Bastian taps his shoulder again.

Geno ignores him again.

"Geno!"

He finally looks up at Bastian.

"Where's your hat?"

Geno touches the top of his hatless head, then shrugs.

"And what about your jacket?"

Geno looks at each of his arms, then back up at Bastian.

"Well?"

Geno shrugs.

"What do you mean you don't know?" Bastian asks. "It's your *good* jacket!"

Geno tugs Bastian's sleeve, again whispering in his ear.

"No, we can*not* check the lost and found," Bastian says. "We're in the middle of a show!"

Geno whispers something else in his ear.

"What do you mean, who's performing?" Bastian asks. "*We* are!"

Geno looks out at the audience as if noticing us for the first time.

"If you don't know where your hat is and you don't know where your good jacket is, do you at least know where your *shoes* are?"

Geno looks down at his bare feet, rocking back and forth on his heels.

"Think hard before you answer."

Geno pinches his chin between his thumb and forefinger, looking up and away like he's in deep thought—then, in a flash, his eyes light up.

"Does that mean you remember where your shoes are?"

Geno nods, yes.

"Well?"

Geno claps his hands, and the tent goes dark. A ferocious growl fills the air, causing the lone girl in the audience to scream, which makes her boyfriend laugh. Geno claps again, and the lights come back on. Standing between Geno and Bastian is a little boy with a face covered in fluffy brown fur. He's wearing a black top hat and a matching coat with tails; the top hat sits just above his dark brow, and the jacket's sleeves hang past his furry fingers. On his feet are a pair of shiny black shoes.

"Ladies and gentlemen," Bastian says, "I present to you the carnivorous canine kid, Pedro the Orphan Wolf Boy!"

Geno lifts the hat from Pedro's head and puts it on his own. He next takes the jacket off of Pedro—revealing his furry arms—and slips it on himself. Finally, he grabs Pedro from beneath his armpits, lifting him up and out of his shiny shoes.

"Aren't you missing something else?" Bastian asks Geno after he slips his feet into the shoes.

Geno shrugs.

"Where's your cane?"

Geno looks around, patting his pockets.

"So, now you don't know where your cane is?"

Geno holds up his finger, requesting time to think.

"Make it fast."

Geno looks around the tent before finally setting his eyes on the cage. He grabs one of the bars and pulls on it. Nothing happens, so he pulls again. Nothing still, so he pulls with all his weight until the bar yanks free, and Geno falls on his butt. He stands up, dusting off his pants. Stepping onto the big piece of plywood, his shiny shoes sound audible clicks.

"Now," Bastian says, "what do you have to say for yourself?"

Geno looks at the audience, clicking his cane against the plywood.

Tap, tap.

Then, with the most angelic voice I've ever heard, he begins to sing.

"If you're blue, and you don't know where to go to/Why don't you go where fashion sits?"

Tap, tap.

"Puttin' on the ritz."

He struts around the plywood, his shoes clicking with each step.

"Different types of wear all day coat, pants with stripes and cutaway coat/Perfect fits."

Tap, tap.

"Puttin' on the ritz."

Geno begins dancing with tremendous skill and precision, light as a feather, clicking away on the plywood stage with his shiny shoes. As he starts the second verse, Geno is joined by the unexpected sound of Pedro playing the ukulele. He plucks with effortless mastery, like the strings are extensions of his furry fingers.

"Come, let's mix where Rockefellers walk with sticks or umbrellas in their mitts."

Tap, tap.

"Puttin' on the ritz."

Geno goes into another breathtaking dance break, flailing his arms like a wild bird who's just been set free.

"If you're blue, and you don't know where to go to/Why don't you go where fashion sits?"

Tap, tap.

"Puttin' on the ritz."

With the song over, Geno and Pedro each take a bow.

"Ladies and gentlemen," Bastian says, "have you been entertained?"

The three of us in the audience applaud.

"Once again," Bastian says, "let's hear it for Geno the World's Shortest Giant and Pedro the Orphan Wolf Boy. I'm Bastian the Boisterous Barker, and it's been our honor to perform for you this evening. Have a great night!"

I expect Bastian to stick around for a chat, specifically about Handsome Harry, but he slips out the back of the tent while Geno and Pedro reset their props, so I follow the giggly couple out of the tent.

Xyla is standing outside, waiting for me.

"Hey, you," she says. "How was the show?"

"It was actually kind of wonderful."

"Good," she says, smiling. "Come with me."

I assume we're headed to her tent, but quickly realize we're walking in the wrong direction. She leads me away from the sideshow tents and midway games until we enter a labyrinth of RVs, trucks, and trailers behind the circus grounds.

"What's all this?"

"This is where we live," she says. "It's also how we travel."

"Everybody has an RV?"

"Most of us share one, but a few of us have our own," she says, stopping in front of one of the trailers. "Here we are."

"This is yours?"

"No," she says. "This is Claudius' office."

"Who?"

"Claudius Xavier," she says. "The Ringmaster."

Chapter Twelve

THE RINGMASTER

THE RINGMASTER SITS IN a worn leather chair behind a cluttered antique desk, his eyes concealed behind red-tinted glasses. A pointy, black goatee frames the thick cigar pursed between his lips. Underneath his buttoned-down shirt—loose at the collar, rolled at the sleeves—are the not-so-subtle hints of a muscular frame. A long mane of black waves hangs over his shoulders.

"Claudius," Xyla says, as we stand in front of his desk, "this is the friend I told you about."

The Ringmaster stands from his chair, scissoring the cigar between two thick fingers as he removes it from his lips.

"Grover Wilcox," he says, extending his free hand across the desk, "it's an honor."

My hand disappears inside his cavernous grip.

"The honor is mine, sir."

"Call me Claudius," he says. "Please, have a seat."

There are two chairs in front of his desk, so Xyla and I each take a seat. The Ringmaster sits back down in his leather chair, running his fingers through his hair.

"So," he says, "Xyla tells me your fireproof."

A pulse of anxiety stings my chest.

"It's okay, Grover," he says, clearly sensing my concern. "I've seen it all. In my time, I've traveled through every continent on the globe, busking and performing, putting on shows for packed and empty houses alike. Along my travels, I've enjoyed the good fortune of meeting amazing people with supernatural gifts, such as you. But *your* gift is of particular interest to me because it was fire that created the world's most famous circus."

"Really?"

"Indeed," he says, exhaling a plume of smoke. "In the 1800s, P.T. Barnum was the proprietor of Barnum's American Museum, which was a grand exhibit of oddities and peculiarities that he ran for twenty-four years. It was what some might call a freakshow. Amongst the attractions were a dwarf named General Tom Thumb who stood twenty-five inches tall, a bearded lady who sprouted her first facial hair at the age of eight, a pair of Siamese twins, a variety of exotic animals, and a mermaid."

"Really?" I say. "A mermaid?"

"No, not really," he says. "It was a small mummified creature about the size of an adolescent child. Barnum claimed to have caught her near the Fiji Islands, but the truth is he was selling a fiction created from the torso of a monkey stitched to the body of a fish. He called it the Fiji Mermaid, and the public believed it was real. Do you know why?"

I shake my head, no.

"Because people *want* to believe," he says. "P.T. Barnum knew this only too well, which is why his museum became an unprecedented success. He had as many as fifteen thousand people a day passing through his doors. Can you imagine that? During the twenty-four years Barnum's American Museum was open, it welcomed in more than thirty-eight million people. I have no doubt his museum would still be open and thriving today if it hadn't been destroyed by fire."

The Ringmaster tugs a drag from his cigar.

"All five stories of Barnum's American Museum were swallowed up by a raging inferno," he says. "Artifacts were lost, exotic animals died. A couple of whales boiled to death in their tank."

"That's awful," I say. "What caused the fire?"

"The Confederate Army of Manhattan," he says. "I doubt you've heard of them. They were a group of southerners who weren't happy with how the Civil War was turning out, so, as a demonstration of their displeasure, they attempted to burn down the entire city of New York. Barnum's American Museum was one of their causalities. But being the strong-willed man that he was, less than two months later, Barnum built a new museum to take its place."

"That's amazing."

"It was amazing," the Ringmaster says. "Unfortunately, it only lasted three years."

"What happened to it?"

"Fire."

"Both museums burned down?"

"Indeed."

"Was it another arson?"

"No, the second fire was simply bad luck," the Ringmaster says. "Barnum used boilers to heat the museum, and unfortunately one of them exploded. But Barnum was nothing if not resilient, because, at the age of sixty years old, he started a traveling circus. Eleven years later, at the age of seventy-one, he merged that circus with another owned by a man named James Baily. They called it Barnum & Bailey's Circus."

The Ringmaster examines the glowing orange embers of his cigar, tapping them over an ashtray.

"When P.T. Barnum died in 1891, his widow sold his half of the circus to James Bailey. Twenty years later, after James Baily died, Barnum & Bailey's Circus was purchased by a group of five brothers named Ringling. The Ringling brothers already had a successful circus of their own, so they combined the two into one and called it the Ringling Bros. and Barnum & Bailey Circus. I have no doubt you've heard of them."

"Of course," I say. "That's the most famous circus in the world."

"Indeed, it is," he says. "So, you see, if it weren't for fire, the most famous circus in the world would never have come to be."

His story gives me goosebumps.

"Can I ask a favor of you, Grover?"

"Sure."

"Would you demonstrate your gift for me?"

"Here?"

The Ringmaster opens a drawer, pulling out a Zippo lighter. With his meaty thumb, he flicks the flame to life.

"When you're ready," he says, reaching his arm across the desk, "please touch the fire."

I hold my hand over the Zippo, letting the flame lick my palm.

The Ringmaster smiles.

"Come," he says, "let's go for a walk."

The Ringmaster moves with the fluid purpose of a great white shark, weaving through the labyrinth of RVs, trucks, and trailers as he leads us onto the circus grounds. He stops at the old-fashioned popcorn wagon, where the same short man I saw yesterday is still manning the machine.

"Grover," the Ringmaster says, "this is Popcorn Pete."

Popcorn Pete smiles, nodding a hello.

"Pete," the Ringmaster says, "tell Grover who created this popcorn machine."

"Charles Cretors."

The Ringmaster looks at me.

"That name probably means nothing to you," he says. "Am I right?"

"I've never heard of him, no."

"Pete," the Ringmaster says, "who was Charles Cretors?"

"He's the man who invented the first large-scale commercial popcorn machine."

"And what year was that in, Pete?" the Ringmaster asks, still looking at me.

"1885, sir."

"Can you imagine that, Grover? The world had no large-scale commercial popcorn machine before Charles Cretors invented it in 1885. In fact, this very machine," the Ringmaster says, rapping his knuckles against the red metal, "was built with Charles Cretors' very own hands. When Walter Grambling, the youngest of the Grambling brothers, took the circus through Wood Dale, Illinois, for a series of shows, Charles Cretors was in attendance. He loved the show so much that, as a show of appreciation, he personally gifted Walter this very machine."

"That's incredible," I say. "It must be worth a fortune."

"Over the years," he says, "I've received countless offers from wealthy men and women who wish to purchase it, but each time I tell them it's not for sale. Would you like to know why?"

I nod, yes.

"Because when I get my hands on something truly valuable, I never let it go."

The Ringmaster continues leading me through the circus grounds until we reach the sideshow tent of Fernando the Fearless Fire Tamer. Inside, there are several foldout chairs, each of them empty except for one occupied by a middle-aged man with a portly belly. He's reading a worn paperback book, oblivious to our presence.

"Fernando," the Ringmaster says, his booming voice capturing Fernando's attention. "How are you today?"

"I'm well," Fernando says, standing up from his chair. "Thank you."

"This is my new friend, Grover Wilcox."

Fernando smiles, shaking my hand.

"Fernando," the Ringmaster says, "I have a request."

"Anything."

"I want you to blow a fireball in Grover's face."

"Sir?"

"It's okay," the Ringmaster says. "Grover is fireproof."

"Fireproof, sir?"

"Yes, he's truly remarkable," the Ringmaster says. "Now, blow a fireball in his face."

Fernando scans me up and down, his face awash with what appears to be skepticism.

"Fernando," the Ringmaster says, his tone much sharper than before. "Please."

Fernando sets down his book and picks up a rod with two large wicks on either end that looks to me like a giant cotton swab.

"Allow me," the Ringmaster says, flicking his Zippo lighter to life and touching it to the wick, transforming the rod into a torch.

Fernando waves the torch from side to side, creating an audible whoosh as the fire cuts through the air, before holding it steady between him and me. He locks his eyes on mine as he takes in a deep breath, holding it in his chest. He gives me a nod, which feels like a signal. As I try to decipher what the signal is for, a terrifying ball of fire blooms from Fernando's mouth. Before I have a chance to process what's happening, the world around me disappears into a brilliant blur of orange.

Chapter Thirteen

THE RUNAWAY

I'M STANDING IN FRONT of my students, trying to teach a lesson on MLA formatting, but all I can think about is yesterday.

The Ringmaster.

Fernando.

Xyla.

I barely remember what happened after the fireball. I know the Ringmaster excused himself, then Xyla and I exited Fernando's tent. At some point, I went home where I could hardly sleep a wink, and now I'm in a classroom trying to teach a lesson on MLA formatting. If you're not familiar with MLA formatting, count your blessings. You'd be better off staring at a blank wall for two hours than listening to me talk about it. This is pretty much what my life has come down to—trapped in a prison of uninspired boredom.

It doesn't seem all that long ago that I was walking in a cap and gown across a stage, and then a few weeks after that, I was standing in front of a roomful of college students to begin my teaching career. At the time, I thought Chandler College hired me because they recognized my raw, untapped talents, but, as it turns out, adjunct professors are a dime a dozen. We come and go, and only a rare few—like myself—are crazy enough to make a career out of being part-time teachers for shit pay. When I was still a college student myself, my only concerns were putting enough coins together to watch a movie and buy a Big Mac once in a while, but now, as a full-fledged adult in the real world, I'm assaulted by an endless parade of bills marching into my mailbox month after month, each of them a bitter reminder that my life is no longer my own.

Most days, I wish I could just run away.

I go to the hospital after my class is over, and I'm surprised to see Mom isn't in the hospital room. I kiss Dad on the cheek, feeling the pricks of his salt-and-pepper stubble against my lips. I wonder if anybody is responsible for shaving his face, or if he'll just continue growing a beard for as long as he's in a coma. It's honestly not a bad look, and I wish he were awake so I could tell him as much.

"Hey, Dad," I whisper into his ear. "I just wanted you to know I'm here, and I love you. Also, I'm fireproof, so that's new. Anyway, I'd really appreciate it if you woke up because I miss you, and I still need you here to teach me about the world."

"Hello."

I nearly jump out of my skin before I realize it's a nurse talking to me.

"Oh, I'm sorry," she says. "I didn't mean to startle you."

"That's okay."

She moves to the other side of Dad's bed, checking the various gizmos and gadgets he's hooked up to.

"You must be Grover."

"I am, yes."

"Your mom's in the cafeteria," she says. "She asked me to send you down there if I saw you."

"Thank you."

I spend a few moments scanning the cafeteria before Mom catches my eye and waves me over. As I get closer, I realize she's not sitting alone.

She's with the Ringmaster.

"Come join us, sweetheart," she says. "I've just been chatting with Claudius."

"Grover," the Ringmaster says, as I sit down beside Mom, "it's so nice to see you again."

"Claudius has been telling me about his circus," she says, smiling at him. "What's it called again? Gambling Brothers?"

"*Grambling* Brothers."

"Oh, forgive me," she says. "Is Grambling a family name?"

"You're forgiven, my dear," he says. "And, yes, it is a family name. However, I can't claim to be kin to the Grambling lineage."

"I just love the way you speak," Mom says, giggling like a schoolgirl. "Anyway, I should get back to Rex."

Mom stands up from the table, and the Ringmaster does the same.

"It was a pleasure meeting you, Claudius."

He takes her hand in each of his.

"The pleasure was all mine, dear."

He sits back down as Mom exits the cafeteria.

"Together again," he says, smiling.

"Um...am I missing something?"

"Whatever do you mean?"

"Are you supposed to be here?"

"Should I be somewhere else?"

"I mean, did we make plans?"

"Would I be here if there weren't a plan?"

"I'm sorry, but I'm confused," I say. "How did you know I was here?"

"Xyla told me about your father," he says. "You and your mother have my deepest sympathy."

"Thank you," I say, "but I'm still confused. I never told Xyla what hospital my dad was at."

"Didn't you?"

"I don't think so."

"You and your mother have been under a great deal of stress," he says, "and stress is no ally to memory."

"Maybe you're right," I say, squeezing the back of my neck, "but how did you know I'd be here *today*? At this time?"

He smiles, running his fingers through his dark waves.

"Lucky guess."

I look around the cafeteria; it's empty except for the Ringmaster and me. I could've sworn there were other people here when I arrived.

"I understand your curiosity around the peculiar circumstances of this meeting," he says, "and I assure you we can investigate those details another time, but the confluence of events that led to this meeting is not nearly as important as the grand event that awaits you."

"What grand event?"

"The removal of life's merciless shackles," he says. "You're an educator, correct?"

"Yes, a college professor."

"Is that your passion?"

"I don't know," I say. "I guess it depends on how you define passion."

"Intense emotion or strong enthusiasm," the Ringmaster says. "Often associated with a powerful drive or motivation toward a clear goal, the embrace of true passion is generally accompanied by a feeling of excitement and joy. Does being a college professor make you feel this way?"

"When you put it that way, I suppose it doesn't."

"So, why do you do it?"

"Everybody needs a job, right?"

"You need basic securities," he says. "I understand *that*, but what I *don't* understand is why you've chosen a profession that you're not passionate about."

"We can't all make a living doing what we love."

"Says who?"

"I don't know," I say. "I guess it's just been my experience."

"Does this job pay you well?"

"Nope."

"So, you've chosen a job that you're not passionate about, *and* it doesn't pay you well?"

"I guess that's the long and the short of it."

"Well, I'd like to change that," the Ringmaster says. "I want you to join my circus."

"To do what?"

"To perform under my big top."

"That's a very flattering offer," I say, "but I'm not a performer."

"I beg to differ," he says. "You have a gift that deserves to be on display, not subjugated by the benign routine of an unfulfilling career."

"I don't know about all that."

"Let me speak plainly," he says. "Right now, you're an easily replaceable cog in a ruthless machine that has neither the ability nor the desire to empathize with your existence. But if you join Grambling Brothers, you'll be so much more than a nameless, faceless cog."

"That does sound nice."

"Join us, Grover," he says. "Whatever you're earning now, I'll double it."

"That's very generous of you, but—"

"I'll triple it."

"It's not that I don't appreciate your offer, but—"

"I'll quadruple it," he says. "Do you understand how valuable you are?"

"I've never thought of myself as valuable."

"Well, you should," he says. "On a separate but related note, your mother informed me about the terrible situation regarding your father's medical insurance."

"She told you about that?"

"Yes, she did," he says. "She also opened up about how worried she is about what the final bill is going to be and how she's going to pay it."

"It's pretty scary," I say. "I just wish there was something I could do to help."

The Ringmaster leans in, resting his elbows on the table.

"Join my circus," he says. "In return, not only will I pay you handsomely, but I'll also pay all of your father's medical bills."

"That's a generous offer," I say, "but we have no idea what we're going to owe."

"It doesn't matter," he says. "I'll gladly pay every cent."

"I don't want to sound ungrateful," I say, "but why would you do that?"

"Because that's how valuable you are to me."

"With all due respect," I say, "how can I know if your offer to pay my father's medical bills is even real?"

"Sometimes, when an offer seems too good to be true, it is both good *and* true," he says. "Nonetheless, your skepticism is warranted. After all, a promise made does not equal a promise kept. If I can present you with a show of good faith, something that demonstrates with absolute certainty that my word is true, will you join my circus?"

"Like what?"

The Ringmaster smiles.

"You'll see."

"This is a lot to take in."

"Whatever you decide, please come see me tomorrow to tell me face-to-face," he says, standing up from the table. "It'll be our final evening in Rancho Cucamonga."

I go back to Dad's room, and, as soon as I walk in, Mom gives me a great, big hug.

"Grover," she says, her cheeks wet with tears, "it's a miracle!"

"What happened?"

"The CEO of the hospital came to speak with me just a few minutes ago."

"What did he say?"

"First of all, son, *she* is a woman," Mom says. "But, more importantly, she told me that we don't have to worry about your father's hospital expenses."

"Really?"

"Yes, apparently a private donor personally contacted her and said they would cover all of the medical costs."

"Are you sure it's real?"

"The CEO gave me her assurance that it's very real," she says. "Can you believe it?"

She holds my hand, laying her head on my shoulder.

"So, what did you and Claudius talk about?"

"I think I'm going to run away with the circus."

THE
CIRCLE

PART TWO

Chapter Fourteen

CALL TO ADVENTURE

I'VE JUST TOLD THE Ringmaster that I'll join his circus. We're sitting across from each other inside his office, and—while I know it's a very big deal and my life will likely never be the same from this day forward—the only thing I can focus on at this very moment is the fact that I'm not wearing any underwear. It's not that I'm averse to wearing underwear, but rather that I ran out of clean laundry, and there isn't a laundry room at my apartment complex. Usually, I take my dirty clothes to my parents' house once a week to clean—well, to be specific, for Mom to clean (she insists, I swear!). But with Dad in the hospital, Mom and I have been far too preoccupied to think about much of anything else, let alone laundry, so it wasn't until I was getting ready this morning that I discovered my lack of clean underwear.

"You've made a wise decision," the Ringmaster says.

"Thank you," I say, trying to adjust the crotch of my pants in a manner that isn't too obvious. "Do you need me to sign anything?"

"That won't be necessary," he says, reaching his hand across the desk. "A gentlemen's agreement is all I require."

I shake his massive paw, surprised at how official it all feels.

"Are you excited for your debut performance?"

"Mostly, I'm nervous."

"That's to be expected."

"I know there's a lot of work to do before I can join the show," I say, "but I'm ready to dig in and learn whatever I need to learn."

"That's an excellent attitude," he says. "Incidentally, you'll be making your debut tonight."

"What? But that's impossible."

"Why is it impossible?"

"I don't have an act," I say. "What will I even do?"

"You'll be fine."

"And what about my job?"

"This is your job."

"I mean my teaching job."

"What about it?"

"I need to let them know that I'm resigning, right?"

"You can handle that today," the Ringmaster says. "I see no issue there."

"So, I'll give them a standard two-week notice?"

"No, that won't work," he says. "We're traveling to our next town after tonight's show. Was I not clear about that?"

"No, you weren't."

"I'm sure I told you as much."

"I don't think so."

"Nonetheless," he says, "you'll debut tonight, and you'll join us on the road after the show."

"I think it would be a mistake to include me in the show tonight."

"Why is that?"

"Because I don't have any idea what I'm doing."

The Ringmaster blows a plume of smoke.

"When the time comes," he says, "you will."

Leaving the Ringmaster's office, I drive straight to the campus of Chandler College so I can speak face-to-face with the Dean of the Language Arts Department, Bill Tilden. I figure I owe him as much since I'll be quitting without notice. Speaking of which, I don't actually know how to quit my job at Chandler College, logistically speaking. At the beginning of each semester, I sign a new contract, so I imagine quitting mid-semester amounts to breaking that contract, and I have no idea what sort of consequences come with that.

Bill is all smiles as I step into his office.

"Grover," he says, coming around the desk to hug me.

You should know that I've never hugged Bill before in my life. I didn't even know that was a thing that could happen. A hug alone would've been strange enough from Bill, but he's also never referred to me by my name before. In the ten years that I've worked at Chandler College, Bill has literally never said more than "hi" or "bye," and even those exchanges were few and far between.

"Congratulations!"

"Thanks," I say. "What for?"

"Your new career in the circus."

"How do you know about that?"

"I spoke with Claudius Xavier just before you arrived," he says. "A fine man."

"He called you?"

"No, he came to my office," he says. "He let me know that you're debuting tonight, so, starting immediately, you won't be available to teach your classes anymore."

"He did?"

"He sure did," Bill says. "On an unrelated note, Claudius insisted on giving me a sizable grant to conduct my research."

"I didn't realize you were in the middle of a research project."

"I'm not," Bill says, laughing, "but I guess I can start one now. I'm thinking there's probably some research to be done in the Bahamas or maybe an Alaskan cruise."

"Good for you, sir."

"We'll miss you around here," he says, clapping me on the back. "Happy trails!"

Leaving Chandler College, I drive straight to the hospital to update Mom on what's happening.

"So, you're joining them tonight?"

"Yeah."

"And you'll start traveling with them after the show is over?"

"That's the plan."

A few moments of silence percolate between us, during which I can't tell how Mom's going to respond.

"Well," she says, finally, "I think that sounds wonderful."

"Really?" I say. "Do you honestly think it's a good idea?"

"I really do, sweetheart," she says. "Life is short, so you need to take advantage of every opportunity that comes your way."

"And you don't think it's crazy?"

She laughs.

"Of course, it's crazy!" she says. "But sometimes a little crazy isn't a bad thing. You know, I have no regrets about getting married after college and becoming a housewife—all of which was my choice, by the way—but I sometimes wonder what my life would've looked like if I made some different choices."

"Like what?"

"Like moving to London to work on my PhD."

"You never told me about that."

"I guess there wasn't much to tell since I didn't go."

"What would you have studied?"

"The work of Joseph Campbell," she says, smiling, "but I'm sure that doesn't surprise you."

Mom has had a lifelong fascination with Joseph Campbell, which I know all about since she started teaching me about him when I was a kid. Now, it might seem like teaching your kid about the leading expert on comparative mythology might be a little heady, but Mom knew I loved comic books, so she enjoyed contextualizing the mythology of my favorite superheroes—like Superman and Batman—with the ancient myths and teachings of Joseph Campbell's work. I really loved these lessons, especially when Mom taught me about the "hero's journey," which is a term Campbell coined in his seminal book, *The Hero with a Thousand Faces*. The idea of the hero's journey is that all stories of heroic figures share the same essential elements, including a call to adventure, a separation from the known world, a confrontation with evil, and a triumphant homecoming.

"It definitely doesn't surprise me that you wanted to study the work of Joseph Campbell," I say, "but I guess I'm sort of surprised you didn't go for it. So, what happened?"

"I was in love with your father," she says, "and we'd just gotten married. Plus, he was in a good place with his career at the firehouse, so I knew he couldn't come with me."

"And you don't have any regrets?"

"Well, I'd be lying if I said I didn't question my decision more than a few times, especially in those first few years," she says. "It was just that nagging feeling of 'what if?'"

"Did the nagging feeling ever go away?"

"It sure did."

"What changed?"

"I had you," she says. "From the moment the doctor handed you to me, I knew I'd chosen the right adventure."

"That helps to hear," I say, "but I'm still kind of scared."

"It's okay to be scared," she says. "That's part of the adventure. Remind me, what was it that Joseph Campbell said about fear?"

I smile.

"The cave you fear to enter holds the treasure you seek."

"There you go," she says, kissing my cheek. "Your adventure awaits."

Chapter Fifteen

CANNIBAL CHICKENS

Arriving back at Grambling Brothers, I realize that I've been so preoccupied with everything else going on that I neglected to pack any clothes or travel accouterments for my rapidly approaching road trip. On top of which, I have no idea what Grambling Brothers' travel schedule is or how often I'll get to come back home. And what about my shitty, little apartment? Does it even make sense for me to keep renting it?

I walk past the empty box office as I enter the mostly vacant circus grounds, making my way into the labyrinth of RVs, trucks, and trailers, weaving aimlessly about as I try to find the Ringmaster's office. It doesn't matter that I was there just a few hours ago, this place still feels like a maze to me. I'm like a kid separated from his parents in the middle of a crowd of towering strangers; the longer I'm lost, the more severe the panic in my brain becomes. Just as it seems the walls of this labyrinth are closing in on me, suffocating my ability to take a deep breath, I find myself standing in front of the Ringmaster's office. I'm not sure how I got here—or if I could find it again—but I'm here now, which is all that matters.

I knock on the Ringmaster's door, and he calls for me to enter. He's looking over paperwork when I sit down at his desk, a lit cigar jutting from the side of his mouth. I watch silently as he traces his finger across the page in front of him from top to bottom.

"Grover," he says, setting his work aside to give me his full attention, "to what do I owe the pleasure of this visit?"

"I guess I still have some concerns about what to expect moving forward."

"What's concerning you?"

"There are some loose ends I hadn't considered."

"If you're speaking of your teaching job, that's been taken care of."

"It's not that," I say. "I don't know what to do about my apartment."

"What needs to be done?"

"I'm not sure if I should keep it or break my lease."

"What would you like to do?"

"I don't know," I say. "I mean, I'm sure I won't be with Grambling Brothers forever, so I'll need a place to live when I'm done."

"You don't want to be with us forever?"

"That's not what I mean," I say, followed by a nervous laugh.

"If you want to break your lease, I'll take care of that, Grover," he says. "What else has you concerned?"

"Really? What if there's a penalty or a fine?"

"I'll take care of it," he says, waving his hand as if to make it disappear. "What else is concerning you?"

"I guess I'm still mostly concerned about debuting tonight," I say. "I literally have no idea what I'm supposed to do."

He nods, pulling a drag from his cigar.

"Have I told you about the history of the Grambling Brothers Traveling Circus Show?"

"No."

"Come," he says, "let's take a walk."

The Ringmaster leads me out of his office and onto the circus grounds.

"In the beginning, the Grambling Brothers Traveling Circus Show was technically *two* shows," he says. "A circus and a sideshow. At that time, I was a performer, so I didn't have a hand in running anything."

"What kind of performer were you?"

"A strongman."

"Like Handsome Harry?"

"I don't know if *any*body is quite like Handsome Harry," he says, "but yes. I was Claudius the World's Kindest Strongman."

"The World's *Kindest* Strongman?"

The Ringmaster laughs.

"General Panda loved eccentric stage names."

"Who's General Panda?"

"He was my former business partner and the proprietor of General Panda's Traveling Sideshow of Wonders and Oddities," the Ringmaster says. "But, before we became business partners, I was a performer in his show. Now, the thing to know about General Panda is he was a cantankerous son of a bitch, which didn't earn him many friends. He needed protection, so he hired me. Along with being a performer in his show, I was also his muscle, and he made sure everybody knew it."

"Like a bodyguard?"

"That's exactly right," he says. "The only thing he asked before hiring me was, 'Can you handle yourself, kid?' I assured him that I was capable in a scrap."

"Did you ever have to fight anybody for him?"

"Never," he says. "Let's just say nobody was in a hurry to test themselves against me."

The Ringmaster pulls a drag from his cigar as we walk through the midway.

"When General Panda wasn't busy pissing people off," he says, "he was a good mentor. He even developed the World's Kindest Strongman gimmick for me. Generally speaking, the strongman gimmick relies purely on size and strength without much concern for portraying a character. So, one of the first and best lessons General Panda taught me was the importance of having a unique persona to package my strongman routine into. With his guidance, I started dressing in dark colors, mostly black. I grew out my beard and wore big hats, long coats, and heavy boots. I even applied dark makeup around my eyes. The idea was to look intimidating, which would allow me to subvert the audience's expectations when they discovered I was both articulate and kind."

The Ringmaster waves hello to Popcorn Pete as we walk past the Charles Cretors popcorn machine.

"I had my doubts in the beginning, before debuting my new persona," the Ringmaster says, "but it worked like gangbusters. Not long after I joined the show, General Panda's Traveling Sideshow of Wonders and Oddities became the hottest ticket in every town we showed up in. Eventually, our success got the attention of Walter Grambling, the youngest of the Grambling brothers and the only one left running their circus."

"What happened to the other brothers?"

"The others had either retired or died," he says. "The Grambling Brothers Traveling Circus—which was its name at the time—had been a successful business for the Grambling family, but attendance was waning, and Walter knew he needed to shake things up. Theirs was a traditional circus with aerial performers, clowns, and such, while General Panda offered more of an exotic freakshow. With his unique business acumen, Walter saw a golden opportunity in combining their two shows, so he made General Panda an offer to merge. Together, they became the Grambling Brothers Traveling Circus and Sideshow of Wonders and Oddities. That remained the name for a long time until I took over ownership and shortened the name to the Grambling Brothers Traveling Circus Show."

The Ringmaster adjusts his red-tinted glasses.

"While General Panda deserves the credit for the World's Kindest Strongmen gimmick," he says, "Walter Grambling made his own contribution to the gimmick when he gave me these glasses, which farmers call chicken specs. Walter knew about chicken specs because he and his brothers grew up on a farm. Such specs were once considered a necessity on farms for taming certain chickens with cannibalistic tendencies. These tendencies were triggered at the sight of blood, so, for example, if a chicken cut itself on a wired fence, they were likely to be attacked by one of the cannibal chickens. To solve this issue, farmers started putting red-tinted specs on their chickens. With the red lenses filtering their vision, the cannibal chickens couldn't distinguish blood from anything else they saw, thereby keeping their killer instincts at bay."

The Ringmaster exhales a plume of smoke.

"Because we were performing in a lot of farming towns," he says, "Walter came up with the idea of adding chicken specs to my gimmick to subliminally suggest danger to the audience."

"Did it work?"

"Like a charm," the Ringmaster says. "Every town we traveled to, Walter would send members of the crew out amongst the population to spread rumors about how dangerous Claudius the World's Kindest Strongman was and how the only thing that kept him from attacking innocent people were his red-tinted glasses. During each of my performances, as I went into my final feat of strength, our clown would interrupt me and snatch the glasses off my face. The audience would invariably gasp in fear as I chased the clown around the big top until he escaped into the audience, giving my red-tinted glasses to a child in the front row. Fully in character, I would stalk towards the child, shoulders heaving, grunting and snarling as if my most primitive and barbaric urges had been triggered. I would stand in front of the child like a crazed animal, letting the audience believe I might do something unspeakable. Just as the tension inside the big top became unbearable, I would drop to one knee and let the child put the glasses back on my face, transforming me back to my non-savage self."

"That sounds like a great act," I say, "but weren't you worried the child might mess up your routine?"

"Never," he says. "The child was a plant. There were always children traveling with us because several of the performers were parents. We rotated a different child into the act in every show."

The Ringmaster stops walking, and I see we're back inside the labyrinth.

"Here we are," he says, knocking on a shabby-looking RV.

The door opens with a strained metallic screech, revealing a young man with shaggy hair and a newsboy cap.

"Hey, boss," he says. "Everything okay?"

"I want you to meet Grover Wilcox," the Ringmaster says. "Grover, this is Canyon."

Canyon nods a hello, shaking my hand.

"Grover will be joining us on the road," the Ringmaster says, "so I'd like him to stay with you."

"The more the merrier," Canyon says. "Is he joining the tent crew?"

"No, he'll be performing in the big top," the Ringmaster says. "I trust you'll help him feel welcome."

"No problem."

"Good," the Ringmaster says. "Grover, I'll see you tonight."

He walks away, leaving me alone with Canyon.

"So, you're a performer, huh?" Canyon says. "What kind of act do you do?"

Chapter Sixteen

CANYON

I WATCH THE RINGMASTER walk away, thinking maybe he'll turn around once he realizes he never addressed my concern about debuting in tonight's show.

"Earth to Grover," Canyon says, waving his hand in front of my face.

"Oh, sorry."

"Just fucking with you, bro," he says with a laugh. "But seriously, what's your act?"

"I don't have an act."

"Are you changing it up or something?"

"No, I mean, I literally don't have an act," I say. "I've never performed before in my life, especially not in a circus."

"Ever?"

"Never ever."

"But didn't Claudius just say you're performing tonight?"

"He did."

"Does *he* know you don't have an act?"

"That's what I keep telling him."

"And he's having you do it anyway?"

"Uh-huh."

"Shit, bro," he says, scratching his head. "Good luck with that, I guess. Anyway, come check out your new digs."

Canyon opens the door to his RV, sounding a very unpleasant metal-on-metal screech.

"This is your RV?"

"Yeah," he says. "I mean, I don't own it. Claudius owns everything around here. But it's mine for as long as I'm with Grambling Brothers."

"Does everyone have an RV?"

"You bet," he says. "But don't call it an RV unless you want to sound like a mark. Around here, we call them wagons."

"Why's that?"

"Back in the day, circuses used to travel by wagon," he says. "That was before they started traveling by train."

"So, it's like an homage to the past?"

"A *what* to the past?"

"An homage."

"What's that?"

"Oh, um...an homage is sort of a way to show respect."

"That's cool," he says. "Yeah, it's an homage, then. This girl right here," he says, wrapping his knuckles against the chrome exterior, "is an Avion LeGrande."

"Is that a popular brand?"

"Not since the seventies, bro," he says. "But back in the day, this hunk of steel was considered the height of luxury. She came with a built-in generator, water heater, air conditioning, a kitchen, and a fully functional bathroom. That's practically a vacation on wheels."

"Sounds great."

"Let me give you the tour."

Canyon steps up into the wagon, and I follow him inside. I don't know exactly what I was expecting, but it's certainly not the picture of luxury that he just described. There are four beds altogether, two on the floor and two elevated above like bunks. Between the beds is a narrow, makeshift hallway that leads to what I assume is the bathroom. The carpet is stained, the upholstery is torn, and there seems to be one very important feature missing.

"Where's the kitchen?"

"We don't have one, bro."

"I thought you said it came with a kitchen."

"Yeah, it *used* to have a kitchen," he says, "but Claudius had it torn out so we could fit more bunks inside. I mean, right now it's only me and Darius in this one, but now we got you with us."

One of the beds is occupied by an unconscious man with a beanie pulled over his eyes.

"That's Darius," Canyon says. "That dude loves his sleep, but he's a hard worker."

"What do you guys do?"

"We're part of the tent crew," he says. "We wake up early, go to bed late, and break our backs in between."

He laughs, but I don't get the impression he actually finds it funny.

"Is there a bathroom?"

"Yeah, the bathroom is back here," he says, leading me down the makeshift hallway.

The bathroom isn't any more impressive than the rest of this hovel on wheels; there's a toilet and a sink, but nothing else.

"When you said it had a fully functional bathroom," I say, "I think I assumed there was a shower."

"Yeah, Claudius took that out, too," he says. "It's for the best, though, because the water heater barely works in this ol' girl, so you'd be showering in ice water."

"Since there's no shower," I say, "where do you guys clean up?"

"Let me show you."

Canyon leads me out of the wagon, and I see several scrapes and dents littered about its dull, chrome frame that I hadn't previously noticed. As we walk through the labyrinth, Canyon talks a mile a minute. He tells me about his family and how, even though his work is grueling, he's grateful for the job because it allows him to give his daughter a good life back home.

"Where's home?"

"Guadalupe."

"Mexico?"

"Nah, Arizona, bro," he says, laughing. "Guadalupe is a tiny little town squeezed between Phoenix and Tempe. It's kind of one of those places where if you ain't looking for it, you won't find it."

"How old is your daughter?"

"Nine," he says. "Her birthday's actually in a few weeks."

"Are you doing anything fun for her?"

"My girlfriend's planning a party," he says, "but I'll be here working with the rest of the crew."

"Can't you take time off?"

"Nah, there's too much work," he says, stopping beside a long trailer. "Here we are."

"What's this?"

"This is our shower, bro," he says. "It's a community bathroom."

He steps up into it, so I follow him inside. After a quick scan, I count six shower stalls and two sinks. Anything metal inside is coated in rust, and it's clear the walls haven't seen the business end of a sponge in a very long time.

"Does everybody use these showers?"

"Nah," Canyon says, "this is just for the grunts. The performers get their own tricked-out wagons, so they've got fancy showers and whatnot. Tell you the truth, I'm surprised Claudius is having you slum with us since you're going to be in the show."

A woman exits the shower wagon, wrapped in a towel and carrying a bag of toiletries. Her hair is wet, slicked back along her neck. Dirt gathers around the edges of her flip-flops as she touches down on the ground.

"Howdy, May," Canyon says. "What are you doing in this shitty joint? Don't you have a shower in your wagon?"

"Yeah, but my plumbing's fucked," she says, "so I've got to rough it with the other roustabouts until it's fixed. Who's your friend?"

"This is my new roommate, Grover."

She offers me her wet hand.

"Nice to meet you, Grover."

"May pretty much runs things around here."

"I wouldn't say all of that," May says. "I'm mainly the prop master."

"The prop master?" I say. "What's that entail?"

"I'm in charge of pretty much anything physical that's used in the show," she says. "If any of the performers need a prop, it's my job to acquire it, maintain it, and ensure it's in the right place at the right time. And for the props we already have, I make sure they're all safe and accounted for between shows."

"She also moves everything from town to town," Canyon says.

"He makes it sound more impressive than it is," May says. "I'm more like a foreman, so, really, I make sure *other* people move everything from town to town."

"That sounds like a lot of responsibility."

"It is," she says, "but it's also pretty easy when you've been doing it as long as I have."

"May also books the towns."

"You'll have to pardon my press agent here," she says with a laugh.

"What goes into booking a town?"

"I make sure we have someplace to perform our show," she says. "That means taking care of contracts, insurance—basically all the stuff Claudius doesn't want to deal with."

"Told you, bro," Canyon says. "She runs this place. She's even the tent boss."

"What's a tent boss?"

"It means I'm in charge of this knucklehead," she says, nodding her head toward Canyon. "It's just more foreman work, really. I oversee the erection of the big top as well as the sideshow tents. Are you joining my tent crew, Grover?"

"Not this guy," Canyon says. "He's performing in the show!"

"Oh, yeah?" she says, looking me up and down. "And Claudius has you staying with Canyon?"

"Right?!" Canyon says with a laugh. "That's exactly what I said!"

"Well, I'm sure Claudius has his reasons," May says. "So, what's your act?"

Canyon laughs before I can answer May's question.

"You're gonna love this," he says, squeezing my shoulder. "Tell her, Grover."

"I don't have an act."

May looks at Canyon, like maybe this is a gag he's put me up to.

"It's true!" Canyon says. "Hand to God."

"I don't get it," May asks. "Do you have a gimmick or anything?"

"I sort of do stuff with fire."

"How long have you worked with fire?"

"I guess it's been a few days now."

"A few days?" she says. "Well, when's your first performance?"

"Tonight."

"Tonight?"

"That's what Claudius tells me."

May looks me up and down again, like maybe she missed something the first time.

"Well, if Claudius is putting you in the show, then I'm sure you'll do great," she says. "It was nice meeting you, Grover."

May walks off, water dripping from her wet hair.

"She's good people," Canyon says.

"You weren't kidding when you said she does everything around here, huh?"

"I'm telling you, bro."

"So, what all goes into putting up the big top?"

"Well, you got the tent boss, which is May, then you got the canvas boss and the pole boss," he says, "and they gotta keep the whole crew organized or shit can go sideways in a hurry because we're pulling ropes, setting up poles, working cranks, all sorts of shit. Even after the big top is up, we gotta make sure the bleachers are secure and the air conditioner is working and the sound system is set up, so, you know, it's a lot of stuff that goes into it. It's like eight or nine hours altogether."

"Did you always work in the circus?"

"Me? Nah," he says, "I used to paint houses. How about you?"

"Up until a few hours ago, I was a college professor."

"No shit?"

"No shit."

"What'd you teach?"

"English composition."

"And now you're in the circus," he says. "Crazy fucking world, huh?"

"You're telling me."

"Anyway, I'm gonna head back to the wagon to catch a few Z's," he says, giving me a fist bump. "I gotta good feeling about you, Grover. I think you're good people."

I walk aimlessly around the circus grounds, feeling woefully out of place and worrying that perhaps I've made a huge mistake. I mean, I'm grateful that my parents won't have to worry about any crippling medical bills, but I'm also worried that the Ringmaster is severely overestimating my ability to perform.

I see Xyla, and the sight of her puts me at ease.

"Hey, I've been looking for you," she says. "Hungry?"

"I can eat."

"Good," she says, "follow me."

Xyla takes me by the arm, leading me to a food truck. There are several long tables and benches set up near the truck, most of which are empty. We walk up to the window, which frames a heavyset man with hairy arms and a dirty apron.

"Welcome, welcome," he says, leaning his arms on the window sill.

"Hi, Vik."

"You brought a friend," he says. "I'm glad to see you're not eating alone today."

"This is Grover Wilcox," she says. "He's joining the show tonight."

"Pleasure to meet you, Grover," he says. "The name's Vik. Welcome to my dukey truck."

Xyla anticipates my confusion before I can voice it.

"Dukey is old carny lingo," she says. "It's what they used to call the cookhouse."

"That's right," Vik says. "It's my job to keep all these rascals fed. Me and my daughters, that is." Vik points his thumb over his shoulder, gesturing to two young women working the grill. "We run this little operation."

"So, it's a family business?" I say. "That's really nice."

"Yeah, I'm a lucky fella," Vik says. "You kids hungry?"

"Yes," Xyla says, "what's on the menu?"

"Today we're making cheeseburgers."

"That sounds perfect."

"Two cheeseburgers, coming right up," Vik says. "Fries or rings?"

"Both."

"Atta girl," Vik says, smiling. "Milkshakes?"

Xyla looks at me.

"Yeah, a milkshake sounds good," I say.

"What flavor would you like, Grover?"

"I'll take whatever's your best."

Vik smiles.

"I like this one," he says to Xyla, rapping his knuckles on the counter. "You kids take a seat, and I'll holler when it's ready."

Xyla leads me to an empty table, and we sit across from each other.

"Do we pay after it's ready?"

"No," she says, "the food is free."

"Really?"

"Yeah," she says, "Claudius takes good care of us."

While the dining area isn't crowded, the people here seem to be taking an interest in Xyla and me.

"Don't mind them," she says. "They're just curious."

"Curious about what?"

"You."

"Are you sure they're not curious because I'm sitting with *you*?"

"Why would you think that?"

"Well, since the first time I visited Grambling Brothers," I say, "people have acted strange when they found out you invited me."

"Strange how?"

"Like they were in disbelief," I say. "Also, a few people strongly implied I should be worried about Handsome Harry."

Xyla doesn't respond right away, which can't be a good sign.

"Harry and I used to be together," she says, "but we're not anymore."

"How long have you been broken up?"

"A few months."

"If he saw us having lunch together," I say, "would I be in danger?"

Vik turns up at our table.

"Here you go, kids," he says, dropping off a pair of cheeseburgers, fries, onion rings, and milkshakes. "Enjoy!"

As Vik walks back to his food truck, Xyla takes a bite of her cheeseburger.

"Don't worry about Harry," she says between bites. "Just focus on your performance."

"I wish I knew what to focus on," I say. "I have no idea what my performance is."

"Why not?"

"Claudius hasn't given me any guidance."

Xyla takes another bite, chasing it with a sip of her shake.

"I know Claudius can be mysterious," she says, "but I promise he wouldn't ask you to perform tonight if he didn't truly believe you could do it."

Chapter Seventeen

KIRKOS

I N ALL OF THE excitement and anxiety of the day, I realize that, along with walking around without underwear, my phone is on the verge of dying. I don't have access to a phone charger, so I'm not sure what to do. I'd ask Xyla for help, but she went off to run errands after we finished lunch. I move aimlessly through the labyrinth until I find Canyon's wagon—which, I suppose, is also *my* wagon now—in the hopes that either he or Darius has a phone charger I can use; it's not until I get here and find the door locked that I realize I don't have a key to get in. I knock a few times, but neither Canyon nor Darius come to my rescue, as they're likely up to their earlobes in Z's.

Since I can't get into my new pad, I continue wandering about the labyrinth until it flushes me out onto the circus grounds. I see Bettie the Bearded Bombshell sitting in a lawn chair in front of her sideshow tent, reading a fashion magazine. She waves as I walk past, and, in spite of my most gentlemanly efforts, my eyes briefly lock in on her magnificent cleavage. I offer a quick hello before hurrying along so as not to prolong my embarrassment. I watch as various members of the Grambling Brothers crew set up their respective midway games and concession stands.

Filling balloons and stacking milk bottles.

Heating grills and popping corn.

As nightfall envelops the big top, the evening's circusgoers begin trickling through the entrance; conspicuous by his absence, Charlie Chuckles isn't there to greet them. The sight of each man, woman, and child who steps into Grambling Brothers is a sobering reminder of my impending debut barreling towards me like a runaway train. Horrifying thoughts of standing in the middle of the big top, isolated and confused, as an angry audience stares down at me, waiting in vain to be entertained, set my brain crackling with the threat of impending doom. Before I have a chance to spiral into a full-fledged, no-holds-barred panic attack, I cross paths with the Ringmaster.

"Grover," he says, "I was just looking for you."

I'm relieved to hear this, as I assume it means I'll finally get some clarification on what I'm supposed to do in the show—or, better yet, maybe he's come to his senses about having me debut tonight at all. The Ringmaster invites me to join him as he heads back into the labyrinth. As we walk, making innocuous small talk, all I really want to do is ask if he truly expects me to perform tonight inside the big top. But, for whatever reason, I'm feeling extra timid, so instead of saying the thing I want to say, I blurt out the first random thought that pops into my head.

"Why don't you have a Ferris wheel?"

The Ringmaster chuckles.

"I take it you're a fan of Ferris wheels?" he asks.

"Yeah, but also, it seems like a Ferris wheel would be a natural fit for the circus."

"You're not wrong," he says, "but the reality is, incorporating a Ferris wheel into our carefully managed ecosystem would require a significant amount of time, effort, and resources. We'd need a team of skilled technicians to conduct inspections and repairs to maintain the Ferris wheel's integrity, not to mention the safety of our patrons. Then there's the tremendous amount of labor and coordination required for transporting the Ferris wheel from town to town, which would entail dismantling each of the components and parts, loading them onto a fleet of trucks, only to reassemble it again once we arrive in the next town. Even after it's put back together, we would have to perform extensive safety checks before operating it for business."

"I guess I never considered all of that."

"And why would you?" he says, smiling. "You've never been on this side of the circus before. But your instincts about the Ferris wheel being a natural fit are quite apt. As a former English professor, I assume you have an appreciation for etymology."

"Sure."

"Are you familiar with the etymology of the word 'circus'?"

"I'm not, no."

"The word 'circus' has its roots in Latin, where it means 'ring' or 'circle,'" he says. "It was originally inspired by the ancient Greek word 'kirkos,' which itself was used to describe circular objects, such as Ferris wheels. Back in ancient Rome, the word 'circus' referred to huge oval-shaped venues where public events like chariot races were held. Eventually, it came to refer to traveling shows that featured acts of entertainment, such as clowns, acrobats, and strongmen. But, for me, I like to think 'circus' transcends language altogether as it recedes into the symbolic nature of the circle itself. Because what is a circle, if not an infinite arching line with no beginning and no end, a metaphor for the yawning wonders of the universe and the mysterious forces that govern it?"

We stop walking as we arrive at the Ringmaster's office.

"Now, let's address what's really on your mind," he says, the orange embers of his cigar glowing bright against the night sky. "Are you ready to make your debut tonight?"

"I wish I could tell you yes."

The Ringmaster smiles, squeezing my shoulder with his thick fingers.

"You're more ready than you think, Grover," he says. "Everything you need is already in you."

"What do you mean?"

"You'll see."

He exhales a plume of smoke before disappearing into his office, leaving me once again alone in the labyrinth.

I decide to call Mom as I continue wandering about. My phone only has a five percent charge left, so I really shouldn't be using it at all, but, with the way everything is unfolding, I'm feeling very much like a scared little boy, so talking to my mom is about the only thing in the world I want to do right now.

"Hi, sweetheart."

It sounds like she's in a wind tunnel.

"What's all that noise?"

"Oh, sorry about that," she says. "I have the window open."

"In Dad's hospital room?"

"No, in my car," she says. "I'm driving."

The wind disappears.

"How's that?"

"Perfect," I say. "Where're you headed?"

"The circus."

"You're coming here?"

"Yes, Claudius invited me," she says. "Didn't I tell you?"

"No, you didn't mention that."

"Well, I know I meant to," she says. "So, are you allowed to tell me what you're doing in the show?"

"I wish I could, but I honestly don't know," I say. "Claudius hasn't given me any clear guidance."

"Maybe he's just been busy," she says. "Have you been practicing whatever it is you all do in the circus?"

"That's the thing," I say. "I don't even know what I should be practicing."

"I'm sure there's *something* you can practice," she says. "Why else would Claudius have hired you?"

There's no way for me to explain this without telling her the whole truth.

But I can't.

Or can I?

Fuck it.

"Okay, I didn't plan on telling you this, but, at this point, I'm not sure it matters anymore," I say, before taking a deep breath. "Here's the thing. I'm fireproof. *Literally* fireproof. I know it sounds crazy, but it's the truth. I don't know how or why, but it happened the same day dad fell into a coma. Anyway, that's why Claudius hired me—because I'm fireproof. Whatever his larger plan for me is, I have no idea, but I feel like I'm heading right into a great, big disaster, and there's nothing I can do to stop it. I'm scared, nervous, terrified—a little bit of everything—and I want to believe this is my Joseph Campbell cave, and on the other side of it will be something amazing, but, if I'm being honest, I wish I'd never agreed to it. Speaking of which, I joined Grambling Brothers in exchange for Claudius agreeing to pay Dad's medical bills. Of course, that gesture alone begs a whole host of questions—mainly, how the hell does he have so much money? But that's beside the point. Anyway, I know I just dropped a whole lot on you out of nowhere, but I promise I'm not crazy."

Silence.

"Mom?"

I look at my phone.

It's dead.

Shit.

How much of that did she hear?

Any of it?

None of it?

All of it?

Wandering about the labyrinth, I hear what sounds like an injured animal crying out in the distance. I try to discern where it's coming from, weaving through wide births and tight squeezes, until I find Charlie Chuckles. He's laboring to breathe while his head hangs back like a rag doll, eyes squeezed shut.

"Are you okay?"

He doesn't answer, which concerns me until I notice there's a young woman bent over in front of him—no more than eighteen or nineteen—with her skirt pulled up over her hips. Her panties are stretched around her thighs, her head bobbing in rhythm with Charlie's staccato thrusts. Her hands are pressed flush against a pristine-looking wagon as she turns her head to shoot me a look.

"Hey, you fucking pervert!" she says. "What the fuck are you staring at?!"

"Sorry," I say, my cheeks hot with embarrassment. "I didn't realize...um...sorry."

"Hiya, kid," Charlie Chuckles says, breathing hard as he digs his gloved fingers into her hips. "Fancy meeting you here."

"You know this pervert?" the woman says.

Before he can answer, the door to the wagon they're fucking against swings open. Charlie Chuckles' cohorts from the Clown Alley Hooligans step out, fully put together in their clown make-up and colorful costumes.

"Jesus Christ, Charlie!" the female clown says. "You can't find someplace else to screw your whore?"

"She's not a whore," he says. "She has a name."

"Oh, yeah? What is it?"

"Fuck if I know."

"Charlie," the male clown says with all the calm and measure of a British butler, "we should be heading to the big top now."

"Yeah, yeah," Charlie says, mid-thrust. "I'll be there as soon as I drop some chowder inside her clam toaster."

"You're disgusting," the female clown says.

"Charlie, if I may," the male clown says, "it's my understanding that you're not to fornicate in public anymore."

"This is hardly in public," Charlie says, speeding up.

"What about this guy?" the female clown says, pointing at me. "He looks public to me!"

"Maybe I invited him."

"Whatever," the female clown says. "Fucking asshole."

She storms off in a huff, and the male clown follows after her, each of them disappearing into the darkness of the labyrinth. Charlie begins making sounds that signal his nearing crescendo, so, not wanting to be anywhere near him when it happens, I hurry away.

As I turn the corner, I run into Canyon.

"There you are," he says. "Claudius is looking for you."

"He is?" I say. "But I just saw him a little while ago."

"Well, he sent me to find you."

Canyon leads me through the labyrinth, and I assume we're headed for the Ringmaster's office, but, in short order, he leads me to the back of the big top. There's an unspectacular entrance in the back of the tent where the Ringmaster is standing; surrounding him in a makeshift circle are each of the big top performers, including Charlie Chuckles, wheezing and out of breath. Canyon nudges me to join the circle before walking away. I'm standing between Charlie Chuckles and Sammy Tawker the High-Wire Walker as everyone's attention is focused on the Ringmaster—everyone except for Handsome Harry, whose menacing glare is trained on me.

"It's that time again," the Ringmaster says. "Time to step into our hallowed big top and entertain the people. Time to stand inside that ring and share your otherworldly abilities. Time to create an unforgettable collection of memories for our awaiting audience. Time to show them that magic truly exists in this world." The Ringmaster looks around at everybody, stopping when his eyes find me. "Before we begin, let's all acknowledge our newest performer."

He walks up to me, resting his hand on my shoulder.

"This is Grover Wilcox," the Ringmaster says, "and he'll be making his Grambling Brothers debut tonight. As you will all soon see, Grover is an extraordinary man with a very unique gift."

There's silence, as everybody's eyes are now trained on me.

"Hi," I say, waving awkwardly.

Silence.

"Now, regarding tonight's performance," the Ringmaster says, "the order will go as follows: high wire, clowns, strongman, clowns, fire, clowns, flyers."

The Ringmaster smiles as music sounds inside the big top.

"Showtime."

Chapter Eighteen

SOLO

A S THE SHOW BEGINS inside the big top, the performers disperse—all except for me and Swift Sammy Tawker the High-Wire Walker.

"Hi," he says. "Grover, right?"

"That's me," I say, shaking his hand. "I saw you perform the other night."

"Cool," he says. "I hope I did alright."

"You were fantastic."

"Thank you," he says. "By the way, welcome to the family."

"Thanks."

"It's always neat to get some new blood injected into the group," he says. "You go on fifth, right? After Harry and the clowns?"

"Yeah, I think so."

"Cool," he says. "I look forward to seeing your act."

I'm relieved he doesn't ask what my act actually is, as the embarrassment of not having a good answer to that question is wearing on me.

"By the way," he says, "did I see you and Xyla together earlier at Vik's?"

"Yeah, that was probably me," I say, wishing all of a sudden that he'd asked me about my nonexistent act.

"You've got some balls," he says. "Good for you."

"What makes you say that?"

"Guys around here usually avoid Xyla."

"How come?"

"Just that whole situation with Harry."

"What situation?"

Applause sounds from inside the big top.

"Sorry," Sammy says, "that's my cue."

He disappears into the big top, leaving me desperate for more information about Xyla and Harry.

"Grover," the Ringmaster says, exiting the big top. "It's almost time. How are you feeling?"

"Not great, to be honest."

"I understand," he says, adjusting his red-tinted glasses. "Tell you what, I'll have more information for you in a little bit."

He disappears into the labyrinth, leaving me every bit as confused as I was before. I begin pacing back and forth for the next several minutes, stopping only when Charlie Chuckles turns up from the labyrinth.

"Hey, kid," Charlie says. "Did you enjoy the show?"

"You mean Sammy's high-wire act?" I say. "I think he's still performing."

"No, I mean before when I was fucking that piece of ass."

"Oh, right," I say. "Sorry about that."

"No, I'm serious," he says. "Did you enjoy it?"

The female clown appears from the labyrinth with the male clown by her side.

"Jesus Christ, Charlie," she says. "Leave the kid alone."

"Mind your business," Charlie says. "I'm not even bothering him. Am I bothering you, kid?"

I shrug.

"See!"

"Grover," the male clown says, extending his hand. "I believe we owe you a proper introduction. My name is Woodrow, and this is my wife, Annie."

"Nice to meet you both."

"Were you there for my big finish?" Charlie says. "My chowder's gonna be dripping out of her snatch for days!"

"Would you shut the fuck up?!" Annie says.

"I'll bet she's sitting in a pool of Charlie pudding right now."

"You're disgusting!"

"Ask nice, and I'll get you a spoon."

Woodrow wraps his arm around Annie, seemingly in an effort to keep her anger from boiling over.

"Grover, please accept our sincerest apology for this Neanderthal," Woodrow says. "I hope you won't let our colorful cohort's exhausting antics stain your opinion of the Clown Alley Hooligans."

The Ringmaster appears from the labyrinth, prompting all three of the Clown Alley Hooligans to straighten up like the school principal just arrived. As quickly as he appears, the Ringmaster disappears into the big top. Swift Sammy exits behind a nice ovation from the audience. This prompts the clowns to climb into their hollow Volkswagen, exposing their giant red shoes as they lift it from the dirt. As Swift Sammy jogs past us, disappearing into the labyrinth, the clowns scramble into the big top.

Not knowing what else to do with myself, I poke my head through the curtain to watch the clowns perform. It's fun to see their act from this perspective, as well as the audience taking it all in. As Charlie and Woodrow get into their dueling red balls routine, I feel a stiff tap on my shoulder. Turning around, I find myself face-to-face with Handsome Harry (well, given how much bigger he is than me, face-to-nipples is more accurate).

"Hey, pipsqueak," he says, poking his finger into my chest. "What are you doing with Xyla?"

The force of his poke is almost as jarring as his use of the word "pipsqueak."

"I...um...I'm not sure..."

Before I can stutter out any more words, Handsome Harry grabs my shirt collar in his large fist, pulling us nose to nose. As his hot breath blows down on me like a raging bull, I notice several people—including some of the other performers—gathering around us in a circle. I've never been in a fistfight before in my life, but I have a terrible feeling that streak is about to come to a very violent end.

My hands are quivering.

My mouth is dry.

I brace myself for whatever Handsome Harry has in store, but before he can do anything else, the clowns exit the big top in their hollow Volkswagen, and the Ringmaster's voice booms inside.

"Ladies and gentlemen," he says, "I present to you Handsome Harry the World's Prettiest Strongman!"

Handsome Harry doesn't move, his fist still gripping my collar.

My heart pounds in my ears.

"Hey, Harry," Charlie says, "you're up."

Handsome Harry waits a beat before letting go of my shirt. Walking past me on his way to the big top, he bumps me with his shoulder, nearly knocking me to the dirt. Quickly after that, the crowd of onlookers dissipates, leaving me with the vibe that they're disappointed with the anti-climactic ending. Aside from me, the only one still here is one of the Soaring Silvas.

"We haven't met yet," he says. "The name's Solo."

I nod hello, still shaken up from my near-death experience.

"And, yes," Solo says, without missing a beat, "I *am* named after the space pirate from *Star Wars*. Technically, my name's short for Solomon, but that was just my dad's sneaky way of naming me after his favorite movie character."

This puts a smile on my face in spite of the fight-or-flight adrenaline that's still buzzing in my veins.

"So, Grover, I've got to ask," he says. "What's up with you and Harry?"

"Honestly, I don't know."

"After that whole production, you don't know why Harry has it out for you?"

"I guess it's something to do with me being friends with Xyla."

"Well, that explains it."

"If you can explain what this is all about, I'd love to hear it," I say, "because I genuinely have no idea."

"Happy to," he says, "but we probably shouldn't hang out here."

"Why not?"

"Harry will be done soon, and I'm guessing you don't want to be around when he comes back," he says. "If you like, you can lay low in my wagon for a while."

"Really?"

"Sure," he says, "follow me."

I'm so relieved, I could cry.

Solo's wagon is very extravagant, and, as he gives me a tour, he proudly shares every posh detail—from the smart control system that allows him to control the lights, temperature, and sound system with his phone to the high-end kitchen with marble countertops and stainless-steel appliances. The living area is set up with a fancy dining table and chairs, a full-grain Italian leather sofa, and a widescreen LED TV, while the wildly spacious bathroom is equipped with heated porcelain tile flooring and a rainfall showerhead. Then there's the bedroom in the back of the wagon with its queen-sized bed, reading lights, and beautiful artwork. But perhaps the most envy-inducing feature of them all is the stacked washer and dryer set.

"I can't believe you can actually do your own laundry here."

"Can't you?"

"I don't even have a washer and dryer in my apartment."

"What about your Grambling Brothers accommodations?"

"I'm in a wagon with four bunks and no hot water."

"Seriously?"

"Yeah."

"That's interesting," he says. "In my experience, Claudius likes to keep the performers comfortable."

"Maybe it's because I haven't performed yet."

"I'm sure he'll upgrade you eventually."

I spot a phone charger beside one of the leather couches.

"May I?"

"Be my guest."

After I plug my dead phone into the charger, setting it face down on a glass-top end table, Solo invites me to take a seat on the Italian leather sofa.

"So," I say, "do all of the Soaring Silvas have their own wagons?"

"No, the family shares one together," he says. "I'm the only one who travels alone."

"Aren't you part of the family?"

Solo snorts a laugh.

"No, way," he says. "I'm more like an unwanted foster kid."

"I don't understand."

"I'm not a blood relative."

"But the rest of them are blood?"

"Yeah," he says. "An important part of the Soaring Silvas gimmick is to present ourselves as a family. The stalky one, Carlos, is the father, and the others are his kids. Ana, Jose, and Paulo."

I do some quick math in my head.

"Four of them plus you make five," I say. "But when I saw you guys perform, there were only four of you."

"I replaced Paulo."

"Which one is Paulo?"

"Lately, he's the one who runs the box office."

"The guy with the black eye and the busted arm?"

"That's him," he says. "He got injured a few months back."

"Did he fall off the trapeze or something?"

"Something like that," he says. "So, what's your act?"

I shrug, shaking my head.

"What's that mean?"

"It means I don't have an act."

"I don't get it."

"I mean, I *literally* don't have an act."

"Aren't you performing in a little while?"

"I don't even want to think about it."

"So, why would Claudius put you in the show if you don't have an act?"

"I'm not sure you'd believe me if I told you."

Solo smiles.

"Oh, okay," he says. "I think I understand. Your special, right?"

"Special?"

"Yeah," he says, "like me."

Solo stands up and shows me his palms.

"Looks normal, right?"

I nod, yes.

"Watch this."

Solo jumps straight up, touching the ceiling with the flats of his hands, and he doesn't come down. He swings his legs back and forth, hanging like his palms are super-glued to the ceiling.

"How did you do that?" I ask after he drops back down.

"My hands can stick to any surface."

"Like Spider-Man?"

"Exactly like Spider-Man," he says, "but only my hands. My feet can't stick to anything."

"Do your hands feel sticky?"

He holds them out for me.

"See for yourself."

I touch his palms, and they feel totally normal.

"As a trapeze artist, it's a great ability to have," he says. "Way better than a safety net."

"Do all the Soaring Silvas have Spider-Man hands?"

"No," he says, "they're world-class flyers who do it the old-fashioned way. Don't get me wrong, I still have to know what I'm doing up there. I've spent plenty of years learning my craft, but it just so happens that I also have the added benefit of sticky hands."

"That's amazing."

"Your turn," he says. "What makes you special?"

"I'm fireproof."

"Well, that's a new one," he says. "No wonder Claudius is so excited about you."

"Unfortunately, it doesn't change the reality that I don't have an act."

Solo leans forward, resting his elbows on his knees.

"You mind if I ask a personal question?"

"Sure."

"Was there any sort of emergency happening in your life when you met Claudius?"

"How did you know that?"

There's a knock at the door.

"Excuse me," Solo says, getting up to answer it.

"Is Grover here?" asks a voice from outside.

"Yeah, we're just hanging out."

Solo steps back as Fernando the Fearless Fire Tamer pokes his head inside the wagon.

"Hello, Grover," Fernando says, waving. "Do you remember me?"

"Of course," I say, standing up. "How are you?"

"I am good," he says. "Claudius sent me for you."

"He did?"

"Yes," he says. "Your performance is next."

My heart drops.

"Next?"

"Please," he says, motioning for me to join him, "we must go."

Chapter Nineteen

GROVER'S FIRST PERFORMANCE

F ERNANDO LEADS ME TO the big top, where the Ringmaster is
waiting outside of the back entrance. I can hear the audience
inside laughing at Charlie, Woodrow, and Annie. The Ringmaster
smiles as he sees us approach.

"It's almost time, Grover," he says. "Once the clowns are done,
I'll introduce you two. I want you each to come in separately. First,
Fernando, and then you. Fernando, after your introduction, give the
audience a little razzle-dazzle. As for you, Grover, after you hear your
introduction, come and join Fernando. Good luck, boys. I'll see you
inside."

Me *and* Fernando? This is certainly a wrinkle I wasn't expecting,
but before I can ask any follow-up questions, the Ringmaster has
already disappeared into the big top. I look to Fernando, hoping he
can shed some light on what's happening.

"I don't know much more than you do," Fernando says. "All
Claudius told me was that you and I are to perform together."

"When did he tell you that?"

"A few minutes ago," he says, "right before he sent me to get you. Did he not tell you the same?"

"No," I say. "This is the first I'm hearing of it."

A rousing ovation sounds inside the big top, followed by Charlie Chuckles and the Clown Alley Hooligans exiting. The clowns move past Fernando and me, disappearing into the labyrinth as the Ringmaster's booming voice begins our introduction.

"Ladies and gentlemen, it's time to prepare your eyes for a spectacle as amazing as it is dangerous, because your next performers trade in the most deadly element known to man. Fire! First up is a man whose mastery of flames will leave you breathless with wonder. A man whose otherworldly ability will deliver your imagination to a realm where fire reigns and danger pours. A man known in every corner of the world as Grambling Brothers' fantastic fiery phenom. Ladies and gentlemen, I present to you Fernando the Fearless Fire Tamer!"

Fernando gives me a thumbs-up before disappearing into the big top. I poke my head through the curtain, watching as he jogs to the center of the ring, where, waiting for him, is a steel barrel filled with dancing fire. From the dirt, Fernando picks up the rod that looks like a giant cotton swab; dipping each end into the flaming barrel, he creates a double-sided torch. As the sparse audience cheers him on, Fernando begins twirling the rod so fast that the flames create the illusion of a fiery circle.

May, the kind lady I met earlier today in front of the community bathroom, turns up in front of me as if from thin air.

"Hey, Grover," she says, "I just wanted to wish you good luck."

"Thank you."

"It looks like you put an act together since this morning."

"Looks can be deceiving."

"So, no act?"

"Nope."

She looks out at Fernando, then back at me.

"Well," she says, offering a half-smile, "I'm sure you'll be fine."

May disappears as Fernando flips the double-ended torch into the air and spins a full 720 degrees on his heel before dropping to a single knee and catching it with one hand behind his back. The audience offers a nice applause for his fiery razzle-dazzle.

"In just a moment," the Ringmaster says, "Fernando will be joined by a man so impossibly special, he's never appeared with any circus anywhere in the world—until tonight." This inspires a ripple of murmurs through the crowd. "He is a man who defies the laws of the scientific universe, whose very flesh is impervious to the hottest flames anywhere on Earth. If fire strikes fear in the heart of man, then your next performer is the man whom fire fears. Ladies and gentlemen, for the first time anywhere, I present to you Professor Grover the Fireproof Man!"

I stand frozen at the back of the big top, my head still poking through the curtains.

"Hey," May says, turning up again. "That's your cue."

I look at her, shaking my head.

"I can't do it."

"Yes, you can."

"How do you know?"

"Because," she says, gently touching her fingers to my cheek, "what other choice do you have?"

I suppose she's right. The only other choice I have is to turn and run the other way—but I also know that's not really an option.

So, I take a deep breath and step fully through the curtains into the big top. The spotlight finds me as I begin walking toward the center of the ring. The Ringmaster walks past me, offering a nod of encouragement as I join Fernando beside the flaming steel barrel.

"I'll take care of you," Fernando says as he circles me. "Just do as I say."

In mid-stride, he brings one end of the double-sided torch to his lips and blows a ferocious fireball into the air, inspiring a chorus of oohs and ahhs from the audience. He then stops in front of me, holding the torch between us.

"Take two steps forward."

I do as he says.

Holding the torch in one hand, Fernando uses his free hand to point at the upper flame, freezing his pudgy digit in place for several dramatic moments. He then methodically rotates his arm until that same pudgy digit is pointing directly at my face. The audience lets out a collective gasp as they interpret Fernando's wordless communication.

"Three nods," he says. "Don't move."

I don't know what that means, but I stay put.

Fernando nods.

Once.

Twice.

Three times.

Immediately following the third nod, a brilliant fireball blooms from Fernando's mouth, causing the audience to shriek in terror. As a matter of reflex, I squeeze my eyes shut while the fireball swallows my head. Even still, I can see a bright orange glow fluttering behind my closed eyelids.

Opening my eyes, I'm greeted by Fernando's smiling face.

"Wave to the people," he says. "Let them know you're okay."

I look out at the audience and wave, triggering a huge ovation.

"Now, hold out your arms," Fernando says, "like Jesus."

I hold out my arms, and, from behind the flaming steel barrel, Fernando picks up a bottle of lighter fluid. Squeezing the bottle, he drenches the front of my T-shirt. As the audience murmurs in anticipation of whatever Fernando has planned, he circles behind me and squirts the back of my T-shirt. With my shirt properly doused, he next squirts lighter fluid on my pants. Tossing the bottle to the side, he positions the torch between us. He takes a deep breath through his nose and nods three times before blowing a fireball at my chest. The force of the fireball feels like a mild gust of wind as it pushes against me. Instantly, my T-shirt goes up in flames, and, in an unexpected reflex of panic, I begin slapping myself to try and put the fire out.

"Let it burn," Fernando says.

As the flames on my T-shirt lick my chin, Fernando circles behind me and blows a fireball against my back, then another against my legs—and then another and another, one fireball after the next, until, for the second time in my life, my whole body is engulfed in flames. The sight of my fiery cocoon inspires shrieks and howls from the audience, and, after several dramatic moments, my T-shirt falls to the dirt. Normally, being shirtless in front of anybody—let alone a paying audience—would be mortifying, as I've spent most of my life harboring severe insecurities about my soft physique, but, in this specific moment, I feel oddly at ease.

With my T-shirt smoldering in the dirt, I'm left—like the proverbial liar, liar—with my pants on fire. Fernando squirts more lighter fluid on my pants, breathing renewed life into the flames.

"Run around the ring," he says, circling his finger in the air. "Let them see you."

I start jogging around the perimeter of the ring, close enough for people in the first couple rows to hear the whoosh of the flames with each stride.

"Go, go!" Fernando says, clapping his hands with each syllable. "Faster, faster!"

I do as he says, picking up speed as I run another full lap around the ring. During my next lap, as my aching lungs remind me of my abysmal cardiovascular condition, I slow down to a trot. Even at this slower pace, the effect of jogging in my flaming pants seems to have heightened the audience's excitement.

Just as I allow myself to be pleasantly surprised with how well everything is going, my flaming pants collapse around my ankles, and I trip face-first into the dirt. The audience bursts into laughter as I struggle to get back to my feet; they continue laughing as I sit in the dirt, kicking the flaming pants off from around my ankles. I jump up to my feet, triumphantly raising my arms in the air to show the audience I'm okay, but they're still laughing. Confused, I look to Fernando, but he's standing slack-jawed and staring down below my waist. I follow his eyes down and see my naked manhood hanging out for all to see.

Shit.

I totally forgot I wasn't wearing underwear, so, except for the shoes on my feet, I'm standing completely naked in front of the audience. Cupping my hands over my sensitive area, all I want to do is run out of the big top and crawl into the first dark hole I can find, but the shock and embarrassment of the moment leave me frozen in place. Fernando is still slack-jawed, and the audience is still laughing when Charlie Chuckles and the Clown Alley Hooligans turn up from behind me in their hollow Volkswagen.

"Hey, kid," Charlie says, opening his door, "lug that big dick of yours in here."

I step inside the Volkswagen, still hiding my manhood beneath my hands. I assume we're going to head straight out of the big top, but Charlie leads us around the perimeter of the ring. The audience goes from laughing to cheering, and just like that, it feels like we're doing a victory lap. Following our victory lap, Charlie leads us out of the big top. We cross paths with the Ringmaster as he heads back to the center of the ring, but he doesn't acknowledge us.

"Alright, kid," Charlie says, once we're outside, "this is your stop."

As soon as I exit the Volkswagen, Charlie, Annie, and Woodrow turn around and head right back inside. Fernando, who is also outside—and, seemingly, unfazed by my exposed nether region—gives me a big hug.

"Great job!" he says. "They loved it!"

"We did good?"

"We did *very* good!"

Fernando excuses himself before disappearing into the labyrinth, leaving me naked and alone behind the big top.

Chapter Twenty

CURTAIN CALL

I'M NOT ALONE FOR long before Solo turns up.

"Great work out there," he says.

"Thank you," I say, shielding my dick with both hands.

"So, were you planning on staying naked the rest of the night?"

"No," I say, "I just don't have any extra clothes here."

"That's no problem," he says. "I'll grab you something to wear. Be right back."

For the second time tonight, Solo has come to my rescue. I don't know why he's decided to be so nice to me, but I'm grateful for it nonetheless. While he's gone, the soaring Silvas arrive in anticipation of their performance. They look at me with some combination of confusion and disdain. Our awkward silence is broken only when Solo returns.

"Hey, guys," he says. "Have you met Grover?"

The barrel-chested patriarch of the Soaring Silvas looks at him, grunting something under his breath that I can only assume is an unflattering remark about me. Any potential for that conversation to go any further is interrupted by the clowns exiting the big top. As the Ringmaster begins his introduction of the Soaring Silvas, Solo quickly hands me the clothes before disappearing into the big top with his compatriots.

As I'm getting dressed, Charlie Chuckles approaches me.

"Nice work out there, kid."

"Thank you," I say, zipping up my fly. "I honestly didn't know what I was doing."

"Improvisation is a good skill to have as a performer," he says. "Not to mention that monster between your legs."

"Pardon?"

"I never would've guessed you were walking around with a third leg, kid."

I'm not sure what the appropriate response is, so I sort of laugh and shrug at the same time.

"I'm serious," Charlie says. "Your back must be on fire twenty-four hours a day."

"Oh, for Christ's sake, Charlie," Annie says. "Give the kid a break."

"I'm not joking around," Charlie says. "If I had a schlong like that, I'd be raking in the dough on Pornhub rather than yucking it up with you two."

"Go to hell," Annie says.

"Already here," Charlie says. "Now, kid, don't get me wrong, my little bean pole is blessed in its own way, but length and girth have never been my cross to bear."

"He's not lying about that," Annie says.

"Fuck you," Charlie says. "You never complained when I was fracking *your* sugar walls."

Woodrow clears his throat.

"Maybe that's enough talk of the past," he says.

"Maybe you're right, Woody," Charlie says. "I'm gonna go rub one out."

"Are you fucking kidding?" Annie says. "It's almost time for the curtain call."

"I won't be long," Charlie says. "But you already knew that."

Charlie disappears into the labyrinth as the rest of the night's performers begin turning up behind the big top—including Handsome Harry. There's a palpable tension in the air as Handsome Harry stands a few feet away from me. I think everyone—myself included—is expecting him to continue where he left off, but, thankfully, Fernando slips in between us, creating a buffer (the buffer is more symbolic than anything else, as I'm sure Handsome Harry could smash both of us at once if he chose to).

Inside the big top, the Ringmaster is wrapping up the show.

"We here at the Grambling Brothers Traveling Circus Show are genuinely humbled and honored that you chose to spend your evening with us," he says. "Now, before you leave, please welcome back our talented performers!"

The Ringmaster first calls for Swift Sammy.

Then Charlie Chuckles and the Clown Alley Hooligans.

Then Handsome Harry.

Then the Soaring Silvas (who are still inside).

Then Fernando.

"And finally," the Ringmaster says, "welcome back our newest performer, Professor Grover the Fireproof Man!"

As soon as I enter the big top, I'm showered with applause. I jog to the center of the ring, joining the rest of the performers. We stand together in a line, shoulder to shoulder. One at a time, each performer takes a bow, and, when it's my turn, I receive the loudest ovation of the night. Though the Soaring Silvas don't say as much, it's very clear from the looks on their faces that they don't appreciate the audience's response to me. The Ringmaster bids the audience goodnight before leading us out of the big top. Once we're back outside, I assume he's going to give us some sort of post-show speech, but the Ringmaster, along with everyone else, disappears into the labyrinth.

Just when I think I'm on my own for the night, Canyon shows up.

"Hey, bro," he says. "How'd you do?"

"Good," I say. "I think it went well."

"That's awesome," he says. "Listen, me and the boys are going to get started breaking down the big top, but the wagon is unlocked for you, so let yourself in when you're ready to call it a night."

"Thank you."

"Also," he says, "you've got some fans waiting for you at the box office."

"Fans?"

"Yeah," he says. "You must've put on quite a show."

I walk to the box office, where I find my mom waiting for me, along with two of my students from Chandler College—a boy and a girl whose names, embarrassingly, I can't remember. Before I can say a word to any of them, Mom wraps me up in a hug.

"When did you learn how to do all that with the fire?"

I interpret her question to mean that she didn't hear any of my fireproof confession over the phone. While I hate to do it, lying feels like the most appropriate option at this point.

"It's just a hobby I've been playing with."

"You never told us about this hobby."

"I didn't think Dad would approve."

"You're probably right."

The boy student raises his hand.

"Yes?" I say.

"How do you do the fire stuff without getting burned?"

"It's complicated."

"That means he's not going to tell us," the girl student says.

"In that case," Mom says, "maybe you can tell us whose idea it was for you to get buck naked."

This makes both students howl with laughter.

"Good grief," I say, my cheeks growing warm with embarrassment. "This is my mother, by the way."

"Oh, we've already met," Mom says.

"Yeah," the girl student says, "we even showed her the video."

"What video?"

"I recorded your performance on my phone."

My stomach drops.

"Um...how much did you record?"

"I got the full monty."

This leads to more laughter.

"We should get going," the boy student says. "But it was awesome watching you perform, Professor."

"Yeah," the girl student says. "Good luck with your new career."

The students walk away, leaving me alone with Mom.

"I guess I should be going as well," she says. "I don't want to leave your father alone for too long."

"How is Dad?"

"He's still stable."

"I don't feel right leaving you alone," I say. "I'll go with you."

"I'm not alone," she says, giving me a hug. "Plus, you're with the circus now, so I want you to enjoy this for however long it lasts. Enjoy every last bit of it, okay?"

I walk Mom to her car before heading back to the labyrinth, where I quickly get lost looking for Canyon's wagon. After nearly twenty minutes, I finally find it. The door is open just as Canyon said it would be, so I let myself in and plop down on an empty bunk. Staring up into the darkness, I replay the show over and over again in my head, smiling as I drift off to sleep.

Chapter Twenty-One

KING POLE

I'M NUDGED AWAKE BY the rumbling and tumbling of the open road. For a few moments, I'm not fully aware of where I am or what's happening, but, soon enough, reality trickles into the folds of my groggy memory, and I remember falling asleep in Canyon's wagon after last night's show. Prying my eyes open, I see Darius asleep in the bunk beside me, while Canyon is manning the driver's seat up front, captaining this rickety ship. I stand up from my bunk, gingerly making my way to the passenger seat, where I plop down in front of a windshield that's as large as it is filthy, framing a glorious morning sky as the road ahead slices through a vast desert of dirt and rocks.

"There he is!" Canyon says, taking a sip from a can of Red Bull.

"Morning," I say. "I didn't realize we'd left."

"Yeah, you were way deep in dreamland, bro."

"Where're we going?"

"Vegas," he says. "We just passed Stateline before you woke up."

I notice a photograph taped to the dashboard. It's Canyon sitting on a brown sofa with a little girl on his lap.

"Is that your daughter?"

"Yeah, she's my little genius," he says. "She wants to be one of those science-y people who lives on a boat and listens to whales."

"I didn't even know that was a thing."

"Me neither," he says with a laugh.

"How did she learn about it?"

"At school," he says. "My girlfriend found out about this private school with good teachers and computers and shit like that, way better than the stuff I had growing up."

"That sounds cool," I say. "How much does that cost?"

"Honestly, I don't know," he says. "The big man pays for it."

"The big man?"

"Claudius," he says. "I could never afford it myself, especially back when I was drowning in medical bills."

"Medical bills for your daughter?"

"Not for her, thank God," he says. "For me."

"What happened?"

"I used to work as a house painter," he says, "so I spent a lot of time up on ladders and shit. Then, one day, I fell." He taps the Red Bull can against his temple. "My head bounced off the pavement like a basketball."

"God, that sounds horrible."

"The falling part was easy," he says. "The only part I remember is waking up in the hospital with my girlfriend crying over me."

"That's wild."

"The doctors told me there were problems with my brain after that," he says. "I was having trouble with my speech and memory and whatnot. After they sent me home, that's when I got the bill. Fuck me, bro, I ain't never seen so many zeroes in my life. Plus, they weren't done with me! There were follow-up visits and speech therapy and prescriptions and whatnot, so those zeroes just kept piling up."

"That sounds rough."

"Yeah, it was," he says. "Not the accident part, though. I grew up tough, so I can deal with bumping my head. But the money part, bro? That shit was a fucking nightmare. My daughter was still young, so she didn't know what all was going on. I just wanted to give her the world, you know, but, with all those bills stacking up, I felt like she wasn't going to have a real chance in life."

"Were you getting disability?"

"Nah," he says. "The house-painting gig was under the table, so I couldn't go to Uncle Sam for help. My girlfriend kept us going as good as she could, waitressing and whatnot, but I needed to figure out how to start bringing in money. Luckily, I met Claudius."

"How'd you meet him?"

"I was just buying donuts for my daughter one day, and Claudius was in there drinking a cup of coffee," he says. "Turns out, Grambling Brothers was in town, so he starts telling me how he needs extra help on his tent crew. Now, me, I know how to hustle, so I start telling him how I'm good with my hands and whatnot, and he asks if I know anything about tents. I tell him I ain't never been camping in my life, but if he's got a paycheck for me, I can figure it the fuck out. That made him laugh, so we kept talking. I tell him about my accident and all the medical bills and whatnot and how I want to send my little girl to a good school, so he offers me a job. He tells me there's a lot of travel and I'll be away from home, but he also offers to pay off my bills, and he even says he'll pay for my little girl to go to any school I want to send her to."

"When he said all that, did you believe him?"

"Fuck no!" he says, laughing. "Where I come from, people don't just hand shit out like Santa Clause. I mean, why the fuck would this man do all that for a stranger he just met in a donut shop, right? But, at that point, I was pretty desperate for a break, so I figured, what's the harm? I'll take the gig, and if he's full of shit, I'll just turn around and go home. The way I saw it, the worst-case scenario is I'd be out of a job." Canyon pauses, tapping his temple again with the Red Bull can. "Well, actually, the *worst*-case scenario would be another accident with my dome. The doctors told me my brain couldn't take another shot like that."

"What would happen?"

"The way they explained it to me, it would be lights out," he says. "A one-way ticket to the pearly gates."

"Shit, that's scary, man."

"Yeah, but it's alright," he says. "I don't gotta climb ladders no more. Plus, my girlfriend hasn't seen one medical bill since I started working for Grambling Brothers."

"Really?"

"She even called all the doctors just to be sure," he says. "They told her we don't owe nothing."

"And your daughter gets to go to her nice private school?"

"Yeah, bro," he says. "She's doing fucking good, too."

"It's uncanny how similar our stories are," I say. "That's almost exactly how Claudius got me to join."

"Is that right?"

"Yeah, my dad's in the hospital right now, and Claudius offered to cover all of the medical costs."

"Oh, yeah?"

"Yeah," I say. "Crazy, right?"

"It's definitely crazy," he says. "Plus, you're also one of the specials, right?"

"Specials?"

"Yeah," he says, "the people with magic abilities and whatnot. Like how you're fireproof."

"You know about that?"

"I hear things," he says, taking a sip from his Red Bull. "If you're wondering, I'm not one of the specials. Darius, neither. We're just a couple of working-class grunts."

"That's cool."

"Remember, May?"

"The nice lady I met yesterday?"

"That's the one," he says. "She's a special."

"She is?"

"Yeah, she can make herself invisible."

"Invisible? Like Sue Storm?"

"Sue who?"

"Sue Storm," I say. "She's part of the Fantastic Four."

"Never heard of them."

"They're comic book superheroes," I say. "Sue Storm is the Invisible Woman."

"I never got into comic books, bro," he says. "I was too busy trying to get laid."

"I guess I was too busy *not* getting laid."

This makes Canyon laugh.

"The funny thing about May is she doesn't talk about being one of the specials."

"Why not?"

"I don't know," he says with a shrug. "We got drunk one night, and she let it slip. But when I asked her about it the next day, she acted like she didn't know what I was talking about."

"That's kind of weird, right?" I ask. "I mean, why would she want to keep it a secret?"

"Around here," he says, "everyone's got secrets."

We arrive somewhere called Summerlin, a very affluent community about twenty minutes from the Las Vegas Strip. All of the trucks, trailers, and wagons are settling in a dirt lot behind a shopping center called Boca Park; in a few hours, this is where the big top will stand. Canyon parks our wagon amongst the labyrinth-in-progress, and we go to Vik's dukey truck for a quick breakfast. Darius stays behind to catch some extra Z's. After breakfast, I tag along with Canyon as he joins the tent crew to begin raising the big top. I watch as the various members of the tent crew pound stakes into the dirt with razor-sharp precision, gradually forming a large circle. Some members of the tent crew lay out large pieces of rolled-up canvas, while others work together to carry over a very tall pole.

"That's the king pole."

I turn to see May standing beside me, appearing as if from thin air. She's wearing blue jeans and a form-fitting flannel shirt with the sleeves rolled up.

"What's the king pole?"

"It's the main pole we use for standing up the big top," she says. "The king pole gives the tent its structure. It also supports its weight and maintains its stability. It kind of does a little bit of everything."

"Sort of like you, right?"

"Yeah," she says, smiling. "sort of like me."

A husky man with a round belly calls for May, whistling with his thumb and forefinger in his mouth.

"I should go see what this guy needs."

"No rest for the weary, huh?"

"Why rest when you can work yourself ragged instead?"

"I guess that's an option."

May laughs.

"Catch you later, Grover."

After May leaves, I continue watching the tent crew work. Once the king pole is erect—anchored with a series of ropes and wires—they crew starts unrolling the large pieces of canvas inside the circle of stakes, pulling each piece together and lacing them with rope. While I'm curious to see the whole process unfold, I remember Canyon telling me it takes several hours to raise the big top, so I decide instead to wander around to see what else is going on.

As I walk through the part of the dirt lot that will eventually become the midway, I see Xyla walking toward me. She waves hello, and, before waving back, I look around to make sure Handsome Harry is nowhere in sight.

"Morning, superstar," she says. "What's it like being famous?"

"I wouldn't know," I say with a laugh. "You're better off asking someone who's actually famous."

"Right now, you're the most famous person I know," she says. "Have you seen the video?"

"What video?"

She smiles, her eyes growing big.

"You don't know about the video?"

"No," I say. "Should I?"

"I take it you haven't been on your phone."

I pat my pockets, triggering a jolt of panic in my chest when I don't feel the familiar rectangle of glass and steel in my pants. For a moment, I worry my phone might've burned up during last night's performance before remembering I left it charging in Solo's wagon. Xyla pulls out her phone, holding it out so I can see the screen. There's a YouTube video queued up titled "OMG this is my professor on FIRE in the circus!!"

She presses play.

I watch Fernando blow fireballs at me, engulfing me in flames. My T-shirt burns off of my torso, followed shortly after by me tripping over my burning pants. The sound of the audience laughing punctuates my clumsy efforts to kick the flaming pants off from around my ankles. When I get back up to my feet, unwittingly nude for everyone to see, my student recording the video yells, "That's my fucking professor!" Mercifully, my cock has been concealed with an eggplant emoji.

"The video's gone viral," Xyla says. "It already has over a million views."

She points to her screen at the official view count.

1,012,977.

"Oh, God!"

"Right now, at this very moment, you may be the most famous circus performer in the whole world," Xyla says. "Not bad for your first night on the job."

"Over a million people have seen me naked?"

"I don't think the naked part is the main takeaway."

As we finish watching the video, Charlie Chuckles—sans clown makeup—runs towards us, waving his phone in the air.

"Hey, kid!" he says. "You're a fucking star!"

"I just saw the video on YouTube."

"Fuck YouTube," he says. "You and your king pole are trending on Pornhub!"

Chapter Twenty-Two

JUGGLING APPLES

I HURRY THROUGH THE labyrinth on the lookout for Solo's wagon. When I find it, Solo is sitting outside on a lawn chair, beneath an attached awning, enjoying a cup of coffee.

"Morning, Grover."

"Hey," I say. "I think I left my phone inside your wagon."

"Door's open," he says. "Pour yourself a cup while you're in there."

I run inside, relieved to find my phone beside the couch where I left it.

"Checking your YouTube views?" Solo asks as I exit.

"You heard about that?"

"Oh, yeah," he says. "I think everybody has."

"Charlie Chuckles said there's an uncensored version of the video on Pornhub."

"Is that right?"

"It's mortifying."

"It could be worse."

"How?"

"You could be anonymous."

I open YouTube and see that the view count has gone up since just a few minutes ago.

"I almost forgot," Solo says. "Claudius wants to see you."

Entering the Ringmaster's office, I see Fernando sitting across from him at his desk. They each turn their heads as I enter, watching me as I take a seat beside Fernando. There's a certain silence in the air that doesn't feel sudden, like the two of them have been sitting here—wordlessly—in anticipation of my arrival. If I wasn't nervous about this surprise meeting before, I most certainly am now.

"So," the Ringmaster says, lighting a fresh cigar between his lips, "last night was interesting."

Gulp.

"How do you feel it went?" he asks, looking at me.

"Um...good? I guess?"

"You thought it was good?"

I wish I could be anywhere in the world but here.

"I mean...I don't know, I guess," I say. "It was my first time, so..."

I trail off because I'm horrified by whatever's happening and I don't know what else to say.

"Well, it seems you and I have different opinions of how your performance last night went."

He pulls a drag from his cigar, blowing a plume of smoke into the air. I'm not sure if I'm meant to respond, so I say nothing as the smoke dissipates between us.

"While you thought last night's performance was *good*," the Ringmaster says, "I thought it was *great*."

Fernando and I perk up in unison like a couple of meerkats.

"I also think you two make a good pairing."

"Thank you," Fernando says, speaking up for the first time since I got here. "And, may I say, I greatly appreciated the opportunity to perform in the big top."

"You're welcome," the Ringmaster says. "For the foreseeable future, I want you two to continue working together."

"It will be my honor," Fernando says with the enthusiasm of a child opening a present on Christmas morning. "Thank you."

"Grover," the Ringmaster says, "I assume you're comfortable with this arrangement."

"Definitely."

"Good," he says. "Incidentally, did Fernando inform you about his supernatural ability?"

Fernando?

Supernatural?

"No," I say.

The Ringmaster smiles.

"As you are now intimately familiar," the Ringmaster says, "Fernando is a fire-breather. Traditionally, fire-breathing is a combination of science and skill. The fire-breather puts a flammable liquid in their mouth, such as paraffin, then sprays it out in a fine mist against an open flame, igniting it into a spectacular ball of fire. Now, with that in mind, is that what you saw Fernando do last night?"

I reflect on the events of last night as best as I can, but my memories are largely a blur.

"Yes," I say, finally, "I think that's what I saw."

"Are you sure?"

"I mean...no, I guess not."

"Let me ask you this," the Ringmaster says. "At any point, did you notice Fernando put a flammable liquid into his mouth?"

"I don't think so, no."

"This then begs the question," he says. "How did Fernando breathe fire without using a flammable liquid?"

I shrug, shaking my head.

"Fernando," the Ringmaster says, "tell Grover how you do it."

"I create it from the inside," Fernando says. "The fire comes from within me."

"Isn't that amazing, Grover?" the Ringmaster says. "Fernando is a genuine fire-breather. If he had wings and a tail, he might pass for a dragon."

"Wow," I say, genuinely amazed. "I had no idea."

"I thought you'd find that interesting," the Ringmaster says. "Now, let's get to more pressing matters. Why were you naked in front of my audience last night?"

My chest tightens.

"I'm sorry," I say. "That was a total accident."

"There were children."

"Claudius," Fernando says, raising his hand, "if I may speak, what happened to Grover's clothes was my fault."

The Ringmaster looks at Fernando, then back at me.

"What's done is done," the Ringmaster says. "Don't let it happen again. Fernando, please excuse yourself. I'd like to speak with Grover in private."

Fernando exits the office without another word, leaving me alone with the Ringmaster.

"So," he says, tapping his cigar over an ashtray, "how are you assimilating?"

"Good."

"Are you making friends?"

"Yes," I say. "I've met some very nice people."

"That's good," he says. "It's important to make friends in the circus. I'm proud to say that, once upon a time, I was friends with Walter Grambling."

"Really?"

"Oh, yes," he says. "Walter and his eleven older brothers grew up on a farm outside of Opelousas, Louisiana. They lived in crippling poverty, but it was also a time when children were not financial liabilities. All twelve Grambling brothers were put to work on the farm just as soon as they were able, helping to grow various fruits, like apples and figs. Walter and his brothers spent much of their childhood selling the family's fruit from a cart outside of the farm. It was while selling fruit that the oldest brother, Irving, discovered he could draw a crowd by juggling apples. The bigger the crowd, the more fruit they sold. It wasn't long before Irving's knack for showmanship got him a job in a small traveling circus. After performing for a few years, Irving got the idea of starting his own circus with his brothers. As you might imagine, the Grambling parents weren't keen on this idea at first, as their boys were the prime labor force that kept the farm viable. So, to put their concerns at ease, Irving came up with the idea of making the circus part of the farm. He assured his parents that the spectacle of a big top would attract paying customers—and he was right."

The Ringmaster stands from his desk and walks to the window. Pressing his fingers against the glass, he gazes outside.

"Irving named their venture the Grambling Brothers Circus," he says. "He even convinced a few of his circus friends to perform in the show. In short order, people from all the surrounding parishes began showing up, and the Grambling Brothers Circus started earning more money than the family farm itself. In the face of their newfound success, it was Walter, the youngest brother, who had the idea of taking the circus on the road. He first proposed traveling to the Yambilee Festival in St. Landry Parish, which, if you couldn't tell from the name, is a festival to celebrate yams. Walter's idea proved to be a hit, as every show they performed at the Yambilee Festival was a turnaway."

"A turnaway?"

"That's circus jargon for sold out," the Ringmaster says. "Following the success at the Yambilee Festival, Irving convinced his parents to retire the farm altogether so he and his brothers could take the circus on the road full-time. Once they hit the road, they altered the name of their show to the Grambling Brothers Traveling Circus."

The Ringmaster raps his knuckles against the window pane before sitting back down at his desk.

"I wish I could've met Irving and the others," he says, "but Walter was the only brother who remained when they merged with General Panda. After a time, Walter quietly disappeared into retirement, but General Panda didn't want to run the circus by himself, so he asked me to run it with him. We successfully ran Grambling Brothers together for several years, right up until the day General Panda went away."

"Where did he go?"

The Ringmaster smiles, exhaling a plume of smoke.

"That's a tale for another day," he says, scissoring his cigar between his thick fingers. "For today, the takeaway I want you to walk out that door with is that this circus has been in my care for a very long time. My responsibility is not simply to the men and women who work under my watch, but to the legacy of Walter Grambling and each of his brothers. As of last night, you're now a part of that legacy, Grover, and it's my hope that you'll come to appreciate the gravity of that responsibility."

The Ringmaster opens a drawer in his desk, pulling out a white envelope.

"With that in mind," he says, sliding the envelope across the desk, "no more nudity."

"You have my word," I say. "Would you like me to see about taking down the YouTube video?"

"No, that won't be necessary," he says. "However, I will see to it that the Pornhub video is removed."

Inside the envelope is a thick stack of cash.

"Is this all for me?"

"You earned it," he says, "and there's going to be more where that came from."

"Oh my God, thank you!"

"Last night was the beginning of something very special," he says. "I look forward to having you here with us for a long, long time."

Chapter Twenty-Three

WEREWOLF SYNDROME

I'M HEADED BACK TO Canyon's wagon to drop off my envelope of cash when I see Bastian the Boisterous Barker and Pedro the Orphan Wolf Boy. They're sitting at a foldout card table outside of what I assume is their wagon. Pedro is leaning back in his chair, arms crossed, as he scowls at a spiral notebook in front of him.

"Don't get frustrated," Bastian says. "It's just homework."

I don't realize I've stopped in front of their table until Bastian speaks to me.

"Hey, Grover," he says. "Heck of a debut last night."

"You were there?"

"No," he says, "but I saw the video."

"Oh, geez," I say. "That's embarrassing."

"Dude, over a million people know who you are now," he says. "I'd give my left nut to be embarrassed like that."

"I'd trade with you if I could," I say. "What are you guys up to?"

"I'm just helping Pedro with his homework."

"There's a school here?"

"No," Bastian says, "but me and some of the other parents try to find learning activities for the kids, so they can get some semblance of an education while we're on the road."

"Pedro's your son?"

"No," Pedro says without looking up.

"He just likes to be particular with the facts," Bastian says. "I'm more like a guardian. And, occasionally, I try to be his teacher, but that's not going very well today."

"What's he working on?"

"An essay," Bastian says. "The instructions say to select two similar things and compare them."

"A compare-and-contrast essay?"

"That's exactly it," he says, sounding impressed. "How'd you know?"

"I'm an English professor," I say. "I mean, I *used* to be an English professor."

"That's swell," he says. "Maybe you can help?"

Bastian shows me his phone with the writing prompt on the screen, and I take a minute to read it.

"This is pretty straightforward," I say, "but I'm not sure it's intended for someone as young as Pedro. How old is he, by the way?"

"Ten."

"Okay, well, that may be part of the issue," I say. "This assignment is intended for a high school or college student."

"Oh, shit," Bastian says. "Really?"

"Yeah, but I can modify it for him," I say. "First, we'll adjust the expectation. This prompt is asking for a five-page essay, so let's change it to one page."

"Okay."

"Pedro," I say, "do you like reading?"

"Uh-huh."

"What kind of books do you like?"

"Comics."

"Perfect!" I say. "I love comic books."

"Aren't you too old for comics?"

"You're never too old for comics," I say. "What's your favorite?"

"Spider-Man."

"Yeah, I like him, too," I say. "Who's your second favorite?"

Pedro rests his chin on his fist, considering his answer.

"Batman, I think," he says. "But I like Superman, too. And Iron Man."

"Let me ask you this," I say. "What do you like about superheroes?"

"Their superpowers," he says, "and their costumes and how they fight and stuff."

"Yeah, that stuff is cool," I say. "You said you like Batman, right?"

"Uh-huh."

"What are Batman's superpowers?"

"He doesn't have any."

"So, if Batman doesn't have superpowers," I say, "does that mean he isn't a superhero?"

"No, he's still a superhero."

"Interesting," I say. "So, what makes him a superhero?"

This briefly stumps him.

"I think maybe because he wears a cape."

"That's it!" I say. "You've figured it out. All superheroes wear capes."

Pedro furrows his brow.

"No," he says. "Spider-Man doesn't wear a cape."

"Shoot, you're right," I say. "So, some superheroes wear capes, but some don't. And some superheroes have superpowers, but some don't. Well, are all superheroes boys?"

"No, some are girls."

"Like who?"

"Wonder Woman. Captain Marvel. Batgirl. Black Widow. Harley Quinn. She-Hulk."

"Wow," I say, "this is getting more and more complicated. It seems like superheroes have some traits that are the same, but then they also have some traits that are different."

I can see Pedro's mind working.

"I have an idea," I say. "You should make a list. In fact, you should make *two* lists."

I take a seat next to him.

"Do you have a blank sheet of paper?"

He tears a sheet from his spiral notebook.

"Thank you," I say. "Can I borrow your pencil?"

He hands me his pencil, and at the top of the page I write "Batman vs. Superman." I draw a line straight down the center of the page, creating two columns. At the top of the first column, I write the word "Same," and at the top of the second column, I write the word "Different."

"Here's what I want you to do for me," I say. "On the side of the page that says 'Same,' I want you to make a list of all the ways that Batman and Superman are the same."

"Like how they both wear capes?"

"Exactly," I say. "And on the side of the page that says 'Different,' make a list of all the ways they're different."

"Like how Superman can fly, but Batman can't?"

"You got it!" I say. "Work on that for a while and see if you can fill up both columns. Then, when the list is done, we can look at it together. Sound good?"

"Okay."

I hand Pedro his pencil, and, with great excitement, he gets to work. Bastian stands up from the table and invites me inside his wagon, where he offers me a beer as he grabs one for himself. I opt for a bottle of water instead.

"That was amazing," he says, taking a drink. "I've never seen him so excited about doing homework before."

"Glad I could help."

"Pedro can be defensive around new people," he says, "mostly on account of his condition. But he warmed up to you really easily."

"If you don't mind me asking," I say, "what condition does he have?"

"It's called hypertrichosis," he says. "Some folks call it Werewolf Syndrome. It just means he grows a lot of hair all over his body. You ever hear of Alice Elizabeth Doherty?"

"No."

"She was a girl born with blond hair all over her body, two inches long," he says. "This was in the late 1800s, so her parents didn't know what the hell to do with her besides put her in the circus. She earned a fortune as a sideshow exhibit."

"Did either of her parents have Werewolf Syndrome?"

"No," he says. "Sometimes it can be passed down, but not always."

"What about Pedro's parents?"

"His mom didn't have it," he says. "I never met his dad."

"Are his parents still alive?"

"It's hard to say," he says. "Pedro's dad was never really in the picture, so I have no idea what his situation is. I knew his mom, though. She was a circus performer. That's how we met."

"What did she do in the circus?"

"Contortionist," he says. "She and I were romantic for a while, and the three of us got along like a nice little family. Then, one day, out of the blue, our circus went under. Just like that, we were out of work. Things got tough in a great big hurry. One day, his mom shows up at my apartment with Pedro and asks if I can look after him while she runs some errands. I haven't seen her since."

"That must've been heartbreaking for Pedro."

"Yeah, it was tough on the kid," he says. "But he eventually bounced back. Kids can be resilient that way."

"How long ago did she leave him with you?"

"I hardly remember anymore," he says. "Five, maybe six years ago. Long enough to know she ain't coming back." He takes a swig of beer. "I was barely keeping a roof over my head at the time, so I had no idea how I was going to take care of the both of us."

"How did you manage?"

"Performing is the only thing I know how to do," he says, "so I developed an act for me and the kid. Things were lean for a while, and we went several stretches without food. There were a lot of nights when Pedro cried himself to sleep in my arms. Then one day, like a miracle, Claudius shows up and offers us a job. We've been with Grambling Brothers ever since."

Bastian leans in, and I get the impression he wants to tell me something more, but he's interrupted by the sound of a flushing toilet. The bathroom door swings open, and out pops Geno the World's Shortest Giant.

"Oh, hey," Geno says, pointing at me, "you're the fire guy."

"Geno," Bastian says, "this is Grover."

"I saw you on Pornhub," Geno says. "Are you really fireproof?"

"Yeah."

"Figures," he says. "Claudius loves the specials."

"Are there a lot of specials here?"

"Depends on what you mean by *a lot*," he says with a shrug. "But there's more than a few."

"Are you two...um...?"

"Special?" he says, finishing my question. "Nope. And, despite the fur, Pedro isn't either. We're just a couple of average joes with unique looks and marketable gimmicks. Anyway," he says, heading for the door, "I'm gonna grab some chow. Nice meeting you, Grover."

He exits, leaving me and Bastian alone.

"So," Bastian says, "can you work with Pedro again tomorrow?"

"Sure," I say. "What time?"

"Same time, if that works for you."

"Yeah, that'll work."

Bastian and I go back outside to check on Pedro, where we find him deep in concentration as he works on his Superman vs. Batman list.

"Pedro," Bastian says, "Grover's going to come back tomorrow to help you some more."

He nods without looking up.

"Trust me," Bastian tells me, "he's very excited."

Chapter Twenty-Four

THE CLOWN ALLEY HOOLIGANS

I LEAVE BASTIAN'S PLACE and wander aimlessly around the labyrinth until I run into Charlie Chuckles.

"Hey, kid," he says, throwing his arm around my shoulders. "What're you up to?"

Even though we don't really know each other, there's something comforting about how chummy he is with me. Plus, I still greatly appreciate how he and the rest of the Clown Alley Hooligans came to my rescue when I was naked in the middle of the big top.

"Nothing," I say. "Just taking a walk."

"Well, shit, you should come with me."

"Where to?"

"I'm headed to a skanky part of town to get my wang doodled."

"You're doing what?"

"I'm gonna get my jack hammered."

"Sorry?"

"I'm gonna get my gas pumped."

"Huh?"

"Kid, is this a bit, or are you really this dense?" he asks. "I'm gonna get some touchy-touchy between my belly button and my asshole."

I stare at him in silence, unsure of what else to say. Luckily, Annie and Woodrow turn up before this gets any more awkward.

"Leave the kid alone," Annie says.

"Mind your business," Charlie tells her. "I wanna see the look on their faces when he pulls that python out of his shorts."

"Wait, what's happening?" I ask.

"Nothing's happening," Annie says. "You're coming with me and Woodrow."

"Don't do it, kid," Charlie says. "There's no happy ending where they're headed."

"C'mon," Annie says, pulling me by my arm.

"Suit yourself, kid," Charlie says. "But, when you end up with Smurf balls, don't come crying to me."

I walk with Annie and Woodrow to Target, which is on the other side of the empty dirt lot where the tent crew is raising the big top. Annie grabs a red shopping cart for us, leaning her elbows on the handle as she pushes it through the store. A burst of air conditioning hits us as we enter. There's a Starbucks near the entrance with a line of people curling out towards the self-checkout area. Woodrow starts making his way over to the line, but, when Annie snaps her fingers, he quickly turns back around to join us.

"Apologies, my dear," he says. "Perhaps on the way out."

"We'll see," Annie says. "So, Grover, what's the story with you and Xyla?"

"What do you mean?"

"You two dating?"

"No, nothing like that," I say. "We're just friends."

"That's not what the birds are singing," she says. "Word is, you two have something romantic happening."

I grab some toothpaste and soap, dropping them into the cart.

"Who said that?"

"Everybody," Woodrow says.

Annie slaps Woodrow's arm.

"It's not *every*body," she says, "but people *are* talking."

"We saw Harry had some words with you last night," Woodrow says.

"Yeah," I say, "that wasn't exactly fun."

I drop a razor and a can of shaving cream into the cart.

"Count your blessings that he didn't do anything more than talk to you," Annie says. "Harry is nobody to trifle with."

"This is true," Woodrow says. "It's my understanding that he's put men in the hospital for merely *looking* at Xyla."

"Oh, God," I say. "Is that true?"

"Stop scaring the kid," Annie says. "But, yeah, it's true."

I drop some face and body towels into the cart.

"Do you know the guy who works in the box office?" I ask.

"Paulo?" Annie says. "Yeah, sure."

"He's pretty banged up with the black eye and injured arm," I say. "Did Harry do that to him?"

Annie and Woodrow look at each other, communicating something with their eyes.

"Tampons," Annie says, turning to walk away. "I forgot to get tampons."

"Make sure you get the ones with extra absorbency," Woodrow says.

"Come help me find them, dear," Annie says, slapping him on the arm.

They hurry off with Woodrow rubbing his bicep, leaving me with the cart. It's pretty clear that they didn't want to answer my question about Paulo. But, why? If Handsome Harry *is* the one who injured him, wouldn't they want me to know that? And why wouldn't the Ringmaster have fired him? Either way, it's obvious that my only option is to stay away from Handsome Harry at all costs.

In the meantime, I need socks and underwear, so I push the cart to the men's clothing aisle. I try to decide between boxer briefs or micro-stretch or stretch knit or no fly or open fly or ride-up sport or...or...or why can't they just keep it simple? Say what you will about the aesthetic abomination of tighty-whities, but at least they're reliable and effective. Just give me something snug, supportive, and cotton.

Wait.

Cotton?

That's no good.

Cotton underwear is way too flammable.

"Can I help you find anything, sir?" says a nice girl in a red shirt.

"I think I need fireproof underwear," I say, thinking out loud.

Silence.

"Everything we have in stock is on the shelf," she says as she hurries away.

I feel bad for scaring her off, but I feel *great* about the idea I may have just stumbled onto.

Fireproof underwear.

Now, I just need to figure out if they actually exist and, if they do, where to find them.

Chapter Twenty-Five

HYPERTRICHOSIS

I'M SITTING ALONE AT a long table, eating lunch from Vik's dukey truck while doing some Google detective work on Alice Elizabeth Doherty. Known professionally as the "Minnesota Wooly Girl," Alice was born in Minneapolis, Minnesota, on March 14, 1887; she died at the age of forty-six from unknown causes in Dallas, Texas, on June 13, 1933.

My internet sleuthing leads me to a few black-and-white photos of Alice—some as a child, some as an adult, some sitting with her family, some sitting alone—and in each of them her face is concealed behind wavy blonde hair that grows from her forehead, cheeks, jaw, and chin; if she closed her eyes, you might think you were staring at the back of her head. Though her face is obscured, preventing any visual cues to indicate her mood, I can't help but detect a sense of sadness in Alice. Perhaps I'm just projecting or making assumptions, but, to me, she looks like a young woman who doesn't enjoy being alive.

One article I read describes Alice as being born to "normal parents," which is essentially the same thing Bastian told me (of course, he didn't use the word "normal," considering its pejorative nature in this context); the article also references Alice's "normal" brother and sister. Another article describes Alice as "one of the most fantastic American freaks of all time," before going on to say that, by the age of two, Alice is the only known person born in the United States with hypertrichosis, which leads her parents to present her as a sideshow attraction. According to a separate article, Alice didn't really enjoy the overwhelming attention she received; however, in an effort to provide financial support for her family, she worked until retiring in 1915.

"Hi, Grover."

I look up from my phone and see May, appearing as if from thin air.

"What's got you so focused?" she asks, sitting down across from me with a plate of food.

"I'm just reading about Alice Elizabeth Doherty."

"The Minnesota Wooly Girl."

"You've heard of her?"

"Oh, sure," she says. "What got you interested in her?"

"I was helping Pedro with his homework earlier," I say, "and Bastian told me about his condition, then he told me about Alice Elizabeth Doherty."

"You were helping Pedro with his homework?" she says. "How sweet."

"It's not a big deal," I say. "I was happy to help."

"Well, I think it *is* a big deal, mister, so good on you," she says. "How are you getting along otherwise?"

"Good so far," I say. "Actually, if it's not too much trouble, maybe you can help me out with something."

"Sure, what's up?"

"I need fireproof underwear."

"That's a first."

"To be honest," I say, "I don't even know if fireproof underwear exist."

"If they do, I'll find them," she says. "When do you need them?"

"Before my next performance."

"So, tomorrow evening," she says. "I'll see what I can do."

"I appreciate it."

"So, what inspired this urgent need for fireproof underwear?"

"Claudius spoke to me this morning," I say. "He made it clear he doesn't want any more wardrobe malfunctions resulting in me being naked in front of the audience."

"Sounds reasonable."

"Truth be told," I say, "I thought he was going to fire me on the spot."

May snorts a laugh, shaking her head.

"Trust me," she says. "Claudius isn't letting you go anywhere."

After lunch, I go back to Canyon's wagon (which, I know, is technically *my* wagon, too, but I'm still getting used to the idea). Canyon and Darius are still setting up the big top along with the rest of the tent crew, so the wagon is empty. Laying on my bunk, I give Mom a call, and we talk for a few minutes—mostly about Dad. She tells me his condition is still the same, and I know I should feel good about this as it means he hasn't gotten any worse, but I'd feel much better about it if there was even a glimpse of him progressing in a positive direction.

There's a knock on the wagon door, so I wrap up my call with Mom to answer it. I find Bettie the Bearded Bombshell standing outside wearing a pinup-style dress that hugs tight around her waist, pushing her voluptuous cleavage up under her beard.

"Hello," she says, her voice even more demure than I remember. "Grover, right?"

"Yes."

I can't tell if she remembers meeting me the other day when she persuaded me into her sideshow tent, but I decide it's not necessary to ask.

"Can I come in?"

"Sure."

She takes a seat on one of the empty bunks, resting her manicured fingers atop her knee as she crosses her legs.

"The reason I'm here is I just spoke with May," she says. "She told me you need fireproof underwear."

"She did?" I ask. "Are you a prop master, too?"

"No," she says, "but I *am* a seamstress, so, from time to time, I make costumes for the other performers. I'm thinking I can make some fireproof underwear for you."

"Really?" I say. "That would be amazing! Have you made fireproof underwear before?"

"Never," she says, "but give me some material and thread, and I can make just about anything."

"I'd appreciate that," I say. "Thank you."

"My pleasure," she says. "Now, at the risk of sounding forward, I was hoping that, in exchange for my help, I could ask *you* for a favor."

"Sure."

"Along with your underwear request, May also told me you were helping Pedro with his homework."

"Oh, yeah," I say. "I just happened to be passing by when I saw Bastian working with him this morning."

"I followed up with Bastian after talking to May," she says, "and he couldn't stop singing your praises."

"That's awfully kind of him."

"You were a college professor?"

"Yeah," I say. "Up until yesterday, that was my gig."

"That's very impressive," she says. "I never went to high school, let alone college."

"Did you ever want to?"

"I'd like to say that I did, but that would be a lie," she says with a laugh. "School was never really my thing. Plus, once I started making money on account of my gift," she says, stroking her beard, "I had no need for being in a classroom. My husband, Lenny, dropped out of school, too, so neither one of us is particularly book smart."

"For what it's worth, you sound plenty smart to me."

"Thank you," she says, squeezing my thigh. "Now, as for my favor, Lenny and I have a daughter who's been traveling on the road with us ever since she was born. We've struggled to help Hannah with her schoolwork on account of the whole dropping out thing, so I was hoping maybe you could help."

"Sure," I say. "I'm working with Pedro again tomorrow, so you can have Hannah join us."

"Oh, thank you!" she says, pressing her breasts against me with a tight hug, her beard tickling my neck. "You don't know what this means to me."

After Bettie leaves, I fall asleep for a nap. When I wake up a few hours later, bleary-eyed and groggy, I find Canyon and Darius asleep in their respective bunks. I tip-toe past them, stepping outside, where I'm greeted by the moon, flanked by an entourage of scattered stars. Walking through the labyrinth and onto the circus grounds, I take a moment to admire the picturesque outline of the Grambling Brothers' skyline; the only thing that would make it better is a Ferris wheel. In the middle of my quiet admiration, Xyla appears from the darkness.

"Hey, you," she says. "Want to go on an adventure?"

Chapter Twenty-Six

THE PG-13 VICINITY

X YLA AND I WAIT for an Uber in front of Target, standing shoulder to shoulder as we look out over the empty sea of asphalt, making small talk under a flickering street light like we've known each other in a hundred different lifetimes.

"One time," I say, "when I was a teenager, I was hanging out with a couple of my friends in a shopping center just like this. It was late on a Saturday night, so all the stores were closed."

"How old were you?"

"I think we were fourteen or fifteen at the time."

"Were there any girls with you?"

"Ha!"

"I'll take that as a no," she says. "Were you at least drinking or experimenting with drugs?"

"Nothing that cool."

"So, what were you doing at a shopping center in the middle of the night?"

"Just walking around and shooting the shit."

"And it was fun?"

"Honestly, it was a blast."

Xyla smiles.

"You're adorable."

"Then again, it stopped being fun when we thought we were about to get murdered."

"Really? What happened?"

"While we were walking down the sidewalk, a car pulled up beside us," I say. "We tried to pretend like we didn't notice it, but it was slowly keeping pace with us."

"That sounds scary."

"Oh, it most definitely was," I say. "It got even scarier when a guy stuck his head out the passenger window and yelled, 'Hey, pussies, we're gonna kill you!' As soon as we heard his door open, we broke into a sprint."

"Oh, my God!"

"You're telling me," I say. "I ran as fast as I could, convinced that it was just a matter of time before they caught up to us."

"What happened next?"

"The car just sped off," I say. "We could hear all the guys inside laughing as they drove away."

"Fucking pricks," she says. "I hate bullies."

"Yeah, me, too," I say. "On the bright side, I learned that I can run reasonably fast when I think I'm going to die."

This makes Xyla laugh, which I love.

"Speaking of which," I say, "during our adventure tonight, will my life be in danger?"

"Who knows?" she says with a shrug.

"Good grief," I say with a laugh. "You really don't know?"

"What kind of an adventure would it be if I did?"

Our Uber arrives before I can ask any more questions, so we slide into the backseat.

"Yo," the driver says, squinting at his phone, "are you, uh...uh...shit. Sorry, how do you say your name?"

"Xyla," she says. "The X sounds like a Z."

"Got it," he says. "So, you guys are headed to New York-New York, right?"

I shoot Xyla a grin, as part of her mysterious adventure has unwittingly been unveiled.

"Yeah," she says, smiling back at me. "New York-New York."

"Cool, cool," he says, pulling out of the parking lot. "So, you two locals?"

"No," Xyla says, "we're in town with the Grambling Brothers Traveling Circus Show."

"That's what's up," he says. "What do you do with the circus?"

"Well, I'm a fortuneteller," Xyla says, "and my friend, Grover, here plays with fire."

"Yo, that's dope!" he says. "Have you guys seen that circus video where the motherfucker is on fire with his dick out?"

"I can do you one better," Xyla says. "The very motherfucker you speak of is sitting right next to me."

"Hold up," the driver says, staring at me in the rearview mirror. "You that same motherfucker from the YouTubes?"

"Guilty as charged."

"With your dick out and everything?"

"I didn't mean for that part to happen," I say, "but, yeah."

"My man," he says, "how the fuck you do that shit without fucking burning to death?"

I look at Xyla, unsure of how much to share.

"He's fireproof."

I guess she settled that.

"Yeah, fucking right," the driver says, laughing. "For real, though, is it like some David Blaine shit or something?"

"Yeah," I say, "something like that."

"Yo, that's what's up," he says. "My man, can I get a selfie with you after the ride?"

"Sure."

Xyla leans into me and whispers, "Looks like you have a fan."

I smile at her remark, but I'm mostly consumed with how erotic it felt to have Xyla's breath on my ear. While the sensation of her words lingers against my skin, the driver calls his boyfriend.

"Baby," he says, practically yelling, "guess who's in my car!" After several wrong guesses—including "them two magic tiger dudes" and "that queen with the rotten Adam's apple"—the driver says, "No, it's that naked fire motherfucker from the YouTubes!" This elicits a high-pitched squeal from his boyfriend. They talk excitedly for a few minutes as the iconic Las Vegas Strip comes into view, which includes a large Ferris wheel that I've never seen before.

"Excuse me," I say, as the driver hangs up with his boyfriend, "is that Ferris wheel new?"

"The High Roller?" he says. "It's been around a minute. That motherfucker is the second tallest Ferris wheel in the whole fucking world."

"What's the tallest?"

"Fuck if I know," he says, "but it ain't in Vegas."

As we approach the intersection of Tropicana Avenue and Las Vegas Boulevard, I see New York-New York and its replica of the Statue of Liberty wearing a giant Vegas Knights hockey jersey. The driver pulls up in front of the hotel entrance amidst a flurry of taxis and limousines, hurrying out of the car to open the door for us. In a quick, seamless motion, he takes out his phone and puts his arm around me, snapping a few selfies.

"My man, what's your Instagram handle?"

"Oh, I'm not on social media."

"But you're the naked fire guy," he says. "How the fuck you not on social media?"

"I know," I say. "I just never got into it."

"Well, shit," he says, "how am I supposed to tag you?"

"I have an Instagram account," Xyla says. "You can tag me, and I'll make sure he sees it."

They take a moment to exchange Instagram handles.

"Real quick," the driver says, "can you do some fire shit for me?"

"Fire shit?"

"Yeah," he says, "something I can share with my followers."

I look at Xyla, unsure of how to answer.

"He'd be happy to."

I guess she settled that.

"Do you have a lighter?" I ask.

The driver pulls a lighter from his pocket, handing it to me. As I flick it to life, the driver starts recording on his phone. I extend my index finger and touch it to the flame, holding it in place for several seconds.

"Oh, shit!" the driver says. "That's what's up!"

"Want to see something else?" I ask, feeling inspired by his enthusiasm.

"Hell yeah!"

I hold the lighter under my chin, pressing the flame flush against my skin.

"No fucking way!" the driver yells, bringing his phone in for a close-up.

I ask for a piece of paper, and the driver hands me a random receipt from his pocket. Keeping the lighter in place, I slide the paper between my chin and the flame.

"My man," the driver says as the receipt burns against my skin, "David Blaine ain't got shit on you!"

After a quick goodbye, he gets back in his car and merges onto Las Vegas Boulevard, while Xyla leads us onto the sidewalk to join the stream of tourists flowing up and down the Strip.

"You were great back there," Xyla says.

"Really?"

"Yes, really," she says. "I think you're better at this than you realize."

As we walk past New York-New York's faux skyscrapers, Xyla intertwines her fingers with mine, awakening a hurricane of butterflies in my belly. We stroll in silence for a while, hand in hand, moving past the MGM Grand, Planet Hollywood, and the Cosmopolitan. Anyone looking at me probably thinks I'm taking in the bright lights and chaotic scenery, but I'm far too overwhelmed by the touch of Xyla's skin to focus on anything else.

Xyla stops us in front of the Bellagio.

"Let's watch the water show," she says. "Have you ever seen it before?"

"Only in the last scene of *Ocean's 11*."

"Oh goody," she says. "I like that your first time is with me."

A faint scent of minerals and chlorine fills the air as a fine mist from the Bellagio's explosive water presentation floats down around us.

As we continue holding hands, a thought occurs to me.

"Hey, I'm just curious," I say. "Are you reading my mind right now?"

"You mean because we're holding hands?"

"Yeah."

"Not exactly," she says, turning to face me. "What would I see if I *were* reading your mind?"

"I don't know."

I turn my head to look at the water show, too timid to hold eye contact with her. She runs her free hand up my chest until her fingers touch my chin, gently guiding my eyes back to hers.

"If you could read *my* mind," she says, "do you know what you would see?"

MILESTONE #4

I close my eyes just as Xyla's lips make contact with mine, guiding me through the most magical kiss I've ever experienced. A pulse of confidence blooms in my belly, inspiring me to run my hands down Xyla's back towards her ass, causing her to moan against my lips—but then, in the very next moment, I lose my nerve and move my hands back up to the PG-13 vicinity of her back.

"So," she says, breaking our kiss, "great water show, huh?"

"The best."

Xyla rests her elbows on my shoulders, causing my body to quiver as she runs her fingers through my hair.

"Confession time," she says. "Whenever we touch, I *do* see inside of you."

"So, you *are* reading my mind?"

"Remember, I can't actually read your thoughts," she says. "I simply see what your mind presents to me."

"And you can't turn it off?"

"No," she says, "not even if I wanted to."

"Do you ever want to?"

"All the time," she says. "Right now, for instance, I wish I could kiss you without seeing anything."

"What do you see?"

"The same two flames that I saw when you visited my tent," she says, "but they're a little different this time."

"Different how?"

"Well, one flame has gotten slightly bigger," she says, grabbing my wrists and running my hands down her back, "while the other has gotten slightly smaller."

Any questions I have about the flames changing size evaporate from my mind as our lips pick up where they previously left off.

Chapter Twenty-Seven

A VIOLENT ONE

O H, WHAT A NIGHT!

I know what you're thinking, by the way, and the answer is no—nothing else happened between me and Xyla beyond that kiss. When our lips finally parted and the world blinked back into focus, we finished watching the Bellagio water show. Afterward, we continued our stroll along the Las Vegas Strip, passing all of the famous hotels, including Caesar's Palace and the Flamingo, until we reached Circus Circus at the end of the Strip. Standing beneath the giant, neon clown in front of the faux big top entrance, I told Xyla all about how my parents brought me to Circus Circus as a kid during my first trip to Las Vegas.

"That's sweet," she said, "and kind of funny that they brought you so close to Naked City."

"Is that like Party City?"

"No," she said, laughing, "it's the neighborhood just north of Circus Circus, right around where the Stratosphere is."

"There's an actual neighborhood called Naked City?"

"Yeah, but I'm sure it's just a nickname."

"How'd it get the name?"

"Back in the day, around the 1950s or so, it was mostly populated by showgirls, as well as other folks who worked on the Strip," she said. "It was affordable and close to all the hotels, so it made sense. As for the name, legend has it that the showgirls regularly sunbathed naked around the pools, thus, it became known as Naked City."

"That's so cool," I said. "How do you know all that?"

"It's just one of the perks of being in a traveling circus," she said. "You tend to learn a little bit about every city you go to. These days, Naked City is infamous for being one of the most dangerous, crime-ridden neighborhoods in Las Vegas."

"Oh, geez," I said. "Are we safe out here?"

"Sure," she said. "You're fireproof, right?"

"Well, yeah, but I'm not bulletproof."

"Okay, let's head into Circus Circus," she said, "where you'll be marginally safer."

"Marginally?!"

This made Xyla laugh again, which, in spite of my newfound paranoia regarding the safety of our immediate surroundings, made me happy. Inside Circus Circus, we watched some of the circus performances and played a few games in the midway before sitting down for dinner at a circus-themed restaurant. After dinner, we went to the casino where Xyla played some slots—including a Wheel of Fortune machine that was bigger than my refrigerator—and several hands of Black Jack while I stood by and watched; she lost more than she won, but you'd never know it based on how much fun we were having. When we left, Xyla ordered us an Uber back to Grambling Brothers. Of course, I was nervous the whole time we were waiting for it outside.

"Let this be a lesson to you," Xyla said with a grin. "Just because you're at the circus doesn't mean you're safe."

The Uber driver that took us back to Grambling Brothers had no idea who I was, so it was a much quieter ride. Xyla and I held hands, and she rested her head on my shoulder the whole way back. While I don't know exactly how long the ride was, it wasn't long enough for me. Back at Grambling Brothers, we shared a nice hug and a quick kiss before parting ways to our respective wagons. And, just in case you're wondering, *I'm* the one who kept the goodnight kiss short and sweet; partly, I wanted to be a gentleman, but mostly, I was super terrified that Handsome Harry might see us together.

I wake up in the morning, still buzzing from my night out with Xyla. Darius is still asleep (as per usual), but Canyon is awake; he invites me to have breakfast with him and May, so, after I take him up on it, we head out to meet her at Vik's truck. As Canyon and I walk through the circus grounds, I hear Xyla calling after me. I turn in time to see her walking my way, phone in hand.

"Grover," she says with a clear tone of excitement in her voice, "he posted it!"

As she catches up to us, Xyla says hello to Canyon before showing me her phone.

"Our Uber driver from last night posted the video of you doing your fire trick."

There I am on her phone, holding the lighter under my chin as the receipt burns to ash.

"He already has over one hundred thousand views," she says.

"Is that a lot?"

"For an Uber driver with hardly any followers," she says, "it's a minor miracle."

"You just keep getting more famous, bro," Canyon says.

"What are you two up to?"

"We were just going to Vik's for breakfast," I say. "You can join us if you like."

"I appreciate the invite, but I already ate," she says. "Find me later?"

"Okay."

Xyla hesitates a moment, like she wants me to kiss her before walking away. Under different circumstances, I definitely would have made a move, but, in the event that Handsome Harry is somewhere nearby, I decide public displays of affection probably aren't a good idea while we're on the circus grounds; while I don't say as much out loud, Xyla seems to get the message before going her own way. Of course, as soon as she's gone, I worry that I may have offended her, and now I'm wondering if I'll ever have a chance to kiss Xyla again.

May is waiting for us at an empty table when Canyon and I get to Vik's. I scan the area for Handsome Harry, and, to my great relief, he's nowhere in sight; the rest of the dining tables are half-full with other performers and crew members. Canyon and I pick up our breakfast from Vik's window, then sit down with May.

"I've been researching fabrics for your special underwear," May says. "Did you know that wool is naturally fireproof?"

"I had no idea."

"Yeah," she says. "Are you interested in wool underwear?"

"Um...no?"

May laughs.

"That's what I figured," she says. "I'm not done looking, so I'm sure I'll find something soon."

"Much appreciated."

"Unfortunately," she says, "I don't imagine we'll be able to get you fireproof underwear before tonight's show."

"Well, I appreciate you going through all the trouble," I say. "I'll just have to figure something out for tonight."

"Speaking of tonight's show," Canyon says, shoveling a forkful of eggs in his mouth, "is Harry still fucking with you?"

"I haven't seen him since the other night," I say, "so, technically no."

"What happens the next time he sees you, though?"

"Hopefully, he realizes that I'm harmless and decides to leave me alone."

"It's not really you that he's worried about," May says. "It's you *plus* Xyla."

"Yeah, he doesn't seem to be a fan of that math."

"He never has been," she says. "If you're not careful, you might end up just like Eddie."

"Who's Eddie?"

"He was a sideshow performer," May says. "Not here at Grambling Brothers, but another circus. I crossed paths with him a few times over the years, as tends to happen with circus folk. Eddie was a real nice guy, all prim and proper. To see him standing with a briefcase in front of an audience, you'd think he was there to do your taxes, but he actually kept knives, spikes, broken glass, and several other sharp and pointy props inside. He did a lot of the classics in his act, like chewing on lightbulbs, sticking knitting needles through his hands, and piercing his ears with butcher knives."

"Fuck," Canyon says, "Eddie sounds like a tough son of a bitch."

"Oh, he was," May says. "Unfortunately for Eddie, he became friends with Xyla."

"What happened to him?" I ask.

"Well, the story goes that Harry and Xyla found themselves working at the same circus as Eddie," May says. "And Eddie, being the kind soul that he was, looked to make them feel welcome. While Harry wasn't keen on being friends with Eddie, Xyla took a liking to him. Now, anyone who knew Eddie knew he didn't have a mischievous bone in his body, so, while I wasn't there, I know with certainty that he wasn't looking to make a play for Xyla. But, as the story goes, Harry didn't like how friendly they were, so he decided to make an example of Eddie."

"What kind of an example?"

"A violent one."

"Oh, yeah, I think I heard this story," Canyon says. "Didn't they have to take Eddie away in an ambulance?"

"That's right," May says, staring me straight in the eyes. "Nobody has seen or heard from Eddie ever since."

"Does Claudius know about what Harry did to Eddie?" I ask.

"Claudius knows everything."

"And he still lets him work here?"

"He's in the show, right?"

"What should I do?"

"Xyla's a nice girl," May says, "but, if I were you, I'd stay away from her."

Chapter Twenty-Eight

SPIRALING DREAD FANTASY

After breakfast, I walk alone through the labyrinth, reflecting on the unsettling potential that I might soon be taken away in an ambulance the next time I cross paths with Handsome Harry. I'm imagining broken orbital bones, punctured lungs, severed tendons, and blood—lots and lots of blood—as a couple of EMTs, both young enough to be my students, whisper grim predictions about my torturous road to recovery while sticking me with needles and measuring my heart rate. Through the ambulance windows, I can see Handsome Harry and the rest of Grambling Brothers watching as I'm driven away, disappearing into the ether of my spiraling dread fantasy.

I'm snapped back into reality when I see Charlie Chuckles sitting with Bettie the Bearded Bombshell in front of her wagon; the two of them seem exceptionally comfortable around each other, with Bettie leaning her whole body into Charlie, shaking with laughter at whatever he said before I showed up.

"Oh, Grover," Bettie says, elbowing Charlie away from her. "I'm glad you turned up. I have something for you."

"You do?"

"Yeah, wait here."

Bettie excuses herself into her wagon, leaving me alone with Charlie.

"Hey, kid, you should've come out with me yesterday," Charlie says. "This sweet little flower milked my shake three times."

"Congratulations?"

"That's not even the best part," Charlie says. "After my third pop, she tells me her hand is tired, but I tell *her* I'm still good to go, so she brings in another girl who makes me pop two more times."

"Geez, how long were you there?"

"I don't know," he says. "A few hours? Either way, I *still* wasn't done. After I wore out the first two girls, they brought in the boss lady to finish the job. Now, she wasn't much to look at, and she handled my cock like a spoon in a garbage disposal, but she got three more pops out of me. You keeping count, kid?"

I shake my head, no.

"That's eight pops," he says. "My cock was redder than a lobster. I could've kept going, too, but the boss lady shooed me out."

"Is eight times even possible in one day?"

"It is if you're me," he says. "There's only one other guy I know of who could do it. You ever hear of Captain Fuckmeister?"

"Can't say that I have."

"He's a legend in the dick business," Charlie says. "Captain Fuck-meister could shoot a load twenty to thirty times a day."

"That's impossible."

"Says the fireproof guy?"

"Fair enough," I say. "But, thirty times a day?"

"You remember *Grunt* magazine?"

"Sounds familiar."

"It's one of those old-school porn rags from back in the day," he says. "I'm sure you kept a sticky issue or two between your mattresses as a kid."

"Well, I mean—"

"Yeah, me, too," he says. "And when I wasn't busy releasing the Kraken, I actually read the articles, which is how I learned about Captain Fuckmeister. There was a lovely think piece written about him and his quest to fuck everybody in Mexico."

"Why would he even try something like that?"

"Because he wanted to be a flicker of light in a dark and unforgiving world."

"By fucking everybody in Mexico?"

"Not all geniuses are appreciated in their own time," he says. "You remember that Japanese kid who dominated the Nathan's Hot Dog Eating Contest a few years ago?"

"Yeah, I think so."

"He's a scrawny little thing who looks like he couldn't finish a Happy Meal without getting a tummy ache," Charlie says, "so, when he turned up for the first time to compete in Nathan's Hot Dog Eating Contest, surrounded by some of the beefiest men from around the world, the kid looked wildly out of place. I mean, nobody in their right mind thought he stood a chance against those guys. So, what's he do? He breaks the fucking record for eating hotdogs. Nobody even came close to him. The world had no idea a human could eat that many hotdogs before that kid did it. Pretty soon other competitive eaters started surpassing their own previous accomplishments, all because one scrawny Japanese kid showed them it was possible."

"That's weirdly inspiring," I say. "I guess it only takes one person to change the world."

"When it comes to yogurt shooters," Charlie says, "nobody will ever match Captain Fuckmeister."

"Are there competitions for that sort of thing?"

"The only man Captain Fuckmeister ever needed to compete against was himself," Charlie says, "and he left this world undefeated."

"He died?"

"How the fuck should I know?" he says. "All I know is Captain Fuckmeister's legendary cock inspired a young Charlie Chuckles to believe he could one day ruin every sock in his drawer before mom called him down for dinner." Charlie actually gets choked up at this point. "Man, I miss those old jerk rags. Now, it's all smartphones and hidden cameras. Speaking of which, did you know Pornhub took your video down?"

"Really?"

"It's crazy, too," he says. "Videos like that never get scrubbed."

"I'm just relieved to hear it's gone."

Bettie exits her wagon with a brown paper bag in hand.

"What are you boys talking about?"

"Grover's monster cock," Charlie says. "Have you seen the dong on this kid?"

Bettie squeals with laughter.

"You're terrible," she says, squeezing Charlie's arm. "Here you go, Grover."

Bettie hands me the brown paper bag.

"What's this?" I say, removing a strange-looking garment from the bag.

"They're a temporary pair of fireproof underwear," she says. "May actually got me the silica fabric I needed for the official pair, but it's a little harder to work with than I anticipated, so I'm not sure how long it'll take me to craft you a proper pair of fireproof underwear. Until then, I made you these."

"Thank you so much," I say. "What are these made of?"

"They're a pair of tighty-whities that I reinforced with foil and duct tape."

"And they're actually fireproof?"

"You bet," she says. "I tested them out over my stove. Fashion-wise, they're not exactly chic, but they'll do. If they don't fit right, let me know and I can make some adjustments."

"I can't believe you did this for me," I say. "Thank you."

"It's the least I can do."

"Don't believe her, kid," Charlie says. "She can do *a lot* more than that."

Bettie squeals again with laughter.

"You need to stop," she says.

"You gonna make me?"

"Maybe I will."

"Oh, yeah?"

I sneak off at this point, deciding I probably don't want to be a part of whatever's happening here.

Chapter Twenty-Nine

BIOLOGICAL

I HEAD BACK TO my wagon to drop off my fireproof underwear before giving Mom a call.

"Hi, sweetheart," she says. "How's the circus?"

"Good," I say. "I have my second performance tonight."

"That's so exciting," she says. "Are you nervous?"

"Very," I say. "How's Dad?"

"He's stable," she says, "but the doctors still don't know squat."

"How are *you* holding up?"

"As long as I'm with your father, I'm fine," she says. "We watch *Live with Kelly and Mark* in the morning, I read the newspaper to him in the afternoon, and at night we enjoy re-runs of *Friends*. Sometimes the nurses come by to keep me company, which is sweet."

"Maybe I should come home."

"Don't you dare," she says. "I'd just turn you right back around."

"I know you would."

After I get off the phone with Mom, I head over to Bastian's wagon for my first official tutoring session with Pedro; the two of them are waiting at the same foldout card table in front of their wagon. As I take a seat next to Pedro, Bettie and Lenny turn up with Hannah. This is my first time encountering Lenny outside of his sideshow tent, so seeing him and his head-to-toe tattoos in the real world is a bit surreal, like crossing paths with a very tall and lanky extraterrestrial.

"Grover," Bettie says, "this is my husband, Lenny."

Lenny extends his hand, swallowing mine up in his long fingers. He smiles and nods, offering a shy hello. For my part, I wonder if he knows how chummy Charlie Chuckles is with his wife—and, if not, I wonder how he'd feel if he ever found out.

"And this is Hannah," Bettie says, patting her little girl on the crown of her head. "Hannah, this is your new teacher."

"Hello, Grover," Hannah says with all the confidence of a used car salesman.

She takes a seat at the table without having to be asked, sitting up straight and folding her hands in her lap. Bettie leans over her, giving Hannah a kiss on the cheek. Lenny crouches down next, his long legs jutting out like a grasshopper as he gives Hannah a hug and a kiss. From this angle, I notice a long sheet of hair growing from the base of Lenny's otherwise bald skull, hanging halfway down his back.

"Be good, baby girl," he says. "I love you."

"Love you, Daddy," Hannah says, her fingers disappearing beneath Lenny's mullet as she hugs his neck.

Once Lenny and Bettie leave and Bastian goes back into his wagon, I get started with Pedro and Hannah. We review Pedro's compare-and-contrast exercise from yesterday, where I'd asked him to make a list of the ways Superman and Batman are different and alike. It's actually a pretty good list, which includes how Superman can fly and Batman can't and how both of them are members of the Justice League.

"I forgot to write down that Superman grows up with his parents," Pedro says, "but Batman is an orphan."

"That's a great observation," I say. "But, you know, Superman is also an orphan like Batman."

"He is?"

"Yeah, he's from the planet Krypton," I say, "but his planet exploded when he was a baby, killing his parents, along with most every other Kryptonian. But, before Krypton exploded, Superman's parents put him on a rocket ship to Earth, which landed in Smallville. That's where he was discovered by his future adopted parents, Jonathan and Martha Kent."

"So, Jonathan and Martha aren't his real parents?"

"They're not his *biological* parents," I say, "but they are very much his real parents."

"Grover," Hannah says, raising her hand, "what does biological mean?"

"It means there is a blood relation," I say. "For example, *your* parents are your biological parents because they made you together."

"How did they make her?" Pedro asks.

"Um...that's a good question."

The kids stare at me, waiting for an answer.

"I think the stork," I say, "but I guess I don't really know the answer."

They seem satisfied with this response, so I quickly pivot back to Superman.

"The main idea is that Jonathan and Martha Kent may not have been Superman's biological parents, but they raised him, loved him, and taught him right from wrong," I say. "What do you think might've happened if Superman's rocket ship had landed somewhere else and he was raised by an evil husband and wife?"

"I think he would've grown up to be a bad man," Hannah says.

"What do you think, Pedro?" I ask. "Do you agree?"

"Yeah," he says, "because they would've taught him to be evil instead of good."

"I think you're both right," I say. "Plus, can you imagine what the world would be like if somebody like Superman, with all of his superpowers, grew up to be an evil villain?"

"That would be scary!" Pedro says.

"Very scary," Hannah says. "I wouldn't want to live in that world."

"Me neither," I say. "So, do you think it was a good thing that he was raised by Martha and Jonathan?"

"Yes," Pedro says.

"And why is that?"

"They taught him how to be a good person."

"Exactly," I say. "In a way, you can say they taught him how to be Superman."

This makes Pedro smile.

"Alright," I say, "I think it's time for a new assignment. I want you each to write a paper about your parents. Specifically, I want you to write about all of the things that make them special to you."

Pedro raises his hand.

"I don't remember that much about my mom," he says, "and I never met my dad."

"That's okay," I say. "What if you write about Bastian?"

"I'm allowed to do that?"

"Sure," I say. "He takes care of you like a mom or dad would, right?"

"Yeah," he says, nodding his head. "Geno, too."

"That's perfect," I say. "You should write about both of them."

Hannah asks Pedro for a sheet of paper from his spiral notebook, as well as one of his pencils, before assuring both of us that she'll show up more prepared for our next class. As I watch them quietly working on their assignment, I find that I'm pleasantly surprised by how much I'm enjoying my familiar new role.

Chapter Thirty

THE TURNAWAY

I T'S ALMOST TIME FOR my second performance in the big top, so I go back to my wagon to try on the foil underwear Bettie made for me. Inside the cramped bathroom at the back of the wagon, I'm finding it very difficult to get undressed, but, after banging my elbows and knees a few times, I manage to get the foil underwear on. The duct tape is cool and stiff against my skin, and the elastic band is pretty much non-existent, so it's sort of like wearing a flimsy biker helmet that's been repurposed into a snug pair of undies. And, considering Bettie never took my measurements, the fit is surprisingly nice; though they're a tad bulky, as I pull my pants up over them, you would be hard pressed to notice I was wearing anything other than a standard pair of underwear.

Exiting the bathroom, I see Darius and Canyon are back from their work with the tent crew. Darius, as usual, is asleep in his bunk, while Canyon is sitting up front in the driver's seat. I walk down the narrow pathway between the bunks and plop down in the passenger seat beside him. He's looking at a sweet picture of his daughter, so I immediately feel guilty for interrupting—but, after doing some quick anxiety calculus in my head, I decide it would probably look strange if I got right back up and walked away.

"Hey, bro," he says.

"Hi," I say. "How was your day?"

"It was good," he says. "Mostly, just maintenance and upkeep. What's new with you?"

"Funny you should ask," I say. "I'm wearing a pair of fireproof underwear that Bettie made for me."

"No kidding?" he says, his eyes darting toward my crotch. "What are they made of?"

"Foil and duct tape."

"And they work?"

"I think so," I say. "Bettie says she tested them out."

"You didn't test them yourself, bro?"

"No," I say, suddenly feeling dumb. "I probably should, huh?"

"Well, Bettie knows what she's doing," he says, "so I'm sure they're fine. How about the foil?"

"What about the foil?"

"Will it burn your skin when it gets hot?"

"The foil is covered by the duct tape, so it's not touching my skin."

"What if it wasn't, though?" he asks. "Can you burn yourself on hot metal?"

"That's a great question," I say. "I actually have no idea."

There's a knock at the door, so I get up to answer it. It's Solo and Fernando the Fearless Fire Tamer.

"Hey, fellas," I say. "Everything okay?"

"Yeah, everything's fine," Solo says. "We just figured you might not want to walk to the big top alone."

"Oh?"

"You know," Fernando says, "just in case."

"In case what?" I ask.

Solo and Fernando give each other a quick look.

"In case Harry still wants to kill you," Solo says.

"Oh, sure, that makes sense," I say, sounding way too casual about possibly running into my co-worker/potential murderer.

While I can't imagine a scenario where either one of them—combined or otherwise—could stop Harry from inflicting any number of violent acts on me, it's still a very kind gesture, so I take them up on it.

"I'm coming, too," Canyon says, joining us at the doorway.

"Maybe that's not the best idea," I say.

"Why not?"

Several reasons come to mind as to why not, but chief among them is that, should things turn violent with Harry, Canyon could be killed—and not just because Harry's a loose cannon with other-worldly physical strength, but because Canyon can't risk any sort of head trauma on account of his brain injury. I'm not sure how to politely bring up the precarious nature of his noggin in front of Solo and Fernando—as I don't know how sensitive he is about sharing that information—so I simply point to my head, tapping my index finger to my temple.

"You're worried about your head, bro?" Canyon asks.

"No," I say, "I'm worried about *your* head."

"Oh, *that?*" he says with a shrug. "It's cool, you don't gotta worry about me."

"You sure?"

"Hell yeah, I'm sure," he says, exiting the wagon. "Let's roll."

The four of us walk to the big top together the way they do in action movies when the main characters move in slow motion on their way to a climactic battle. I've never been part of a crew like this before, especially one willing to fight a bully for me, and I must admit, it feels pretty cool.

Arriving at the big top, there's an audible hum of excitement in the air as a long line of people makes its way inside. All of the performers, including Handsome Harry, are already huddled at the back entrance. The Ringmaster is there, too, which may be the only reason Harry hasn't made a move to break my neck. Fernando and Solo stand on either side of me, while Canyon stands behind us, arms crossed.

"Shouldn't you be standing with the Silvas?" I whisper to Solo.

"It's okay," he whispers back. "They won't miss me."

Charlie Chuckles walks over to us, squeezing in between me and Fernando.

"Did you hear, kid?" he asks, putting his arm around my shoulders. "We've got a genuine turnaway tonight."

"Oh," I say. "That's great."

"Yes, it is great," the Ringmaster says, the sound of his voice snapping everybody into quiet attention. "This is our first turnaway in a very, very long time, and it's clear to me that there is one very specific individual to thank for it." The Ringmaster turns his attention to me. "Grover, after one night with us, you've proven to be an invaluable addition to our family. The YouTube video of your debut performance, which has clearly captured the attention of the masses, now has over 10,000,000 views."

"10,000,000?" I say. "I thought it was around 1,000,000."

"That was yesterday," the Ringmaster says. "It seems you've officially gone viral."

Charlie responds with a loud hoot, which inspires polite applause from the rest of the performers (except for Handsome Harry).

"With Grover's newfound celebrity in mind," the Ringmaster says, "there will be a change in tonight's lineup. The order goes strongman, clowns, high wire, clowns, flyers, clowns, and fire. Clear?"

As the group nods their affirmation, the Soaring Silvas seem none too pleased with their new spot in the lineup—and, by the disgusted looks on their faces, I suspect they're also not happy with me taking their spot.

With the show underway, Solo invites Fernando, Canyon, and me to hang out in his plush wagon. We shoot the breeze like a group of old pals, and, amidst the small talk, I ask Fernando how he blows fire without an ignition source. Without missing a beat, he opens his mouth to display a small orb of fire on his tongue, no bigger than a marble. Forming his lips into an O like a kid preparing to blow a bubble, Fernando unleashes a ball of fire. Solo and Canyon jerk back as the fireball audibly whooshes before disappearing.

"Bro," Canyon says, "that was some serious *Game of Thrones* shit!"

This garners a laugh from the rest of us.

"Is that fire on your tongue all the time?" I ask.

"No," Fernando says, "but I can conjure it at will."

"How?"

"To be honest, I don't really know," he says. "For me, it feels as natural as taking a deep, mindful breath."

"Does it burn your mouth?" Canyon asks.

"Not my mouth, no," Fernando says, "but I'm not fireproof like Grover, so I must be careful not to touch any other part of my body with it."

"How about spicy food?" Canyon asks.

This garners another laugh from the group.

"Actually, yes," Fernando says. "Spicy food *does* affect my mouth."

"Bro," Canyon says, shaking his head, "magic is strange."

"Are you the only one?" I ask. "I mean, does anybody else have the same power?"

"My father had it," Fernando says. "But he also knew how to blow fire the traditional way, and he made sure to teach me as well. Father believed it was important to understand the dangers of fire-breathing as a matter of respect."

"How do traditional fire-breathers do it?" Solo asks.

"Kerosene," Fernando says.

"I would've assumed alcohol."

"That's a common assumption," Fernando says, "but alcohol is much too dangerous for fire-breathing."

"Why's that?" Canyon asks.

"It doesn't burn fast enough," he says, "so it's easier to injure your mouth. But, with kerosene, it burns as soon as the mist touches the flame. So, as long as it is done correctly, the fire never touches your mouth."

It's time for Solo to join the Soaring Silvas in the big top for their performance, so he gets up to leave. Before he excuses himself, Solo invites Canyon, Fernando, and me to keep hanging out in his wagon. We take him up on his offer, continuing to make small talk until it's time for Fernando and me to close the show.

"For the final performance of the night," the Ringmaster says to the packed audience, "it is my unrivaled honor to present you with a performer who, just two nights ago, made his Grambling Brothers debut. A debut that has already been viewed more than 10,000,000 times on YouTube." At the mention of the video, the big top fills with cheers and applause, cascading into a chant of "Grover, Grover, Grover." The Ringmaster continues, "He is a man who defies the laws of the scientific universe, whose very flesh is impervious to the hottest flames anywhere on Earth. If fire strikes fear in the heart of man, then your next performer is the man whom fire fears. Ladies and gentlemen, I present to you Professor Grover the Fireproof Man!"

The spotlight tracks me as I make my way to the center of the big top, igniting the audience into an explosion of excitement. Fernando and I start our act, going through all the same beats from our debut performance. When my T-shirt burns off, leaving me naked from the waist up, Fernando blows a fireball against my bare chest, which drives the audience wild. This naturally leads to Fernando burning off my pants, which, once they've collapsed from my legs, leave me wearing only my sneakers and Bettie's duct-tape-and-foil underwear. Fernando, for good measure, improvises a new beat by blowing an extra fireball against the underwear before offering a comedic shrug to the audience when they don't burn off; this gets a huge laugh.

At the conclusion of the show, all of the performers stand together in the center of the ring for our curtain call before exiting the big top. I make a point of walking with the Ringmaster just in case Handsome Harry has any plans to get me alone.

"Another successful performance," the Ringmaster says. "I do believe you're a natural, Grover."

"Thank you," I say. "Fernando's been a great mentor."

"I expected he would be."

Our small talk winds to a natural end as we approach the labyrinth, but, not wanting to abandon the security of the Ringmaster's presence, I try to keep it going.

"Did you know there's a Ferris wheel on the Las Vegas Strip?"

"Yes, I'm aware."

"An Uber driver told me it's the second tallest Ferris wheel in the world," I say. "I'm not sure where the tallest one is, though."

"Dubai."

"Pardon?"

"The tallest Ferris wheel in the world is in Dubai."

"Wow, you really do know everything."

The Ringmaster smiles.

"Have a good evening, Grover."

Once the Ringmaster fades away into the labyrinth, leaving me alone, I walk towards the midway, hoping I might find Xyla. But, instead of finding the object of my affection, I see Handsome Harry loitering near Xyla's tent like a grizzly bear sniffing around a campfire. My stomach drops at the sight of him, so I hurry away in the opposite direction, speed-walking all the way back to my wagon.

Chapter Thirty-One

BROKEN

IN THE MORNING, I wake up to a text message from Xyla inviting me to her place for tea. In the message, she gives me a general idea of her location and says to look for a small, silver wagon. As much as I don't want to tempt fate by potentially having Handsome Harry see me anywhere near Xyla's wagon, I can't bring myself to turn down her invitation, so I brush my teeth, then head out. After ten or fifteen minutes of wandering about the labyrinth, I find a wagon with a chrome exterior and rounded edges, like a van that aspires to be a dolphin.

Before I can knock, Xyla opens the door and lets me in.

"This is a neat wagon."

"Groovy, right?" she says. "It's a Hunt House Car."

"Cool," I say, pretending to know what that means.

"Ever heard of it?"

"Nope."

"I hadn't either, before I got it," she says. "Claudius told me it was manufactured in the 1930s."

"That explains the retro look."

The inside isn't quite big enough for a tour, so I take a few moments to look around and take it in. There's an open bathroom and toilet directly behind the driver's seat, and a two-grill stove and sink where the passenger seat would be. Xyla's bed is built into one side of the wagon, and an eating nook is built into the opposite side. Aside from the compact, minimalist nature of her traveling home, I'm struck by how different the décor is from her fortuneteller tent. I guess I was sort of expecting spicy incense and colorful fabrics, but instead it looks more like a staged room in IKEA.

"Sorry about the cramped space," Xyla says, before inviting me to sit down at the eating nook. "I know it's not as gaudy as some of the other wagons, but it's perfect for me. Plus, it's easy to drive, which I like."

"How did you end up with it?"

"Claudius got it for me after I broke up with Harry," she says, putting some water in a kettle. "As you can probably guess, he and I used to live and travel together. That wagon was much bigger than this, but Harry did all the driving, so I didn't have to worry about ever getting behind the wheel. After the breakup, I told Claudius I needed my own wagon, so he got me this old girl.

As the kettle starts whistling, Xyla takes it off the stove and pours steaming hot water into a couple of very nice cups—porcelain, I think—before dunking two tea bags shaped like pyramids; inside the pyramids are dried fruit and hearty tea leaves that look like potpourri.

"That smells amazing," I say as Xyla hands me my cup. "What is it?"

"It's called Winter Dream," she says. "Do you take sugar?"

"Yes, please."

She spoons some sugar into my cup, stirring it in for me.

"Thank you."

I take a sip as she sits beside me in the nook.

"How is it?"

"Delicious."

"Good," she says, smiling. "I'm glad you like it."

While small talk feels like the appropriate speed for morning tea, my anxiety about Handsome Harry gets the best of me, and I initiate a much heavier topic.

"So...um...do you know who Eddie is?"

"Eddie who?"

"I don't know his last name," I say, "but May told me he was a sideshow performer at another circus where you and Harry worked."

"Oh," she says. "Eddie."

"The way May told it, Harry wasn't happy about you and Eddie being friends."

"Is that all she said?"

"She also said Harry hurt him," I say, "badly enough that he was taken away in an ambulance. Did all of that really happen?"

Xyla sighs.

"Harry was jealous of Eddie," she says, setting down her cup. "Well, really, Harry was jealous of everybody when it came to me. It was a toxic part of our relationship that I tried to pretend wasn't as bad as it really was. Anyway, Eddie didn't deserve what happened to him."

"So, it's true?"

"Unfortunately."

"What happened afterward?" I ask. "Did anybody call the police or anything?"

"No."

"Why not?"

"In my experience," she says, "circus folk don't like involving the law."

"So, what usually happens in that sort of situation?"

"For better or worse, we tend to police our own."

"And after all that, you stayed with Harry?"

"I didn't know what else to do," she says. "I guess staying was easier. But, you have to understand, things weren't always bad with me and Harry."

"How did you two even end up together?"

"I was working in New Orleans," she says. "I knew a palm reader out there who had her own shop, and she let me work there. Harry was busking nearby on Bourbon Street, so I'd see him around. At the time, he went by Harry Hercules. One day I was out for a walk, and I stopped to watch his act. As soon as he finished, he approached me for a chat."

"How did that go?"

"To be honest, he was surprisingly charming," she says. "Things moved quickly from there. After a few dates, I left my gig in New Orleans and hit the road with Harry. We developed our own act and took it from town to town."

"What kind of act?"

"It was still his strongman act, but I joined in as his lovely assistant."

She frames "lovely assistant" in finger quotes.

"So, no strongman-fortunetelling hybrid?"

"No, but I still did some fortunetelling on the side," she says, "mostly when we needed extra money. Eventually, we landed here with Grambling Brothers. That's when he started going by 'Handsome Harry.'"

"What prompted the name change?"

"Claudius."

"He likes his unique names, huh?"

"He sure does," she says. "It was also Claudius' idea to call me the 'World's Prettiest Fortuneteller.'"

More finger quotes.

"Were you happy with the new name?"

"I didn't love it, but I went with it," she says. "I was just grateful to have job security. Before Grambling Brothers, Harry and I joined other traveling circuses as often as we could, but that work never lasts."

"Why not?"

"Their seasons always end eventually."

"Seasons?"

"Most circuses don't travel year-round," she says. "Grambling Brothers is the rare show that does."

I suspect I should be more interested in Grambling Brother's non-stop travel schedule, but, at the moment, I'm more consumed with Xyla's history with Handsome Harry.

"If you don't mind me asking," I say, "why did you two break up?"

"He couldn't keep his dick in his pants."

"Oh."

"A tale as old as time, right?" she says. "I'd see him flirting with girls all the time after shows, but I convinced myself there was nothing to worry about. Then one day I walked in on him fucking one of his admirers."

"And that was the end?"

"That was the end."

"How did Harry take it?"

"About as well as you'd imagine," she says, cracking a grin for the first time in several minutes. "Afterwards, I told Claudius I was done with Grambling Brothers."

"Really?" I say. "You wanted to leave?"

"Yeah, I needed a clean break."

"So, what happened?"

"Claudius wanted me to stay," she says, "and he can be very persuasive."

"What did he say?"

"Mainly, he gave me his word that Harry wouldn't be a problem for me moving forward."

"That's nice that he gave you some assurance," I say, "but, honestly, I can't believe he let Harry stay."

"What's probably more relevant than that is once Claudius finds someone with a supernatural ability, he never lets them go."

"Wait a minute," I say, nearly dropping my cup. "Are you saying Harry is supernatural?"

"I thought you knew."

"I had no idea," I say. "What can he do?"

"He has supernatural physical strength."

"Oh, Jesus," I say, feeling woozy. "Exactly how strong is he?"

"I'm not sure how to quantify it," she says, "but I know he can lift a car."

I grab a handful of my T-shirt as my chest tightens.

"Grover?"

I'm having trouble breathing.

"Are you okay?"

The room is spinning.

"Let me get you some water."

My hands feel numb.

"Here you go."

Xyla hands me a glass of water, but, when I try to take it, it slips through my fingers, shattering on the floor.

"Shit," I say. "I'm sorry."

"It's okay."

I stand up from the nook, steadying myself with my sweaty palms pressed flat atop the table.

"I should go."

"I think you should stay," Xyla says, laying her hand atop mine. "Please."

I hesitate a moment before sitting back down.

"Just breathe," she says, stroking my back. "In through your nose, out through your mouth."

I close my eyes and take a deep breath.

In through my nose.

Out through my mouth.

"Good," she says, "nice and steady."

In.

Out.

In.

Out.

"How are you feeling now?"

My chest begins to relax as my fingers tingle back to life.

"I'm okay," I say, opening my eyes. "I'm sorry about your cup."

"Don't worry about it."

I slide off the couch to my knees so I can pick up the broken glass.

"That's not necessary," Xyla says. "I'll clean it up."

"Okay," I say, standing up. "I'm sorry."

"You don't have to keep apologizing," she says, squeezing my hand. "I promise it's okay."

"Thank you," I say. "I really should be going, though."

"You sure?"

"Yeah," I say. "Thank you for the tea."

"Anytime."

I forget to say goodbye before exiting, leaving Xyla to clean up my mess.

Chapter Thirty-Two

THE HANDSOME HARRY DILEMMA

M Y HEAD IS SPINNING as I leave Xyla's wagon and walk aimlessly through the labyrinth, contemplating this new wrinkle in the Handsome Harry dilemma. I mean, Harry was scary enough when I thought he was just a muscled-up meathead with unchecked jealousy issues, but now that I know he can—quite literally—tear my arms off, he's downright pee-in-my-pants terrifying. As much as I hate to admit it, I think I may have to start keeping my distance from Xyla.

I'm snapped out of my Harry-inspired angst when I hear someone call my name. Looking up, I see Bettie the Bearded Bombshell sitting under the awning of her wagon in a polka-dot string bikini, a glamour magazine resting against her golden thighs as she waves me over. "I was hoping you'd pass my way," she says. I'm not really in the right headspace to socialize, so my intention is to quickly let her know I can't stay, but, before I can, she excuses herself into her wagon. A few moments later, she returns with a small piece of clothing in her hands.

"These are your fireproof underwear," she says, handing them to me. "The *official* ones."

I hold the underwear at the waistband, looking them over as a soft breeze flutters the gray fabric like a flag. The material is a little rough to the touch and thicker than a regular pair of underwear, but, all in all, they look like proper boxer briefs.

"Wow," I say, "they look so normal."

"They *are* normal," she says, "and fireproof."

"How did you manage to get them done so fast?"

"The expedience is mostly thanks to May," she says, "though I was the one up most of the night making them."

"Well, I can't thank you enough."

"It was my pleasure, hun."

"So, what are they made out of?"

"Silica fabric."

"Never heard of it," I say, "but I'm guessing it's not meant for underwear."

"No, it's not," she says, giggling. "Silica fabric is a fireproof material used for things like curtains or blankets, but May had the bright idea that I might be able to fashion a pair of underwear out of it."

"Looks like she was right."

"May's rarely wrong," she says. "Now, because silica fabric is primarily intended for industrial applications, the tricky part was figuring out how to work with it."

"How do you mean?"

"My sewing machine wasn't up to the task," she says, "so I let May know and, in very short order, she dropped off a Juki TL-2010Q on my doorstep."

"That's a mouthful," I say. "Sounds like a *Star Wars* droid."

This makes Bettie laugh.

"I'll tell you what," she says, "it probably cost as much as a *Star Wars* droid."

"Oh, no," I say. "How much was it?"

"I didn't see the receipt," she says, "but I know it wasn't cheap."

"Well, I'll happily pay May back as soon as I see her."

"You can try," she says, "but May won't take your money."

"You don't think?"

"No way," she says, "that sort of thing gets taken care of around here."

"Wow," I say, "that's so generous."

"Get used to it," she says, "because, from what I hear, Claudius is quite infatuated with you."

"He is?"

"You've got a viral video on YouTube, after all, and last night's show was a turnaway," she says, "so I'm thinking you may be Grambling Brothers' next golden goose."

"Who's the current golden goose?"

"I don't know if you could tell from your first show," she says, "but we've been goose-less for a while now."

"I don't get it," I say. "The show is so great, I can't imagine how it's not filled up every night."

"It's tough to get people's attention anymore," she says. "You practically have to light someone on fire to make them care."

This makes me laugh.

"Now, before I forget, let's get back to business," she says, running her long, manicured fingernails across the fireproof underwear. "I need you to try these on for me."

"Sure," I say. "I'll go try them on in my wagon."

"Oh, pishposh," Bettie says, "you can change inside my place."

She opens the door before I can protest, leading me inside her wagon. I expect to see Lenny and Hannah as I enter, but they're nowhere around.

"Lenny took Hannah out for some daddy-daughter time," Bettie says, practically reading my mind, "so I've got an empty nest for a little while."

"Which way is your bathroom?"

"You don't want to change in front of me?"

Silence.

"Just joshing with you," Bettie says with a laugh. "The bathroom is straight back."

I nod a quick thank you before hurrying to the bathroom. Stepping inside, I find it's roomier than the bathroom in my wagon, but not by much. As I take my pants off and slip into the fireproof underwear, Bettie knocks on the door.

"How's it going in there?"

"Great," I say. "I've got them on."

"Perfect," she says, "let me see, hun."

"Really?" I say, a bouquet of butterflies blooming in my belly.

"No need to be shy," she says. "You'll be modeling these in front of a packed house soon enough."

She's right, of course, so I muster up a bit of courage before stepping out of the bathroom.

"Oh, they look good on you," she says, looking me up and down. "*Really* good."

It feels like she may be flirting with me, so I'm not sure how to respond. I'm also now acutely aware that while I'm out here in my new fireproof underwear, Bettie is practically naked in her polka-dot bikini.

"How do they feel?" she asks, slowly circling me.

"Fine," I say. "I mean, good. They feel good."

"Lovely," she says. "Now, keep in mind, silica fabric isn't designed for comfort, so the main thing we want to concern ourselves with is the fit."

"Okay."

"They're not too tight?" she asks, sliding two fingers between the waistband and my pelvis, her long, manicured fingernails brushing against my manhood.

I try to speak, but I'm immediately distracted as Bettie's incidental contact causes an involuntary pulse of excitement inside my fireproof underwear. I'm not sure if this pulse has intentions of becoming a full-fledged erection, but, just in case it does, I don't want it to happen in front of Bettie, so I turn around and hurry toward the bathroom. Before I can take two steps, I trip over my feet and hit the floor with a thud. I turn over onto my back, waiting for the shock of pain to dissipate as Bettie squats down near my head. She leans over to check on me, but all I can focus on are her exquisite breasts pushing out beneath her burly beard and the one adventurous nipple threatening to break free from its polka-dot prison.

"You okay, hun?"

I'm too embarrassed to respond, so I scramble to my feet and sprint into the bathroom.

"Are you hurt?" Bettie asks through the door.

"I'm okay," I say, pulling my pants up over my new pair of fireproof underwear.

Exiting the bathroom, I offer a hurried thank you before making a beeline for the door. I think Bettie tries to offer me a drink, but I'm already outside, moving as fast as I can without bursting into a sprint. I look back long enough to see Bettie standing in the doorway, a mischievous smile on her face.

After speed walking for a few minutes, I slow down to a stroll and wander about the labyrinth until I unexpectedly run into Fernando near Vik's dukey truck. He's standing beside a steel barrel trashcan with a large flame dancing inside, which is odd, not only for the dramatic and unexpected visual but because it's still morning and the weather is pleasantly warm.

"Grover!" he says, giving me a big hug. "Perfect timing, my friend. I was just working out a new idea for our act."

"Oh, yeah?" I say. "What is it?"

"You're looking at it," he says, gesturing toward the flaming trashcan. "I think it would be very fun for the audience to see you climb inside with the fire."

"Interesting," I say. "Where in the act would we do it?"

"After you're naked," he says. "To see your bare skin consumed by flames, the audience won't have any idea how you're not burning alive."

"I love that idea," I say. "Though, as I think about it, what if it's *too* hard to believe?"

"What do you mean?"

"If it's too hard to believe," I say, "the audience might assume we're somehow faking it."

"But we're not."

"Yeah, but they don't know that."

"Good point," he says, folding his arms. "What do we do?"

"I don't know," I say, folding my arms. "Let's think about this."

We stand together in silence, staring into the flaming trashcan, quietly hoping for a good idea to present itself. During our impromptu meditation, Xyla turns up beside us. Now, I know my plan for the safety and preservation of my bodily health—as of less than an hour ago—was to steer clear of Xyla, but, as soon as I see her, I don't want her to go away.

"Feeling better?" she asks.

"Yeah."

"Glad to hear it," she says, smiling. "What're you guys up to?"

"We're working on a new section for our act."

"Fun," she says. "What is it?"

"Well, Fernando came up with this idea of having me stand in a flaming trashcan after my clothes have burned off."

"That sounds cool," she says. "Standing naked in fire will look amazing."

"Well, not *totally* naked," I say. "I have fireproof underwear now."

"Since when?"

"Since this morning," I say. "Bettie made them for me."

"And they work?"

"Bettie says they do."

"Have you tested them?"

"Not yet."

"Where are they now?"

"I'm wearing them."

"Perfect," she says. "Jump in the can."

"What?" I say, laughing. "Are you crazy?"

"Why is that crazy?"

"Well, first of all, these are new clothes I bought the other day."

"That's okay," she says. "Take them off."

"Now I *know* you're crazy."

"What's crazy about that?"

"I'm not going to get naked here."

"You won't be *totally* naked."

"Well, now I just think you're being a troublemaker."

"Maybe," she says. "Or maybe I'm just trying to get you naked."

This makes Fernando laugh, so I laugh with him, though I'm feeling more bashful than tickled at the moment.

"But, seriously," I say, desperate to shift the subject away from me getting naked, "we're trying to solve a problem with the new section of the act."

"What's the problem?"

"We're concerned that if the spectacle of me standing in the flaming trashcan is too hard to believe, then the audience will assume it's fake."

"I see," she says. "So, you want to ensure the audience knows with certainty that you're standing naked in a flaming trashcan."

"Precisely," I say. "I mean, not *completely* naked, but yes."

"What if you roast marshmallows?"

"Roast marshmallows?" I say. "I don't follow."

"If you roast marshmallows while you stand in the trashcan," she says, "then it'll prove to the audience that the fire is real."

"Ah, yes," Fernando says. "This is good. We can even hand out marshmallows to the audience at the beginning of the performance and tell them not to eat them because they will be used in the grand finale."

"Oh, I like that," Xyla says. "It'll create wonderful anticipation."

"After Grover climbs into the trashcan," Fernando says, "I will go around and collect the marshmallows. Then, we will roast them in front of the audience while Grover stands in the fire."

"And after they're roasted," I say, "we can give them back to the audience."

"Yes," Fernando says, "it's perfect!"

"I just had a thought," Xyla says. "Will the trashcan itself burn you?"

"How do you mean?"

"It's steel," she says. "Are you impervious to hot metal as well as fire?"

"Canyon actually asked me the same thing yesterday."

"And?"

"And I have no idea."

"You haven't been tempted to find out?"

"Well, given that the only way to find out is by voluntarily touching a hot piece of metal," I say, "I haven't made it a priority."

This gets a good laugh out of Xyla and Fernando, even though I wasn't trying to be funny—but then, rather abruptly, Xyla falls deathly silent as a look of concern washes over her face.

"Grover," she says, staring straight ahead, "jump into the trashcan."

Before I can ask why, I see Handsome Harry stalking towards us from Vik's truck, a half-eaten grilled cheese sandwich hanging from his fingers.

"Grover," Xyla says, a restrained panic in her voice, "do it now."

I hesitate a moment, my anxiety freezing me in place, until Xyla looks me square in the eyes.

"Now!"

Without a second thought—either for the logistics of actually getting inside or the potential of searing my skin against the red-hot steel—I grab the lip of the trashcan and lift myself up, swinging one leg over, then the other, until both of my feet are compressing the flaming garbage beneath them. As Harry bounds closer, tossing his sandwich aside, I crouch down and hug my knees, letting the angry flames whoosh up around me. A small crowd of onlookers forms around us as Harry gets closer, and my clothes become fully engulfed.

On the bright side, I realize the scorching steel of the trashcan didn't burn my skin, so it seems that I am—in fact—impervious to hot metal. On the not-so-bright side, Harry is now standing directly in front of me, a crazed look on his objectively handsome face.

"Harry," Xyla says, stepping between us, "leave him alone."

There's a calmness in her voice, perhaps because this isn't the first time she's tried to calm Harry down. If her calm tones ever worked before, they're not working now, as Harry pushes her aside, never taking his eyes off of me. However unsettling it is to be face-to-face with this terrifying man who wants nothing more than to cause me great bodily harm, I'm gradually feeling more and more safe inside my protective flames. Harry reaches his hands toward me before quickly snatching them back as they touch the fire.

Stepping away from the flaming trashcan, he curses while blowing on his fingertips. He cocks his head to the side, a low growl sounding in his throat as he tries to figure out his next move. I'm still feeling secure inside the flames even as Harry straightens his head, a snarling smile opening his lips. Whatever idea he's come up with, I assume I'll still be safe—that is until Handsome Harry lifts his tree trunk of a leg and kicks the trashcan. It feels like I've been hit by a car as the trashcan topples over, launching me onto the dirt in a wild tumble. Now that I'm removed from the protective fire, Harry stomps towards me with renewed confidence.

"Grover," Xyla says, "run!"

I scramble to my feet—still on fire in spite of the tumble—breaking into a sprint as Harry chases behind me. Running harder than I've ever run in my life, I wind through the labyrinth and away from the raucous rumblings of the onlookers, eventually finding myself alone in the midway as my flaming clothes peel away from my body, leaving me naked but for my sneakers and fireproof underwear. My heart races as I glance back and see Harry closing the gap between us, gaining ground with the ferocity of a runaway train. Desperate to keep my precarious distance from Harry, I try pumping more speed into my legs, hoping to tap into an undiscovered reserve of energy, only to find that I've already pushed my body well past the point of exhaustion.

Up ahead, near the Cretors popcorn machine, I see Harry and I aren't the only two people in the midway anymore as Lenny and Hannah return from their daddy-daughter date, each of them visibly confused at the sight of me running for my life. With my legs on the verge of collapse, I glance back one last time to see Harry even closer than he was before—arms stretched out, fingers clawed—just a few long strides away from his prey. Finally, after giving it all I had to give, my body crumbles to the dirt, leaving me to gasp for air as Harry leaps into the sky like a ravenous lion. Time slows down to an insufferable drip as the shadow of his massive frame swallows me whole, his body so close to mine that I can smell the rancid musk of rage fuming from his pores.

And then, inexplicably, in pure disregard for the laws of physics, Handsome Harry goes from hovering above me to violently flying away—directly to my left—like he's been T-boned by an invisible Mack truck. His body crashes into the Cretors popcorn machine, glass shattering like confetti as the red and yellow steel crumples against the weight of Harry's overwhelming brawn. As Harry groans in pain, I sit up and look around the midway to see if anyone else witnessed the improbable turn of events that saved my life, but, as it was before I collapsed to the dirt, Hannah and Lenny are the only other two people in sight.

By the looks of it, sweet little Hannah might be in shock, the poor thing. While Lenny stares at Handsome Harry laying half-conscious atop the Ringmaster's precious popcorn machine, Hannah stands frozen in an odd posture: one leg bent forward and the other posted straight back at a 45-degree angle, her arms stretching forward with her hands splayed open to the sky like she's pushing against an invisible wall.

Standing up to my feet, I brush the dirt from my knees as I gingerly make my way toward Hannah. My intention is to offer some comfort and perhaps an explanation of what she saw, but I stop short of saying anything when I notice Hannah's normally kind eyes squinting angrily against her furrowed brow. Before I can work out exactly what's happening with her, Lenny collapses to the dirt, lying unconscious at his daughter's feet.

Chapter Thirty-Three

THE LEGEND OF GILES COREY

Handsome Harry and I are inside the Ringmaster's dimly lit office, sitting side by side in front of the boss's desk, hands folded in our respective laps like a couple of kids who've been summoned by the principal. I'm still very naked, but for my fireproof underwear, so I'm grateful for the lack of light in here. Harry is sporting several fresh cuts and scrapes from his violent—and still quite inexplicable—collision with the Cretors popcorn machine. I don't know how long we've been in the Ringmaster's office; it feels like hours, though minutes is more likely. Sitting in his worn-down chair, fingers interlaced atop his desk, he's yet to say anything to either one of us.

"So, Harry," the Ringmaster says, finally speaking, "who's responsible for breaking my popcorn machine?"

Harry shrugs.

"What's that?"

"I don't know."

"You don't know?"

Harry shakes his head, no.

"So, it wasn't your body that crushed the very machine Charles Cretors personally gifted to Walter Grambling?"

"Well, yeah," Harry says, "but I didn't do it."

"So, you *did* it, but you *didn't* do it," the Ringmaster says. "Do I have that right?"

Harry shifts in his seat.

"Sounds like quite the paradox," the Ringmaster says. "How do you explain it?"

"Something moved me."

"Emotionally?" the Ringmaster asks.

"No," Harry says, "it moved my body."

"Fascinating," the Ringmaster says. "What exactly moved your body, if it wasn't you?"

Harry shrugs, shaking his head.

"If I didn't know any better, I'd think you were describing witch-craft."

Perhaps tired of interrogating Harry, the Ringmaster shifts his attention to me.

"What do you think, Grover?"

"About what, sir?"

"The destruction of my Cretors popcorn machine," he says. "Do you think it was witchcraft?"

"I don't know," I say. "Probably not."

"Do you not believe in witchcraft?"

"I mean, I guess it's possible," I say, unsure of how seriously I'm meant to regard his question. "But I've never seen it before."

"Never?" he asks. "Are you sure?"

"I think so."

"Have you ever met a witch?"

I start to say no before stopping myself.

"When I was a kid, my Aunt Ruthie told me *she* was a witch," I say. "But I'm not sure that counts."

"Why wouldn't it count?"

"I'm not sure she actually *was* a witch."

"But she *could've* been a witch?"

"I guess it's possible."

The Ringmaster flicks his Zippo lighter, puffing a fresh cigar to life.

"It sounds like you're hard to convince without concrete evidence," the Ringmaster says. "If you were in charge during the Salem witch trials, I dare say there would've been far fewer executions. Incidentally, do you happen to know how the Puritans executed accused witches during the Salem witch trials?"

"They were hanged."

The Ringmaster smiles.

"Very good," he says, scissoring the cigar between his thick fingers. "Most people assume they were burned at the stake."

"The burnings mostly happened in European countries."

"It sounds like you're quite knowledgeable about the Salem witch trials."

"Not really," I say, "but my aunt told me a little bit about it."

"Did she know a lot about the Salem witch trials?"

"I think so, yeah."

"Did she ever tell you about Giles Corey?"

I shake my head, no.

"Giles Corey was a man accused of being a witch during the Salem witch trials," the Ringmaster says, "and, as a consequence of that accusation, he was killed. But, unlike the other accused witches, Giles Corey wasn't hanged."

"Was he burned?" Harry asks.

"No, he wasn't burned either," the Ringmaster says. "You see, during the Salem witch trials, you couldn't be executed simply for being *accused* of witchcraft. After you were accused, the Puritans asked you to make a plea—guilty or not guilty—at which point they were free to hang you to death, assuming they found you guilty."

The Ringmaster exhales a plume of smoke.

"You have to hand it to the Puritans," he says, examining the glowing orange embers of his cigar. "As witch crazy as they were, they disguised their mania as law and order. The Salem witch trials lasted just over one year, from 1692 to 1693, and during that year, over two hundred men and women were accused of witchcraft, including Giles Corey. Of those two hundred accused, do you know how many were found guilty?"

I shake my head, no.

"Thirty," the Ringmaster says. "And all thirty of them were executed by hanging. But Giles Corey wasn't one of those thirty."

"I thought you said they killed him," Harry says, clearly riveted.

"Here's the thing," the Ringmaster says. "When the Puritans accused Giles Corey of witchcraft, he refused to give them a plea. His wife, Martha, was also accused of witchcraft, but, unlike her husband, she quickly offered a plea of not guilty and, shortly thereafter, was found guilty and hanged to death. But, since Giles wouldn't enter a plea, the Puritans couldn't hang him on account of their own legal loophole. So, in the absence of a plea, the Puritans pivoted to their next best option."

"What was that?" Harry asks.

"Torture," the Ringmaster says, sliding his ashtray to the middle of the desk. "The Puritans' goal was to make Giles Corey suffer until he gave them what they wanted, so they dragged him into a public square, laying him down on the ground as a crowd of locals circled around him." The Ringmaster draws an invisible circle around the ashtray with his fingertip. "They placed a wooden board on top of his body, then set a heavy stone on top of the board. Beneath the weight of this heavy stone, Giles Corey was given an opportunity to enter a plea, but he refused. So, another stone was set on top of him, and, again, the Puritans asked for a plea, but Giles Corey refused. So, another stone was placed on top of him, followed by another refusal. It went on like this for three days until Giles Corey was eventually crushed to death."

The Ringmaster pulls a tug from his cigar.

"Death by pressing," he says. "Even though the Puritans didn't get to put a noose around his neck, Giles Corey still ended up giving them exactly what they wanted. Now, Harry, let me ask you again. Who's responsible for breaking my popcorn machine?"

Silence.

"Well?"

"It's *his* fault," Harry says, pointing at me.

"Are you sure?" the Ringmaster says, stabbing the ashtray with his cigar.

"Uh-huh."

"There's nothing you want to take responsibility for?"

Harry shakes his head, no.

"Okay then," the Ringmaster says, removing his red-tinted glasses. "Very well."

Without warning, the Ringmaster shoots his arm across the desk, snatching Harry's neck with his meaty fingers like a viper attacking its unsuspecting prey. The Ringmaster stands from his seat and walks around the desk, lifting Harry into the air by his throat. His massive bicep bulges beneath his sleeve as Harry's face turns red, his toes frantically searching for the floor beneath him.

"Grover," the Ringmaster says with all the calm of a Buddhist monk, "I'm sorry your first days with Grambling Brothers were affected by the actions of this crude man-child. You have my word that, from this moment forward, Harry will never bother you again."

The Ringmaster tightens his fingers around Harry's throat, prompting his legs to flail like a marionette.

"Stop!" I say as Harry's face changes from red to purple, saliva foaming from his mouth. "You're killing him!"

"Perhaps that's what needs to happen."

"Please," I say, "you don't have to do this."

"Don't I?"

"No."

"Do you think Harry would offer you the same courtesy if the situation were reversed?"

"It doesn't matter," I say. "Just please let him go."

"Are you sure that's what you want?"

"Yes."

"Very well."

The Ringmaster releases Harry from his grip, dropping him to the floor with a pronounced thud. A shallow cloud of dust kicks up around his limp body, and I fear he may already be dead until the color returns to his face and he takes in several deep gulps of air.

"Grover," the Ringmaster says, putting his red-tinted glasses back on, "you may be excused."

I stand up from my seat without another word, stumbling past Harry's heaving shoulders as he sobs on the floor, a thick string of drool hanging from his chin. Opening the door, a stretch of sunlight cuts through the darkness as I exit the Ringmaster's office.

Chapter Thirty-Four

NOT NOW, NOT EVER

A BALL OF TERROR pulses in my chest, my body shaking uncontrollably as I stand outside the Ringmaster's office. I move to wipe the tears streaking down my face, freezing when I hear shuffling inside the office. The door slowly opens, and Handsome Harry steps out, making his way down the short set of steps. He stops beside me, wiping his nose with the back of his hand before clearing his throat.

"Thank you," he says.

He's staring straight ahead as he speaks, looking at nothing that I can clock.

"Sure," I say.

He walks away without another word, his big, powerful shoulders slouched as he disappears around the corner. I stand exactly where I am for several unsettling minutes after he's gone, paralyzed with confusion, when Xyla shows up.

"Grover," she says, "are you okay?"

I shake my head, no.

She gives me a big hug, and I lay my head against her neck, a fresh stream of tears wetting her skin.

"What happened?" she asks. "Did Harry hurt you?"

I shake my head, no, unable to speak another word without getting choked up. If I could, I'd tell Xyla that I just watched the Ringmaster nearly murder Handsome Harry, and, apparently, I'm the only reason he's still alive. I'd also tell her that whatever supernatural strength Harry has was totally useless against the Ringmaster.

"It's okay," she says, filling the silence, "we can talk about it later. Want to put some clothes on?"

I forgot that I'm standing here practically naked, so I nod in the affirmative. Xyla takes my hand and guides me away from the Ringmaster's office, handling me as gently as she might a scared child. It's the first time that we've held hands like this on the circus grounds without worrying about Handsome Harry. Xyla takes me to my wagon, and I grab some fresh clothes while she waits outside.

I get dressed quietly as Canyon is sleeping in his bunk. A silver ring hangs from his neck, laced by a thin gold chain. It looks like a wedding band, and—if it is—I wonder why he's not wearing it on his finger. I've never been one to wear rings myself, so I'd understand if that's why he prefers it around his neck. After quietly contemplating Canyon's ring for a few minutes, a cool mist of calm settles over me.

I rejoin Xyla outside, and we walk about the labyrinth, hand in hand. I see Hannah sitting with a coloring book while Bettie files her nails. Lenny's not with them, which is unsettling because the last time I saw him he was passed out in the dirt. I want to make sure he's okay, so I start walking their way. Hannah spots us before we get there and runs over to give me a hug. When she's done with me, she wraps her arms around Xyla's waist.

"Okay, Hannah," Bettie says from her lawn chair, "leave these lovebirds alone."

Hannah squints against the sunshine as she flashes us a smile before going back to her coloring book.

"How's Lenny?" I ask.

"He's in bed," Bettie says, "but he'll be fine."

"What happened to him?"

"Nothing we haven't seen before," she says, standing up from her lawn chair. "I should probably go check on him. Hannah, come on, baby."

Hannah jumps from her chair, following Bettie inside their wagon.

"I hope I didn't say anything out of line back there," I say to Xyla as we continue walking. "I was just concerned about Lenny is all."

"It's okay," Xyla says, "she knows you meant well. What happened to him anyway?"

"I'm not sure," I say. "Earlier today, after Harry crashed into the popcorn machine, I saw Lenny pass out."

"Did Harry collide with him or something?"

"No, they weren't even close," I say. "Lenny and Hannah were just standing by and watching Harry chase me. Then, the next time I looked over at them, Lenny crumbled to the dirt, passed out unconscious."

"That sounds scary," she says, "but I guess if Bettie's not worried, he'll probably be okay."

"I hope so."

"Plus, Hannah was in good spirits," she says, "so that seems like a good sign."

"Speaking of Hannah, I had no idea you two were so close."

"Me neither," she says with a laugh. "I'm pretty sure she only hugged me so I wouldn't feel left out."

"She's a sweet girl that way."

We stop in front of Xyla's wagon, and she invites me in. It's not that I don't want to spend more time with her, but my brain is still processing the crazy day I've had, so I'm just not up for it.

"Rain check?"

"Sure," she says. "Find me later?"

"You bet."

I walk the circus grounds past the sideshow tents and the midway games and the empty spot where the Cretors popcorn machine used to be. Popcorn Pete is standing there, seemingly unsure of what to do with himself. We chat for a few minutes, and, while he's putting on a happy face, I sense a tangible sadness beneath the surface. He tells me the Ringmaster was very kind to him after breaking the news of what happened and promised to bring in a new popcorn machine for him to oversee.

We part ways as I get a call from Mom.

"Hi, sweetheart," she says. "How's circus life?"

"Never boring," I say, deciding not to fill her in on the Handsome Harry drama. "How's Dad?"

Silence.

"Mom?"

"I don't want you to worry," she says, "but his vital signs took a dip."

"What? When?"

"A little while ago," she says. "I'm not exactly sure, but I didn't want to concern you since the doctors aren't panicked just yet."

"Maybe I should come home."

"That's not necessary, sweetheart," she says. "The doctors and nurses are taking extra good care of your dad. Plus, I'm here with him every day."

"Okay," I say, "but you'll let me know if you need me to come home?"

"Of course."

"Promise?"

"Promise."

As I hang up with Mom, I see Paulo Silva approaching the box office with a cup of coffee in hand and a burrito tucked under his injured arm. I'm curious how he's going to open the door in the back of the box office to let himself in, so I watch him for a few moments. He stares at the door for a minute before cursing to himself. At the risk of being intrusive, I decide to see if I can help.

"Need a hand?"

"I'm fine."

"You sure?"

A few awkward moments of silence pass.

"Keys are in my pocket," Paulo says, turning his hip toward me.

"Oh," I say, "should I...I mean...do you want me to get them?"

"Never mind."

"No, no," I say, "let me help."

I slide my fingers into his pocket, and—good lord—it's a tight fit. My palm is pressed flush against his thigh as I feel the keys with my fingertips. There's not quite enough room for me to grasp them, so I have to go deeper. I manage to get my middle finger on the keyring, and I try to quickly drag it up, but, in my haste, I lose my grip, so I have to slide my hand back in. During this second journey down Paulo's pants, I'm pretty sure I make contact with one of his testicles. He flinches, and I whip my hand out of his pocket.

"I'll figure it out," he says. "Thanks anyway."

"Let me try one more time."

On my third attempt, I finally manage to pull the keys out. Paulo tells me which one is for the box office, and I open the door for him. He sets down his burrito and coffee inside before coming back out to get the keys.

"Thank you."

"Happy to help."

Another awkward silence follows, as neither of us seems to know what to do next.

"Hey," I say, "you mind if I ask what happened to your arm?"

"Just some bad luck."

"What kind of bad luck?"

Paulo looks around before stepping closer.

"You seem like a nice guy," he says, "and I appreciate your help here, so I want to offer some advice."

"Okay."

"Stay out of trouble," he says, "and don't ask too many questions."

"I'm sorry, I didn't mean to pry."

"The truth is," he says, lowering his voice to a whisper, "I'm not allowed to talk about it."

"You're not allowed to talk about your bad luck?"

"Not now, not ever."

Wandering the circus grounds, I pass the big top, where I hear grunts of effort and exertion inside. Curious, I slip through the front entrance and see the Soaring Silvas and Solo rehearsing on the flying trapeze. Solo is standing on one of the opposing platforms when he sees me and waves. I take a seat in the bleachers, as close as I can get, and tilt my head up to watch. Solo grips the trapeze with his Spider-Man hands and leaps from the platform, arching his legs back like a crescent moon, then kicking them forward to generate momentum. As he reaches the apex of his swing, Solo releases his grip on the trapeze and tucks his body into an aerial somersault that lasts for three breathtaking revolutions before catching the outstretched hands of Carlos—the elder Silva—who hangs by his knees from the opposing trapeze.

I stay glued to my seat until the end of the rehearsal. Solo, Carlos, Jose, and Ana climb down the rope ladders to solid ground. Solo stops to say hi, while the rest of the Soaring Silvas walk past me as if I'm not here.

"If it makes you feel better," Solo says, "they don't like me either."

"I was actually just talking with Paulo before coming here."

"No kidding?" he says. "How'd that come about?"

"He needed help getting into the box office," I say. "I got the impression he didn't want me around before I helped him out."

"That makes sense," he says. "I'm sure he wants to stay loyal to his family."

"I don't even know what I did to make them hate me."

"They were Grambling Brothers' featured act before you came around," he says. "You took their spot."

"That's fair," I say. "But why don't they like *you*?"

"I'm not one of them," he says. "I replaced Paulo."

"You didn't injure him, right?"

"No, not at all," he says with a laugh. "They're just a very tight-knit family. I'm confident that they would've hated whoever replaced him."

"How did you end up replacing him, anyway?"

"It's kind of a long story," he says, "but what it comes down to is my mom is sick."

"What's wrong with her?"

"Breast cancer."

"I'm so sorry."

"Thank you," he says. "She lives in Puebla, Mexico, and we couldn't afford the sort of health care she needed for chemo. Then I met Claudius."

"How'd you meet?"

"I was jogging in the park, and he was sitting on a bench," he says. "He struck up a conversation with me, and we got to talking about the circus. I told him I was a trapeze artist, and he told me this was a lucky coincidence for him because he needed to replace an injured flyer. What are the chances, right?"

"One in a zillion, I'd bet."

"Then he asks if I'd be interested in joining his circus."

"Just like that?"

"Just like that," he says. "I told him I couldn't accept the offer because I was going to Mexico to be with my mother. He asked me to reconsider, so I told him she has cancer and needs my help. He tells me he can get her the best medical treatments available if I join his circus. I tell him I can't afford it, and he says he'll cover all the costs. It was too good to refuse, so here I am."

"Has your mom gotten her medical treatments?"

"Yeah," he says. "Her body has responded well so far, and the doctors are cautiously optimistic."

"And the medical costs?"

"All taken care of."

"Wow," I say, "that's pretty much exactly what happened to me."

"How so?"

"My dad's sick," I say. "He's in the hospital right now."

"What's wrong with him?"

"He's in a coma," I say, "but the doctors don't know what's wrong."

"That's rough," he says. "How did Claudius find you?"

"Xyla told him about me," I say. "He offered to take care of my dad's medical costs if I joined Grambling Brothers."

"And here you are."

"Where do you think his money comes from?" I ask. "I mean, is Grambling Brothers that profitable?"

"Look around this place," he says. "Does it look profitable to you?"

"Not really," I say. "So, how is he able to help all the people he makes deals with?"

"Your guess is as good as mine," he says. "But, as long as he holds up his end of the bargain, I'm not worried about finding out."

It's showtime.

The performers gather behind the big top, and the Ringmaster gives a pre-show talk. He announces the lineup, which has Fernando and me closing the show again. Fernando lets me know that the flaming trashcan and marshmallows will be ready for us tonight, so we can try the new finale we talked about earlier in the day. As the Ringmaster heads inside to kick things off, everyone disperses except for Handsome Harry and me.

"Hi," I say.

Harry nods a silent hello.

"So, that was kind of crazy what happened earlier, right?"

Harry doesn't respond.

"I mean, that wasn't normal," I say, "was it?"

"I don't know what you're talking about."

"I'm talking about that crazy meeting we had in Claudius's office this morning."

"Nothing happened this morning."

I look at him, confused.

"Are you being serious?"

"Whatever you think you saw," he says, "you're better off never mentioning it again. Not now, not ever."

Chapter Thirty-Five

A NEW WORLD

AFTER TWO NIGHTS IN Las Vegas, Grambling Brothers packed up and hit the road for Albuquerque, New Mexico. I'm currently sitting shotgun with Canyon as he navigates our wagon along the rocky orange landscape of the American Southwest. The ink-black sky and its endless tapestry of stars have filled the windshield for the entirety of our drive until, inside of a few fleeting minutes, the black gives way to purple, then to orange, and finally to blue—right before our eyes, a new morning is upon us. Darius is asleep in the back as we drive through Arizona, just about four or five hours away from Albuquerque.

"I appreciate you driving," I say. "If you get tired or anything, let me know, and I can take over for a stretch."

"Long drives relax me," Canyon says, pulling the thin gold chain up from beneath his shirt, "so I don't mind being the wheel man."

Pinching the silver ring that hangs from the chain, Canyon brings it to his lips, giving it a kiss.

"Is that your wedding ring?" I ask.

"No way," he says with a chuckle. "Me and my lady aren't legal like that. We like to keep Uncle Sam out of our business." He lets the necklace dangle from his fingers for a moment before slip-ping the ring back beneath his shirt. "It was my dad's wedding ring. My mom gave it to me after he died."

"I'm sorry to hear he passed."

"Thanks, bro," he says. "My old man was a truck driver, so he was on the road a lot, but he was crazy in love with my mom. Every morning at sunrise, when he was away from home, Pops would kiss his ring for my mom. And my mom was always awake before sunset, so she could kiss her ring at the same time. So, now every morning at sunset, I do the same thing."

"Sounds like that ring means a lot to you."

"It means everything to me, bro," he says. "Besides my little girl and my lady, it's the most valuable thing I've got."

"How old were you when he died?"

"Young," he says. "Just a kid."

"What happened to him?"

"Heart attack, I think," he says. "My mom never really talks about it, so I'm not too sure."

"My dad's in the hospital right now," I say. "He's in a coma."

"Shit, bro," he says. "What happened to him?"

"The doctors don't know yet," I say. "My mom is with him every day, so she keeps me updated. But I can't help but fear the worst. I know I'm not a kid or anything, but I'm not ready to lose my dad."

"I don't know what's worse," he says. "Seeing it coming or being caught by surprise. For me, it happened so out of the blue, I couldn't even wrap my head around it. Those first few weeks after he died, it just felt like he was out on the road like normal. Sometimes when I'd be playing with my toys in front of the TV, lost in my own world, I'd hear the front door open and, for just a second, I'd think Pops was home."

I turn to look out the passenger window, not wanting Canyon to see me cry.

"My mom gave me his ring after the funeral," he says. "I wanted to wear it like he did, but my fingers weren't big enough, so she got me this necklace."

"That's sweet," I say. "He's always with you, huh."

"Always," he says. "I never take it off, either. Not ever, not for nothing. This ring will be around my neck till the day I die."

I wake up in Albuquerque, my shoulder wet with drool, unaware that I'd fallen asleep. Canyon and Darius are already gone, presumably to start their day with the rest of the tent crew. I wander through the reassembled labyrinth until I find the community bathroom, where I take a shower and brush my teeth. After putting on some fresh clothes, I head out to the circus grounds, where the tent crew is setting up the big top in a large field of weathered grass that feels like it used to be populated by cowboys and saloons. There's a random pink train car nearby, and brick walls covered with vibrant, childlike paintings. Out beyond the weathered grass are tangerine-colored mountains with flat peaks, a rusty water tower, and a strange-looking structure that resembles a giant salt shaker.

May turns up beside me, as if from thin air.

"Have you ever been to these parts before?"

"Albuquerque?" I say. "Never."

"Technically, we're in a town called Bernalillo," she says, "but it's part of Albuquerque."

"Is this a regular stop for Grambling Brothers?"

"Oh, yeah," she says. "Historically, blue-collar towns like this were the lifeblood of the circus."

"Really?"

"You bet," she says. "Affordable entertainment for the whole family that would appear in the dead of night without notice or explanation. Word would spread from mouth to ear like a virus, and everyone showed up to the big top ready to forget about their difficult lives for a little while. Would you believe that fewer than 10,000 people live here?"

"Is that right?"

"You could fit every citizen of Bernalillo inside Madison Square Garden with room to spare," she says. "I always make a point of putting towns like this on our schedule. They tend to appreciate us more than the big cities."

"Claudius lets you plan where the show travels?"

"You bet," she says. "That's all up to me."

"He must really trust you, huh?"

"You can say that."

"So, you probably know what happened with me and Handsome Harry in his office the other day."

"I hear things," May says. "For example, I happen to know that Claudius is very happy to have you here."

"Well, it's nice to be appreciated."

"You're more than appreciated," she says. "You're his new favorite toy."

I'm tempted to ask May if it's true what Canyon told me—that she can make herself invisible—but I chicken out.

"Since you're his right-hand gal," I say, "maybe you can convince Claudius to add a Ferris wheel."

"A Ferris wheel," she says. "Why would I do that?"

"I don't know," I say, feeling silly for mentioning it. "It just seems appropriate for the circus."

"Maybe under someone else's watch," she says, "but traveling the country with a big ol' wheel is one headache I can do without."

Someone with the tent crew calls out for May.

"Looks like I'm needed," she says, turning to walk away. "I'll see you around."

A flash of nerve jolts through me.

"Hey, May?"

She turns around mid-stride, giving me her full attention as she walks backward.

"Yeah?"

"Can you make yourself invisible?"

She smiles.

"Can't we all?"

The midway feels like a ghost town, as nobody else is around. The solitude is strange, but nice. I know it won't be long before there are people everywhere, but for now I get to have it all to myself, alone with my thoughts. Speaking of which, I still haven't quite wrapped my head around what all happened in the Ringmaster's office—not just the fact that he's strong enough to hold Handsome Harry in the air with one hand while simultaneously choking him very nearly to death, but also the fact that he's uncomfortably willing to take a man's life. I suppose it could've all been a show for my benefit, and maybe the Ringmaster never had any real intention of killing Handsome Harry—but, even if that's true, I don't think Harry was in on it.

An unexpected rustling sound startles me as I stroll through the midway and realize I'm not as alone as I thought. After a hurried survey of my surroundings, I see Charlie Chuckles standing inside a midway booth; he's leaning against the short wall, his head hanging back like he's asleep on his feet. My initial instinct is to mind my own business, but then a flash of panic zips across my chest as it occurs to me that Charlie may be in the throes of a medical emergency. As I hurry over to check on him, Charlie turns his head and sees me coming.

"Hey, kid!" he says, smiling through yesterday's grease paint. "How's it go...oh...ooohhh, yeah, baby!"

Charlie briefly collapses, his knees buckling as he catches himself with his elbows on the short wall. Just as I get close enough to ensure he's okay, Bettie the Bearded Bombshell rises up from behind the booth, pearls of moisture hanging from her mustache.

"Hi, Grover," she says, wiping her lips with the back of her hand.

"Sorry," I say, backing away from the booth. "I'll get out of here."

"It's okay," Bettie says. "I was just leaving."

"That's funny," Charlie says. "I was just coming."

Bettie squeals with laughter as she bends over to slap the dirt from her knees.

"Grover," she says, looking up at me, "were you planning to work with the kids today?"

"Um, yeah, I think so."

"Oh, good," she says. "Hannah had a great time the other day. What time should I drop her off?"

"I'm not sure," I say. "Probably the same time as before."

"Perfect," she says, smoothing out her dress over her thighs. "See you then."

Charlie and I stand in silence, watching her walk away.

"That's one hell of a woman," he says. "Her mouth belongs in a goddamn museum."

"Charlie, what the fuck?"

"What?"

"What's going on here?"

"Bettie just gave me a hummer," he says. "I thought that was obvious."

"I figured that much out."

"So, which part's confusing you?"

"She's married!"

"No shit."

"So, why is she giving you a blowjob in the midway?"

"We had nowhere else to go."

"No, I mean, why was she giving you a blowjob *at all*?"

"Oh, I don't know, maybe because she's a fucking saint."

"What about Lenny?"

"Lenny can ask for a blowjob if he wants one," Charlie says, "but it's up to Bettie whether she does it or not. It's a new world, kid. You've got to get consent."

"What I mean is, why is she blowing *you* when she's already married to *Lenny*?"

"I don't know what to tell you, kid," he says. "Love's complicated. Anyway, I need to go clean my dick. See you tonight."

Charlie shuffles away, pulling a wedgy from his jumpsuit as he goes.

Just when I think I'm alone again, Xyla turns up from out of nowhere.

"I've been looking all over for you," she says. "Ready for our next adventure?"

Chapter Thirty-Six

THE ROOM

XYLA TAKES ME TO a cool spot called 505 Pinball, which is an arcade devoted solely to pinball machines. There are all sorts of themed machines here, from Metallica and *Back to the Future* to Aerosmith and *The Walking Dead*. I'm particularly enamored with a *Star Wars* machine, replete with miniature models of the Death Star, X-wings, and the nostalgia-inducing sounds of R2-D2's beeping and whirring.

"How'd you find this place?"

"It's not my first time in Albuquerque," she says. "One of the perks of circus life is all the many places you get to visit."

I pull back the handle on the *Star Wars* machine, shooting my ball into a galaxy far, far away.

"So," I say, "you'll never guess what I saw today."

"What?"

"Charlie Chuckles getting a blowjob from Bettie the Bearded Bombshell."

"They let you watch?" she says. "Kinky."

"No," I say, laughing, "I happened upon them."

"It sounds so classy when you say 'happened upon them.'"

I laugh some more.

"Isn't that crazy, though?" I say. "I mean, Bettie's married."

"You're sweet to worry about her marriage."

"I just think it would suck if this broke up their family."

"You're right," she says, "they're a very sweet family. Speaking of which, I meant to tell you that when their daughter hugged me the other day, I saw inside of her."

"You saw inside Hannah?"

"Yeah."

"What did you see?"

"Do you remember the first night you visited my tent when I told you that I'd only ever seen one other vision like what I saw inside you?"

"Yeah, with Lenny," I say. "Two bolts of lightning floating side by side."

"Well, I saw the exact same bolts of lightning inside of Hannah."

"Really?" I say. "Has that ever happened before?"

"No," she says, "I've never seen an identical vision inside two different people."

"So, Hannah and Lenny have the same images inside of them," I say. "What does that mean?"

"Your guess is as good as mine."

"Could it be that parents and kids have similar images inside of them?" I say. "Sort of like having the same color eyes or something?"

"I don't think it works like that," she says. "I saw inside my mom once when I was a kid, and it was an image that meant nothing to me. But when I asked her about it, she freaked out."

"What happened?"

"She was tucking me into bed," Xyla says, "and when she kissed me, I saw a room inside of her. It had brown walls with striped curtains fluttering against an open window. Mind you, I saw inside my mom all the time, but I didn't know I was special. I just assumed it was something everybody could do. So, when I told her about what I saw, I didn't think much of it."

"What did she say?"

"She asked who told me about that room, and I told her no one told me about it," Xyla says. "She thought I was lying, and she begged me to tell her the truth. I tried to convince her I wasn't lying, but she didn't believe me. Later that night, I heard her arguing with my dad about it."

"How did that go?"

"Not good," she says. "She asked my dad why he told me about the room, and he insisted he hadn't told me anything."

"Did she believe him?"

"Nope," she says. "She just kept yelling, 'How else can she know about that room?' He tried to be calm with her, explaining she was wrong, but nothing he said could change her mind. He finally raised his voice and said, 'Why would I tell our little girl about that awful room? I'm not a fucking monster!' Then my mom started crying, and the arguing drifted into something quiet after that, and I couldn't make out any more words."

"Did you ever find out the significance of the room?"

"No, we never talked about it again," she says. "Anyway, that's enough sad childhood shit for today. It's time for the next stop on our adventure."

Xyla next takes me to a comic book shop called Astro-Zombies, which has a magnificent mural of superheroes fully covering the street-side view of the building; it's got characters from Marvel and DC engaged in an epic battle with heroes like Batman, Spider-Man, and the Teenage Mutant Ninja Turtles on one side and the Joker, Magneto, and the Green Goblin on the other. I try to explain to Xyla that it's cool because these characters don't exist in the same comic book universe.

"You're so cute," she says, before taking my elbow and guiding me inside.

We walk around the shop, looking at the many comic books, toys, and vinyl albums on display. They even have a Ceiling of Fame with signed doodles from well-known comic book folks, like Skottie Young and Brian K. Vaughn, and celebrities, like Samuel L. Jackson.

"This is easily the best comic book store I've ever seen in my life."

"Glad you like it."

The clerk behind the counter approaches us as we look at the different doodles on the Ceiling of Fame.

"It's you," he says. "Your Fireproof Man, right?"

"Um...yeah," I say, stunned to be recognized in public.

"I've watched your YouTube video at least a hundred times."

"I appreciate that," I say. "Thank you."

"Are you performing here?"

"Yeah, we'll be in town for a few nights," I say. "The first show is tomorrow night."

"Really?" he says excitedly. "I'll be there!"

"We look forward to seeing you."

"Hey, will you draw something on our ceiling?"

"Oh, I'm not an artist."

"That's okay," he says. "Whatever you draw will be great."

"I don't know—"

"Please!"

Xyla nudges me with her elbow, flashing a smile.

"Sure," I say, "why not?"

The clerk disappears for a minute, returning with a step ladder and a black Sharpie. I climb the ladder and quickly sketch a crude drawing of a man on fire before signing my name beside it. Stepping down from the ladder, I'm startled to see Handsome Harry standing behind me.

"I'm not looking for trouble," he says. "Just buying some comics."

"You like comic books?"

"Since I was a kid."

"Who's your favorite?"

"The Hulk," he says, holding up a stack of Hulk comics.

"Cool," I say. "Which series is that?"

"*The Immortal Hulk*," he says. "Have you read it?"

"No, I don't think so."

"Well, it's great," he says. "Basically, the Hulk can't die in this series, no matter what happens. Bruce Banner even gets killed in the first issue, but when the Hulk comes back, Banner comes back to life."

"How does Bruce Banner become the Hulk if he's dead?" I ask. "Doesn't he have to get angry or whatever?"

"Not in *The Immortal Hulk*," he says. "In this series, Bruce Banner is kind of like a werewolf, so every night at sunset, he changes into the Hulk."

"That's neat," I say. "So, even if he hasn't lost his temper or anything, he changes into the Hulk?"

"Yeah, it doesn't matter how he's feeling," Harry says. "When the sun goes down, he becomes the Hulk, no matter what."

"That's interesting."

"Basically, Bruce Banner and the Hulk share a body," he says. "Bruce uses it during the day, and the Hulk uses it at night."

"And they can't die."

"Exactly."

"That sounds good," I say. "I should check it out."

"Yeah, you definitely should."

Harry looks over at Xyla, like he's just noticed her.

"Hi, Xyla."

"Hey, Harry," she says. "How've you been?"

"Fine."

"I heard you had an encounter with a popcorn machine."

"Oh, you heard about that?"

"I think everybody heard about that."

"It was the strangest thing," he says. "It's like I wasn't in control of my own body."

"Maybe the Hulk took over."

This makes Harry guffaw, and I realize I've never seen him smile before, let alone laugh. I very much prefer this version of Harry to the one who wanted to kill me.

"Anyway," he says, "I'll see you around."

I offer a quick goodbye as he turns to walk away.

"Well, well, well," Xyla says.

"What?"

"I think you two just became friends."

"Whatever."

"I'm serious."

"He literally tried to kill me a couple of days ago."

"Harry is nothing if not complicated."

"You really think we're friends now?"

"In all the time I've known him," she says, "Harry's never been that nice to anybody unless he wanted to fuck them."

"I guess I'm flattered?"

"Don't worry," she says. "I'm pretty sure you're not his type."

Chapter Thirty-Seven

THE TIP OF THE SWORD

Aꜰᴛᴇʀ Xʏʟᴀ ᴀɴᴅ I return to the circus grounds, I go to Bastian's wagon for Pedro's next tutoring session. Bastian is grateful for my timing, as he and Geno are heading out to a local bar for some cocktails. I take a seat beside Pedro at the card table after Bastian and Geno split.

"Is Hannah coming?" he asks.

"I don't know," I say. "Does she know we're starting?"

"I'm not sure," he says, jumping from his seat. "I'll go get her!"

Pedro sprints away, returning a few minutes later with Hannah sprinting by his side. They slap the card table at the same time when they arrive, laughing and out of breath.

"Who won?" Pedro asks.

"Looked like a tie to me," I say.

Pedro and Hannah look at each other in disbelief.

"Rematch after school?" Hannah says.

"Deal!"

The kids take their seats, and we get started by talking about their last assignment, where I asked them to write about their parents. Pedro begins by reading from his Spider-Man notebook; as we'd discussed during our last session, he focused his paper on Bastian and Geno. He makes a very poignant comparison in his paper between them and Superman's adoptive parents, Jonathan and Martha Kent. "Jonathan and Martha taught Superman good lessons about how to be a good person," he reads, "just like Geno and Bastian teach me good lessons. So, your parents don't have to be biological to teach you how to be good and kind." I tell him what a great job he did, making sure to acknowledge his use of the word "biological," since he just learned it a few days ago.

In the middle of the tutoring session, Sammy Tawker the High-Wire Walker turns up with a young lady—about twelve or thirteen years old, I suspect—clutching a math textbook to her chest.

"Hi, Grover," Sammy says, "sorry to interrupt. This is my little sister, Tonya."

"Nice to meet you, Tonya."

She smiles, shaking my hand.

"I just ran into Bastian," Sammy says, "and he said you're running a tutoring school right now."

"It's not really a school or anything," I say. "I'm just helping out."

"That's awesome," he says. "Tonya needs help with her math homework, and I have no idea how to do it."

"Well, I'm more of an English teacher, so math is sort of the opposite of what I do," I say, "but I can try to help."

"Awesome!" he says. "Any help you can offer would be better than what I can do."

Tonya pulls up a chair at the card table as Sammy heads off to go wherever he's going. I ask the kids to introduce themselves, but, apparently, they already know Tonya; it makes sense that all the kids around here probably know each other. I fill Tonya in on what we're doing before asking Hannah to share her work with us. She's written a very sweet paper about how her mom's beard tickles her when she gives her hugs and how, when her dad puts her on his shoulders, she can see the whole world. When she's finished reading, Hannah asks Tonya if she wants to go next.

"I'm sorry," Tonya says. "I didn't know there was homework."

"It's okay," I say. "You can do the next assignment."

"What's the next assignment?" Pedro asks.

"Well, Tonya needs help with math," I say, "so maybe we can all work on that together."

Pedro and Hannah love this idea, so I ask Tonya if I can see her book.

Introduction to Algebra.

Uh-oh.

"You're learning algebra?" I ask.

"I'm trying to," she says, "but I don't really understand it."

I tell the kids to do some journal writing about any topic they like, so I can look through Tonya's algebra book. I graze the introductory chapter, reading about constants and coefficients while also trying to make sense of several strange symbols that somehow look familiar and foreign all at once. It feels like I'm in high school all over again, struggling to understand even the most basic math lessons.

A large shadow casts over the algebra book as the towering figure of Handsome Harry stands over me. He's holding one of his new Hulk comic books.

"You never told me yours," he says.

"Pardon?"

"I told you my favorite superhero," Harry says, "but you never told me yours."

"Oh," I say. "Well, I like a lot of superheroes, but if I had to pick one, I'd say the Flash."

"The Flash?" he says. "Really? All he does is run fast."

"Well, that's not *all* he can do," I say. "He can also pass through solid objects and travel through time."

"He can pass through solid objects?"

"Uh-huh."

"How?"

"Well, you know how solid objects are made up of molecules."

"What are molecules?"

"Hmm...I'm not sure I know how to explain it well," I say. "As best as I understand it, a molecule is the smallest particle of an object. All the particles of an object bind together to make it whole. Make sense?"

"I think so," Harry says. "But what's that got to do with the Flash?"

"Even though molecules come together to make a solid object, there's still space between the molecules," I say, "and the Flash has the ability to vibrate his body at such a high speed that he can move his own molecules through the spaces between other molecules."

"That's pretty cool," he says. "What about the time-travel thing?"

"I think the time-travel thing also works with the Flash's vibrating ability," I say. "But he also has to use something called the Cosmic Treadmill, which looks sort of like a regular treadmill, but when the

Flash runs on it, he can break the time barrier and travel any-where in time."

Pedro eyes Harry's comic book.

"You like the Hulk?" he asks.

"Yeah," Harry says.

"Do you like him more than Spider-Man?"

"I like the Hulk more than I like *every*body."

"Why?"

Harry doesn't answer right away, as he seems to be construct-ing a response in his head. While we wait for his answer, I invite him to sit down with us at the card table, and before long, he's engaging with Pedro in an animated debate about the merits of the Hulk versus Spider-Man. Once they parse through the Hulk and Spider-Man's various supernatural abilities, they get into some of the more nuanced reasons why they like each hero. While Pedro talks about how he likes that Spider-Man is a teenage kid under his mask and Harry talks about how he likes that the Hulk's alter-ego is a brilliant scientist, Hannah leans into my ear.

"Mr. Grover," she whispers, "is Harry your friend now?"

"Yeah," I say, "I think he is."

"Okay, that's good."

Tonya becomes fascinated with the Hulk versus Spider-Man discussion, which leads her to ask a series of probing questions:

Does Spider-Man actually like spiders?

Is green the Hulk's favorite color?

Does Spider-Man have time to do his homework?

Why doesn't the Hulk wear bigger clothes?

Do either of them get paid to be superheroes?

Pedro and Harry are mostly stumped, but they try their best to answer Tonya's questions, which only sends them deeper down their geeky rabbit hole. While everyone is otherwise occupied, I try again to make sense of Tonya's algebra book.

"Hey, Grover."

I turn to find Bettie the Bearded Bombshell's world-class cleavage inches away from my nose.

"Hi," I say, quickly lifting my gaze to look her in the eyes.

"You busy?"

"Just working with the kids."

Bettie leans in.

"Can we talk privately?" she whispers, which is way sexier than she probably meant for it to be.

I don't know what she needs to talk to me privately about, but I'm guessing it has something to do with catching her with Charlie Chuckles earlier. I'd much rather pretend that I never saw what I saw, but I figure I can't say as much here, so instead I say, "I'm not sure I should leave the kids in the middle of our tutoring session."

"I think they'll be fine," she says, squeezing my shoulder. "Please?"

"Okay."

I'm sitting across from Bettie and Lenny inside their wagon, feeling some combination of curiosity and awkwardness as I hold a steaming cup of chai tea latte that Bettie made for me. She appears uneasy, while Lenny is stoic, his large tattooed hands folded in his tattooed lap.

"First of all, let me get the uncomfortable part out of the way," Bettie says. "I want to apologize for what you saw earlier when I was with Charlie."

She rests her hand on Lenny's thigh.

"Lenny had to remind me that sometimes the absurdities of circus life can become so normal that it's easy to forget what *normal* actually looks like," she says, framing the word "normal" with finger quotes.

"It's okay," I say.

"Thank you," she says. "Believe it or not, there used to be a time when sucking off Charlie in public would never have occurred to me as being normal."

Lenny unfolds his hands, squeezing Bettie's knee. She laughs, dropping her eyes with embarrassment.

"As you can tell," Lenny says with his soft voice, "my wife is very comfortable talking about sex. Maybe a bit *too* comfortable."

She squeals, covering her face.

"I'm so sorry, Grover," she says. "Here I am wanting to make things better, and I think I'm making them worse."

"It's okay," I say again.

"Lenny and I talked about this before inviting you over, and he said, 'Make sure Grover is comfortable talking about this sort of thing before you get into it.' And I agreed with him, but here I am getting into it without asking if you're comfortable."

"Getting into what?"

"Sex."

Lenny drops his head, laughing.

"I mean, *talk*!" Bettie says. "Sex *talk*."

She covers her face again.

"Lord, help me," she says. "Okay, let's start over."

She takes a deep breath, folding her manicured fingers atop her lap.

"Grover," she says, like we're about to begin a job interview, "are you comfortable talking about sex with us?"

"I think so."

"Just so you know," she says, "you don't have to say you are just to protect my feelings."

"How about this?" Lenny says. "Give us an opportunity to open up to you, and you can tell us if you want us to stop."

"That sounds fair."

Lenny looks at Bettie, giving her a nod to continue.

"We just wanted a chance to talk to you before you got the wrong idea about what you saw with Charlie and me," she says. "We're in the lifestyle."

Lenny cringes.

"He hates that term," Bettie says, laughing.

"What term?"

"The lifestyle," Lenny says. "It just means we're swingers."

"Oh."

"So, when you saw Bettie with Charlie," he says, "they weren't fooling around behind my back."

"Well, that's a relief."

"We figured it would be," Bettie says. "Being in the lifestyle just means we sometimes have sex with other couples. But we also have hall passes."

"Hall passes?"

"A hall pass means we have permission to have sex with other people separate from each other," Lenny says. "When Bettie was playing with Charlie earlier, she was using her hall pass."

"I had an itch to scratch," Bettie says, "and Lenny was still recovering, so that's how you ended up finding me sucking off Charlie in the midway."

"I appreciate the explanation," I say. "Maybe I should get back to the kids now."

Lenny and Bettie look at each other, both of them nodding in the affirmative.

"Okay," Bettie says, "but before you go, there's something else we wanted to talk to you about."

"It's probably easier if we show you," Lenny says.

We sit in silence for a few moments when suddenly my cup begins vibrating in my hands, and the steaming chai tea latte inside floats up until it's hanging in midair, stretching and pulsating like the inside of a lava lamp. As seamlessly as the tea floated up into the air, it lowers back down into the cup, not a single drop out of place.

"What the hell?!"

"It's okay," Lenny says. "What you just witnessed is my special ability."

"Lenny's telekinetic," Bettie says.

"Telekinetic?" I say. "Is that the one where you can move objects with your mind?"

"Yes," Lenny says. "It's technically part of our act, except the audience isn't supposed to know. For example, I use it with my sword-swallowing gimmick."

Lenny walks to the back of the wagon, retrieving his sword.

"Here, touch the blade," he says, holding it in front of me.

I pinch the steel between my fingers, careful to avoid the sharp edge.

"Solid, right?"

"Uh-huh."

"Now, watch."

Tilting his head back, Lenny points his chin towards the ceiling and lifts the sword over his head. Dipping the tip of the sword into his mouth, he gingerly slides it down his throat, his sternum pushing out against the pressure of the blade. Once the sword disappears with only the handle in sight, Lenny carefully pulls it back out.

"Did you catch the telekinesis?"

"No," I say, "not at all."

Lenny holds the sword in front of me again, flicking the steel with his fingernail, sounding a ping. Then he snaps his fingers, and, in an instant, the sword droops toward the floor like a limp slice of pizza. He makes a twirling gesture with his finger, and, as he does, the limp steel rolls up towards the handle in a tight spiral.

"I never actually swallow the sword," he says. "I just roll it up as I push it down my mouth."

"What about your chest?" I ask. "I saw the impression of the sword pushing from inside."

"Like this?" he asks, pressing his chest out in the shape of the sword.

"You can affect your own body with telekinesis?"

"Sure," he says.

"That's amazing," I say. "Why not let the audience in on it?"

"We tried in the beginning to let audiences in on it," he says, "but they couldn't wrap their minds around it."

"We'd tell them Lenny was telekinetic," Bettie says, "and then he'd demonstrate it for them. But they were too consumed with *how* he was doing it, like it was a trick to be figured out. We told them over and over that there was no trick, that Lenny was truly moving objects with his mind, but their limited understanding of what's possible wouldn't let them believe it."

"We eventually evolved the act into something easier for audiences to digest," Lenny says, "showing them things like sword swallowing."

"What about when you stick the eight-inch needles through your forearm?"

"That part's real," he says. "I like to mix things up."

"Are there limits to it?" I ask. "Like, can you lift a car?"

"In theory, yes," he says, "but the size and weight of an object matter. If I tried to lift a car, for example, I'd only be able to do it for a short period of time. Plus, the effort would wipe me out for at least a few hours."

"Is that what happened the other day, when you passed out?" I say. "Did you throw Harry into the popcorn machine with telekinesis?"

"That wasn't me who threw Harry."

Lenny looks at Bettie. She smiles and gives him a nod before he turns his attention back to me.

"It was Hannah."

"Hannah?" I say. "How?"

"She's telekinetic, too," Bettie says, "like her dad."

"Really?" I ask. "Does anybody else know?"

"No," Bettie says. "Just us."

"And now you," Lenny says. "I'm sure you can appreciate how very protective we are of Hannah, so we gave this quite a lot of thought before deciding to tell you."

"I appreciate you confiding in me," I say, "but why did you decide to tell me?"

"Hannah really likes you," Lenny says, "and you've had a very positive impact on her in a short amount of time. The other day, when Harry was chasing you, Hannah's first instinct was to protect you. Without thinking, she used her telekinesis to throw Harry into the popcorn machine."

"From the time she was old enough to understand," Bettie says, "we've taught Hannah the importance of keeping her ability secret. Even still, we figured she was likely to let it slip and tell you about it herself at some point."

"Which is why we decided to tell you ourselves," Lenny says. "It wasn't a decision we came to easily, because the fewer people that know, the easier it is for us to keep Hannah safe."

"Is she in danger?"

"No," Bettie says, "but she could be if the wrong person found out about her."

"The part that was most concerning to us is not that Hannah used her telekinesis to protect you," Lenny says, "but that she used her ability out in the open where others could see it."

"Was anybody else there?" I ask.

"I don't think so," Lenny says. "Just you and Harry."

"Well, I can tell you that Harry has no idea what happened to him," I say. "That much I know for sure."

"That's comforting to hear," Bettie says.

"Protecting Hannah's secret isn't the only reason she's not supposed to use her telekinesis," Lenny says. "It also protects *me*."

"How so?"

"It's sort of hard to explain, but, essentially, Hannah and I are connected to the same telekinetic power," he says. "The reason for that is beyond my understanding, but I know it's true. The way it works is that when Hannah uses her telekinesis, it makes me extremely weak, like she's draining my battery to charge her own."

"Oh, I get it," I say. "That's why you collapsed?"

"Exactly."

"Lenny was laid up for the rest of the day after that," Bettie says. "He couldn't even pull himself out of bed until the following morning. And even then, just barely."

"Does Hannah get weak, too?"

"No, not at all," Lenny says. "When I use telekinesis, she's just fine."

"The one exception we learned," Bettie says, "is that if Hannah and Lenny use telekinesis at the same time, they're both fine afterward."

"How does that work?"

"Like I said, it's beyond my understanding," Lenny says. "But the main thing for us is keeping it secret, and we feel like we can trust you."

"You absolutely *can* trust me," I say. "I won't say a word."

Chapter Thirty-Eight

THE CATCH

O UR FIRST PERFORMANCE IN Albuquerque is another turn-away (and, perhaps on a totally related note, the YouTube video of my debut performance is approaching half a billion views). After Fernando and I close the show, we receive a rousing response from the sold-out audience. The following morning, I slip out of my wagon with the intention of grabbing breakfast at Vik's dukey truck, but to my surprise—and confusion—I'm intercepted by Paulo Silva. He invites me to have breakfast with him at a local Mexican restaurant as a way of thanking me for helping him out at the box office the other day.

The restaurant is called Abuelita's New Mexican Restaurant, which is a quaint spot within walking distance from Grambling Brothers. It sits behind a small dirt parking lot next door to a closed-down floral shop, a web of antiquated telephone wires hanging overhead. A hostess greets us inside, asking if we'd like a table, but Paulo tells her we're meeting people. Before I have an opportunity to ask who we're meeting, I see the Soaring Silvas—minus Solo—sitting at a table together.

Carlos.

Ana.

Jose.

Their eyes move in unison, locking in on me as Paulo leads us to the table. None of them seem pleased with my presence as Paulo invites me to take a seat.

"You guys know Grover, right?"

Silence.

"Hi," I say, trying not to sound as awkward as I feel. "It's nice to officially meet you all. I love watching you perform."

Ana stares at her menu.

Jose does the same.

"C'mon," Paulo says, "you're all being rude. Grover is our guest."

"It's okay," I say, standing from the table. "I can go."

"No," Paulo says, "please stay."

Though I really would prefer to leave at this point, I sit back down.

"*Papai*," Paulo says to his father, "Grover is a good man."

Silence.

"Please, *papai*," Paulo says. "Say something."

Carlos closes his fingers into fists, setting them aggressively atop the table.

"He is *not* circus."

"But, *papai*—" Paulo begins before his father cuts him off with a sharp look.

Carlos leans his elbows on the table, locking his eyes on mine.

"My family is circus," he says. "We perform for generations. My father and *his* father before him. They teach us to build our bodies. To develop our skills. To earn our place. But, *you*? You are not circus. You are one of the *aberrações*."

"*Papai*!" Paulo says.

I have no idea what that word means, but I assume it wasn't flattering.

Ana puts down her menu.

"It means you're one of the freaks," she says.

"Freaks?"

"The ones who are not human," Jose says. "The ones whose bodies go against God."

"My family worked very hard to earn our place," Carlos says, his fists still clenched atop the table. "You have earned nothing but are given everything. My family has given everything to Grambling Brothers, but we continue to be punished. First, with Paulo—"

"*Papai*!" Paulo says, cutting him off. "*Silêncio*."

Carlos bangs the table with his fists, rattling the silverware.

"Your body is broken, *filho*," he says. "I am tired of being quiet."

"Please, *papai*," Paulo says. "Not now, not ever."

Carlos grunts, looking away.

"You're right," I say. "Up until recently, I was a teacher. I had to work hard to earn that job. If somebody came in and replaced me without the same level of effort, I'd be upset, too. I appreciate hard work, I really do. I learned it from my dad."

Silence.

"What does your father do?" Paulo asks.

"He's a firefighter."

This captures Carlos' attention.

"That is very hard work," he says.

"He's my hero," I say. "But he's in the hospital now."

For the first time since I sat down, Carlos' face softens.

"Your father is not well?"

"He's in a coma, and he won't wake up," I say. "The doctors can't figure out what's wrong with him."

Carlos nods, dragging his fingertips through his beard.

"And Claudius," Carlos says, "he is helping your father? With money?"

"Yes," I say, "how did you know?"

He waves off my question like a pesky fly.

"So, this is why you are here," he says, "to take care of your father?"

"Yes."

Carlo nods, leaning back in his chair.

"We have all sacrificed much to be here," Carlos says. "What is your father's name?"

"Rex," I say. "Rex Wilcox."

"Rex Wilcox," he says, smiling. "Very American."

I laugh.

"I will add Rex Wilcox to my prayers."

"That's very kind," I say. "Thank you."

"Now," he says, opening his arms, "we eat."

After breakfast, I go back to my wagon, where I find Canyon sitting alone in the driver's seat, a half-empty bottle of Jack Daniel's resting in his lap. I climb in, settling into the passenger seat. With his thumbs, Canyon is pinning a bent photo of his daughter against the steering wheel, staring at it like it might disappear if he looks away.

"I don't really count the days anymore," he says, the scent of whiskey heavy on his breath. "There was a time I knew how long, but now I don't bother."

"Canyon?"

"It just sort of happens," he says. "We all agreed to it, but we didn't really understand. Now, we can't take it back."

"Take what back?"

He gives me a half-smile, like he's only just realized I'm here.

"I just miss my little girl."

"When's the last time you saw her?"

He shrugs.

"You don't know?"

"Last time I saw her was before I started working here."

"When was that?"

"I don't really count the days anymore," he says. "She's in Arizona with her mother. They're gonna have a birthday party for her. Cake. Presents. *Piñata*. I wish I could be there."

"Arizona's just a few hours away, right?" I say. "Ask Claudius for some time off."

"He won't let me go."

"Why not?"

"He always tells me to hang tight," he says. "Just a few more days. Always a few more days. But I don't really count the days anymore."

I take a hard look at him.

"Are you okay, Canyon?"

"My little girl goes to a fancy private school, right?" he says, choking up. "My lady tells me she's happy there." He pulls the wedding ring from beneath his T-shirt, tears rolling down his cheeks. "My pops would've done the same thing for me."

"You need to be with your daughter."

"I can't."

"Why not?" I ask. "You're not a prisoner here."

Canyon snorts a laugh before taking a hard swig of Jack Daniel's.

"You're a smart guy, Grover, maybe the smartest I ever met," he says, the bottle prepped for another swig. "How is it you ain't caught on yet?"

"Caught on to what?"

"The catch."

"What are you talking about?"

He kisses the wedding ring, slipping it back under his T-shirt.

"You'll figure it out," he says, climbing out of the driver's seat. "We all do eventually."

"Figure what out?"

He shuffles to his bunk, plopping face-down on the mattress.

"Canyon," I say, "what will I figure out?"

Chapter Thirty-Nine

PENDULUM

A FTER A FEW DAYS in Albuquerque, Grambling Brothers next travels to the coastal city of Galveston, Texas. As usual, Canyon handles the wheel while Darius sleeps in his bunk. I also sleep for a few hours before taking my familiar spot in the passenger seat beside Canyon. As we make our way through Amarillo, Canyon's not as chatty as he's been on our previous road trips, and I can't help but think it has something to do with the strange conversation we had back in New Mexico. I chalk most of what he said up to being drunk and sad, so I haven't mentioned it since. We exchange a bit of inconsequential small talk between Dallas and Houston before finally reaching our destination of Galveston.

Grambling Brothers takes over a relatively small parking lot in an area called the Strand, which is a neat little touristy spot with Victorian architecture, loads of shops and restaurants, and what appears to be a pirate ship out in the water. After showering and brushing my teeth in the community bathroom, I go to Vik's for breakfast. I still have Tonya's algebra book with me, as I continue to try—and mostly fail—to grasp the algebraic concepts inside. On my way to Vik's, I see Pedro and Handsome Harry; they're still carrying on their spirited Spider-Man versus Hulk debate. At the moment, they're arguing over who would win in a fight.

The crux of Harry's argument is the Hulk is too big and strong and would kill Spider-Man, while Pedro posits that Spider-Man only has to avoid the Hulk until he changes back into his frailer human form of Bruce Banner, at which point he could break every bone in his body. Harry says the pain of his broken bones would turn Bruce Banner back into the Hulk, and the transformation would heal his injuries. Pedro says Spider-Man would just repeat the same strategy of avoiding the Hulk and attacking him after he's changed back to Bruce Banner. I offer a quick hello as I pass, but neither of them seems to notice.

At Vik's, I order French toast and scrambled eggs before taking a seat with the algebra book. I pour over the same page over and over again, but none of it sticks. It feels like I'm trying to learn a foreign language that nobody speaks anymore.

"What do you got there?" Vik asks, setting down my breakfast. "Algebra, huh?"

"Yeah."

"Studying for the SATs?" he says with a laugh.

"No, but it feels like it," I say. "I'm helping Sammy's little sister with her algebra."

"I didn't know you knew math like that."

"I don't," I say, "and that's the problem. I've been tutoring some of the other kids, but we mostly focus on reading and writing, which I'm good at. But Tonya needs help with Algebra, which is my Kryptonite."

"So, you're trying to learn Algebra, so you can teach it to Tonya?"

"Yup."

"That's one of the kindest things I've ever heard."

"It's not a big deal," I say, "especially since I can't seem to learn it anyhow."

"Sounds like you need someone good at math to help you help Tonya."

"That would be a miracle."

"Well, in that case," he says, "call me Mr. Miracle."

"You're good at math?"

"To be honest with you, Grover," he says, "I'm *great* at math. In my former life, before I picked up the spatula, I was something of a math wizard."

"What did you do for work?"

"I was a CPA," he says. "I spent my nine-to-fives computing taxes, inspecting account books, organizing financial records, and other matters that would bore you to tears."

"I guess you'd have to be a math wizard to do that sort of work."

"Truth be told, math is overrated in accounting," he says. "It's like mastering the art of sword fighting only to slice bread for a living. Doing taxes is more about analyzing and interpreting data, but it helps if you're good at math."

"So, maybe you can help me tutor Tonya?"

"I'd love to," he says. "I can help with the other kids, too. Who else you got?"

"Pedro and Hannah."

"Great," he says, "we'll give them all math lessons."

"You're a lifesaver, Vik," I say. "Thank you."

"My pleasure."

"So, if you were an accountant," I say, "how'd you get into the food business?"

He smiles.

"Food tastes better than numbers."

I head back to the wagon after breakfast, where I find Canyon sitting in the driver's seat again, just like the other day. I climb inside and join him up front, expecting to see another bottle of Jack Daniel's, but his lap is empty. He's just sitting there, smiling at the dirty windshield.

"I owe you one, bro," he says. "Thank you."

"For what?"

"You told me what I needed to hear."

"I did?"

"You caught me in a strange moment back in Albuquerque," he says. "I was feeling sorry for myself, but when you said I should just leave and see my daughter, that hit me in my fucking heart."

"I'm glad I could help," I say. "So does that mean you're going to see her?"

"Yeah, I'm going to Arizona tonight."

"That's great," I say. "Claudius gave you some time off?"

"He doesn't know," Canyon says. "Nobody does."

"Are you driving our wagon?"

"No way," he says. "I've got to be like a ninja, bro."

"Wait, you're sneaking out?"

"Yeah, I'm gonna Shawshank this joint."

"How are you getting there?"

"I'm just gonna take a walk," he says. "When I get far enough away, I'll catch a cab or something. Maybe I'll hitchhike. I'll figure it out."

"I don't understand," I say. "Why can't you just tell Claudius you're leaving?"

"Look, I shouldn't say what I'm about to say, but fuck it," he says. "One way or another, I'm done with this place. You know how you made a deal with Claudius in exchange for joining Grambling Brothers?"

"Yeah."

"Well, we all did," he says. "Everybody who works here made their own deal. And because of that, we're all prisoners here."

"What are you talking about?"

"What I'm talking about is you ain't leaving Grambling Brothers, bro," he says. "Once you make a deal with Claudius, that's a wrap."

"Says who?"

"Who do you think?"

"That doesn't make sense," I say. "What happens if you leave?"

He opens his mouth to speak, stopping himself before the words slip out.

"I don't know why I can't say it," he says, shaking his head. "I'm breaking loose, and I still can't make myself say it."

"Say what?"

"It doesn't matter," he says. "The only thing that matters is it's my daughter's birthday, and I'm gonna be there. Fuck, bro, I'm so excited to see my little girl."

"Are you coming back?"

"Yeah, I'll be back."

"Promise?"

Canyon pulls the necklace from beneath his T-shirt.

"Remember what I told you about this ring," he says, "about how I never take it off?"

"Yeah."

Canyon lifts the necklace up over his head and hangs it from the rearview mirror, leaving the ring to sway like a pendulum in front of the dirty windshield.

"This right here is my promise to you," he says. "As long as this ring is here, you know I'll be back. The only problem is—"

He stops himself again.

"What is it?"

"Nothing," Canyon says unconvincingly. "All I gotta do is get back before we leave for New Orleans. I do that, maybe he won't know I'm gone." He leans toward me, his demeanor becoming more serious than I've ever seen. "Look, bro, I need you to do me a favor."

"Sure, anything."

"If anybody asks where I'm at—especially Claudius—I need you to cover for me."

"What do I say?"

"Say anything," he says, "just don't tell him I'm gone."

"What happens if he finds out?"

Canyon leans in closer, lowering his voice to a hush.

"We don't talk about that," Canyon says. "Not now, not ever."

Chapter Forty

PARANOID

"HI, MOM."

"Hi, sweetheart," she says. "Where are you calling from this time?"

"Galveston."

"Texas?"

"Uh-huh."

"Wow, you're really making the rounds."

"Yeah, Claudius keeps us busy."

"It must be so nice to travel and see different parts of the country," she says. "Are you still having fun?"

"Oh, yeah," I say, "it's a good time."

"And now you're in Texas," she says. "Tell me something interesting about Galveston."

"Um, let me think," I say. "Oh, they have a pirate ship."

This makes her laugh.

"Where is this pirate ship?"

"So far as I can tell, it's in the middle of the city."

"Goodness gracious," she says, still chuckling. "Why in the world do they have a pirate ship?"

"You got me."

We enjoy a bit more small talk before I decide to broach a heavier topic.

"How's Aunt Ruthie?"

"She's good," Mom says. "Unfortunately, I haven't been to visit her since Dad's been in the hospital."

"I'm glad she's doing well," I say. "She's been on my mind lately."

"What got you thinking about Aunt Ruthie?"

"Remember my friend, Canyon, I was telling you about the other day?"

"Is he the one who helps with the big top?"

"Yes," I say. "Anyway, the last few days he's been acting sort of strange."

"Strange how?"

"Lately, he's seemed sort of...I don't know. Disconnected, I guess."

"Disconnected?"

"From reality."

"I see."

"He's been reminding me of how things were with Aunt Ruthie before she was diagnosed with...um...sorry, remind me what she was diagnosed with."

"Paranoid schizophrenia."

"Yes, that."

"How's he been acting?"

"Well, last time I talked to him, he told me we were trapped here in Grambling Brothers."

"Trapped how?"

"Trapped like prisoners," I say. "He thinks Claudius is keeping us here against our will."

"That definitely sounds like a break from reality."

"And another time, he told me that one of the ladies who works here can make herself invisible."

"Really?" she says. "That's pretty strange."

"Yeah," I say. "I'm not even sure why he told me."

"Is she anybody significant?"

"Actually, yes," I say. "She's one of Claudius' most trusted hands."

"Interesting," she says. "What does she do?"

"She does a little bit of everything," I say, "handling props, organizing travel, getting insurance stuff handled, things like that. And, more informally, I suspect she's something of a confidant to Claudius."

"Interesting," Mom says. "So, along with feeling like he's a prisoner, perhaps Canyon thinks this invisible woman is spying on him for Claudius."

"I don't know," I say. "I think he considers her a good friend. In fact, when he first introduced me to her, he went out of his way to tell me what a great person she is."

"Well, if you thought somebody was secretly watching *you*—and that same somebody was in a position to adversely affect your well-being—wouldn't you also say glowing things about them?"

"When you put it that way, I guess it makes sense," I say. "As far as him feeling trapped, he told me earlier today that he's planning to sneak out."

"He's looking to escape, huh?"

"Yeah, and he asked me to cover for him."

"Sounds like he trusts you," she says. "Did he say what he thinks will happen if he gets caught sneaking out?"

"I asked him, but he said he couldn't talk about it."

Mom is quiet for a moment.

"Unfortunately, blurring the line between what's real and what's not is a predominant symptom of paranoid schizophrenia."

"That's what I was afraid of," I say. "Just the other day, I was sitting with him, and he started talking like we were in the middle of a conversation. At the time, I assumed he was talking to me, but now I think he didn't even realize I was there. It's like he was talking to a ghost."

"Sounds like he may have been having a hallucination," she says. "Your Aunt Ruthie had hallucinations, too. She was convinced that the government was watching her, but, like Canyon, she could never tell me what they wanted. All she knew was they wanted to harm her, so she had to keep herself on guard at all times. When she saw that one Jim Carey movie, she felt quite validated."

"Which one was that?"

"The one where he's the star of a reality TV show, but he doesn't know it," she says. "You know, the one where the whole city is one big TV set filled with actors and hidden cameras."

"Oh, *The Truman Show*," I say. "That's one of my favorites."

"Aunt Ruthie loves it, too," Mom says. "Like Canyon, Truman's suspicious that somebody powerful is watching his every move—and, of course, he turns out to be right. Also like Canyon, Truman decides he's going to escape his prison."

"Yeah, that's right."

"With paranoid schizophrenia, if things get bad enough, the afflicted person will eventually act on their delusions," she says. "For Truman, in order to escape, he needs to sail across the ocean, even though he has a crippling fear of water."

"Yeah, he wants to go to Fiji."

"That's exactly right," she says. "Truman believes his long-lost love was taken there after being kidnapped by mysterious men. You'll also recall that the creator of the TV show tries to stop Truman from escaping by generating a huge storm in the middle of the ocean during his getaway."

"But Truman keeps pushing forward," I say. "He doesn't stop until his boat crashes into a wall at the end of the TV set, which is painted to look like the sky."

"When he gets out of the boat," she says, "do you remember what happens next?"

"The creator begins talking to him."

"And can Truman *see* the creator?"

"No," I say, "his voice comes through a speaker."

"Just a voice in the sky," she says. "And Truman talks back to the voice, even though he doesn't see anybody there. He never once questions *why* a voice in the sky is talking to him, either, because, in his reality, it all makes sense. Your Aunt Ruthie called it a masterpiece."

I'm quiet for a moment, gobsmacked by Mom's razor-sharp insights.

"You know, as I think about it," I say, "Canyon told me he suffered a severe head injury before joining Grambling Brothers. Could that have something to do with how he's acting?"

"It's possible," she says. "There's been evidence that suggests traumatic brain injuries may trigger schizophrenia, but it could also be that Canyon is simply tired or stressed out."

"He does work very hard," I say. "Plus, he's been missing his family a whole lot lately. The day that he seemed to be talking to someone who wasn't there, he said he couldn't remember the last time he saw his daughter."

"That'll do it," Mom says. "Believe me, there are moments in this hospital room where I don't know what day it is or what I'm even doing here."

"That makes sense."

"As for Canyon," she says, "the best thing you can do is keep an eye on him. If his behavior appears to worsen, you'll probably want to talk to Claudius about getting him help."

"I'll do that."

"I know you will."

"So, how's Dad?"

Mom sighs on the other end.

"What is it?"

"I don't want you to worry," she says, "but his vitals have gotten weaker."

"Weaker since the last time?"

"Yeah."

"Well, that settles it," I say. "I'm coming right home right now."

"Sweetheart," she says, "there's nothing you can do here."

"I can help you watch over Dad."

"The doctors think he's stable now."

"That's not very reassuring."

"Trust me, they're keeping a very close watch on him," she says. "If things get bad enough, you know I'll tell you, right?"

"Promise?"

"Cross my heart."

"Okay," I say. "Give Dad a kiss for me."

"Done."

I know I told Mom that I wouldn't come home, but the truth is, I can't imagine hanging back while she carries the burden of Dad's condition all by herself, so, after we get off the phone, I walk to the Ringmaster's office. As I reach his door, I realize this is the first time I've been back since he nearly choked Handsome Harry to death, so I can't help but feel a bit uneasy as I enter.

"Grover," he says, as I sit across from him. "To what do I owe this visit?"

"I just got off the phone with my mom."

"Oh?" he says, lighting a fresh cigar. "And how is Lucy?"

"She's well," I say. "But my dad's not doing great."

"I'm sorry to hear that," he says. "How bad is it?"

"I don't know," I say. "My mom hasn't been giving me a whole lot of details, but I have a bad feeling he's going downhill."

"Is there anything I can do?"

"Actually, yes," I say. "I'd like to request some time off to be with him."

"Consider it done," he says, exhaling a plume of smoke. "Being with your father right now is the right thing to do."

"Thank you," I say. "I knew you'd understand."

"Grambling Brothers is a family," he says, "and you're part of that family, Grover."

"You don't know how much this means to me."

"If it helps," he says, "I'll even make the travel arrangements."

"You'd do that for me?"

"Of course."

I'm so relieved, I could cry.

The Ringmaster pulls a drag from the cigar, his cheeks collapsing behind his charcoal beard.

"Let's get through tonight's performance," he says, "then we'll talk about it further in the morning."

"That sounds great."

"Since you're here," he says, "there's another matter I'd like to discuss with you."

"Sure."

"Where's Canyon?"

A sharp bolt of panic zips across my chest.

"Canyon?"

"Yes."

"I don't know."

"That's a shame," he says. "I was hoping you would."

He taps his cigar over the ashtray, sprinkling down a tiny shower of orange embers.

"Did you know he's missing?"

A knot cinches in my chest.

"Missing?"

"Yes," he says. "I know you two have grown close, so I was hoping you might have some information regarding his whereabouts."

"Sorry," I say, the knot cinching tighter. "I don't know where he is."

"That's disappointing," he says, leaning back in his chair. "But if you don't know where Canyon is, what can be done, right?"

"Right."

The Ringmaster pulls a drag from his cigar as he stands from his desk, turning his back to me as he looks out the window.

"Have you ever heard of the spotted lanternfly, Grover?"

"No."

"They're pesky little things," he says. "To look at them, they appear harmless—like lovely moths with bright, beautiful colors—but they are far from harmless. While spotted lanternflies don't harm humans directly, they can harm the natural environment humans depend on for survival. Crops and vineyards worth billions of dollars often get obliterated by this little creature that, to the untrained eye, looks as inconsequential as a stray leaf falling from a tree. But, because they pose such an immediate threat, when a spotted lanternfly is identified, there's only one surefire way to deal with it."

He hammers his fist on the window seal, triggering the sound of cracked wood.

"Smash it."

The Ringmaster turns from the window, locking his dark eyes on mine.

"My old friend, General Panda, taught me about the lanternfly," he says. "He was fascinated with entomology. That's the study of insects—but I'm sure you knew that."

I didn't.

"General Panda wasn't an expert by any stretch," he says, "but he always took a particular interest in the strange and peculiar parts of nature that often get overlooked. I suppose that's how he ended up in the sideshow business. Speaking of General Panda, I recall you once asked me what happened to him, and I told you that was a tale for another day. Do you remember that?"

I nod, yes.

"Well, today is that day."

The Ringmaster pulls a drag from his cigar, exhaling a plume of smoke as he sits back down at his desk.

"General Panda betrayed me."

"Betrayed you?" I say. "What did he do?"

"He kept a secret from me."

The knot in my chest cinches even tighter.

"Now," the Ringmaster says, "I'm forgiving of many things, but secrecy is not one of them. General Panda's secret was that he had a gift."

"What kind of gift?"

"Like you, he was fireproof."

"Really?"

"Yes," he says, "but, *unlike* you, General Panda hid this from me."

"Did you want him to perform in the show or something?"

"No, that wasn't my concern," the Ringmaster says. "I simply don't like being lied to."

"How did you find out?"

"General Panda was a philanderer," the Ringmaster says. "He had a weakness for the flesh, particularly the female form. He had affairs with many of the women who worked for Grambling Brothers, and I often warned him that he was playing a dangerous game. One night, a very talented knife thrower that he'd left scorned had a mental breakdown, and she set General Panda's wagon on fire while he slept inside. By the time the fire died out, the wagon had burnt to a crisp. I expected to find the blackened remains of my dear friend inside, but what I found instead was General Panda fast asleep on his charred bed. He had no idea the knife thrower had attempted to burn him to death. With his secret revealed, rather than coming to me and confessing his truth, General Panda thought it best to run away."

The Ringmaster leans in, resting his elbows on the desk.

"But I found him."

"How did you find him?"

The Ringmaster smiles.

"I have my ways."

"What happened after you found him?"

"We don't talk about that," he says, stabbing the ashtray with his cigar. "Not now, not ever."

The Ringmaster excuses me, so I stand from the desk and head for the door.

"Grover," he says, before I step outside, "you will tell me if you hear from Canyon, won't you?"

I nod, yes.

"Thank you."

Chapter Forty-One

CONSEQUENCES

E VERY ADULT AT GRAMBLING Brothers—from the performers to the tent crew—is standing shoulder to shoulder inside of the big top, forming a large circle with Canyon at its center.

Hands in his pockets.

Shoulders slouched.

Spotlight overhead.

Just a few hours ago, we performed another turnaway. From the beginning of the show to the end, everything felt perfect. Xyla was in the audience for the first time to watch me perform, and as we walked back to her wagon after the show, hand in hand, she told me how much she loved it. She also told me she hadn't watched a show inside the big top for a very long time.

"Not since Harry and I broke up."

"You didn't miss it?"

"I didn't think I did," Xyla said, "not until tonight."

We sat on the couch inside her wagon, making out like teenagers, passionate and clumsy, letting our hands roam over each other's clothes—and occasionally underneath. I felt like I was in the middle of a fairytale, my very own happily ever after, when Xyla abruptly stopped.

"What is it?" I asked.

"Something changed."

"What do you mean?"

"The two flames," she said. "They're different."

"Different how?"

"One of them is bigger," she said. "Significantly bigger."

"What about the other one?"

"It's much, much smaller, like it might soon disappear."

That's when we heard Handsome Harry knock at the door.

"We're going to the big top," he said, before quickly walking away.

Xyla looked at me, an urgent expression on her face.

"We have to go."

I followed her out of the wagon, no questions asked, and we seamlessly merged with all the others like a run of salmon swimming upstream. As we entered the big top, I saw several people standing in place around the perimeter of the ring. Xyla found a spot next to May, and I took the spot beside Xyla, still unsure of what we were doing there. Everyone was quiet, staring straight ahead. Charlie, Woodrow, and Annie all stood side by side. Fernando. Sammy. Bastian and Geno. Carlos, Ana, Jose, and Paulo. Vik. Solo. Darius. And there were others, several of whom I hadn't met yet. Lenny and Bettie entered the big top last, standing in the spot beside me.

We all just stood there.

Still.

Silent.

I looked at Xyla, but she didn't meet my eyes.

Without warning, Canyon's body was launched into the center, tumbling across the dirt like he'd been ejected from a moving car. I held my breath as he pushed himself up to his hands and knees, laboring to his feet. A switch sounded overhead, and the spotlight beamed down on him, leaving the rest of us in shadow.

And that brings us to now.

This moment.

Hands in my pockets.

Shoulders slouched.

The Ringmaster appears from the shadows, joining Canyon in the center, his large frame towering over him from behind. He raises his hands in the air like a preacher about to begin a sermon.

"Here we are for another gathering of the Circle," he says, "for once again we must rectify a devastating betrayal."

The Ringmaster lays his hands on Canyon's shoulders.

"Standing here before you is Canyon, the agent of our most recent betrayal," he says. "Canyon has been a loyal member of our family for some time now. Like each of you that forms this Circle, Canyon made the choice to join Grambling Brothers. He was not forced, nor was he coerced. He made this choice fully of his own free will. And in so doing, just like all of you, he became part of our family. So, when Canyon ran away a few days ago, he didn't simply abandon me, and he didn't simply abandon you. He abandoned *us*. But, through the grace of a power greater than any of you can possibly imagine, Canyon now stands before us, prepared to accept the consequences of his betrayal."

The Ringmaster removes his red-tinted glasses, placing them in his pocket. From behind, he wraps his powerful fingers around Canyon's neck, lifting him into the air. Canyon grabs the Ringmaster's wrists, flailing his worn sneakers above the dirt. As easily as you might toss a crumpled sheet of paper, the Ringmaster hurls Canyon through the air. His screams fill the big top until he lands hard on the ground, his head bouncing off the dirt as the momentum tumbles him across the Circle, stopping at the feet of Handsome Harry.

Harry stands like an obedient soldier, hands behind his back, staring straight ahead as Canyon groans in front of him. The Ringmaster stalks over to Canyon, his heavy boots grinding footprints in the dirt as he lifts him to his feet. Canyon's knees are buckled, and he's unable to stand on his own strength. The Ringmaster lifts him up in the air again, this time pressing him over his head, arms fully extended, as he walks back to the center of the Circle with Canyon resting atop his powerful hands.

Beneath the spotlight, the Ringmaster heaves Canyon up into the air, where he hangs for several excruciating moments—eyes wide, limbs flailing—until he falls violently to the dirt. Canyon's arms quiver as he pushes himself up to his hands and knees before the Ringmaster kicks his ribs with enough force to once again lift him off the ground. As Canyon crashes back down, he wraps his arms around his belly, weeping like a child. The Ringmaster kicks him again, this time sending Canyon skidding across the dirt until he stops at my feet.

He struggles to breathe, blood leaking from his nose and mouth. Canyon looks up at me, his eyes pleading for mercy. I make a move to help him, but Lenny grabs my wrist, stopping me. The Ringmaster walks to Canyon, crouching down and grabbing him by the throat as he lifts him again off his feet. I know he's still conscious because his eyes are open, but Canyon offers no resistance. He clutches the Ringmaster's forearm with his quivering fingers, but it seems more of a benign reflex than a desperate act of survival. The Ringmaster takes a moment to look at me, locking his eyes on mine, before throwing Canyon down to the dirt with such force that the ground shakes beneath my feet. Blood leaks from his ears, merging with the crimson rivulets streaming from his nose and mouth as they pool into a dark puddle in the dirt.

Leaving Canyon's limp body at my feet, the Ringmaster walks back to the center of the Circle.

"Canyon's betrayal has been rectified," he says as he retrieves the red-tinted glasses from his pocket. "From this moment forward, no one in this Circle shall speak of what they saw."

The Ringmaster sets the glasses back on his face.

"Not now, not ever."

Everyone in the Circle begins to file out of the big top as quietly as they had entered, while Canyon remains unconscious, inches from where I stand. I don't move until Xyla takes me by the wrist, guiding me away.

"What about Canyon?" I ask.

Xyla presses her finger to her lips, shaking her head.

I look to the center of the big top, expecting to see the Ringmaster. But he's already disappeared.

Chapter Forty-Two

LET THE DEVIL IN

I can't close my eyes without seeing Canyon's face. His eyes looking up at me, blood leaking from his ears. The Circle was the most horrible thing I've ever witnessed, and I hope it's something I never have to see again. I haven't slept a wink as the sunrise slips through the window of our wagon.

Canyon's bunk is empty. I don't know what that means, but I fear the worst. I exit the wagon and wander through the labyrinth, determined to find out if he's okay. As I see others going about their day, I anticipate we'll offer one another an acknowledgment of the collective horror we experienced last night in the big top—perhaps a slight nod or a knowing glance.

But that's not what happens at all.

I see the tent crew packing up the big top.

I see the Soaring Silvas practicing yoga.

I see Vik serving pancakes and coffee.

I see Bettie and Lenny playing a board game with Hannah.

It's as if last night never happened.

"Grover."

It's the Ringmaster, his voice hitting me like a splash of cold water.

"Come with me."

I sit across from the Ringmaster in his office, wishing I could be anywhere else in the world but here.

"How're you feeling?"

"Good," I say, unable to look him in the eyes.

"Good?" he asks. "Are you sure?"

I shrug, not knowing what else to say.

"After last night," he says, "I wouldn't expect you to feel *good*."

Now, I look up, meeting the Ringmaster's eyes through his red-tinted glasses.

"I know what you're thinking," he says. "Not now, not ever."

"I thought that was the rule."

The Ringmaster smiles.

"Do you follow the rules, Grover?"

"I try to."

"That's a clever answer," he says. "It leaves a sliver of daylight, just enough to let the Devil in."

The Ringmaster lights a fresh cigar.

"So," he says, "have you?"

"Have I what?"

"Have you let the Devil in?"

My chest tightens.

"I respect authority," I say. "I always try to follow the rules."

"There's that 'try' word again."

He exhales a plume of smoke.

"Why are you afraid to answer 'yes' or 'no'?"

"I guess it's not that simple."

"Isn't it, though?" he asks. "If a rule has been established and you're clear on what that rule is, then how is it *not* simple? You either follow it or you don't, yes?"

I nod, yes.

"So, have you ever broken a rule?"

"I'm sure I have."

"So, you *try* not to break the rules, but sometimes you do," he says. "Is that a fair assessment?"

I nod, yes.

"It seems then there are rules you *are* willing to break."

The Ringmaster leans back in his chair, lacing his fingers over his chest. I'm suddenly aware of how hot it is in here as a bead of sweat rolls down my temple.

"Relax," he says. "We're just talking. Now, about last night, how are you *really* feeling?"

The anxiety constricts my breathing like there's a bowling ball resting on my sternum.

"Don't worry," he says, "there is no punishment for an honest answer."

"Okay," I say. "I feel awful about what I saw last night."

"And why do you feel awful?"

"Canyon is my friend."

"You feel awful only because Canyon is your friend?"

"No, I mean, I would feel awful about seeing that happen to anyone," I say. "But it was especially awful seeing it happen to Canyon because he's my friend."

"I understand," he says, pulling a drag from his cigar. "When was the last time you saw Canyon?"

"Last night."

"Inside the big top?"

"Yes."

"Are you curious about where he is now?"

"Yes, of course."

The Ringmaster smiles.

"I thought you might be," he says. "The truth is, I sent Canyon home."

"Home to his family?"

The Ringmaster exhales a plume of smoke.

"Yes," he says, "and I made sure he received proper medical attention before sending him off."

"How long will he be home?"

"For good."

"For good?"

"Yes."

"Really?"

"Really," he says. "I'm not a fool, Grover. I'm fully aware of what motivated Canyon to break the rules. I'm also aware that one might see Canyon's reasoning as justified, perhaps even noble. Nonetheless, rules were broken, and consequences were earned. This is why we have the Circle. While some may see the Circle as an arena for horrific torture and pain, I see it as a mechanism for communal purification. By enduring his punishment inside the Circle, Canyon was cleansed of his betrayal, thus clearing the path for him to return home to his family."

"That's great," I say. "I'm happy for him."

"I figured you would be."

"I wish I could've said goodbye."

"That's circus life," the Ringmaster says. "Given Canyon's departure, you'll now be sharing a wagon with Solo."

"Really?" I ask. "Does Solo know that?"

"He does."

"What about Darius?"

"Darius will be fine," he says. "I'd recommend using what time we have left here in Galveston to move your belongings to your new home."

"Okay."

"Now, in spite of what we discussed here today," the Ringmaster says, "I trust you know not to speak of last night's events ever again."

I nod, yes.

"Good," he says. "Not now, not ever."

On my way back to my wagon—well, my *former* wagon—I see May watching over the tent crew as they load up the trucks.

"Morning," I say, walking over to her. "How's it going?"

"It'll be a lot better once we get everything packed for New Orleans."

"I'm assuming you know about Canyon."

May shoots me a look.

"It's okay," I say. "I just left Claudius' office."

May rests her hand on my back, leading me away from anyone within earshot.

"I hope you're not talking about what I think you're talking about."

"No, I'm not talking about last night," I say. "I'm talking about Claudius sending Canyon home to his family."

"That's what he told you?"

"Yes."

"Well, then," she says, "it must be true."

May's response strikes me as odd.

"Is there something you're not telling me?"

"Sorry," she says, walking away, "I've got to get back to work."

I'm feeling very unsettled following our brief chat, but I try to shake it off as I head back to my former wagon. As I climb inside, my eyes are briefly blinded by a bright reflection of light coming from the windshield. There, hanging from the rearview mirror, I see Canyon's ring—the very same ring he told me he would never leave behind. Removing the ring from the mirror, I exit the wagon to look for May. As soon as I find her, I show her the ring.

"Did Canyon ever tell you about this?"

"Yeah, it belonged to his dad."

"That's right," I say. "Canyon told me it was the most valuable possession in his life."

"He told me the same thing."

"Did he also tell you that he never took it off?"

"Yes."

"So, why is it here?"

Silence.

"If Canyon is truly home with his family," I say, "why didn't he take his ring with him?"

May's eyes well up with tears.

"I really do have to get back to work," she says. "I'll see you in New Orleans."

Chapter Forty-Three

THE MAN ON THE BLACK THRONE

I BELIEVED HIM.

The Ringmaster lied to me, and I believed him.

I can't stop thinking about Canyon and his family. The thought of his daughter losing her father, his girlfriend losing her partner. It breaks my heart. I'm sure the Ringmaster has already talked to them, telling them whatever version of the truth he wants them to hear.

"You're being terribly quiet," Solo says.

I'm sitting shotgun in his wagon, staring out the window as he drives us to New Orleans. At the start of the trip, he told me it would take us six or seven hours to get there, but I'm not exactly sure how long we've been on the road. I suppose I haven't been that great of a co-pilot, given that my mind has been pretty well occupied.

"Sorry," I say. "I guess my mind is somewhere else."

"It's alright," he says. "I understand what you're going through."

"You do?"

"Sure," he says. "The circus is a strange, transient life. People come and go in and out of our lives. One minute they're here, the next—*poof*—they're gone."

"I guess I had to learn that the hard way."

"We all do."

Silence.

"Anyway," he says, staring out at the road ahead, "I'm sorry about your friend."

"Thank you."

We leave it at that.

As we arrive in New Orleans, the tent crew is already setting up the big top in the sprawling parking lot of a Furniture Mart. Solo parks his wagon amongst the other vehicles that make up the labyrinth before excusing himself to take a well-deserved nap. I should probably do the same as my body is exhausted, but I can already tell sleep won't come easy for me any time soon, so I choose instead to take a walk.

I'm barely outside a few minutes when I run into Xyla. It's the first time I've seen her since the Circle. She smiles and gives me a hug, like everything is exactly as it was before—and to be honest, it's kind of a relief.

"Have you ever been to New Orleans?"

"No," I say, "never."

"These are my old stomping grounds, you know."

"So, I've heard."

"Care for a guided tour?"

"Sure," I say, "that sounds nice."

We start on Bourbon Street, which is very chaotic with drunken tourists at every turn. The buildings are charming and old, laced with bright neon lights and signs advertising ten-dollar cocktails. Every other door that isn't an entrance to a bar or restaurant with vibrant live music leads into one of the many strip clubs on Bourbon Street. Wrought-iron balconies hang over our every step, each crowded with wobbly men throwing beads out to any girl willing to lift her shirt.

Xyla next leads me down Royal Street, which runs parallel to Bourbon Street. It's much quieter here with fewer people moving about. From front to back, Royal Street is populated with a variety of classy shops, galleries, and cafés.

Xyla next takes me to Café Du Monde on Decatur Street.

"Have you ever had a beignet?"

"A what?"

She laughs.

"I'll take that as a no," she says, smiling. "C'mon, you'll love it."

We walk beneath an awning with green and white stripes, weaving through crowded tables and chairs until we reach an order window. Behind the window, several men and women in white collared shirts and black bowties work feverishly amidst a persistent fog of flour and sugar. Xyla orders us six beignets and two café au laits, which we take to an empty table beneath the striped awning. Opening the bag of beignets, she invites me to look inside at the cozy huddle of golden squares.

"They're basically donuts," she says, "but better."

"What makes them better?"

She pushes the bag across the table.

"Find out for yourself."

I pinch a piping hot beignet from the bag—at least I *assume* it's piping hot since I can't actually feel the heat against my fingertips—and take my first bite.

"Well?"

"Delicious."

Xyla leans in and gives me a kiss, getting powdered sugar on her lips. I take another bite, which Xyla follows up with another kiss. I chase the sugar and kisses with a sip from my café au lait, which goes down like a cozy caffeinated hug. All in all, it's been a lovely day, and I'm awash with joy—but, as quickly as the joy washes over me, thoughts of Canyon float back to the surface.

"What's the matter?" Xyla asks.

"I can't stop thinking about Canyon."

"Grover—"

"I know, I know," I say, conceding her concern. "Not now, not ever."

"I've been where you are," she says. "It's hard to get used to, especially the first time."

"So, you've seen that more than once?"

"Unfortunately," she says. "But I find that the not-talking-about-it rule helps me get through it."

"For me, not talking about it makes it worse."

"If you like, you can talk about it with me."

"Aren't you worried about breaking the rules?"

She smiles, resting her hand on mine.

"There's nobody here but us."

I take a deep breath.

"Is it always like what happened to Canyon?"

"No," she says. "In my experience, the punishments are different every time."

"Why are they different?"

"Claudius has never explained that to us," she says, "but the punishments always appear to be tailored to whoever is inside the Circle."

"I've never witnessed anything like what Claudius did to Canyon," I say. "I mean, I've seen violent movies and stuff, but I've never seen anything like that in real life. And I know that, in the grand scheme of things, I didn't know Canyon all that long, but he was still my friend, so watching that happen to him was devastating. What really wrecks me is thinking about his daughter and girlfriend back home."

"I didn't know he had a daughter."

"That's the reason he ran away," I say. "He wanted to be with her on her birthday."

"Damn," she says, "that's so sad."

"The thing is, he was going to come back," I say. "That's what he told me the night before he left."

"You knew he was running away?"

"He asked me not to say anything."

"Sounds like he trusted you."

"Not that it did him any good," I say. "The truly fucked up part is Claudius called me into his office this morning to feed me a cheerful lie."

"What did he tell you?"

"He said Canyon was okay and that he sent him back home to be with his family."

"Are you sure he was lying to you?"

"I'm certain of it."

"How do you know?"

I reach my hand beneath my shirt collar and pull out the necklace with Canyon's ring.

"This belonged to his dad," I say. "His mom gave it to him when he was a kid after his dad died. Canyon told me it was the most valuable possession he owned, and he never went anywhere without it. But he knew I was worried about him leaving, so, to put me at ease, he left it behind in our wagon as a means of assuring me he would be back. Now, he's gone, and all that's left of him is this ring."

Xyla looks away, her eyes welling up with tears.

"This place is so fucked up," she says, shaking her head.

"That's becoming more and more clear to me with every passing moment."

"Unfortunately, there's more to it than what you've seen."

"What do you mean?"

Xyla takes a deep breath, staring out into the distance.

"I know things."

"What kind of things?"

"Things about Claudius," she says. "Things I wish I never knew."

She wipes a stream of tears from her cheek.

"What is it?" I ask.

Xyla covers her face with her hands.

"We're his prisoners, Grover," she says. "We're his fucking prisoners."

"So, it's true?"

She looks up at me, surprised.

"You knew?"

"Canyon tried to tell me the night before he ran away," I say, "but I didn't believe him."

"Sounds like he was definitely a better friend to you than I've been."

"That's not true," I say. "You've been great."

More tears stream down her cheeks.

"I need to tell you something else," she says. "But once I do, you'll never want to talk to me again."

"You don't know that."

"Yes," she says, "I do."

"Aren't you the one who told me fortunetellers don't predict the future?"

She takes a deep breath.

"The first thing you need to know is that before Harry and I joined Grambling Brothers, we got into some legal trouble in Utah."

"What kind of legal trouble?"

"We were arrested."

"For what?"

"Selling drugs."

"No kidding?"

"Yeah, but we were small time," she says, "*very* small time. In the movie of my life, selling drugs wouldn't even make the final cut."

"What kind of drugs were you selling?"

"Weed and molly, mostly," she says. "Our customers tended to be college kids looking to spice up their weekend."

"How did you get into it?"

"Harry knew a guy who knew a guy," she says. "Selling drugs was never anything I planned on getting into, but busking on street corners didn't always pay the bills. For the most part, it was easy money, right up until we got arrested in Salt Lake City."

"How did you end up getting arrested?"

"We tried to sell to an undercover cop."

"Shit," I say, "I guess that'll do it."

"Given how small time we were, we probably would've gotten probation and maybe some community service," she says. "But, thanks to Harry, that didn't happen."

"What did Harry do?"

"He resisted arrest," she says. "He was like the proverbial bull in a China shop until they managed to put him down with an overwhelming collection of tasers, pepper spray, and billy clubs. Unfortunately, Harry ended up hurting a few cops before they got him under control. Broken bones and dislocated joints, for the most part. Anyway, if there was ever a chance they were going to take it easy on us, that went out the window with Harry's temper tantrum. I don't remember half the charges they threw at us, but suffice it to say we were going to get much more than community service. After a day or so of sitting alone in my jail cell, a guard told me I had a visitor. He took me to a small room with a table and two chairs. One of the chairs was empty, and the other was occupied by Claudius."

"You already knew Claudius?"

"No," she says, "I'd never seen him before in my life."

"How did he know you were there?"

"He said he'd read about Harry and me in the local paper," she says. "I assumed he was going to offer me legal advice, but instead he started telling me about his circus and how he wanted me and Harry to come work for him. I let him know that, unless he could magically make my legal woes go away, I wasn't in a position to accept his offer.

He assured me that he actually *could* make my legal woes go away, and all I had to do was accept his offer."

"Did he know about your supernatural abilities?"

"I'm sure he did," she says, "otherwise I doubt he would've been interested. Anyway, I told him I'd happily join his circus if he could actually get me out of trouble. Within an hour, Harry and I were free."

"Just like that?"

"That's the Claudius way."

"How were things after you joined Grambling Brothers?"

"Things were cool as far as work goes," she says. "But my relationship with Harry was on a downward trajectory. So, when we inevitably broke up, I told Claudius I wanted to quit."

"How'd that go?"

"He asked why, and I told him I didn't want to be around Harry anymore," she says. "So, he told me in no uncertain terms, 'You can't leave.' And when I asked him why, he said, 'We made a deal.' Now, I'm no pushover, so I told him in no uncertain terms that if I wanted to leave, there was nothing he could do to stop me."

"You really told him that?"

"I did."

"I can't imagine standing up to Claudius like that," I say. "What happened?"

"He asked me to look inside of him," she says. "It seemed like a request out of left field, but I thought nothing of it, so I pressed my fingers to his temples and closed my eyes. In an instant, I was alone inside a fiery elevator going down. It was the most visceral vision I'd ever experienced. The flames were right on top of me, and I didn't want to be there anymore, but Claudius held my fingers in place against his temples. When the elevator stopped, the doors slid open to reveal an endless landscape of fire and brimstone. In the middle of it all was a large man sitting on a tall black throne. At this point, Claudius started talking to me like he knew exactly what I was looking at. 'Go to him,' he told me, so I started walking toward the man on the tall black throne. His face was obscured by flames, but, when I was finally in front of him, I saw exactly who it was."

"Who was it?"

She squeezes her eyes shut, sending a fresh river of tears down her cheeks.

"It was *him*," she says. "It was Claudius. When I opened my eyes, he said, 'Do you understand now?' I told him yes, and that was it. I never talked about leaving Grambling Brothers again."

"What did he mean when he asked if you understood?"

"I'd say it means he's a very bad man," she says, "but you have to be human before you can be a man."

"He's not human?"

She shrugs.

"Who knows?" she says. "Whatever he is, Claudius is evil."

"That's definitely a lot to wrap my head around," I say, "but I don't understand why you thought I wouldn't want to talk to you anymore."

"There's more," she says. "After I looked inside of Claudius, he told me he was feeling generous and asked if I wanted a new deal."

"What kind of deal?"

"He said he would set me free if I could find someone special to replace me."

"Did you accept the new deal?"

"Yes."

"What happened?"

"I found *you*."

Chapter Forty-Four

A TURN FOR THE WORSE

A STREAK OF PAIN constricts my chest like a taut rubber band as I stumble away from Café du Monde, the shrapnel of Xyla's betrayal fresh in my heart. She's talking to me as I walk away, her words dissolving into an empty mist of sound as I wade through the fog of anger and confusion inspired by her revelation. I move through the endless procession of tourists until I find myself back on Bourbon Street, surrounded by crowds of joyful men and women laughing it up with their bright red drinks and Mardi Gras beads. Walking past the pink doors of Larry Flynt's strip club, I hear the unmistakable voice of Charlie Chuckles calling my name.

"Grover!" he says, hugging me like we haven't seen each other in ages. "Are you out here looking for some fresh poon to hide that donkey sausage in?"

"No," I say, "I'm just sort of lost."

Charlie's jovial face quickly takes the form of a concerned elder.

"Are you alright, kid?"

"No."

"Can I help?"

"I just want to go home."

"Alright," he says, "let's go."

Charlie waves down a cab for us, and we head back to Grambling Brothers.

"You want to tell me what's going on?"

I offer a half-hearted shrug.

"C'mon, kid," he says, "what is it?"

"I don't think we're allowed to talk about it."

"Oh, I see," he says. "Not now, not ever, right?"

"Isn't that the rule?"

"Sure," he says, "but we haven't said anything we're not supposed to. So, what's on your mind?"

"What's on my mind is that I'm a prisoner in Grambling Brothers."

Charlie pats my knee.

"Sorry, kid," he says, "that's a tough truth to reckon with. Seems to me you got smartened up quicker than most of us."

"I think I liked it better when I didn't know."

"I don't blame you," he says, "but there's no un-ringing that bell. If you don't mind me asking, was it worth it?"

"Was what worth it?"

"Whatever deal you made," he says. "Was it worth it?"

I think about my dad in his hospital bed and my mom sitting by his side.

"Yeah," I say. "I think it was."

"There you go," he says. "Things worked out."

"It's just not fair," I say. "I had no idea what I was agreeing to."

"None of us did."

"What's worse is I just found out I was recruited."

"By Claudius?"

"No," I say. "Xyla."

"Really?"

"Yeah," I say, "apparently Claudius told her that she could leave Grambling Brothers if she found somebody to take her place."

"And she gave him you, huh?"

I nod, yes.

"That's heavy, kid."

Silence.

"Remind me," he says, "how long have you been with Grambling Brothers?"

"A few weeks."

"That's what I figured," he says. "So, if Xyla made a deal for her freedom, why isn't she gone?"

Why *is* Xyla still here?

I'd ask her myself, except I'm currently avoiding her, and I haven't seen her since Café du Monde, which was a few days ago. Well, I suppose I should be more specific and say I haven't *spoken* to her. Of course, I've seen her. How can I not in this claustrophobic prison of ours? Each time I see her, a wave of hurt and anger triggers inside of me, followed by a paradoxical wave of joy and gratitude, because my brain and my heart can't separate all of the wonderful memories from that very terrible one.

I've spent these last few days in New Orleans just going about my regular business. Every show has been a turnaway, and my infamous YouTube video has ticked over half a billion views. I've also spent time working with the kids. Vik's joined in to help with math, just like he said he would. Handsome Harry started attending our sessions as well, as he and Pedro are practically inseparable these days. Harry enjoys the lessons and even does the same homework as the kids; he's bright, too, though I can tell he's never really gotten a formal education. What I appreciate is he's not the least bit self-conscious about learning side by side with Pedro, Hannah, and Tonya. I suppose that sort of confidence probably comes with having mountains of muscles and supernatural strength. All in all, he's been a very welcome addition to our education crew.

I try my best to keep distracted, but Canyon is never far from my thoughts. When I'm not performing, tutoring the kids, or grabbing a bite to eat at Vik's, I mostly hang out in Solo's wagon, contemplating what the rest of my life will look like. Traveling from town to town, performing with Fernando—or maybe one day I *won't* perform with Fernando. Maybe the Ringmaster will decide he wants me to perform with someone else or *nobody* at all. Maybe he'll put me in the sideshow. Maybe he'll choke me half to death in his office. There's truly no telling what he'll do or when he'll do it.

The only constant I can count on is that I'm trapped in this peculiar prison where the Ringmaster feeds me, shelters me, pays me a generous wage, and asks for nothing in return except that I do the job I've agreed to—and, of course, that I never, ever leave him. On its face, it seems like a very nice arrangement, which may be why nobody else is kicking and screaming for their freedom. Or it could just be they've already come to terms with the same reality I'm slowly but surely wrapping my head around.

Grambling Brothers finishes its stay in New Orleans, and the tent crew does their usual amazing work of breaking everything down and packing up. Once the last door closes, we hit the road for Tallahassee, Florida. It's a short trip from New Orleans—roughly five hours all told. I ride shotgun with Solo as we drive through the night. My intention was to keep him company during the trip, but I fall asleep without ever realizing my eyes had closed. I may as well have traveled by time machine, because I didn't so much as blink before finding myself in the swampy humidity of Florida's capital city.

Solo's wagon is already parked in the labyrinth when I wake up; he's fast asleep in his bed, so I tip-toe around until I find my phone. I see that I have several missed calls from Mom, as well as a single text message: *Call me as soon as you see this.*

I fear the worst, my hand quivering as I make the call.

She answers on the first ring.

"Oh, Grover."

She's crying, making no effort to hide it.

"What's wrong?"

"It's your father."

"What happened?"

"He's taken a turn for the worse."

My whole body begins to shake.

"What's that mean?"

"I'm so sorry, sweetheart," she says. "Your father is dying."

The taste of hot tears touches my lips.

"What happened?" I ask. "I thought he was stable?"

"His vital signs keep dropping," she says, "but it's happening faster than before. The doctors and nurses have been doing everything they can for him, but nothing is making a difference. Dr. Boudreaux sat me down to give me the hard news."

"How long does he have?"

"Maybe a few days," she says. "If he makes it through the end of the week, it'll be a miracle."

"Oh, God," I say. "A week?"

"Grover," she says, "it's time for you to come home."

GROVER'S **FINAL** PERFORMANCE

PART THREE

Chapter Forty-Five

LOVE RULES

I HAVE A PLAN.

Sort of.

I'm going to run away like Canyon.

What choice do I have? My father is on his deathbed, and I need to be there. It doesn't matter if I'm imprisoned in the Ringmaster's nefarious circus, I need to get home as soon as possible. We have our performance here in Tallahassee tonight, so I'll stick around for that—going through the motions, keeping everything looking as normal as possible—then after the show, everybody will go about their business. Some will go to sleep, others will wander about town, but nobody will be looking for me.

Especially not the Ringmaster.

I hope.

We have another show tomorrow night. That means if I'm right and nobody comes looking for me, I'll have a twenty-four-hour head start. I don't know what Canyon did when *he* ran away—what precautions he took or how he got caught—but I need to do better. In order for my plan to work, I have to assume the Ringmaster knows everything and then act accordingly. So, I can't buy a plane ticket because he can probably access that information. I can't buy a train ticket for the same reason. Or a bus ticket. I need to disappear in the wind, leaving no trace, like a ghost. And, even then, I have to assume the Ringmaster will eventually find me. After what happened to Canyon, I'm not going into this believing I can run away for good. I'm just hoping to spend a few final moments with Dad, a chance to say goodbye before he takes his last breath.

I'm sure you're wondering how I plan on pulling this off, right? The plan is to hitchhike back home to Rancho Cucamonga from Tallahassee. Now, I've never hitchhiked before in my life, but it seems like the safest option available to me, as well as the closest I can get to being off the grid. Being off the grid matters because I need to make it as difficult as possible for the Ringmaster to track me down. A quick calculation on Google Maps tells me that driving from Tallahassee to Rancho Cucamonga takes just under thirty-five hours—that's assuming I drive nonstop, which probably isn't possible. But if I can get enough rides to stay on the road for at least ten hours a day, then I can be home in three or four days.

Nobody can know I'm running away. I've made some friends here—*good* friends—friends I'm confident I can trust, friends who I know would cover for me if I asked them to, but I don't want to ask that of anyone. When the Ringmaster inevitably finds me, I don't want anybody to be punished for it.

This is my choice.

My plan.

My execution.

Mom can't know either. She doesn't even know that I'm coming home. I told her I'd be unreachable for a few days and that I'd try my best to get back. I'm leaving my phone behind because I have to assume the Ringmaster can track it. Without a phone, I won't just be out of touch with Mom—I also won't be able to get updates on my father. I'll have no idea if he's dead or alive before I get to the hospital. Once again, Dad has become Schrödinger's cat—both alive and dead at the same time.

The first Tallahassee performance is complete, another turnaway with a vibrant audience. From Fernando blowing fireballs in my face to me standing tall in my fireproof underwear, the crowd loved everything we gave them. Even the Ringmaster is particularly satisfied with the night's performance, and he tells us as much during his post-show speech. Everything truly feels perfect, and if circumstances weren't what they are, I could almost actually imagine myself staying.

Nonetheless, the show is done.

My final performance.

Everyone has gone their separate ways to do with the night what they will. I walk the circus grounds, taking it all in. I know it's my prison, and it should feel bad here, but I've collected a lot of good memories in a relatively short amount of time. I walk past the sideshow tents and through the midway, the scent of popcorn and cotton candy still hanging in the air. As I approach the exit, I stop and turn to take one last look at the big top—that whimsical cathedral where I discovered a life I never knew possible. Regardless of the evil man who runs it or his ever-mysterious motives, we put smiles on people's faces. We give audiences a reason to cheer, a reason to laugh, a reason to step away from their everyday lives and let their hearts fill with wonder—and I got to be a part of it, if only for a little while. I wish it didn't have to end like this.

I'll miss performing.

I'll miss tutoring the kids.

I'll miss Vik's dukey truck.

I'll miss my friends.

I walk through the exit, past the empty box office, half-expecting the Ringmaster to grab my shoulder before I can leave. But there is no last-minute effort to keep me in his circus prison. The only thing between me and my getaway is the muggy night air hanging over Tallahassee like a damp sheet.

From the darkness, emerging like a specter in the night, I see Xyla.

"Where are you headed?" she asks.

"Just taking a walk," I say.

"I haven't seen you around."

"I guess I've been busy."

"Can we talk?"

"Now's not a good time."

"When *is* a good time?"

"I don't know," I say. "I've got to go."

I walk into the empty parking lot.

"I'll go with you," she says, catching up with me.

"You don't even know where I'm going."

"That's okay."

She's at my side, walking with her arms crossed.

"I need to be alone," I say. "You should go back."

"Grover," she says, "are you doing what I think you're doing?"

Silence.

"Grover?"

She grabs my arm, forcing me to stop.

"My dad's dying," I say. "He only has a few days left. I need to see him."

"My god," she says, "I'm so sorry."

"I've got to go."

"I'll go with you."

"No way."

"Why not?"

"First of all, I'm not sure I can ever trust you again," I say. "But, second of all, you and I both know this probably won't end well."

"All the more reason for me to go with you."

"You don't have to sacrifice yourself just because you feel guilty."

"That's kind of the best reason to sacrifice myself, don't you think?"

"That's not funny."

"I'm not being funny," she says. "It's my fault you're in this situation at all. I was selfish and desperate, and when I thought I found a way out, I took advantage of it—of *you*. And for what? I'm just as trapped as I ever was. What's worse is I'm pretty sure I'm falling in love with you, so there's that."

"Don't say that."

"It's true."

"You barely know me."

"I don't make the love rules."

"Well, as much as I want to believe you," I say, "you can't blame me if I have a hard time buying anything you're selling."

"That's fair."

"And as far as tagging along with me, I still don't think it's a good idea."

"I know I did a very bad thing," she says. "I betrayed you even before I knew you. But if I knew you then the way I know you now, I never would've done it."

"What's done is done."

"Let me make it right."

"How?"

"Let me help you get home."

Chapter Forty-Six

LEAP OF FAITH

I KNOW WHAT YOU'RE thinking.

What if Xyla's conning me again? What if she's secretly working with the Ringmaster? What if she plans on keeping tabs on my whereabouts she can report back to him between here and Rancho Cucamonga? And what if I can't say no, because, in spite of all the clear and objective evidence that says I shouldn't trust her, I'm probably falling in love with her too?

As a precaution, I tell Xyla she has to leave her phone behind. Without hesitation, she takes it behind the box office and smashes it with a rock.

"How's that?" she asks.

"You didn't have to do that."

"You should probably do the same."

She's right, so I hurry back to my wagon to retrieve my phone before taking it behind the box office and smashing it with the same rock. My stomach turns as I look over the shattered remains of my digital connection to the world. I probably should've written down a few phone numbers first, but it's too late for that now. I dig a shallow hole in the dirt to bury our crushed phones, and, after filling in the makeshift grave, we exit the circus grounds. We walk aimlessly for a while, neither of us saying a word, just moving for the sake of moving. Xyla asks if I have a plan, so I tell her my idea of hitchhiking across America.

"That's one way to go," she says, "but do you have a plan that might work?"

"You didn't have to come, you know?"

"Lucky for you, I did."

"We'll see about that."

"Let's go there," she says, pointing at a Waffle House.

"We shouldn't stop for food until it's necessary."

"We're not eating."

"What're we doing, then?"

"Getting a ride."

"From who?"

"Trust me."

I shoot her a look.

"Fair enough," she says, holding her arms in the air like I've just stuck a gun in her chest. "Think of it instead as a leap of faith."

"Why should I?"

"Because I have an idea that's just crazy enough to work."

I follow her to the Waffle House, passing an eighteen-wheeler parked along the curb on our way inside. I've never been to a Waffle House, but I'm instantly put at ease by its generically familiar décor, which reminds me of every diner I've ever been to with my parents.

We're greeted by a kind hostess behind a podium.

"Welcome to Waffle House," she says. "How many?"

"That depends," Xyla says. "Maybe you can help me out."

"How's that, darlin'?"

"Do you know who the rig belongs to?" she asks, pointing her thumb over her shoulder in the direction of the eighteen-wheeler.

The hostess looks around the dining room, which is relatively empty. There's a young couple on a date, an old man sitting at the counter drinking coffee, two young ladies who look like they came straight from their shift at the strip club, and a middle-aged man eating alone in a booth.

"That's the fella right there," the hostess says, nodding in the direction of the middle-aged man.

"Perfect," Xyla says, "we're with him."

We walk past the hostess, making our way toward the man at the booth. I look back at the hostess, thinking maybe I'll need to explain our actions, but she doesn't seem at all invested in our hijinks. Before we get to the booth, Xyla stops me.

"Stay back until I need you."

"Where should I go?"

"Sit at the counter."

I want to ask how I'll know when she needs me, but she's already gone, joining the man at the booth. I take a seat at the counter, positioning myself close enough to listen in on whatever Xyla is up to.

"Hello, handsome," she says. "Mind a little company?"

"Not at all."

"I'm Xyla."

"Roger."

"It's a pleasure to meet you, Roger," she says. "Is that your rig out there?"

"Sure is."

"Good," she says, "I'd like to make you an offer."

"I didn't make you for a lot lizard," he says, smiling.

"Not *that* sort of offer."

"You sure?"

"What kind of girl do you take me for?" she says, giggling as she squeezes his forearm, her dainty fingers dwarfed by his vascular muscles.

"The truth is, Roger, I need a favor," she says. "I'm traveling across the country, and I need a ride for as far as you can take me."

"You can ride with me as long as you want."

"That's what I was hoping you'd say."

Xyla looks my way, beckoning me over with a nod of her head. I walk to the table, but I'm not sure if I should sit or stay standing.

"You got a problem, bud?" Roger asks.

I stutter a few monosyllabic sounds, none of which add up to a cohesive sentence.

"It's okay," Xyla says, "he's with me."

"*This* guy?"

"It's not romantic," she says, squeezing his arm. "He's my brother."

Xyla grabs my wrist, pulling me into the booth beside her.

"We've been traveling cross country," she says, "just trying to get some family time in since our grandmother passed away. She raised us on account of our parents not being around. Our car broke down back in Orlando, so we've been hitchhiking ever since. Unfortunately, Grover here just found out his dog is sick and might be dying."

Roger looks at me with what I think might be empathy.

"How long have you had your dog?"

"I don't know," I say. "It feels like my whole life."

"What's his name?"

"Rex."

He wipes his meaty fingers across his lips.

"I bet Rex needs you."

"Not as much as I need him."

"Where is he?"

"California."

Roger stands up from the booth, dropping a twenty-dollar bill on the table.

"I'm going as far as Jackson, Mississippi," he says. "You're both welcome to ride with me till we get there."

"Thank you," I say. "You don't know how much this means to me."

Roger heads outside without another word.

I look at Xyla.

"What just happened?"

"I looked inside of him," she says, "and I saw a grainy, black-and-white memory of a little boy playing with a dog."

"I can't believe it worked."

"See," she says, smiling, "aren't you glad I'm here?"

Roger's truck is both cramped and deceptively roomy.

"We'll be to Jackson in seven hours," he says, starting it up. "I'd take you further if I could, but Jackson's home for me."

The truck has a dashboard housing a matrix of lights and buttons that look way too complicated for a vehicle without wings. There's a monitor with a GPS map and several large cup holders that can comfortably accommodate a gaggler of Big Gulps. Behind the front seat is a built-in bed, which is where I'm currently sitting. Xyla's in the passenger seat, while Roger navigates us down the road from the driver's seat. There's a small closet with a few clothes hung up, while the majority of Roger's wardrobe lays crumpled on the floor beside a box of Top Ramen noodles, a dented can of baked beans, and a carton of Pall Malls. There's a single shelf back here occupied by a stack of Stephen King novels and a couple of porn magazines. Taped to the wall is a faded Polaroid of a handsome Siberian husky.

Roger and Xyla make small talk for the next several hours, which I only sort of pay attention to until my eyes grow heavy. Next thing I know, Xyla's waking me up at a rest stop somewhere in Jackson.

"This is where we part ways," Roger says. "I hope you get to Rex in time."

"Thank you," I say, shaking his hand.

Xyla and I exit the truck and watch Roger drive away into the burgeoning sunrise.

Chapter Forty-Seven

THE BRAVE SIDE

"Now what?"

"We get another ride."

"How?"

Just as soon as the word leaves my mouth, a beat-up van blasting music I've never heard before pulls into the rest stop. I'm no good with recognizing the make and model of most any vehicle, but I know that this model of van is what Dad likes to call a "shag wagon." The side door slides open, and a cloud of pungent smoke billows out along with a small group of twenty-somethings making their way to the bathroom. There's an equal split of men and women in the group—six altogether. I turn to Xyla to make a lame Cheech & Chong joke, but she's already walking towards the shag wagon. I stand back, watching her strike up a conversation with the driver, smiling and laughing at whatever it is they're talking about. As the shag wagon's other passengers return from the bathroom, Xyla starts talking to them as well; they all seem quite happy to meet her.

Xyla waves me over, so I join them.

"This is Grover," she says, looping her arm around mine.

A chorus of laid-back hellos floats my way.

"Nice to meet you all."

"They're on a road trip to Austin for EDF," Xyla says, "just like us."

"No kidding?"

I have no idea what EDF is, but I'm guessing Xyla already knows this.

"They said we can ride with them," she says. "Isn't that great?"

"It's better than great."

"Pile on in," the driver says. "EDF awaits."

EDF, as it turns out, is the Electronic Dreamland Festival, an annual event that takes place in Austin, Texas. We're about eight hours from Austin, at which point we'll have to figure out our next move. I'm not sure how far Austin is from California, but, for now, the only thing that matters is we're moving west. The twenty-somethings started their road trip from Montgomery, Alabama, and, considering they're a group of young people on their way to a music festival, the shag wagon isn't nearly as raucous as you might assume it would be. There's definitely drug use (mostly weed and mushrooms) and lots of odd music that I don't ever need to hear again in this lifetime, but, by and large, the twenty-somethings are pretty cool.

The shag wagon has no seats except for the two in front. While the driver mans the wheel, the other twenty-somethings sit on the floor with Xyla and me, as well as an array of crumbled fast food bags, empty beer cans, and beat-up backpacks. I don't know any of their names, but it hardly matters as everyone in the shag wagon is enamored with Xyla. Along with her effortless charm, she holds their collective imaginations by giving each of them a tarot reading. I listen in on the first couple before laying on the floor, fingers clasped behind my head.

There's a little window in the roof about the size of a box of cereal that welcomes in a cozy haze of sunlight. I feel the sun on my lids as I close my eyes, Xyla's voice cradling me in the darkness like a lullaby as each bump in the road rocks me gently to sleep.

My eyes open, and I'm startled to discover my head is on Xyla's lap. She's stroking my hair, soothing me as I come to. A different twenty-something is driving now, while the previous driver is curled up under a heavy blanket. The rest of the twenty-somethings are either asleep or lost in their smartphones. I start to sit up, but Xyla eases me back down.

"Rest," she says. "We'll be in Austin soon."

Closing my eyes, I enjoy the sensual touch of her fingers against my cheek.

I open my eyes in Austin as the shag wagon parks in front of a Holiday Inn Express. The twenty-somethings file out through the sliding door. Xyla and I exit last, sliding the door shut behind us.

"We're less than two miles from Zilker Park," the driver tells us, slipping her backpack over her shoulders.

"Zilker Park?" I ask.

"That's where EDF is."

"Oh, right," I say. "I guess I'm still waking up."

"We can meet up in the morning and walk there together," she says. "Do you guys have a room here?"

"No," Xyla says. "We're booked in a different hotel."

"Oh, which one?" she asks. "We can give you a ride."

"That's so sweet of you," Xyla says, "but we're happy to walk. Thanks again for letting us ride with you all."

"Of course," she says. "I hope we see you at EDF."

"You can count on it."

The driver hurries off to join the rest of the twenty-somethings inside the Holiday Inn Express.

"Now what?"

"This is your adventure," she says. "I figured you had a plan."

"Really?"

"Of course not," she says. "You hungry?"

"I can eat."

"Austin is supposed to have legendary barbecue."

"Sounds good to me," I say. "Where to?"

"Your guess is as good as mine."

We head towards the highway and start walking down the side-walk.

"Is this even the right direction?"

"Would you believe me if I said yes?"

"Sure."

"Then, yes, it is."

After walking for about an hour, we find a roadside barbecue joint. It's a small concrete box with a kitchen inside, but no dining room. Xyla and I join a row of customers lined up at the ordering window; we wait in line for about ten minutes before finally ordering. Most of the customers are taking their food to go, but we take ours to a flimsy plastic table beside the concrete box. I dig into a delicious pile of charred, smoky goodness, while Xyla enjoys a pulled pork sandwich.

"I'm sorry, Grover."

I look up and see Xyla has stopped eating.

"For what?"

"Everything."

"Oh, that," I say, setting my fork down. "It's okay."

"No, it's not," she says. "But thank you for saying that."

"I'm a big boy," I say. "You didn't twist my arm to take Claudius' offer."

"But I led you to him," she says. "I all but presented you on a silver platter."

"Are you trying to talk me out of forgiving you?"

"Wait, you forgive me?"

I shrug.

"I haven't decided yet."

"So, you're thinking about it?"

"Don't get your hopes up," I say, "but I haven't ruled it out."

"I may regret asking this," she says, "but why?"

"Why what?"

"Why are you even *considering* forgiving me?"

"Because I understand why you did what you did," I say, "and if I were in your shoes, I can't say with certainty that I wouldn't have done the same thing."

"Well, you kind of *are* in my shoes now," she says, "only you've chosen to do something incredibly brave."

"There's a thin line between brave and foolish."

"However thin that line is," she says, "you're on the brave side."

After dinner, we put our feet back on the pavement, offering our thumbs to every car that crosses our path. The night sky is black as ink, with a generous collection of stars flanking the moon. We walk for about two hours before a woman with short salt-and-pepper hair pulls over in a beat-up pickup truck.

"I'm headed to El Paso," she says. "Where're you two going?"

"California," Xyla says. "Can we get a ride?"

"Depends," she says. "Are you guys serial killers?"

"No, ma'am."

"You on drugs?"

"Nope."

"You running from the law?"

"Something like that."

This makes the woman smile.

"Outlaws, huh?" she says. "Get in."

"Yeah?"

"Yeah," she says. "We outlaws need to stick together."

Chapter Forty-Eight

THE STALE STENCH OF REGRET

H ER NAME IS IRMA.

She's nice and very talkative. Aside from her unsubtle attraction to Xyla, it's clear to me that Irma picked us up more out of loneliness than any overwhelming act of humanity. A few hours in, we make a pitstop at McDonald's for black coffee, apple pies, and French fries. Xyla does most of the talking, sharing stories of her life traveling the country as a fortuneteller. When Irma asks how it all works, Xyla gives her the long version because we've got a lot of road in front of us. After that, she offers to give Irma a tarot reading.

"I appreciate the offer, darlin', but no thank you," Irma says. "I'm happy to listen to most anything that comes out of that beautiful face of yours, but I'm not one to reckon with the future before it's time."

After nearly eight hours on the road, Irma lets us know we're approaching her final stop in El Paso.

"Where can I drop you kids off?"

"How about the next motel you see?"

Irma finds us a less-than-desirable motel in the middle of nowhere.

"You two made for great company," she says. "I'll be rooting for your happily ever after."

Xyla and I offer a quick goodbye before watching Irma disappear down the road.

"So," Xyla says, "shall we get a room?"

"We can't stop," I say. "We've got to keep moving."

"We need to rest," she says. "Not to mention, we don't exactly have a ride at the moment."

"We don't have time to rest."

"Grover," she says, "we've been moving nonstop for the better part of two days. It's okay for us to take a break."

"But...my dad."

"I promise I'll do everything I can to get us to your dad as soon as possible," she says, "but if we don't get at least a little rest, neither one of us will make it to California."

"Fine," I say, "but I don't want to stay for more than a few hours."

"Deal."

We enter the front lobby, which is a tiny room scarcely big enough to fit two grown adults, let alone the clerk behind the ragged counter. I can't tell if he's an older man or if he's simply clocked a whole lot of rough miles on his life's journey. He barely notices as we enter, leaving Xyla and me to stand in front of the counter for nearly a minute before he even lifts his eyes.

"What do you want?" he says, finally looking up.

"We'd like a room," she says. "Just for a few hours."

The clerk grunts as he stands from his stool, turning to the wall behind him, where a matrix of keys hangs on wooden pegs. He grabs a key before typing something into his wildly antiquated computer.

"Cash or card?"

"Cash," Xyla says, pulling out some money.

"Let me," I say, reaching into my pocket.

Xyla waves me off as she pays for the room. We exit the tiny lobby with key in hand, and it doesn't take long to find our room, as there are only a dozen or so on the whole property, all of which face the parking lot. Xyla opens the door, and we're greeted with the stale stench of regret and poor choices. The walls look sticky, the carpet is grimy, and everything that passes for décor is either orange or brown.

"This is...um...charming?" I say.

Xyla laughs.

"That's one way to put it."

She sits on the bed and takes her sandals off, lifting her feet onto the mattress without letting them touch the carpet. She pats the bed, inviting me to join her, so I sit down, folding my hands in my lap.

"Relax," she says. "Take your shoes off."

"Have you seen the carpet?" I ask. "I don't think my feet would ever forgive me."

"Fair enough," she says. "Besides, I'm sure this bedspread has had worse things on it than your shoes."

"Oh, god," I say, jumping to my feet, "you're probably right!"

Xyla laughs as she gets off the bed, seamlessly stepping into her sandals. She yanks the bedspread off the mattress, revealing a rea-sonably white sheet.

"Better?"

"Let's hope so."

Xyla reclines on the bed as I reluctantly remove my shoes, surrendering to the weary comfort of the shabby room. We scoot back, sitting up against the headboard, our bodies just inches apart. Back in New Orleans, when I left Xyla at Café Du Monde, the only feelings that made sense were anger, sadness, and betrayal, and I truly believed that, for as long as I lived, those would be the only feelings I'd ever have for Xyla Peppermint again. But, sitting here on the bed, our fingertips achingly close, all those terrible feelings seem totally foreign and so very far away.

"Be honest," I say, "do you think there's a chance we get away with this?"

"You mean, sneaking away to California without Claudius finding out?"

"Uh-huh."

"Would you believe me if I said yes?"

"Sure."

"Then, yes."

Silence.

"Let's say there's a reality where we *do* get away with it," she says. "Will you miss the circus?"

"I don't know," I say. "I'd definitely miss the people."

"The audience?"

"No, I'd miss the performers and the crew," I say. "As a college professor, I never really had coworkers. I'd drive to school, teach my class, then go home. But Grambling Brothers provided me with a sense of community that I didn't realize was missing in my life."

"What about friends and family?"

"Well, my parents are great," I say, "but I'm an only child, and I'm not all that close with any of my extended family, except for my Aunt Ruthie, and I haven't seen her in years. As for friends, I lost touch with anybody I cared to know after high school."

"I can relate," she says. "For the last few years, Harry was the only family I had."

"I imagine that's how he wanted it."

"I'd love to heap the blame on him," she says, "but the truth is, I made it easy for people to stay away."

"How so?"

"By not making an effort," she says. "I never went out of my way to make friends or let anybody get close to me."

"Why not?"

"I don't know," she says. "I guess making friends as an adult never came easy to me, so not making an effort was the path of least resistance."

"But you got along great with Roger," I say, "and the kids in the van and Irma, so you definitely know how to make friends."

"That's different," she says. "Making fast connections with people and putting them at ease has been my job for a long time. But making genuine connections that lead to friendship—that's a game I never got good at."

"I guess meeting people has never been easy for me, either."

"You could've fooled me," she says. "From what I saw, you made friends with everybody at Grambling Brothers."

"Really?"

"Oh, yeah," she says. "I bet they'd vote you homecoming king if they could."

"Get out of here."

"It's true," she says. "The only ones who don't like you are the Soaring Silvas."

"You noticed that, huh?"

"Yeah," she says, "but they don't like anybody."

"Believe it or not," I say, "I think I made friends with them back in New Mexico."

"See," she says, laughing, "that's exactly what I'm talking about. You make friends with everybody, even the folks who don't want to be your friend."

This makes me smile.

"If I could do it all again," she says, "I'd embrace all of the potential friendships that I let slip through my fingers."

"It's never too late."

"I wish that were true," she says, "but I don't think I'll be doing much of anything after the fallout comes from this little scheme of ours."

"Right," I say, "I nearly forgot that part."

Silence.

"Can I ask you a question?"

"Anything," she says.

"I understand you brought me to Claudius because I'm fireproof," I say, "but when we met at Chandler College, you didn't know I was fireproof."

"That's true."

"But you still invited me to the circus that night."

"That's also true."

"Why?"

"Why did I invite you?"

"Yeah."

"I don't know," she says, "there was just something about you. Maybe it was your eyes or the unassuming way you carried yourself. There was a gentleness about you, something kind and pure that I found attractive."

"So, you invited me because you were attracted to me?"

"Is that so crazy?"

"Honestly, yes."

"You know, I don't think you realize how special you are," she says, "and it has nothing to do with being fireproof. As much as I regret getting you tangled up in this whole mess, I can't say I regret the opportunity it gave me to spend time with you."

"I enjoyed that part, too," I say. "I mean, I didn't love the part where Harry tried to kill me and all."

Xyla laughs.

"I'm glad you think it's funny."

"It's only funny because even *Harry* likes you now."

"He may like me *now*," I say, "but I thought I was dead in the water the day he chased me through the midway. The only reason he didn't manage to murder me is because Hannah saved my life."

"Bettie and Lenny's daughter?"

"Yeah...oh, wait," I say. "Shit."

"What?"

"I wasn't supposed to say anything."

"Say anything about what?"

"I sort of made a promise to keep it a secret."

"A secret?" she says. "Well, now you have to tell me."

"If I tell you, you can't tell anybody else."

She looks around the motel room, then back at me.

"I don't know if you forgot our situation," she says, "but who do you think I would tell?"

"I know, I know," I say, "but, promise me anyway."

"You have my word."

"Okay," I say. "Hannah is telekinetic."

"Really?" she says. "I had no idea."

"Nobody does," I say. "Bettie and Lenny keep it a secret."

"Why is *that* a secret?"

"They don't want Claudius to find out."

"That makes sense," she says. "So, how exactly did Hannah save you from Harry?"

"She used her telekinesis," I say. "When she saw Harry chasing me, she threw him into the popcorn machine."

"So, *that's* what happened?" she says. "I just figured he tripped or something."

"Crazy, right?" I say. "Betty and Lenny filled me in on the truth of what happened a few days ago. They said they figured it was only a matter of time before Hannah let it slip, so they wanted to tell me themselves before asking me to help keep their secret. They also told me *Lenny* is telekinetic."

"No kidding?" she says. "So, it's genetic?"

"Yeah, I guess so."

"Is Bettie telekinetic, too?"

"No, just Lenny and Hannah," I say. "They're actually connected by their telekinetic power."

"Connected how?"

"When Hannah uses her telekinesis, it makes Lenny sick," I say. "Well, I don't know if *sick* is the right word, but it drains him. After Hannah saved me from Harry, Lenny passed out in the dirt, and he was bedridden for a day or so afterward. They told me that they've raised Hannah to understand the importance of not using her powers, both for Lenny's physical wellbeing as well as to ensure Claudius doesn't learn what she can do."

Xyla is quiet for a few moments before jumping from the bed and pacing around the room.

"Whoa!" I say. "What's happening?"

Her eyes dart wildly from side to side, as if she's unraveling a puzzle in her mind.

Suddenly, she stops moving.

"Grover," she says, locking eyes with me, "I think I've figured it out."

"Figured *what* out?"

"Your dad," she says. "I know what's wrong with your dad!"

Chapter Forty-Nine

THE AVENGERS ANALOGY

"IT'S HANNAH," XYLA SAYS. "She's the key."

"I don't understand," I say. "Hannah's the reason my dad is dying?"

"No, what I mean is you and Hannah are the same."

"You lost me."

"Okay, let me think," she says, pacing around the room again like a caged animal. "Remember when I told you Lenny and Hannah had identical lightning bolts when I looked inside of them?"

"Yeah," I say, "you saw two bolts of lightning, side by side."

"And remember how I said they were similar to the two flames I saw inside of you?"

"Yes."

"Okay, now keep that in the front of your mind," she says. "Remember how you told me that after the first time you caught on fire, you learned your dad was sick?"

"Yeah, my mom called me a few minutes after I put the fire out."

"Exactly!"

"Exactly what?" I ask. "I don't follow."

"One minute you were completely engulfed in flames," she says, "and the next your dad fell into a coma."

Xyla stops pacing and stares at me.

"It makes sense, right?" she asks.

"I don't know," I say. "Are you saying what I think you're saying?"

"What do you think I'm saying?"

"I think you're saying that my dad is basically like Lenny and I'm like Hannah?"

"Exactly!" she says. "Except, instead of telekinesis, I think your dad's fireproof."

"My dad? Fireproof? That's impossible!"

"It's the only thing that makes sense," she says. "Look, you've used your power nearly every day since your dad's been in the hospital, right? That means he wouldn't have time to recover, which is why he hasn't woken up."

"Oh, shit."

"Plus, there's probably even a compounding effect."

"What do you mean?"

"Your dad's condition probably gets worse every time you use your power."

"Shit, am I killing my dad?"

"Not on purpose."

"Fuck, fuck, fuck."

"On the bright side," she says, "every day that you *don't* use your power, your dad is probably getting stronger."

"You think so?"

"Maybe."

"How long ago was my last performance?"

"About two days," she says, sitting back down on the bed. "Let me take a look inside of you."

She touches her fingers to my temples.

"What do you see?"

"The two flames have changed," she says. "They're almost equal in size now, and they're also closer together."

"How close?"

"Practically touching."

Xyla and I stay in the motel room for a few more hours. She manages to fall asleep, and, in spite of all the new information buzzing in my head, I do as well. After we wake up, we treat ourselves to a couple of showers before checking out and getting back on the road. It's officially our third day, and, along with the possibility that my dad may be getting better, I'm feeling encouraged by the fact that the Ringmaster hasn't found us.

As we walk down the road, offering our thumbs to each car that passes, my heart swells with the thought of my dad waking up. If Xyla's theory is accurate, then it's only a question of how long I have to abstain from using my powers in order for Dad to fully recover. I'm so overwhelmed with optimism and hope that I've become virtually useless in our hitchhiking efforts. Luckily, Xyla manages to hook us up with a ride on another eighteen-wheeler. I hardly register getting into the truck or even learning the driver's name. After eight breezy hours on the road, we pull into a truck stop in Yuma, Arizona.

"This is as far as I go," she says.

We thank her for the ride as we exit the truck. I don't know exactly where Yuma is on the map, but I know Arizona isn't too far from California, which means I'm almost home. Since we're already at a truck stop, Xyla is quickly able to get us another ride with a new truck driver. This one is headed for Hesperia, California, which is great news because that's only an hour or so away from Loma Linda Medical Center.

As we pile into the cab, the truck driver tells us the ride to Hesperia is roughly four hours. Xyla squeezes my hand and tells me she's going to sleep in the back, which is fine by me given how much she's already done to aid in my precarious voyage home.

His name is Niko.

He has pockmarked skin and an old photo of a feathered showgirl taped to his dashboard. On his left hand, the tip of his ring finger is missing, leaving it dwarfed among the neighboring digits. I'm free to notice these details because, for the first hour or so of our drive, Niko doesn't say a word as he's fully consumed with political talk radio.

"You know what the fucking problem is, don't you?" he says.

I assume he's talking to the radio, but quickly realize his question is for me.

"Oh," I say. "No, I don't think I do."

"It's all those rich Washington fat cats up in their ivory towers," he says. "They don't give a fuck about the working man. All they care about is making their next billion dollars."

"I guess it's better to be a have than a have-not."

"You got that right, bub," he says, snorting a laugh. "What's your name again?"

"Grover."

"I'll tell you what, Grover," he says. "You put *me* in charge, and I'll fucking fix this whole broken country."

This sort of conversation is usually not my lane, but I figure the polite thing to do is engage.

"What would you do?" I ask.

"Hell, I don't fucking know," he says, "but you got guys like you and me out here working our dicks off for crumbs, while the rest of the bread is sitting in bank accounts in the Bahamas, where those rich assholes don't have to pay a goddamn penny in taxes. Not a *fucking* penny!" Niko pounds his fist on the steering wheel to punctuate his point. "You know what? Fuck it. I know *exactly* what I would do. I would fucking get rid of capitalism."

"That sounds pretty extreme."

"Extreme is the only thing that'll shake up the status quo, bub," he says. "Elect me president right now, and the first thing I'd do is sign an executive order to make this a fucking socialist country. I mean, shit, with fucking capitalism, you've got working men running around like fucking rats fighting for every last piece of cheese just to fucking survive. You know what that makes us?"

"What?"

"A country of fucking rats," he says. "But you make this country socialist, and the next thing you know is you get people working together. Everyone gets an equal share of the cake, and no more rich fucking fat cats living the high life off my fucking sweat."

"Is that how socialism works?"

"How the fuck should I know?" he says. "The public education system is garbage in this country."

"Well, I don't know much about economics," I say, "so I can't speak to the merits of replacing capitalism with socialism. But I do think you're right in that people are better off when they work together."

"Fuck yeah, bub."

"It's kind of like the Avengers."

"Who the fuck are they?"

"They're a team of superheroes," I say. "Iron Man, Captain America, Thor—"

"Shit, I don't know from no fucking superheroes."

"All you really need to know is that, individually, each member of the Avengers has the potential to do amazing things," I say, "but when they come together, they can literarily save the world."

"Right on," he says. "We need to Avenger the fuck out of this country."

Niko turns up the volume, and for the next couple hours he vacillates between yelling at the radio and engaging me with his very passionate views on drug laws, abortion rights, illegal immigration, mainstream media, fake news, and most any other topic designed to separate people into self-righteous tribes. At some point during the drive, I noticed a series of cassette tapes on Niko's floor. Aside from being surprised that anybody still listens to cassette tapes, the bigger surprise is that it's the audiobook of Joseph Campbell's *The Hero with a Thousand Faces*. I mean, what are the odds that I'd hitch a ride with a random truck driver who, like me, is a fan of Joseph Campbell? I don't know if it's a sign or anything, but it feels like a good omen.

"You like Joseph Campbell?" I say, picking up the box set.

"That motherfucker?" he says with a snarl. "No fucking way!"

"But you have his audiobook?"

He looks over and sees the box set in my hand.

"Yeah, well, I'm banging a college professor," he says. "She gave it to me, thinking I might like it, I guess."

"And you listened to it?"

"Beginning to end."

"And you didn't like it?"

"Fuck no," he says. "You like him?"

"Yeah, I love Joseph Campbell."

"That's too bad for you, bub."

"What do you have against Joseph Campbell?"

"He's a fucking fascist!"

Admittedly, I'm not all that learned in the ways of fascism, but I can say with confidence that Niko is wrong in his assessment of Joseph Campbell—of course, I wouldn't actually say that out loud to him, as he's a very intimidating man, but I am nonetheless interested in exploring his oddly strong viewpoint.

"What makes you think Joseph Campbell is a fascist?"

"It's that whole deal with the monomyth."

"The hero's journey?"

"Yeah, that whole gimmick is a fucking fascist concept."

"How do you figure?"

"It's like this," Niko says. "The hero's journey is way too fucking focused on the individual, which is the whole fucking problem with this goddamned country. It's too many fucking individuals looking out for themselves."

"But, to be fair, that's not really what the hero's journey is about."

"Yeah, yeah, yeah, I know what the fucking hero's journey is about," he says, waving his hand as if to swat my words out of the air. "It's about one guy going out into the scary world to embark on an adventure where he faces a series of trials and tribulations before eventually defeating a big, bad villain, which leads to his personal growth."

In spite of his sarcastic tone, I have to admit that was a surprisingly apt synopsis.

"Okay, but in Campbell's explanation of the hero's journey," I say, "one of the main things he talks about is how the hero meets a wise figure along his journey."

"So, what?"

"Well, it means that the hero's journey isn't all about the hero as an individual," I say. "He makes friends along the way who help him out."

"Yeah, but that's the problem," Niko says. "The hero's friends are putting in work, but when the story's over, the hero's the only one people wanna talk about. I'll tell you what—I wanna see a movie where the hero *and* his friends are all together in the end, killing the bad guy together, all of them getting the credit they deserve. None of this nonsense where one man defeats the bad guy all by himself."

"I like that idea," I say. "A story like that would essentially acknowledge that everybody involved is on their own hero's journey, which, in the end, would sort of make it a *collective* heroes' journey."

"Fuck yeah," Niko says. "Now, that's closer to real life than Joseph Campbell's fascist bullshit."

"Actually, the more I think about it, that's exactly what happens in the Avengers," I say. "In every Avengers movie, it takes a collective effort from all the heroes in the climactic scene to defeat the bad guy."

"That sounds like something I can get with."

"But I still can't agree with you about Joseph Campbell being a fascist."

"Yeah, well, what the fuck do I know anyway?" Niko says with a shrug that feels more like an olive branch than a concession. "If there's only one thing I *do* know, it's that, from the moment we're born to the day we die, we're all just bouncing around this planet like a billion aimless pinballs trying to make sense of a senseless world."

Once we arrive in Hesperia, Niko stops for gas at the Pilot Travel Center. Xyla stirs awake as the truck rumbles to sleep.

"This is where we part ways," Niko says.

We thank him for the ride as we exit the truck, making our way into the food mart, where Xyla charms the clerk behind the counter into ordering us a cab. Once the cab arrives, Xyla and I slide into the back seat. She holds my hand, intertwining our fingers together.

"What do you see?" I ask.

"The two flames are the exact same size now."

"Are they still getting closer?"

"Yes," she says. "They're actually beginning to overlap."

"Like they're joining together?"

"Yes."

"Do you think that's a good thing?"

"I think it is," she says. "I really do."

For the remainder of the drive to Loma Linda Medical Center, I'm like an antsy kid waiting for Christmas morning. I watch every freeway sign pass overhead, clocking the miles and counting down as we get closer and closer until we make our final exit. We drive through Loma Linda for only a few minutes, weaving through a few bends and turns, before arriving at the hospital. I pay the cab driver his fare plus a generous tip and nearly trip over myself as I hurry towards the hospital entrance.

Three days ago, we started this improbable journey, and I have to admit, I didn't have high hopes of making it this far. But, after seventy-two hours of cross-country travel, working against any reasonable probability of success, we made it. The joy is so overwhelming that I start to cry.

"Ready?" Xyla says, wiping the tears from my cheeks.

"Ready."

We step into the lobby, cooled by the fresh burst of air conditioning. Despite not having been here for a few weeks, I remember exactly which halls to walk down, which elevator to take, and which floor to get off on until my dad's room is just a few steps away.

Xyla stops before we enter.

"Do you want me to wait out here?"

"No," I say, taking her hand. "I want you with me."

We enter Dad's hospital room, and he still appears to be in a coma. Mom's at his bedside, smiling when she sees me.

"Grover!"

"I got here as soon as I could."

"I'm so happy to see you, sweetheart," she says. "Look who else is here."

I look to the corner of the room, and my heart sinks.

"Hello, Grover," the Ringmaster says. "I've been waiting for you."

Chapter Fifty

THE MYSTERIES OF THE WORLD

R ED-TINTED GLASSES.

Charcoal beard.

Legs crossed, hands folded in his lap.

"What are you doing here?"

"I'm here to offer my support," the Ringmaster says, standing from his seat.

He walks to the bed and stands opposite me, leaving my dad as a buffer between us.

"Lucy," the Ringmaster says, "if it's not asking too much, do you think perhaps Grover and I can speak privately for a few minutes?"

"Yes, of course," Mom says. "I'll go get some coffee in the cafeteria. Would anybody else like something?"

"I'm fine, Mom."

"I'm fine, too," Xyla says. "Thank you."

"Claudius?" Mom says. "Coffee?"

"You're too kind," he says. "I'll have whatever you're having, my dear."

He pulls a large bill from his pocket, handing it to her.

"No," she says, "that's not necessary."

"Lucy, please," he says, "let me have the pleasure of buying you coffee."

Mom smiles, stifling a giggle as she accepts the money.

"You boys enjoy your top-secret chat," she says. "I'll be back in a bit."

Mom exits the room, leaving me and Xyla alone with the Ringmaster.

"How was your trip, Grover?"

"How did you know where to find me?"

"Maybe it was witchcraft," he says. "Maybe it was a lucky guess. Does it really matter?"

"I guess not," I say. "What happens now?"

"We'll get to that," he says. "Now, answer my question. How was your trip?"

Silence.

"Did you and Xyla have some nice bonding time together?"

Silence.

"Grover," the Ringmaster says, "if I'm the only one talking, this is going to take all night."

"What do you want?"

"I want to know if you and Xyla bonded during your trip."

"Yes, we did."

"Xyla," the Ringmaster says, looking at her, "do you agree?"

"Yes," she says, crossing her arms.

"Oh, my," the Ringmaster says, "did you see that, Grover? I don't think she's happy to see me. How about you? Are *you* happy to see me?"

"Thrilled," I say. "So, how does it work?"

"How does what work?"

"Do you drag me back, kicking and screaming?"

"Now, now," the Ringmaster says, "you have the wrong idea about me. I would never make you come back against your will."

"So, I don't have to go back?"

"That decision will be entirely up to you."

"And if I decide not to go back?"

"Then, I'll be on my way."

"Just like that?"

"Just like that."

The Ringmaster runs his thick fingers down his beard.

"But, if I may play fortuneteller for a moment," he says, "I predict that before I walk out of this hospital room, you will make the decision to return to Grambling Brothers."

"I doubt that."

The Ringmaster smiles.

"You want to see something interesting?" he asks, lifting my dad's hand from the bed.

"Don't you touch him!"

"If you feel that strongly about it," the Ringmaster says, "come and stop me."

While I have no illusion that I can do anything physically imposing to the Ringmaster, I can't just stand by and do nothing.

"Don't," Xyla says, holding me back.

"You'd be wise to mind her," the Ringmaster says. "Besides, I think you're going to like what I have to show you."

With his free hand, he retrieves his Zippo lighter from his pocket.

"What do you think will happen if I touch your father with this flame?" he says, flicking the Zippo to life.

"Leave him alone."

"That's not really an answer, Grover," he says, "so I'll ask again. What do you think will happen if I touch your father with this flame?"

"I don't know."

"Interesting," he says, turning his attention to Xyla. "Do you think he truly doesn't know?"

Xyla shrugs.

"I see," he says, shifting his eyes between Xyla and me. "That's how we're going to play this?"

Silence.

"Fine."

The Ringmaster moves the flame just below my dad's limp palm.

"Stop!" I say.

"If you want me to stop," the Ringmaster says, "give me an honest answer."

I look at Xyla.

"Keep your eyes on me," the Ringmaster says, "and give me an answer."

"I don't know," I say. "I think maybe he would be unharmed, I guess."

The Ringmaster smiles.

"Thank you for your honesty, Grover."

"Now, let him go."

"Not just yet," the Ringmaster says. "I think we need to find out for certain."

He lowers Dad's hand until the flame presses flush against his palm.

"Would you look at that?" the Ringmaster says, turning Dad's hand over. "It appears you're not the only fireproof member of your family. But you knew that, didn't you, Grover? Tell me, how did you know the fire wouldn't burn your father's flesh?"

"I don't know."

"Enough with the coy routine," the Ringmaster says. "Tell me how you knew."

Silence.

"Well?"

"Xyla."

"Xyla?"

"She had a theory."

"Did she now?" the Ringmaster says, looking at Xyla. "And what inspired this theory?"

"I think you already know," she says.

"Maybe I do," the Ringmaster says, "but I want to hear *you* say it."

"When I look inside of Grover, I see two flames."

"Go on."

"Over the last few weeks, one flame has gotten progressively bigger, while the other has gotten smaller."

"Fascinating," the Ringmaster says. "Be a dear and look inside Grover's father, please."

Xyla looks at me, silently asking for permission. I nod my approval, and she touches her fingers to Dad's temples.

"Well," the Ringmaster says, "what do you see?"

"Two flames."

The Ringmaster holds his hands to his cheeks, feigning shock.

"How do these flames look compared to the flames you see inside of Grover?"

"They look identical."

"Interesting," the Ringmaster says. "Would you say the two flames are the same size?"

"Yes."

"And how close together are they?"

"Very close," she says. "They're overlapping."

"Would you say the two flames are becoming one?"

"It looks that way."

"Thank you," the Ringmaster says. "You may stop now."

Xyla gently removes her fingers from Dad's temples.

"Now, let's talk about what happens next," the Ringmaster says. "Grover, I have some good news for you. Your father is going to wake up."

"He is?" I ask. "How do you know?"

The Ringmaster smiles.

"The mysteries of the world are mysteries for a reason," he says. "I want you to stay here with your father for a few days until he wakes up."

"You're really going to let me stay to see him wake up?"

"Yes, of course."

"What's the catch?"

"No, catch," the Ringmaster says. "I want you to be here to see your father's recovery with your own eyes. And after he wakes up, I want you to return to Grambling Brothers to accept the consequences of your actions."

"You said I didn't have to go back."

The Ringmaster walks around the bed, approaching me and Xyla.

"To be precise," he says, "I told you I would never make you come back against your will."

"So, I don't have to go back?"

"No," he says, "not if that's you're will."

The Ringmaster snatches Xyla's arm, pulling her into his body.

"But, before you make your final decision," he says, "you may want to know this next bit of information. Xyla's coming back with me. So, if *you* choose not to come back, *she* will suffer the consequences of your actions."

"That's not fair," I say.

"I beg to differ," the Ringmaster says. "I'm giving you the option to stay with your family and live out the rest of your life any way you see fit. I believe that's extremely fair. So, what's it going to be?"

"Stay here," Xyla says. "Don't go back."

"I can't let you suffer my consequences."

"I don't care about that," Xyla says. "Whatever it is, I deserve it."

"You would really do that for me?"

"Yes."

"Ticktock, Grover," the Ringmaster says. "What will it be?"

I look at my dad, then Xyla.

Silence.

"Well?"

"I'll go back."

"Splendid," the Ringmaster says. "And because I'm feeling generous, you have my permission to spend one full day with your father after he wakes up. When that day is complete, you will rejoin us at our next stop."

"Where will that be?"

The Ringmaster smiles.

"Salem, Massachusetts."

Chapter Fifty-One

COMING TO AN END

M OM RETURNS TO THE room with two cups of coffee. I'm
standing at Dad's bedside, hands resting on the rail, looking
over my superhero.

"Where did your friends go?"

"They had to get back to the circus."

"That was fast," Mom says. "Too bad Claudius couldn't stay for
his coffee."

She hands me the warm foam cup that was intended for the
Ringmaster.

"Thank you."

"Was there an emergency?"

"Claudius has his hands in everything," I say, "so there's always
something."

"Bless his heart," she says, sipping from her cup. "Does that mean
you have to leave, too?"

"No," I say. "In fact, Claudius insisted I stay for a few days."

"That man is too kind."

I sip from the Ringmaster's cup.

"How long was Claudius here?"

"Just a few minutes," she says. "I assumed he was with you, but he told me you two traveled separately. That was so sweet of him to come out all this way."

"Yeah," I say, "it was unexpected."

She sips from her cup.

"And your friend had to leave, too?"

"Claudius needed her back with him."

"I'm sorry I didn't have a chance to properly meet her," Mom says. "What's her name?"

"Xyla."

"Oh, that was the fortuneteller?"

"Yeah."

"Then I'm doubly sad I didn't get to meet her," she says. "Maybe next time."

"Next time, for sure."

Mom gives me a look.

"Is everything okay, sweetheart?"

There are so many things I want to tell her right now. I want to tell her that the Ringmaster is evil, and he may not even be human. I want to tell her that he had no intention of ever letting me come back here to see her or Dad or anybody outside of Grambling Brothers ever again, and the only reason I'm here now is that I risked my life to run away. I want to tell her that Dad—her husband, her rock, her forever sweetheart—will wake up soon. I want to tell her that I know this as surely as I know he's fireproof, just like his son. I want to tell her that after he wakes up in a few days, I'll return to Grambling Brothers, and she'll never see me again. I want to tell her that the Ringmaster has bad intentions for me, and whatever those intentions are, I don't expect to come out the other side alive. I want to tell her that I saw the Ringmaster kill the first friend I made in the circus right before my eyes. I want to tell her that the rest of the circus stood in a circle and watched, and nobody—including me—did anything to stop him. I want to tell her that the Ringmaster's going to turn me into a cautionary tale, something his prisoners can whisper about when they think he's not near. I want to tell her how very much I love her and Dad. I want to tell her that I appreciate everything they've ever done for me, and I'm grateful to spend my final days with them.

But I don't say any of that.

"Yeah," I say, "everything's okay."

Chapter Fifty-Two

FIRE-MAN

TIME HAS BLURRED TOGETHER since I got home, so I'm not sure how long I've been here, but I know it's been at least a few days. Dr. Boudreaux comes and goes, taking tests, giving updates, and speaking in exotic medical terms. There's optimism in his tone because Dad's vitals are getting stronger. Nurses bring extra meals so Mom and I don't have to leave the room; sometimes they even bring McDonald's or Starbucks, because that's the sort of dazzling effect my mom has on people—especially strangers—charming them without realizing she's being charming, making them laugh and smile, happy just to be in her presence. She calls each nurse by their first name, asking about their husbands and wives, boyfriends and girlfriends, children and grandchildren, nieces and nephews; she wants to know how one did on their science test and if another had a happy birthday. She does it all effortlessly, making each one of them feel like they're her best friend, because, in those moments, that's exactly what they are.

She's asleep now in the chair that's become her second home.

I'm glad she's resting.

Three days.

I think I've been here for three days.

It could be more.

I don't think it's been less.

"Grover?"

There are only three of us in the room.

Me.

Mom.

"Dad?"

Oh, my God.

He's awake.

He blinks his eyes, looking around the room.

He's confused, maybe a little scared.

"It's okay," I say, hurrying to his bedside. "You're safe."

He tries to sit up, but his body is tethered to wires and tubes.

Mom opens her eyes.

"Rex?"

He sees her.

"Lucy."

She jumps from her chair and wraps her arms around him in defiance of every tube and wire that gets in her way. His arms take her in, fingertips digging into her sweater, clinging like his life depends on it. I leave the room—partly to find a doctor, but mostly to give them the privacy this moment deserves. I see one of the kind nurses, and, before I can say a word, she responds to the look on my face, sprinting to Dad's room. I follow her in, and we find Mom lying in the bed, her cheek cradled against Dad's broad chest, quietly sobbing as he strokes her hair.

Dr. Boudreaux is puzzled, but pleased. He, along with the other doctors, spend hours coming and going, running tests, trying to gather any bit of information that will help them understand the strange miracle they find themselves audience to. Word spreads quickly throughout the hospital, from nurses and receptionists to janitors and volunteers, all of them coming by to see the miracle firefighter who came back from the dead. Once the excitement and commotion subside, Mom and I are left alone with Dad.

For all the talk of miracles, I know exactly why Dad is awake. I also know why he lay in a coma for so many weeks. Of course, I can't tell Dr. Boudreaux—or any of his colleagues—that my father and I share a mystical fireproof power, because that would just sound crazy.

But what about Dad?

Can I tell *him*?

What if he already knows?

Perhaps, at some point in his life, just like me, he discovered he was fireproof, but instead of doing something frivolous like joining the circus, he decided to become a superhero.

Fire-Man.

Like all the best superheroes, he chose to use his power for the good of mankind.

Is it possible that his power is connected to anybody else?

Were my grandparents fireproof?

Did *they* tell him about his powers?

Dad always told me that he'd dreamt of being a firefighter from the time he was a kid. Maybe knowing he was fireproof informed his childhood dream. Then again, maybe he *didn't* know about his powers, and the fact that he's fireproof was simply a cosmic gift from the universe for the man whose northern star has always guided him to do the right thing. It's entirely possible that he grew up carving a path for his life through the will of his determination, fueled by the petrol of his childhood dream, all the while being oblivious to his supernatural ability.

Was he born fireproof?

Could he walk through a burning building as a toddler?

Did his power lay dormant until he was an adult?

Does he know *I'm* fireproof?

If so, was he ever going to tell me?

I suppose the only way I can know the answer to any of my questions is to ask him, but how do I even bring it up without sounding like a crazy person? Of course, if he does already know, then I won't sound crazy at all.

I wouldn't be so anxious about any of this if I knew we had more time together, but now that he's awake, the Ringmaster will expect me to return to Grambling Brothers. I know there's no reasonable way for the Ringmaster to know Dad is awake, but I'm pretty well convinced he was aware the very moment it happened.

Mom and Dad have been acting like a couple of teenagers since he woke up, trading whispers and stealing kisses. The nurses think it's adorable, and, truth be told, so do I. A few hours after Dad wakes up, his eyes get heavy. You'd think after being in a coma for all that time, he'd have gotten all the rest he needs; if I'm being honest, now that he's awake, I never want him to close his eyes again.

Mom senses my concern without me having to voice it.

"He'll be fine," she says. "Won't you, honey?"

"You bet," Dad says with his gravelly post-coma voice while unfurling a manly yawn.

"Grover and I will grab some dinner," Mom says. "Are you hungry, dear?"

Before he can even consider answering, Dad is already snoring.

Mom and I go down to the cafeteria and order the daily special, which is a bean and cheese burrito, French fries, and a fountain drink. I assumed I wasn't hungry, but the moment I smell the food, I'm famished. The last time Mom and I sat in here sharing a meal feels like a lifetime ago; at that time, I was still a college professor, and Dad was cocooned in a medical mystery. Being here now under better circumstances is incredibly cathartic.

Looking up from my burrito, I see Mom crying.

"What happened?"

"I'm okay," she says. "These are happy tears, I think. Maybe they're exhausted tears. Either way, nothing's wrong. Everything is wonderful."

"It's been a scary few weeks," I say. "Crying for any reason is pretty appropriate."

"It really has been scary," she says. "He was dying, you know? That's what Dr. Boudreaux told me. He believed it, and I believed *him*. I had to find a way to be at peace with never seeing your father look at me again. Never saying good morning, never kissing me good night. I wasn't ready for it, but I had no choice. I just sat in that room, overwhelmed with the reality that I would soon be grieving the death of my husband, my best friend, the love of my whole little life, while also having to manage things like funeral arrangements and canceling credit cards and putting the house up for sale."

"You were going to sell the house?"

"I wasn't going to live there all by myself," she says. "It's too big for just me. Plus, all the memories would be too much to be around. I wasn't looking forward to any of it, but I understood our love story was coming to an end, and there was nothing I could do about it. Then, like a fairytale, your father opened his eyes—and just like that, our love story began a new chapter."

"A new chance for a happy ending."

"That's exactly right," she says. "The three of us still have a lot of years left to be a family, and I couldn't be more grateful."

Dad enjoys a bowl of red Jell-O as I tell him about my recent adventures in the circus.

"So, you're a circus performer, now?" he says, turning to look at Mom. "Is he being serious?"

"Quite serious," she says, smiling. "I watched him with my very own eyes."

"Well, shit," he says with a laugh. "How did that happen?"

"A few days after you went into your coma, I met a man named Claudius Xavier," I say, "and he made me an offer to join his circus."

"Doing what?"

"A fire act."

"A *fire* act?" he says, squinting his eyes. "Are you pulling my leg?"

I grab my phone from my pocket and queue up the YouTube video, which now has well over a billion views. Dad watches with wonder as Fernando blows fireballs on me, engulfing my clothes in flames. He laughs hard when my clothes burn off, and I run around naked in front of the audience.

"That's really you?"

"Yeah," I say. "I've been traveling and performing the whole time you've been here."

"Your son has become quite a sensation," Mom says. "They've been selling out shows all over the country, thanks to Grover."

"That's amazing, but what about teaching?" he asks. "Are you still a college professor?"

"No," I say, "but I *am* still teaching. There are kids who travel with Grambling Brothers, and they need help with their school-work, so I tutor them."

"That's pretty cool, bud," he says. "My son, the circus performer. So, what I saw in the video, that's your fire act?"

"Yeah," I say. "My partner, Fernando the Fearless Fire Tamer, lights me on fire, and I remain unharmed."

"Unharmed?"

I nod, yes.

"How do you pull that off?"

I think this is the moment. It's time for me to show him that I'm fireproof, then let whatever happens happen. Hopefully, he'll know exactly what he's looking at, and we can have an honest conversation about our shared power, and maybe he can even shed some much-needed light on this whole surreal phenomenon—or maybe he'll be confused and gobsmacked, and I'll have to tell him that not only am *I* fireproof, but so is *he*.

"Let me show you," I say. "I need a lighter."

"You're looking at the wrong fella," Dad says. "I don't even have underwear, let alone a lighter."

This makes Mom laugh.

"I'm pretty sure the nice girl behind the front desk smokes," she says. "I'll go see if she has one."

Now that I'm alone with Dad, I consider just blurting it all out to him, but Mom returns with a lighter before I have a chance.

"You're not going to do anything dangerous, are you?" she asks, handing it to me.

"No, not at all."

I flick the lighter to life.

"All right, Dad," I say. "I'm going to show you something amazing."

"Great."

"And after I do," I say, "I'm hoping you may be able to explain it to me."

"Explain what?"

"You'll see," I say. "Just watch."

I hold my left hand above the lighter, lowering it until my palm touches the flame.

"Fuck!" I say, yanking my hand away from the flame.

Mom and Dad laugh like I'm doing a bit.

"What happened?" Dad asks.

"It hurt," I say, blowing on my palm. "The fire burned my skin."

"Well, that's what fire does," he says, laughing. "Is this what you wanted me to explain to you?"

Mom and Dad laugh some more, so I go along with it like it was all a joke before excusing myself to the bathroom. I flick the lighter to life and press the flame against my palm, and it feels exactly the way fire is supposed to feel when it touches living flesh.

"Shit."

I'm not fireproof anymore.

Chapter Fifty-Three

DESTINY

T HE STAKES ARE CLEAR.

I made a deal with the Ringmaster, and now it's time for me to make good on it. I can whine about the Ringmaster not playing fair or how he withheld the finer details of our deal to ensure I gave him what he wanted, but it wouldn't change anything. I'd still have to rejoin Grambling Brothers, or else Xyla will suffer the consequences.

My consequences.

Now, I know what you're thinking.

She deserves it, right?

She betrayed me first.

But what's any of it matter?

In the end, the Ringmaster personally escorted her back, so even if I choose to stay here with my family, what reason do I have to believe he won't do the exact same thing to me? Let me answer that one for you. I'm confident that regardless of what decision I make here today, I'm destined to end up back at Grambling Brothers one way or another. Well, maybe "destined" isn't the right word, because I don't think destiny has anything to do with it. You might say it's just one incredibly unfortunate stroke of bad luck, but I wouldn't agree with that either. I don't think luck is any more involved than destiny. It's easy to get caught up in the whole winding cosmic mystery of it all.

Who is the Ringmaster?

What powers does he have?

How far-reaching is his grasp?

Is he all-knowing?

Is he the devil incarnate?

Is he just a man?

The one thing I can say with absolute confidence is this:

I don't know.

Here's something else I'm confident about—even if I got the answers to all of my questions, it wouldn't matter. From the moment I came out of my mom's womb, my life was my own. Free will was my inheritance. Then I met the Ringmaster, and he made me an offer. He didn't threaten my life or the lives of anyone I love. He didn't twist my arm or imply that I had to take his deal or else. He simply presented me with a very seductive offer. If I hadn't accepted his offer, the Ringmaster would not be in my life today—of that, I have no doubt.

But I *did* accept his offer.

Me.

Grover Wilcox.

Sound mind, sound body.

And now it's time to go back and take my place in the Ringmaster's circus prison. When I return, I'll have to confess that I'm no longer fireproof. Without my power, there's no telling how he'll have me live out my sentence. Maybe he'll stick me in the midway. Maybe he'll have me take over for Paulo in the box office. Maybe he'll put me on the tent crew, reducing me to a life of backbreaking manual labor.

Forever.

And I'll have no choice but to do it.

No matter how tired I get.

No matter how tedious it becomes.

No matter how desperately I wish for better circumstances, I'll be stuck doing an incredibly difficult job, and my reward at the end of the day will be to simply exist so I can do it all again tomorrow.

And the day after that.

And the day after that.

And it'll go like this, on and on and on, until the day death finally takes mercy on me. And even then, I can't be sure the Ringmaster won't be waiting for me on the other side.

I keep the goodbyes brief.

I can't handle it any other way.

Dad is up on his feet, hugging me under his own power.

Mom is already crying.

"Don't be sad," I say. "I'll be back."

It doesn't matter if it's true.

It only matters that she believes it.

Chapter Fifty-Four

YOU

S PEAKING OF GOODBYES, I want to take this opportunity to also say goodbye to you. I know you're still here, but I think it's best to acknowledge we'll be parting ways soon. You've stuck with me on this strange journey much longer than you had any obligation to. Even when things turned bleak, you were there.

But I don't expect you to stay till the end.

This is my burden.

Not yours.

Chapter Fifty-Five

SALEM

I'M SITTING ON AN airplane, 40,000 feet in the sky, traveling across the country. I've never been to the Northeast in my life, let alone Massachusetts, and certainly not Salem. I land at Logan International Airport in Boston; as it turns out, there isn't an airport in Salem. I have no luggage, so I move through the airport easily—almost *too* easily—until I'm standing outside in the brisk, cool air. With a quick bout of internet research, I learned that public transportation in these parts is not hard to navigate. If I wanted to, I could extend my final march to Salem for another hour and a half by traveling on the Line 88 bus, subway, and train for less money than most people spend at Starbucks.

I *could* do that.

But I don't want to.

There's no use in prolonging the inevitable. What would I even do with an extra ninety minutes of freedom besides spend it worrying about the future? The sooner I get to the future, the sooner I can stop fretting over it.

So, I jump into the first cab I see.

"Where to, pal?"

"Salem."

"Where at in Salem?"

"Do you happen to know where the circus is?"

"Nope."

"In that case, drop me off anywhere you like," I say, "as long as it's in Salem."

"How about I take you to the witches?"

"Perfect."

The cabbie drops me off at the Salem Witch Trials Memorial, which seems like a good enough spot to get started on my wild goose chase. I hand him some cash without counting the bills, and he seems more than satisfied as I exit the cab. The memorial is mostly antiquated tombstones, dying grass, and narrow dirt trails laced around the graves. A few large oak trees surround the tombstones, gangly branches hanging over the remembered dead like gnarled fingers frozen in time. A thick wall of stacked stone blocks borders the graveyard; several elongated slabs stick out from the wall like granite benches, each of them engraved with names and dates.

One reads:

MARGARET SCOTT
HANGED
SEPT 22, 1692

Another reads:

JOHN WILLARD
HANGED
AUGUST 19, 1692

Yet another reads:

SARAH GOOD WILLARD
HANGED
JULY 19, 1692

Then, I see a familiar name:

GILES COREY
PRESSED TO DEATH
SEPT 19, 1692

As I stand over the memorial for Giles Corey, the Ringmaster turns up beside me, a lit cigar jutting from the side of his mouth. I know I should be shocked. After all, how in the world did he know I'd be in this exact place at this exact moment?

But the truth is, I'm not shocked.

However mystic or unexplainable his presence is, I've come to expect nothing less from the Ringmaster.

"Grover," he says. "I'm pleased you showed."

"We made a deal, right?"

"Indeed, we did."

We walk past bookshops and cafes, restaurants with yellow umbrellas, and postmodern water sculptures beyond my grasp of artistic appreciation.

"How's your father?"

"Do you care?"

"Of course, I do."

"He's great," I say. "Strong and healthy as he ever was."

"Good," the Ringmaster says, "that's exactly what I was hoping for."

We walk past wrought iron fences, small buildings resembling medieval castles, and statues celebrating Puritan heroes. Eventually, all of the brick-and-mortar gives way to a sweeping landscape of green grass and lush trees resting low to the ground like a dense emerald fog. I can see the circus grounds just beyond the leaves and branches.

"This is Gallows Hill Park," the Ringmaster says. "Admittedly, not the most sensitive name, but it's a fine stop for a circus."

We walk past the labyrinth and the empty box office, stepping through the wooden arch painted to look like the big top, and, for the first time since I fled in the middle of the night, I'm back inside of the Grambling Brothers Traveling Circus Show. We walk past the sideshow tents and the midway games, stopping when we reach the big top.

"Professor Grover the Fireproof Man," the Ringmaster says, "are you ready for your next performance?"

"About that."

"Yes?"

My chest tightens.

"I can't perform for you anymore."

"But, Grover," he says, "that wasn't our deal."

"I know," I say. "What I mean is I *literally* can't perform my act."

"And why is that?"

"I'm not fireproof anymore."

"You're not?"

"No."

"Are you certain?"

"Yes."

"Good," he says, dropping his cigar to the dirt and grinding the orange embers beneath his boot. "Follow me."

He disappears into the big top, so I follow him inside. As my eyes adjust to the dimness, I see my friends and colleagues standing shoulder to shoulder in the form of a large circle.

Chapter Fifty-Six

THE LEGEND OF GROVER WILCOX

T HE CIRCLE.

It's so obvious now.

I can't believe I didn't see it coming.

As I step further into the big top, the Circle opens up, letting me inside. My fight-or-flight instinct is telling me to turn and run, to get the hell out of here as fast as I can—but I know that won't work. The Ringmaster will just find me and bring me back. As I walk toward the center, the Circle closes behind me. The spotlight overhead snaps to life, shining a cone of light down to the dirt below. Framed inside the conical light is a wooden pole standing erect in the dirt. Gathered around the pole is a tall pile of tree branches, and just above them, about a foot or so off the ground, is a platform big enough to house two adult feet. I've never seen a burning-some-one-at-the-stake apparatus in person before, but I have no doubt that's exactly what I'm looking at.

The Ringmaster enters the Circle from the opposite side, stalking towards me with a thick twine of rope hanging from his fingers. My fight-or-flight instinct is once again kicking in, but, no matter how violently my heart beats against my chest, I know as surely as I've ever known anything in my life that there's no use trying to run away. The Ringmaster stares at me through his red-tinted glasses, unblinking, each step bringing him closer and closer until he's standing right in front of me.

Face-to-face.

"Grover Wilcox," he says, "do you understand what's happening?"

I nod, yes.

"It didn't have to end this way," he says. "It's important to me that you know that."

The Ringmaster takes a few steps backward towards the wooden pole, opening his arms like a crucifix.

"Follow me."

I do as he says.

"Take your place."

I step onto the platform, standing with my back against the wooden pole as he wraps the heavy rope around my arms, chest, and belly, cinching it into a knot so uncomfortably tight that I know, even without having to try, I can't break free. It's a strange feeling to cooperate so freely in my own execution. For what it's worth, I don't want you to think I've lost my will to live. Like somebody stranded in the middle of the ocean, staring into the wide-open jaws of a great white shark, I want to live. Like somebody heaved over the highest ledge of the Empire State Building, gazing at the clouds as they move further and further away, I want to live. But, regardless of my desperate want to live, I know that boxing a row of razor-sharp teeth is every bit as futile as screaming at the sky to reason with gravity.

The inevitable is undefeated.

I look around the Circle at all the familiar faces.

Charlie.

Annie.

Woodrow.

Fernando.

Sammy.

Harry.

Solo.

Carlos.

Ana.

Jose.

Paulo.

Bastian.

Geno.

Pete.

Bettie.

Lenny.

Darius.

May.

Vik.

Xyla.

There are others in the Circle, including the midway workers and members of the tent crew, many of whom I never had the pleasure of meeting. I wish I'd had the opportunity to know them all, to learn their names, and exchange a few kind words on our way to oblivion.

As it was with my first experience with the Circle, the children are mercifully not present.

No Pedro.

No Tonya.

No Hannah.

The Ringmaster claps his hands, prompting May to step out of the Circle. She drags a steel barrel to the center, setting it beside the pile of tree branches. Before walking away, May catches my eye and mouths the words, "I'm sorry." Taking her place back in the Circle, she positions herself directly in my line of sight—chin up, hands behind her back. I wish I'd had an opportunity to tell her she has nothing to be sorry about, but that's just one more regret I'll have to take with me.

The Ringmaster reaches his arm into the steel barrel, pulling out a large red can of gasoline. Removing the cap, he showers the branches before doing the same to me, soaking my clothes and wetting my hair. Gasoline runs down my face, burning my eyes; the strong fumes overwhelm my nostrils and turn my stomach. The Ringmaster reaches back into the barrel, pulling out Fernando's giant torch rod. He wets the wick with gasoline before igniting it with his Zippo lighter. Torch in hand, he gives his focused attention to the gathered audience.

"Here we are for another gathering of the Circle," the Ringmaster says, "for once again we must rectify a terrible betrayal."

My chest tightens.

"To begin, let me tell you about the legend of Grover Wilcox. Once upon a time, Grover had an accident in his kitchen, an accident that resulted in his entire body becoming engulfed in flames. Once the flames expired, Grover discovered his flesh was fireproof.

But what Grover did not yet know was at that very same moment, his father slipped into a mysterious coma. With his new-found fireproof ability, Grover made a deal to join the Grambling Brothers Traveling Circus Show, where he became Professor Grover the Fireproof Man. But there was something *else* that Grover did not yet know—his father was *also* fireproof. As it turns out, the father and son were connected by their supernatural power, and it was *because* of their connection that the father fell into his coma."

Pinpricks of anxiety flood my fingertips.

"What Grover would soon learn is the connection he shared with his father operated like a metaphysical tug-of-war, each of them drawing from the same mystical source. On that day in the kitchen, when his body was engulfed in flames, Grover yanked that metaphysical rope so severely that his father's body could no longer remain conscious. And with each of Grover's performances inside the big top, his father grew weaker and weaker, marching him towards death's door. When Grover learned of the transactional nature of his fireproof ability, he decided to betray his Grambling Brothers family by running away, disappearing in the still of the night. Within a few days, the metaphysical tug-of-war achieved stasis, and Grover's father came back to life. Following this miraculous recovery, Grover felt remorse over his betrayal and returned to his Grambling Brothers family, taking his place at the center of the Circle where he stands before you now, awaiting the consequence of his actions—to be burned at the stake."

This last part isn't a surprise, but hearing it out loud still leaves me weak in the knees.

"Because Grover is fireproof, it stands to reason that burning him at the stake is really no consequence at all," the Ringmaster says, "unless, of course, Grover is no *longer* fireproof."

The Ringmaster brings the torch towards my face, causing me to jerk my head away from the heat. This triggers a collective gasp from the Circle.

"It turns out that, as a consequence of bringing his father back to life, Grover had to abandon his own fireproof power. Therefore, burning him at the stake *will* lead to his death." The Ringmaster locks his eyes on mine, giving me his full attention. "Or will it?"

I hold his gaze, unflinching, the heat from the torch still warm on my cheek.

"There *is* a possibility that Grover can survive being burned at the stake."

I break eye contact, looking past the Ringmaster.

"In fact, there are *two* possibilities."

Something is wrong.

"Just like the seminal incident in his kitchen, burning Grover at the stake could trigger a new metaphysical transaction between him and his father, reconvening their mystical tug-of-war. Should that happen, Grover's fireproof power would return, shielding him from death. But, as a consequence, Grover's father most certainly would die."

Someone is missing.

"Or," the Ringmaster says, removing his red-tinted glasses, "Grover's fireproof power may simply *not* return, in which case he would burn to death in the center of the Circle."

It's May.

"Which possibility will it be?"

May is missing.

"Let's find out."

The pressure around my torso eases as the ropes begin to loosen. The Ringmaster's eyes shift, perhaps sensing something is amiss. He walks behind me, and, for the time being, I am no longer the center of his attention. There is a brief commotion, punctuated by a woman's scream. When the Ringmaster comes back around, each of his hands is full—in one hand, he holds the torch, and, in the other, he holds a handful of air. The Ringmaster shoots a snarling stare at his empty hand.

"Show yourself."

A human figure begins to appear from thin air. For a few moments, the figure is as translucent as a still body of water. As its form becomes more and more opaque, it is objectively clear that the Ringmaster is in fact holding May, gripping her by the back of her neck like a kitten as her feet dangle above the dirt. With a twist of his wrist, the Ringmaster rotates May's body around, forcing her to look him in the eye.

"There you are."

May kicks her legs, struggling to no avail.

"Worry not," the Ringmaster says, waving the torch, "there will be fire enough for you both."

No sooner have the words left his mouth when the torch flies from the Ringmaster's hand like it's been yanked by an invisible cord, skidding across the dirt. His eyes grow big, as this was clearly unexpected.

"Another betrayer," he says, surveying the Circle. "I wonder who it could be?"

Still holding May, the Ringmaster locks his eyes on Lenny, whose arms are stretched out in front of him, palms flat, like he's pushing an invisible wall.

"You've chosen the wrong side," the Ringmaster says, walking towards him. "Now, you too will—"

His words are cut off as Lenny's face pinches into a defiant scowl, his telekinetic powers pushing the Ringmaster backward against his will. As the heels of his heavy boots drag through the dirt like a pair of worn plows, the Ringmaster drops May to the ground and leans into Lenny's telekinetic force, walking towards him—one labored step at a time—as if through an angry blizzard.

"You think this can stop me?"

Lenny sets one foot back, his heel digging into the dirt as he struggles to hold the Ringmaster at bay. As Lenny's resistance threatens to falter, the Ringmaster steadily advances, gaining ground with increasing ease. Lenny drops to one knee, determined to maintain his defense, his hands still raised in the air despite his dwindling energy. His efforts, unfortunately, appear to be for naught as the Ringmaster moves comfortably into striking distance. Just as the Ringmaster extends his arm, his massive fingers dangerously close to Lenny's throat, a sudden, powerful force propels him backward like he's been struck by an invisible Mack truck. The Ringmaster soars through the air for at least twenty feet before crashing back down to earth, tumbling to a stop in a cloud of dust.

It's Hannah.

She's positioned herself beside her father—arms extended, palms flat.

I expect Lenny to fall unconscious now that Hannah is here using her telekinetic power, but, if anything, he seems to be growing stronger. As I watch the father-and-daughter duo pin the Ringmaster to the dirt with their telekinesis, I recall Lenny's earlier explanation that, so long as he and Hannah use their supernatural gift simultaneously, his strength doesn't deplete. Lenny rises to his feet alongside Hannah, each of them advancing toward the Ringmaster, who struggles against their combined effort with his back pressed against the ground. With the Ringmaster otherwise occupied, May hurries back to me, continuing her efforts to untie my bindings. The Ringmaster's struggle is short-lived as he manages to get back to his feet, but instead of targeting Lenny, he is now moving towards me and May. Lenny and Hannah do their best to slow him down, but, in spite of their combined power, they cannot fully impede the Ringmaster's progress.

No longer willing to stand by, Xyla breaks away from the Circle and runs to me, joining May in her efforts to untie me. As the Ringmaster inches closer and closer, they seem to be making progress, but not fast enough, as he is now upon us. Before the Ringmaster can make his next move, a defiant roar sounds from the Circle, followed by the sound of Handsome Harry's galloping footsteps. Charging like a bull in Pamplona, Harry buries his shoulder into the Ringmaster's gut, driving him back down to the dirt. Lenny and Hannah rush over to them and resume their tandem telekinesis—this time from much closer proximity—pinning the Ringmaster to the ground with renewed vigor.

Charlie Chuckles breaks from the Circle next, joining May and Xyla's efforts to set me free until, finally, the heavy rope falls to my feet. Xyla throws her arms around my neck as I step down from the platform. As grateful as I am to be free, I know we're not yet safe. The Ringmaster pushes himself up to a sitting position in spite of the combined efforts of Harry, Lenny, and Hannah, and it seems only a matter of time before he's back to his feet.

A wild scream sounds from the Circle, and I turn my head in time to see Darius sprinting towards the Ringmaster, tears streaking down his face; there's no doubt in my mind that those tears are for his fallen friend, Canyon. Despite having no supernatural abilities to speak of, Darius joins Harry, Lenny, and Hannah in their efforts to hold the Ringmaster down.

Solo breaks from the Circle next, running toward the group of rebels and leaping through the air, his body landing on top of the Ringmaster's legs. He laces his arms around the Ringmaster's ankles, gripping his boots with his Spider-Man hands as he fashions himself into a human straight jacket. As Solo does his thing, Handsome Harry wraps the Ringmaster's waist in a bear hug, squeezing with all of his supernatural strength. Darius, for his part, bravely lays his body atop one of the Ringmaster's arms like a soldier sacrificing himself against a live grenade. All the while, Lenny and Hannah continue their duel telekinetic efforts. As the struggle progresses, a collective realization fills the big top: the Ringmaster isn't strong enough to take on everyone all at once.

Vik and his two daughters break from the Circle next, followed by Fernando, Sammy, the Soaring Silvas, the Clown Alley Hooligans, and on and on until the Circle collapses completely into a dogpile on top of the Ringmaster.

Xyla squeezes my arm before leaving me to take her inevitable place in the dogpile.

May joins next.

The only two people inside the big top who aren't participating in the collective effort to restrain the Ringmaster are me and Charlie Chuckles. I move to join the dogpile, but Charlie stops me.

"Not you," he says.

"But I need to help."

"You already have," Charlie says. "You're the reason this mutiny is happening at all."

I look at my friends piled atop one another, scratching and clawing against the otherworldly power of the Ringmaster.

"Go on, kid," Charlie says, nodding his head toward the exit. "Get out of here."

"I think I should stay."

"What for?"

"To do my part."

Charlie looks at the dogpile of men and women fighting for their lives, then back at me.

"Maybe your part is to stand witness," he says. "Somebody needs to tell the story of what happened here, right?"

"Are you sure?"

"Yeah, I'm sure," he says. "This was our burden long before it was yours, and it's well past time we did something about it."

"What are you going to do?"

"What we should've done a long time ago," he says. "End it."

I hurry to the exit as Charlie joins the dogpile. Beneath all of the bodies and the struggling and the screaming, the Ringmaster is fully out of sight. Stepping outside, I see Pedro and Tonya standing together, holding hands. I go to them, standing beside Pedro, who takes hold of my hand with his furry fingers.

"Is Hannah okay?" he asks.

"Yes," I say, "she's okay."

"Did she help?" Tonya asks.

"Oh, yes," I say. "She was a *huge* help. If it weren't for Hannah, I don't think I would have gotten out of there alive."

Together, the three of us watch the big top, listening to the escalating sounds of violence and struggle inside. A deep, guttural roar fills the air, shaking the earth beneath our feet as a fog of thick, black smoke billows out through the curtains, rising up towards the heavens. One by one, as more and more smoke fills the sky like a mystical oil spill, each member of the Grambling Brothers Traveling Circus Show exits the big top.

Everyone except for the Ringmaster.

Handsome Harry exits last and heads straight toward me. He presents me with a clenched fist, unfurling it to reveal the Ringmaster's red-tinted glasses resting in his palm. He nods, urging me to take them, so I do. I'm not sure why he wants me to have the glasses, but my sense is they're meant to be a reminder of what was—and, perhaps more importantly, what we never want to be again. With all of us outside and standing together, we silently watch the tower of flames swallow up the big top until it crumbles down into an ashen heap of glorious freedom.

Chapter Fifty-Seven

SCHRÖDINGER'S RINGMASTER

S O, WHAT HAPPENED TO the Ringmaster?

The last time I saw him with my own eyes, he was inside the big top—but was he still inside when it burned to the ground? I think so, but I don't really know for sure. Like Schrödinger's cat, the Ringmaster is both dead *and* alive at the same time.

For now.

Bear with me, I'll circle back to this idea in just a bit.

First, I want to take a deep breath and enjoy the fact that right now everything is good. That'll change eventually because that's just how life goes, but right now—as I say these words—all is right with the world. From the moment I caught fire in my kitchen until a few months ago, when I watched the Ringmaster's big top turn to ash, my life existed in a perpetual present tense, like I'd been dropped onto a moving treadmill and was so busy trying to keep my legs in motion that I didn't have time to think about what was happening—or why. Now that I'm off that metaphorical treadmill, let me give you a rundown of what's happened since Grambling Brothers burned to the ground.

Dad is good.

So is Mom.

I talk to them every day, mostly on FaceTime, as I've been busy traveling the country. Dad went back to work at the firehouse, but, for the first time that I can remember, he's actually talking about retiring—sooner rather than later—so he can spend more time with Mom. As far as Dad being fireproof, I haven't had an opportunity to ask him about it.

Okay, that's not true.

I tried to slip one past you.

The truth is, I haven't *looked* for an opportunity to ask him, and, if I'm being totally honest, I don't expect I ever will. Maybe Dad *does* know he's fireproof, and he's fully capable of explaining the metaphysical mystery of it all—or maybe he has no idea. Either way, I'm perfectly okay with that remaining a mystery for now.

Xyla's good.

She and I are officially a couple, too.

Crazy, right?

By "officially," I mean that I asked her to be my girlfriend. I even said the words, "Do you want to be my girlfriend?" like we were in high school or something. We were in my childhood bedroom when I asked, as she'd gone with me to visit my parents for a few days before we got back on the road for work. She giggled for several minutes before saying yes.

So, there you go. Grover Wilcox has a girlfriend, and that's pretty darn cool. Also, Xyla's still doing her fortuneteller thing, but now that the Ringmaster isn't around to call the shots, she dropped the "World's Prettiest Fortuneteller" gimmick—though, as far as I'm concerned, she's the world's prettiest everything.

Lenny, Bettie, and Hannah are good.

I've expressed many thank yous to both father and daughter for saving my life. Hannah wasn't even supposed to be there in the Circle, but thank God she was. I've asked her a couple of times how she knew I needed help in the big top that day, but she's always coy with her answers, usually shrugging her shoulders or running off to play with one of her friends. I think that, however much the kids of Grambling Brothers were shielded from the more sinister aspects of their circus community, they knew more than they let on about what was happening around them.

Bettie tells me that Hannah's been expressing a rapidly growing interest in joining the family business, so she and Lenny have begun training her to be part of their act. The family rule remains that Hannah mustn't use her telekinesis unattended, but now that she wants to join the show, Lenny and Bettie have begun allowing her to practice her supernatural ability; of course, she can only practice in the presence of Lenny, ensuring that they use their telekinetic abilities simultaneously. And, even though they've embraced the idea of Hannah joining the show, Lenny and Bettie still want her to focus on being a kid and continuing her education.

Speaking of education, I'm still working with Hannah, Pedro, and Tonya on their schooling, but there have been some significant developments. When the Ringmaster's big top burned down, the Grambling Brothers Traveling Circus Show—for all intents and purposes—went up in smoke right along with it. But the circus itself didn't go away; all of the performers and crew members were still around, as was most of the physical infrastructure, such as the midway booths, the box office, and the sideshow tents. In the immediate aftermath, everybody was motivated to stay together and keep our circus going, so we all agreed to do just that. The first significant decision we made as a group was to rename it.

We're now called Canyon's Grand Traveling Circus, and a portion of all our profits go towards a trust fund set up for Canyon's daughter. While we're all grateful that the Ringmaster is out of the picture, the reality was our rebranded circus was left without a host to lead audiences through our show, so I suggested Bastian the Boisterous Barker take on the role. Everyone loved the idea, especially Bastian, and he's been doing a fantastic job for us.

We next needed an Operations Manager. Since nobody knew more about the inner workings of this circus than May, she was the obvious choice. Because May was the Ringmaster's right-hand gal, you might assume there would be some trust issues, but given how selflessly she risked her life to save mine, sparking the great mutiny that ultimately brought down the Ringmaster, she more than earned the group's trust moving forward. One of May's first orders of business—after enduring my nagging for several weeks—was to finally add a Ferris wheel to our traveling repertoire.

We next needed someone to handle our finances, so Vik agreed to step in as our Financial Manager. His dukey truck is still very much a part of our traveling circus, but Vik lets his daughters run it full time now.

While all of the talents agreed to stay with Canyon's Grand Traveling Circus, we did lose one performer.

Me.

It should come as no surprise that doing a fire act based on being fireproof doesn't really work when you're not fireproof. Incidentally, my famous YouTube video is still up and, once in a while, it ticks some new views, but, by and large, public interest has plateaued. As it is with most viral moments, folks eventually lost interest and moved on to the next shiny thing. Since I couldn't perform anymore, I assumed my time with the circus was over and I'd go back to my previous life as a college professor. I told May as much not long after we voted her in as Operations Manager, but she had another idea. May wanted to create an official education program within Canyon's Grand Traveling Circus, and she wanted me to run it. I warned her that I had no experience running a program like that, but May wasn't deterred.

"We all have to start somewhere," she told me.

May's vision was for me to continue doing the work I'd already started with the kids while also building out a formal program. That meant I'd get to continue being a teacher—which, as it turns out, I enjoy more than I previously realized—while also remaining part of the circus. In the months since I've taken on the role of Education Director, May has hired several new people, many of whom have brought their kids on the road with us.

Hannah, Pedro, and Tonya love seeing the program grow around them, and they take particular pride in being the original students. I also love seeing it grow, which is why I've been extra diligent in my efforts to build something special. I've even partnered with an accredited homeschool program, so the kids aren't simply sitting through lessons and doing homework for their own sake, but they're now earning school credits that will allow them to transfer into a regular school if they ever want to, while also giving them the opportunity to one day attend college.

Along with making sure the kids are set up for success, I'm actively developing the program to accommodate adult education as well. Handsome Harry was the first to sign up, and he's done marvelous work, especially in the field of literary analysis. I recently helped him write a research paper examining the influence of *The Strange Case of Dr. Jekyll and Mr. Hyde* on the creation of the Incredible Hulk. Overall, since my field of expertise is limited to reading and writing, I've brought more teachers into the program to travel with us, so the kids can get proper instruction in other fields, such as math, science, and history.

I think that brings you up to speed on everything, which leaves us with that one nagging question.

What happened to the Ringmaster?

Well, I'm told that after I exited the big top, everyone applied their collective efforts to burning the Ringmaster at the stake. It's a pretty gruesome way to go, but if anybody deserved it, it was Claudius Xavier—if that's even his real name. By the time the sirens filled the air and the Salem Fire Department arrived to put out the flames, the big top was reduced to a pile of ashes. Amongst the ashes, there was no trace of the Ringmaster—no bones, no teeth, no nothing—like he was never there.

So, is the Ringmaster dead?

I truly don't know.

None of us do.

Maybe all physical traces of the Ringmaster were simply eviscerated in the fire, though that's pretty unlikely since it takes roughly three hours to cremate a corpse. Maybe his powers were more vast than we ever knew, and he slipped out of the fire without harm. Maybe years will pass as he bides his time, letting us become more and more comfortable in his absence, allowing the memories of his existence to fade until we forget about him altogether, setting up a shocking return for his ultimate revenge. Maybe we overestimated his powers all along, and he truly did burn to a crisp right along with the big top. Maybe I'll live the whole rest of my life without ever seeing the Ringmaster again.

Maybe.

Here's what I know for sure.

If I allow the Ringmaster to haunt my every waking thought, then it won't matter if he never comes back, because he'll always be there. So, as far as I'm concerned, the Ringmaster is dead and gone.

It doesn't matter if it's true.

It only matters that I believe it.

WRITE A REVIEW

Thanks so much for reading *Grover Wilcox Goes to the Circus*. If you enjoyed the book, I hope you'll write a review on Amazon.

Reader reviews from good folks like yourself are like gold for authors, so it'd mean a whole lot to me if you could.

SOCIAL MEDIA

BookBub
Facebook
Goodreads
Instagram
YouTube
X

BOOK TRAILERS (on YouTube)

Inside the Outside
The Vampire, the Hunter, and the Girl
The Vampire, the Hunter, and the Witch
The Vampire, the Hunter, and Frank
Dolph the Unicorn Killer & Other Stories

PODCAST

The Martin Lastrapes Show Podcast Hour

ABOUT THE AUTHOR

MARTIN LASTRAPES is the critically-acclaimed author of *Inside the Outside*, *The Vampire and the Hunter Trilogy*, and *Dolph the Unicorn Killer & Other Stories*. He studied at Cal State San Bernardino, where he earned a Bachelor's Degree in English and a Master's Degree in Composition. This is his fifth novel.

Made in the USA
Monee, IL
05 October 2024

67202326R00277